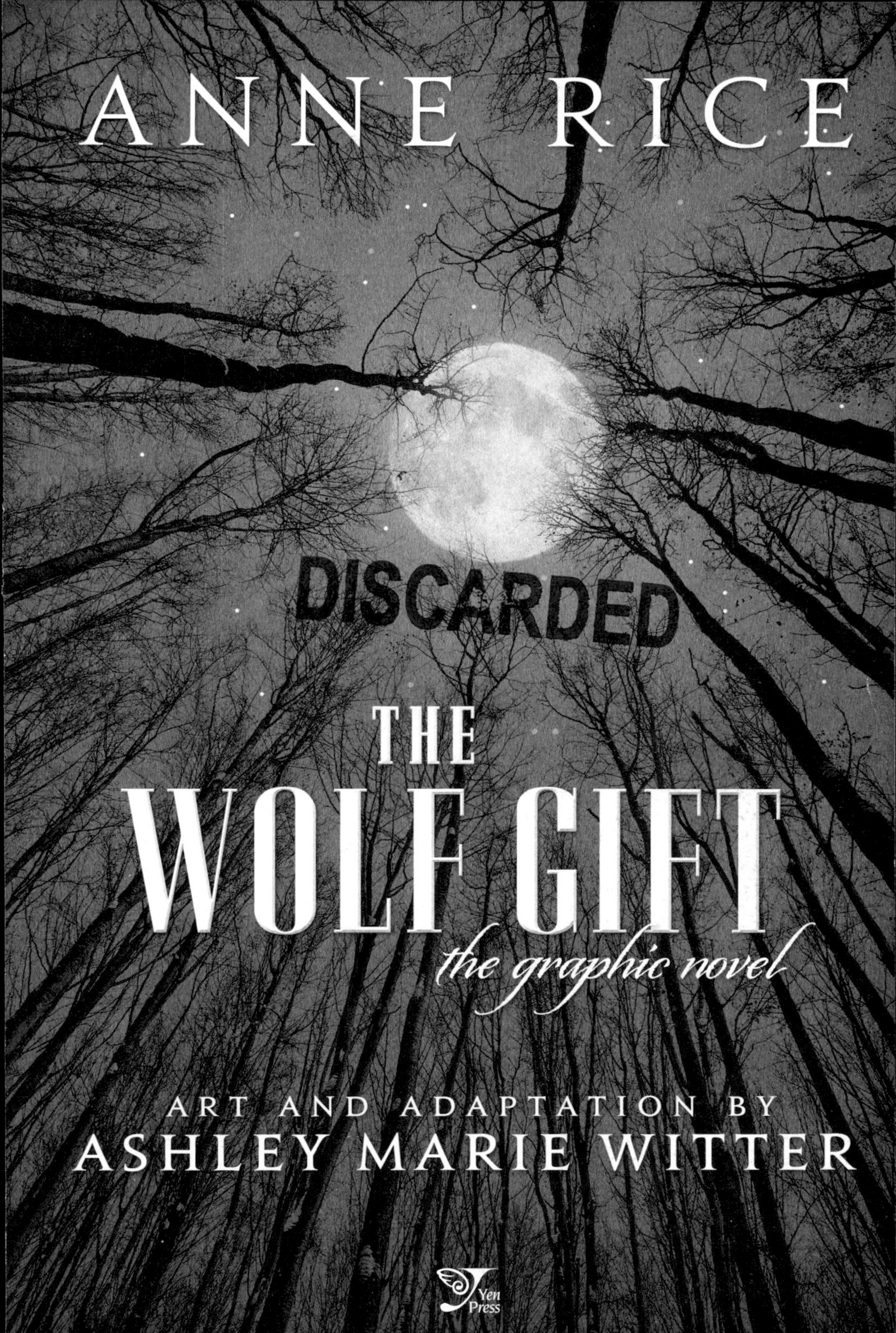
ANNE RICE
DISCARDED
THE WOLF GIFT
the graphic novel
ART AND ADAPTATION BY
ASHLEY MARIE WITTER
Yen Press

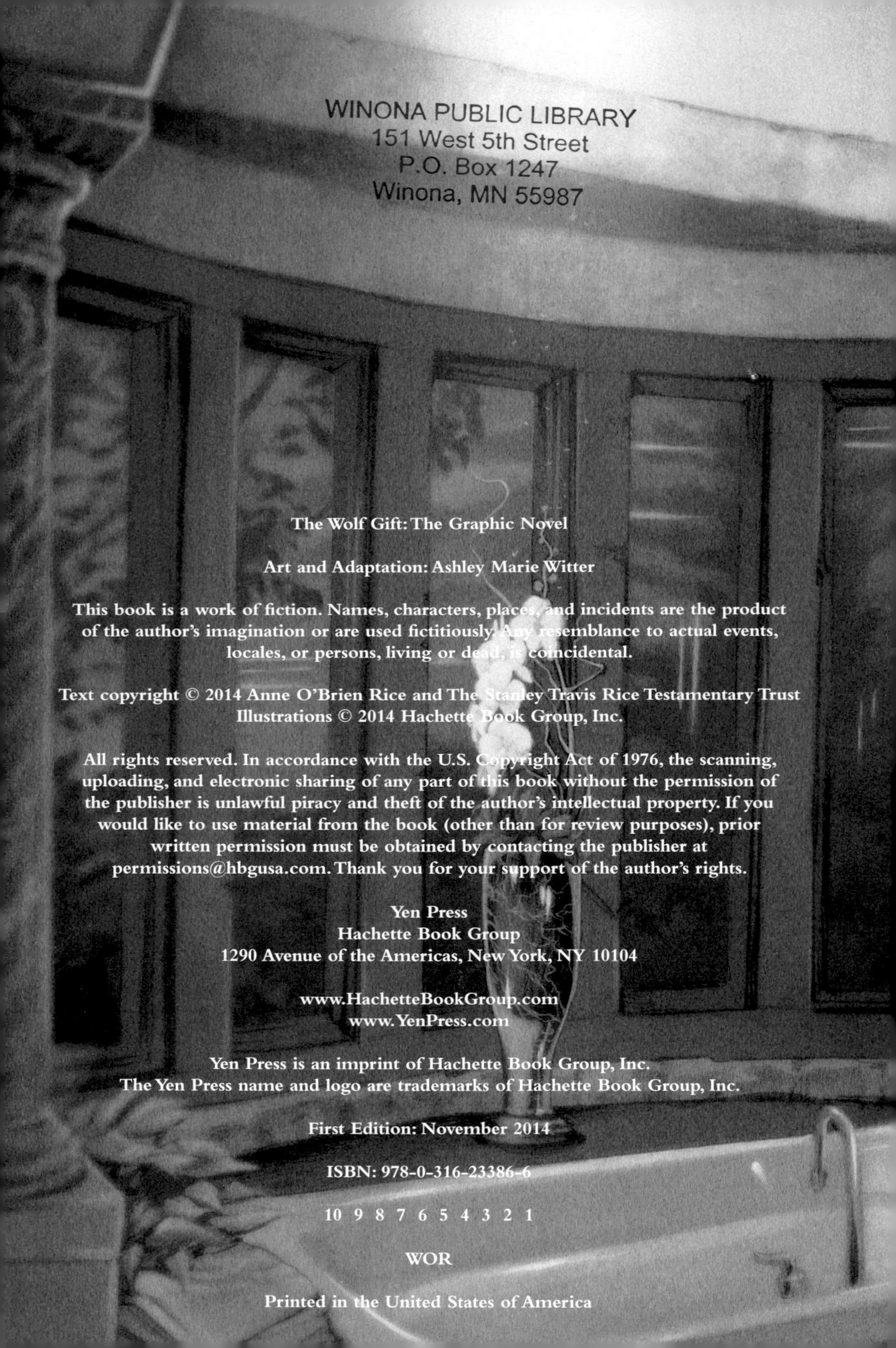

The Wolf Gift: The Graphic Novel

Art and Adaptation: Ashley Marie Witter

Yen Press
Hachette Book Group
1290 Avenue of the Americas, New York, NY 10104

www.HachetteBookGroup.com
www.YenPress.com

Yen Press is an imprint of Hachette Book Group, Inc.
The Yen Press name and logo are trademarks of Hachette Book Group, Inc.

First Edition: November 2014

ISBN: 978-0-316-23386-6

10 9 8 7 6 5 4 3 2 1

WOR

Printed in the United States of America

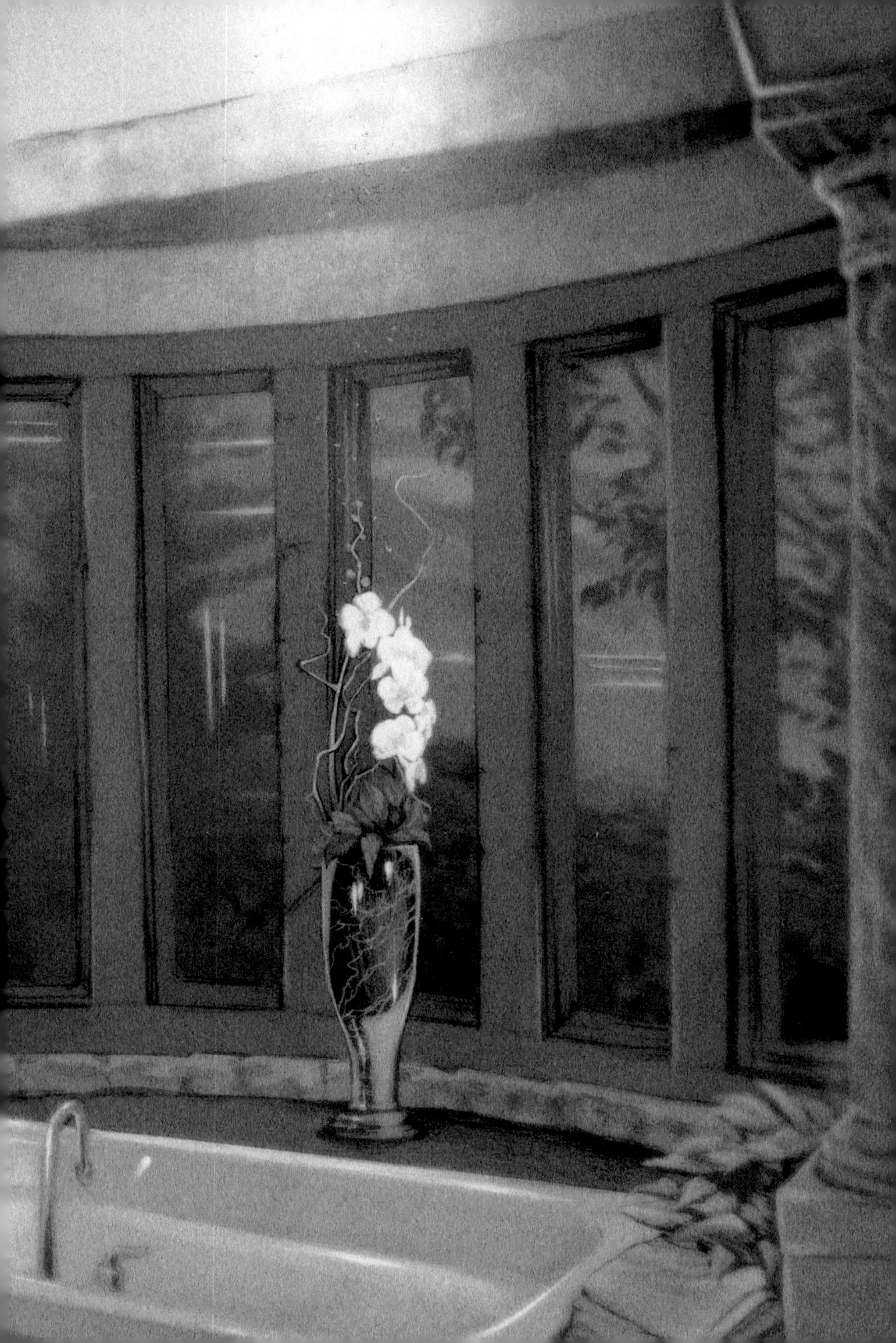

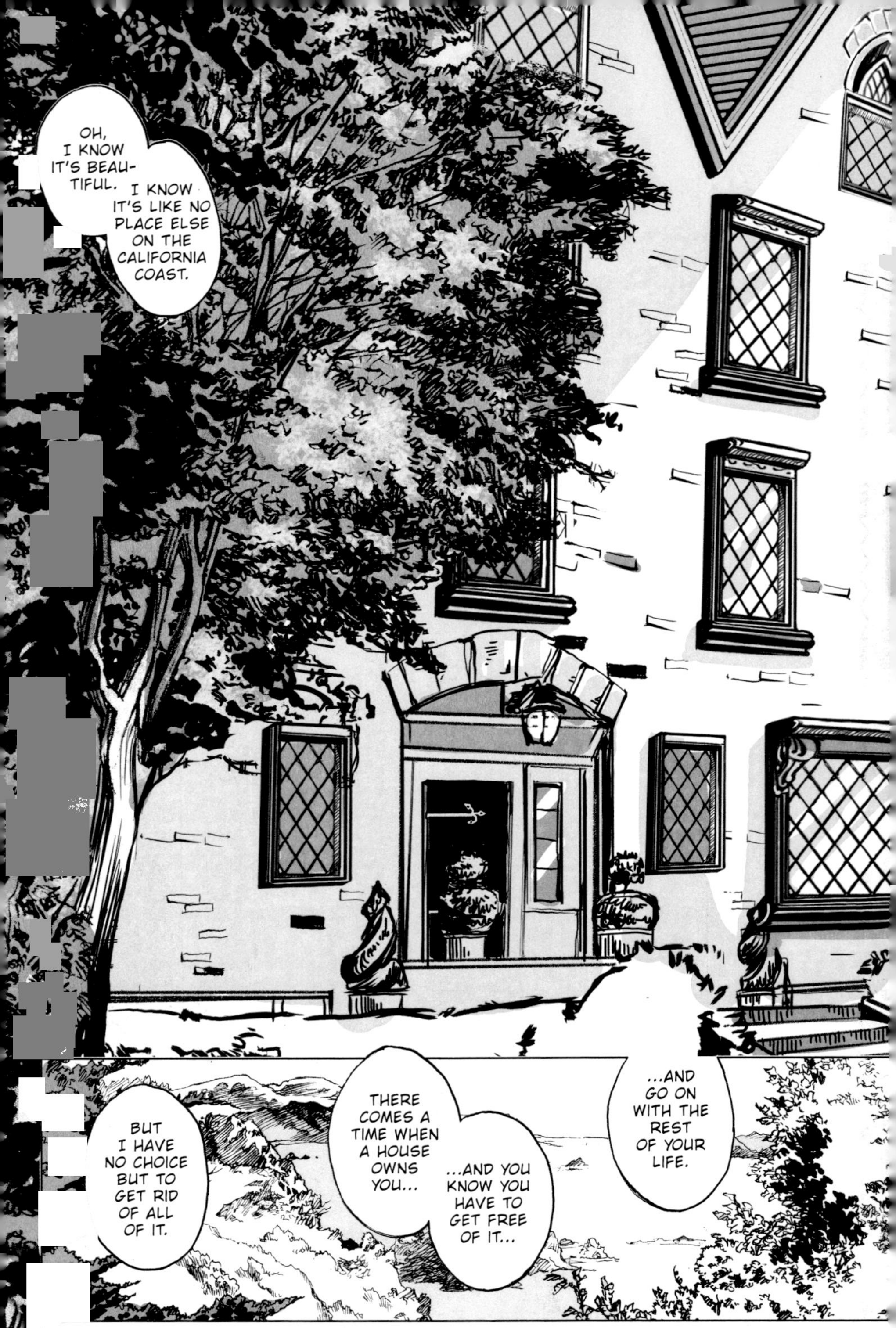
OH, I KNOW IT'S BEAU-TIFUL.
I KNOW IT'S LIKE NO PLACE ELSE ON THE CALIFORNIA COAST.
BUT I HAVE NO CHOICE BUT TO GET RID OF ALL OF IT.
THERE COMES A TIME WHEN A HOUSE OWNS YOU...
...AND YOU KNOW YOU HAVE TO GET FREE OF IT...
...AND GO ON WITH THE REST OF YOUR LIFE.

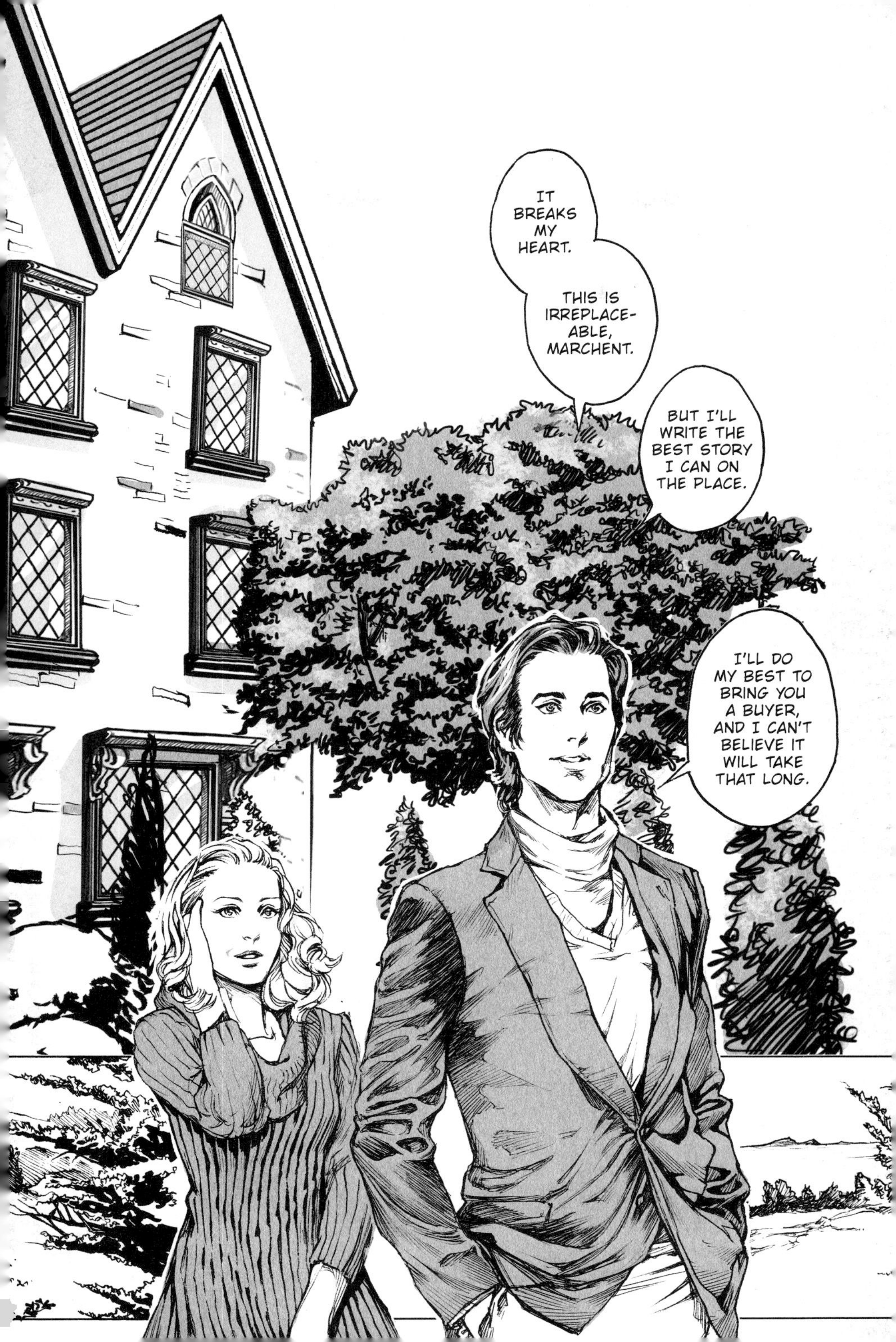
IT BREAKS MY HEART.
THIS IS IRREPLACE-ABLE, MARCHENT.
BUT I'LL WRITE THE BEST STORY I CAN ON THE PLACE.
I'LL DO MY BEST TO BRING YOU A BUYER, AND I CAN'T BELIEVE IT WILL TAKE THAT LONG.

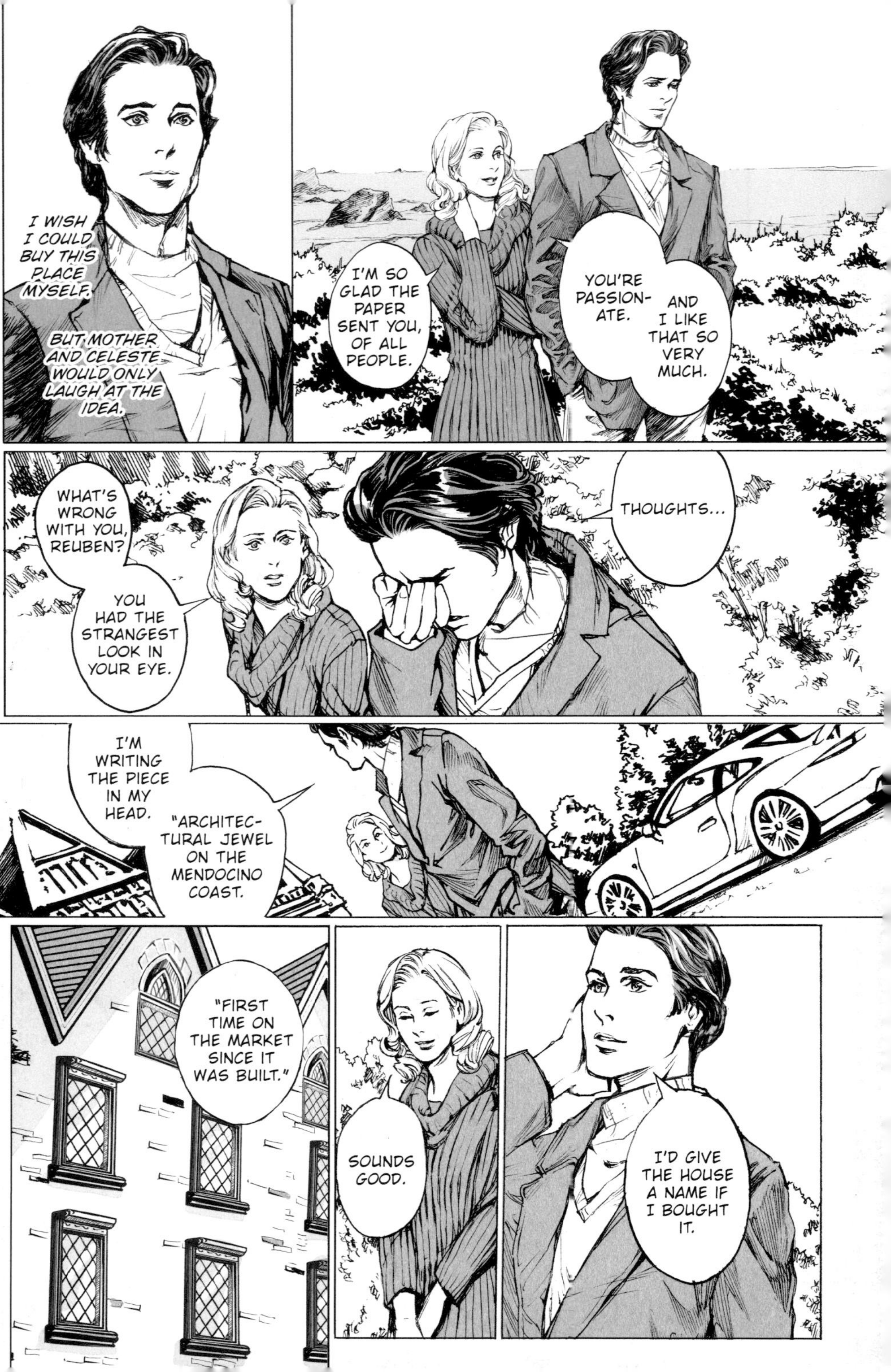
I WISH I COULD BUY THIS PLACE MYSELF.
BUT MOTHER AND CELESTE WOULD ONLY LAUGH AT THE IDEA.
I'M SO GLAD THE PAPER SENT YOU, OF ALL PEOPLE.
YOU'RE PASSION-ATE.
AND I LIKE THAT SO VERY MUCH.
WHAT'S WRONG WITH YOU, REUBEN?
YOU HAD THE STRANGEST LOOK IN YOUR EYE.
THOUGHTS...
I'M WRITING THE PIECE IN MY HEAD.
"ARCHITEC-TURAL JEWEL ON THE MENDOCINO COAST.
"FIRST TIME ON THE MARKET SINCE IT WAS BUILT."
SOUNDS GOOD.
I'D GIVE THE HOUSE A NAME IF I BOUGHT IT.

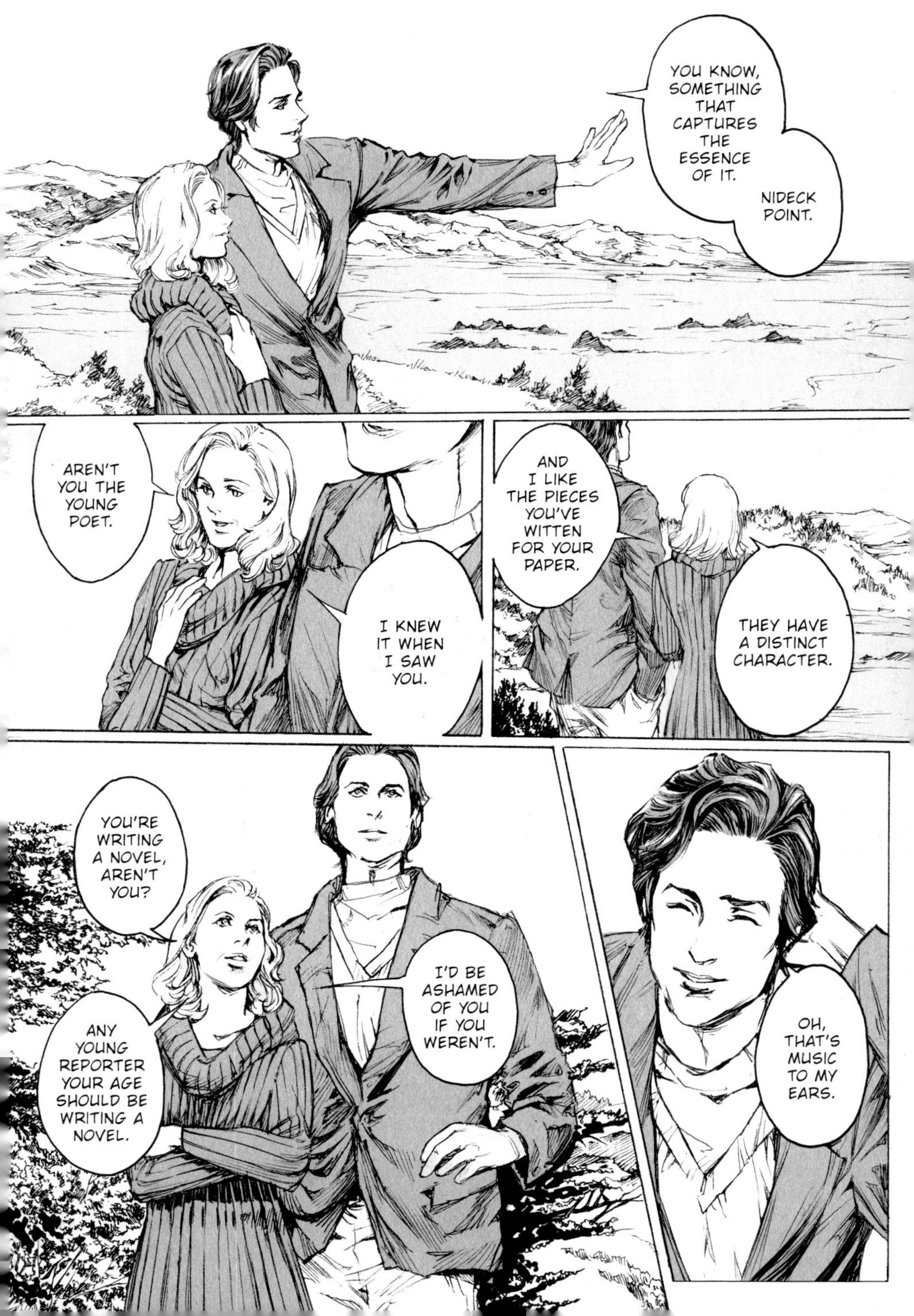
YOU KNOW, SOMETHING THAT CAPTURES THE ESSENCE OF IT.
NIDECK POINT.
AREN'T YOU THE YOUNG POET.
I KNEW IT WHEN I SAW YOU.
AND I LIKE THE PIECES YOU'VE WITTEN FOR YOUR PAPER.
THEY HAVE A DISTINCT CHARACTER.
YOU'RE WRITING A NOVEL, AREN'T YOU?
ANY YOUNG REPORTER YOUR AGE SHOULD BE WRITING A NOVEL.
I'D BE ASHAMED OF YOU IF YOU WEREN'T.
OH, THAT'S MUSIC TO MY EARS.

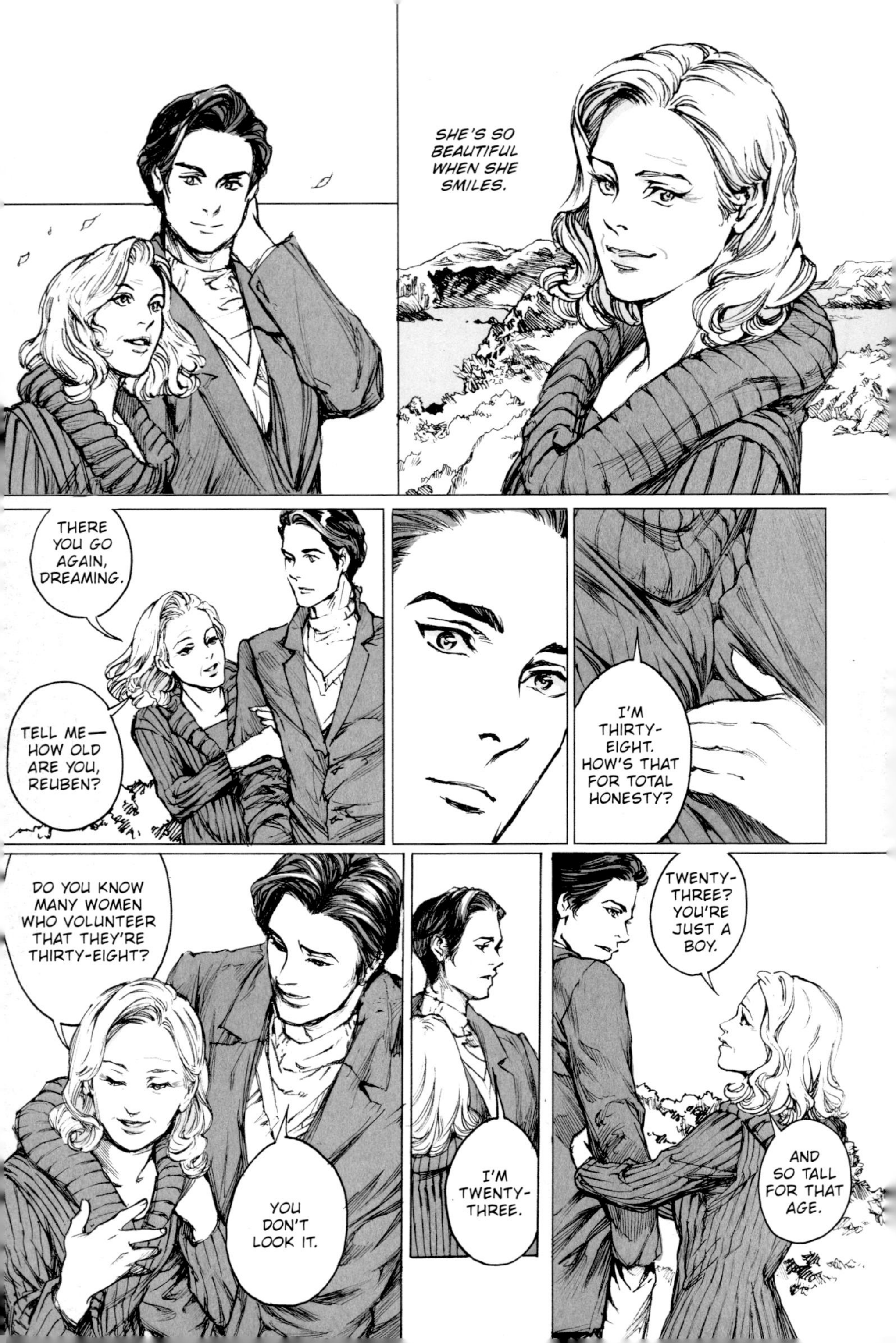
SHE'S SO BEAUTIFUL WHEN SHE SMILES.
THERE YOU GO AGAIN, DREAMING.
TELL ME— HOW OLD ARE YOU, REUBEN?
I'M THIRTY-EIGHT. HOW'S THAT FOR TOTAL HONESTY?
DO YOU KNOW MANY WOMEN WHO VOLUNTEER THAT THEY'RE THIRTY-EIGHT?
YOU DON'T LOOK IT.
I'M TWENTY-THREE.
TWENTY-THREE? YOU'RE JUST A BOY.
AND SO TALL FOR THAT AGE.

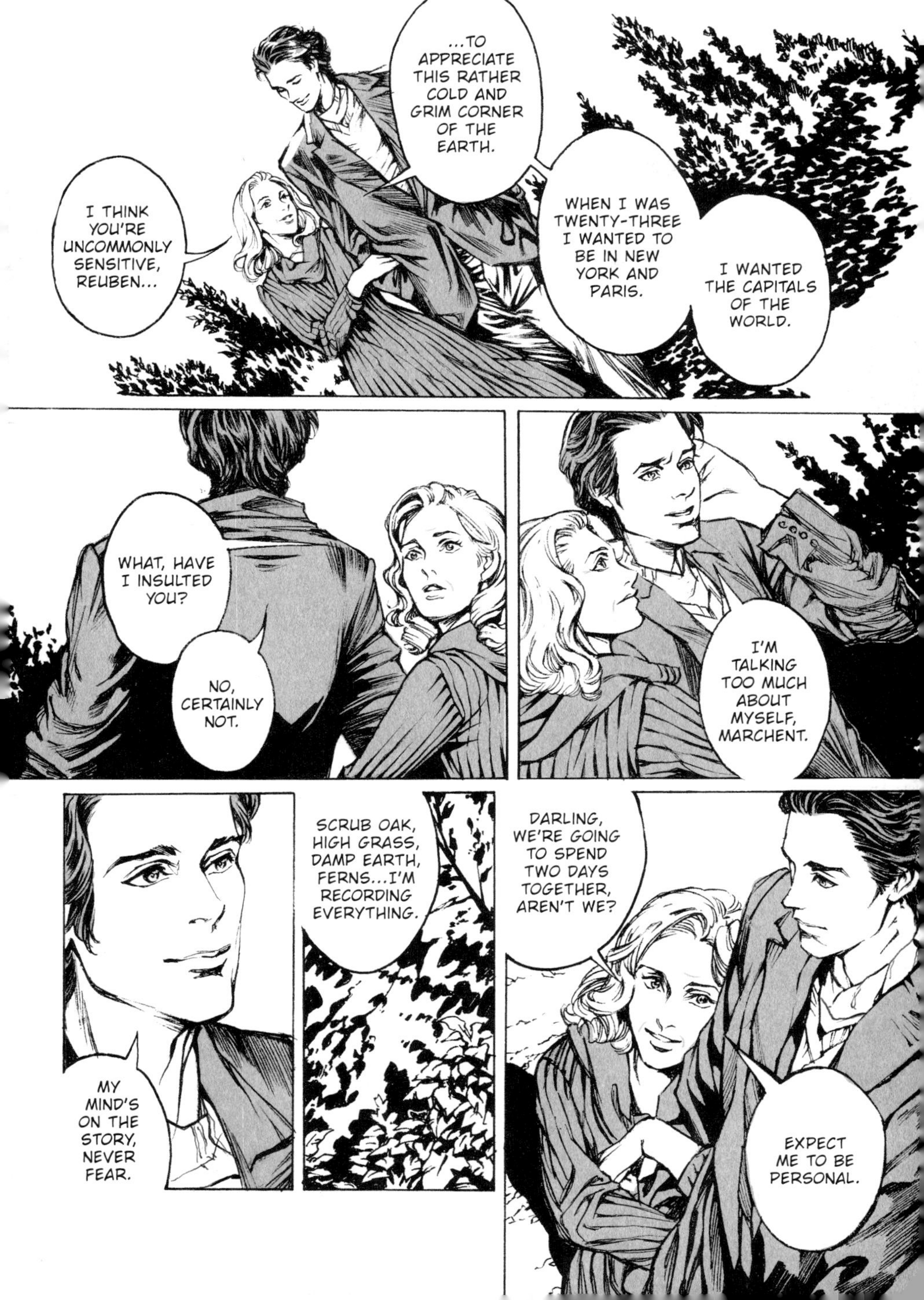

...TO APPRECIATE THIS RATHER COLD AND GRIM CORNER OF THE EARTH.
I THINK YOU'RE UNCOMMONLY SENSITIVE, REUBEN...
WHEN I WAS TWENTY-THREE I WANTED TO BE IN NEW YORK AND PARIS.
I WANTED THE CAPITALS OF THE WORLD.
WHAT, HAVE I INSULTED YOU?
NO, CERTAINLY NOT.
I'M TALKING TOO MUCH ABOUT MYSELF, MARCHENT.
MY MIND'S ON THE STORY, NEVER FEAR.
SCRUB OAK, HIGH GRASS, DAMP EARTH, FERNS...I'M RECORDING EVERYTHING.
DARLING, WE'RE GOING TO SPEND TWO DAYS TOGETHER, AREN'T WE?
EXPECT ME TO BE PERSONAL.

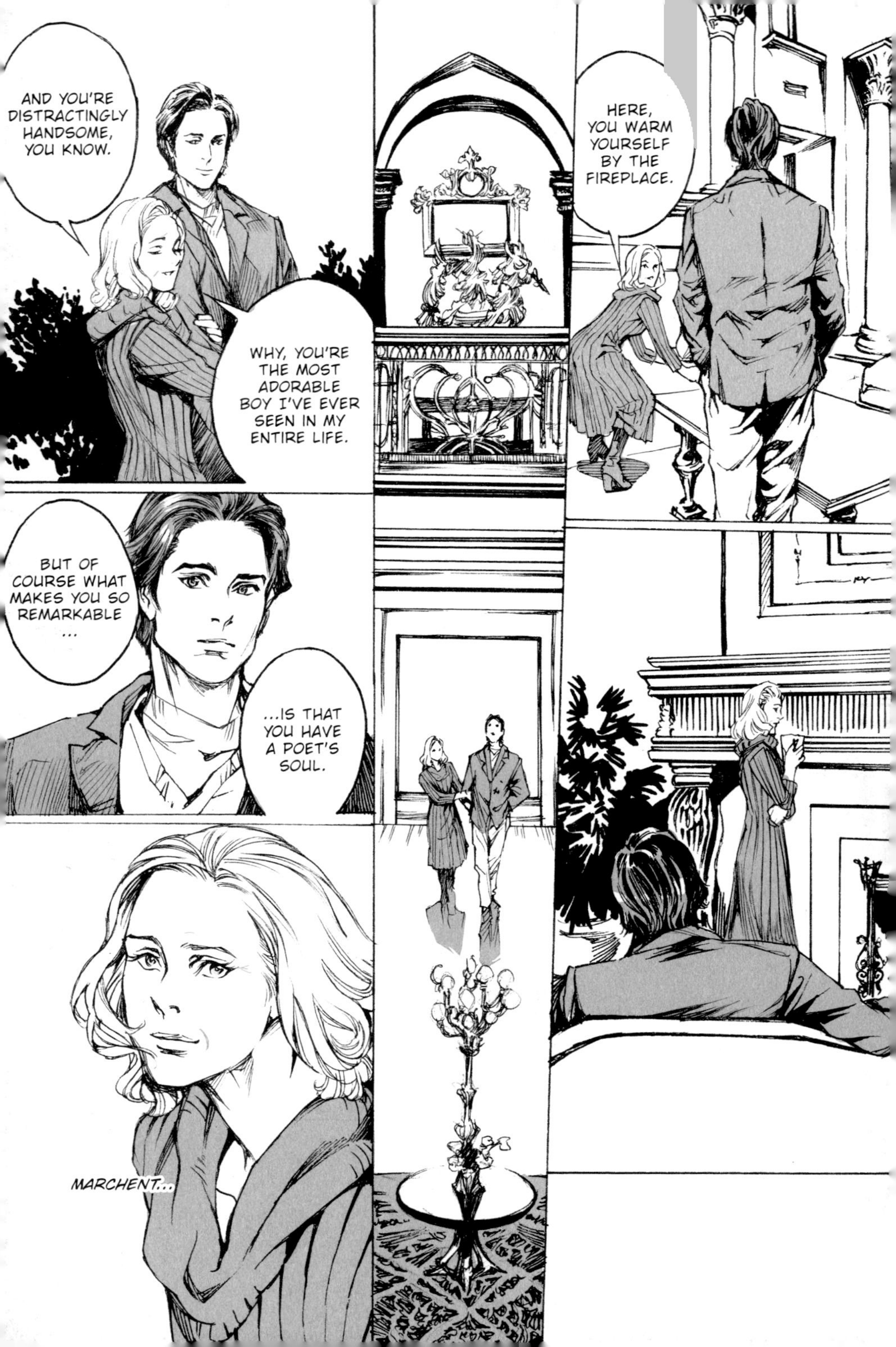
AND YOU'RE DISTRACTINGLY HANDSOME, YOU KNOW.
WHY, YOU'RE THE MOST ADORABLE BOY I'VE EVER SEEN IN MY ENTIRE LIFE.
HERE, YOU WARM YOURSELF BY THE FIREPLACE.
BUT OF COURSE WHAT MAKES YOU SO REMARKABLE ...
...IS THAT YOU HAVE A POET'S SOUL.
MARCHENT...

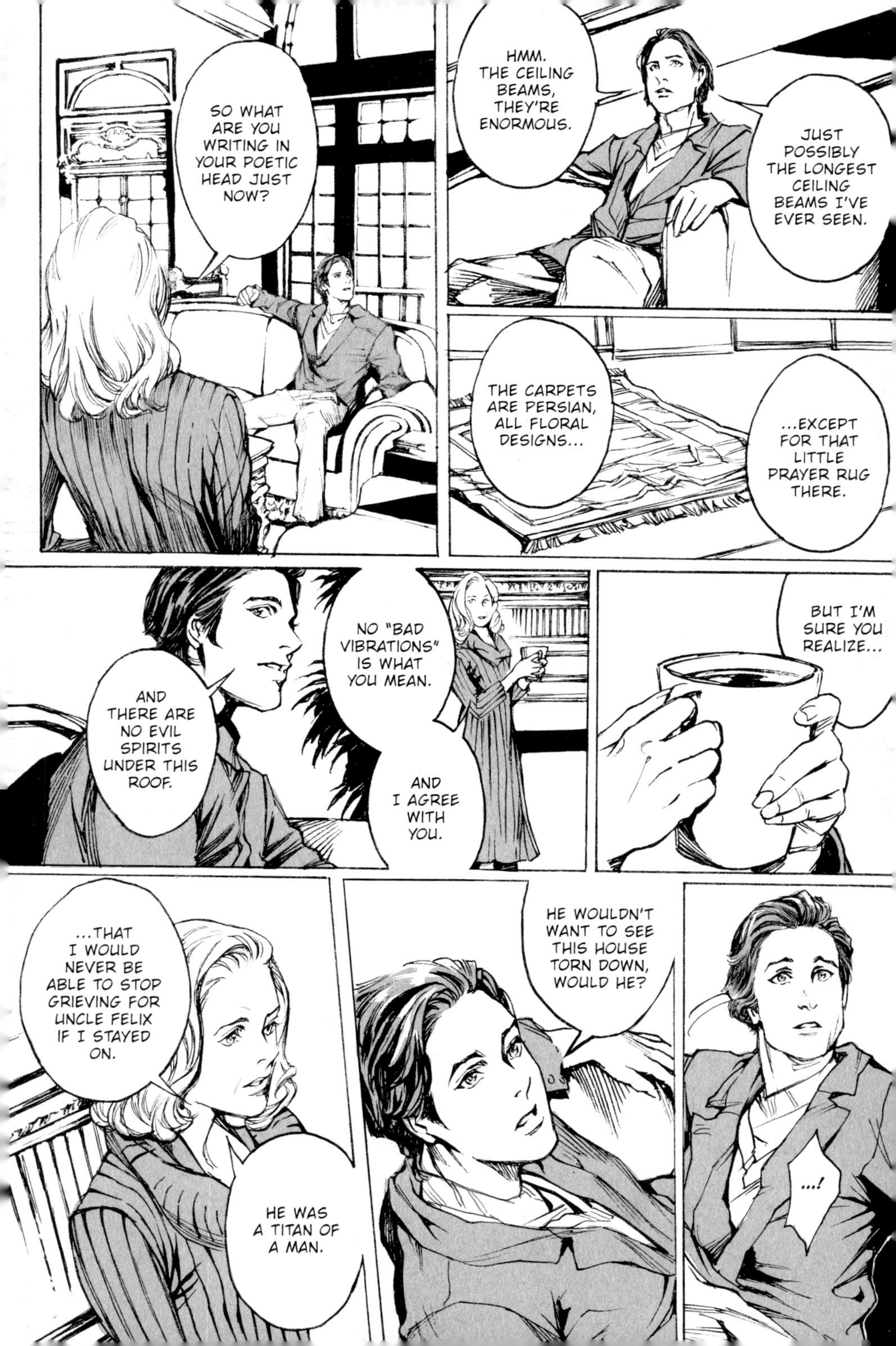
SO WHAT ARE YOU WRITING IN YOUR POETIC HEAD JUST NOW?
HMM. THE CEILING BEAMS, THEY'RE ENORMOUS.
JUST POSSIBLY THE LONGEST CEILING BEAMS I'VE EVER SEEN.
THE CARPETS ARE PERSIAN, ALL FLORAL DESIGNS...
...EXCEPT FOR THAT LITTLE PRAYER RUG THERE.
AND THERE ARE NO EVIL SPIRITS UNDER THIS ROOF.
NO "BAD VIBRATIONS" IS WHAT YOU MEAN.
AND I AGREE WITH YOU.
BUT I'M SURE YOU REALIZE...
...THAT I WOULD NEVER BE ABLE TO STOP GRIEVING FOR UNCLE FELIX IF I STAYED ON.
HE WAS A TITAN OF A MAN.
HE WOULDN'T WANT TO SEE THIS HOUSE TORN DOWN, WOULD HE?
...!

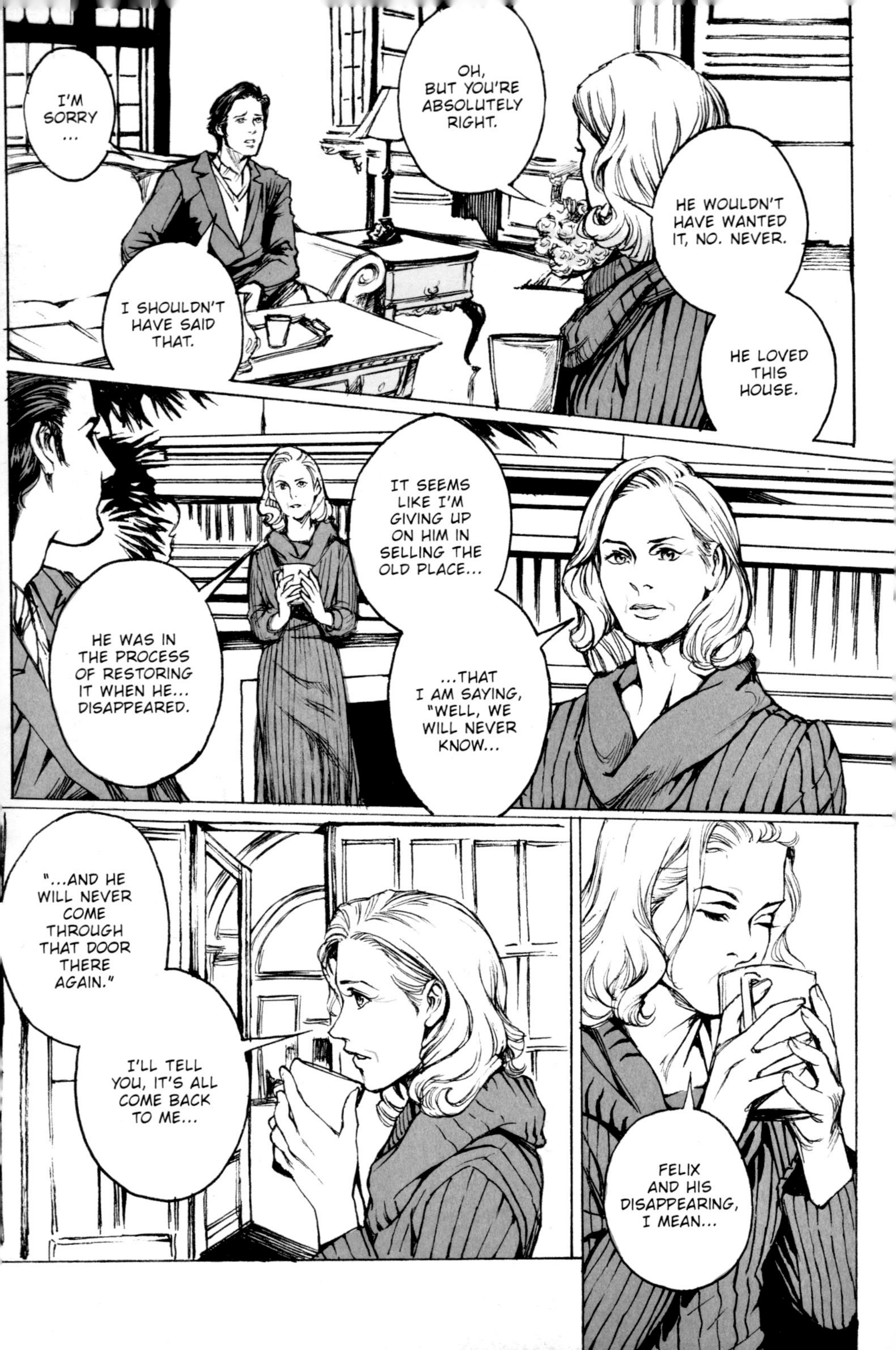
I'M SORRY ...
OH, BUT YOU'RE ABSOLUTELY RIGHT.
I SHOULDN'T HAVE SAID THAT.
HE WOULDN'T HAVE WANTED IT, NO. NEVER.
HE LOVED THIS HOUSE.
HE WAS IN THE PROCESS OF RESTORING IT WHEN HE... DISAPPEARED.
IT SEEMS LIKE I'M GIVING UP ON HIM IN SELLING THE OLD PLACE...
...THAT I AM SAYING, "WELL, WE WILL NEVER KNOW...
"...AND HE WILL NEVER COME THROUGH THAT DOOR THERE AGAIN."
I'LL TELL YOU, IT'S ALL COME BACK TO ME...
FELIX AND HIS DISAPPEARING, I MEAN...

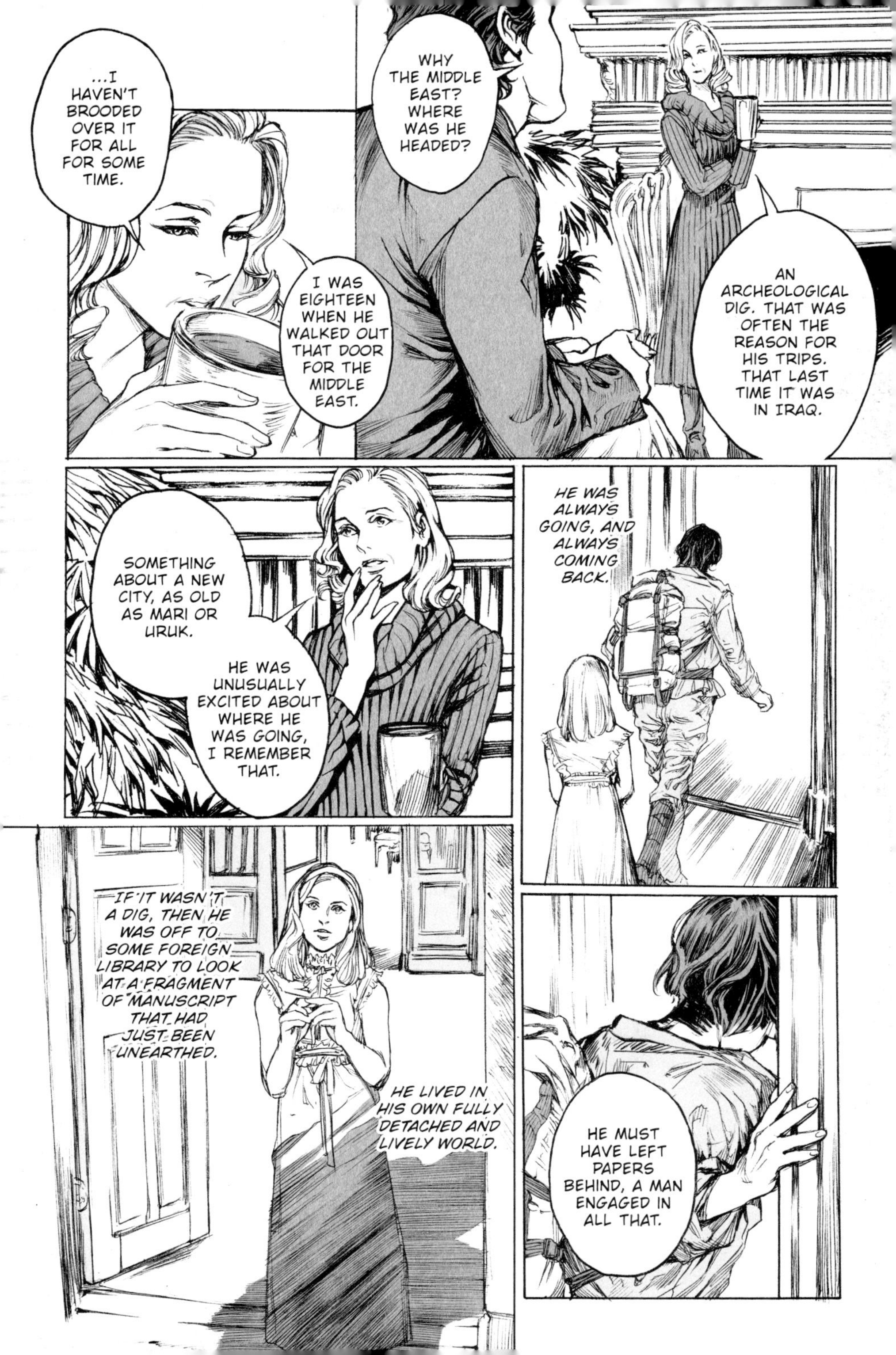

...I HAVEN'T BROODED OVER IT FOR ALL FOR SOME TIME.
WHY THE MIDDLE EAST? WHERE WAS HE HEADED?
I WAS EIGHTEEN WHEN HE WALKED OUT THAT DOOR FOR THE MIDDLE EAST.
AN ARCHEOLOGICAL DIG. THAT WAS OFTEN THE REASON FOR HIS TRIPS. THAT LAST TIME IT WAS IN IRAQ.
SOMETHING ABOUT A NEW CITY, AS OLD AS MARI OR URUK.
HE WAS UNUSUALLY EXCITED ABOUT WHERE HE WAS GOING, I REMEMBER THAT.
HE WAS ALWAYS GOING, AND ALWAYS COMING BACK.
IF IT WASN'T A DIG, THEN HE WAS OFF TO SOME FOREIGN LIBRARY TO LOOK AT A FRAGMENT OF MANUSCRIPT THAT HAD JUST BEEN UNEARTHED.
HE LIVED IN HIS OWN FULLY DETACHED AND LIVELY WORLD.
HE MUST HAVE LEFT PAPERS BEHIND, A MAN ENGAGED IN ALL THAT.

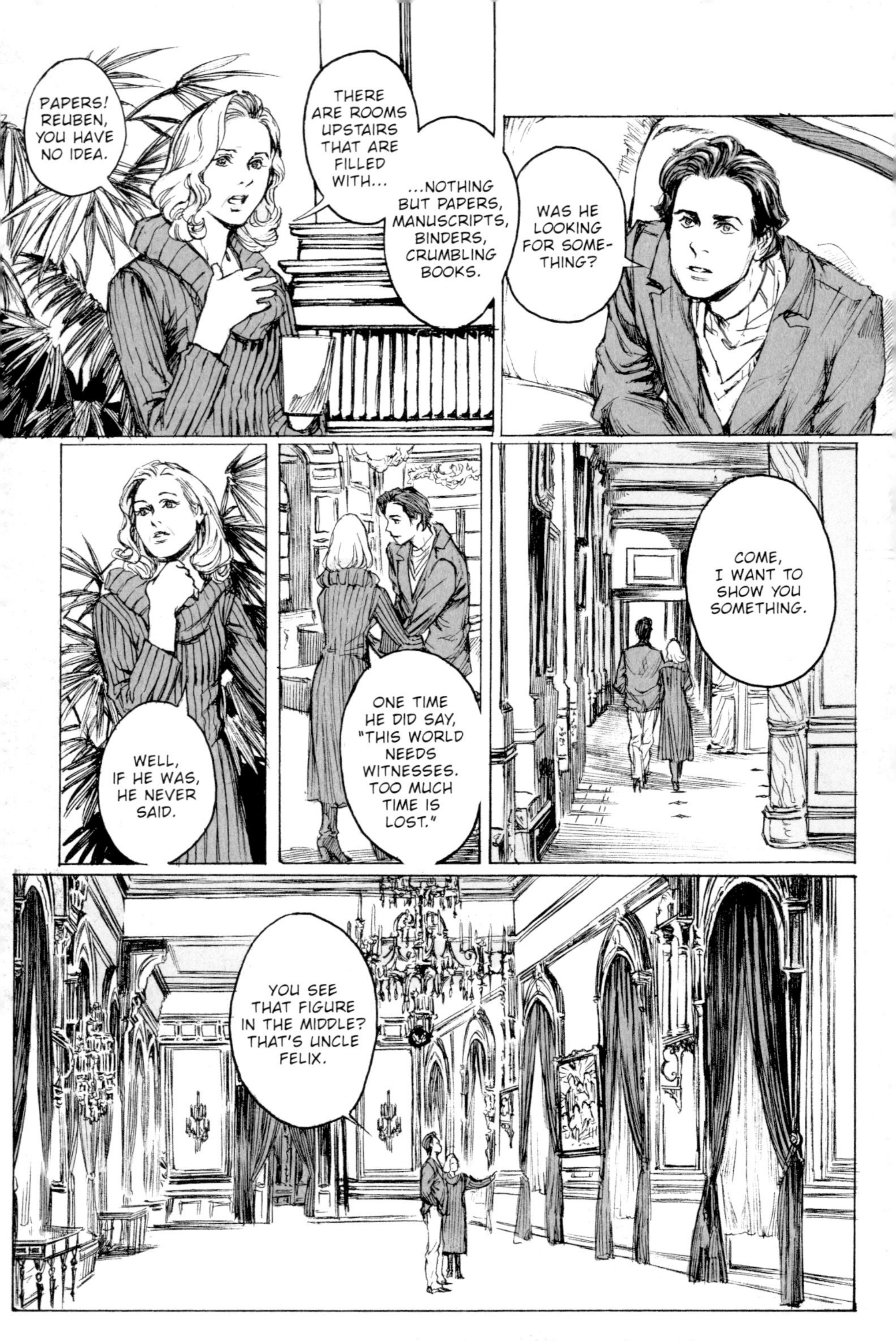
PAPERS! REUBEN, YOU HAVE NO IDEA.
THERE ARE ROOMS UPSTAIRS THAT ARE FILLED WITH...
...NOTHING BUT PAPERS, MANUSCRIPTS, BINDERS, CRUMBLING BOOKS.
WAS HE LOOKING FOR SOME-THING?
WELL, IF HE WAS, HE NEVER SAID.
ONE TIME HE DID SAY, "THIS WORLD NEEDS WITNESSES. TOO MUCH TIME IS LOST."
COME, I WANT TO SHOW YOU SOMETHING.
YOU SEE THAT FIGURE IN THE MIDDLE? THAT'S UNCLE FELIX.

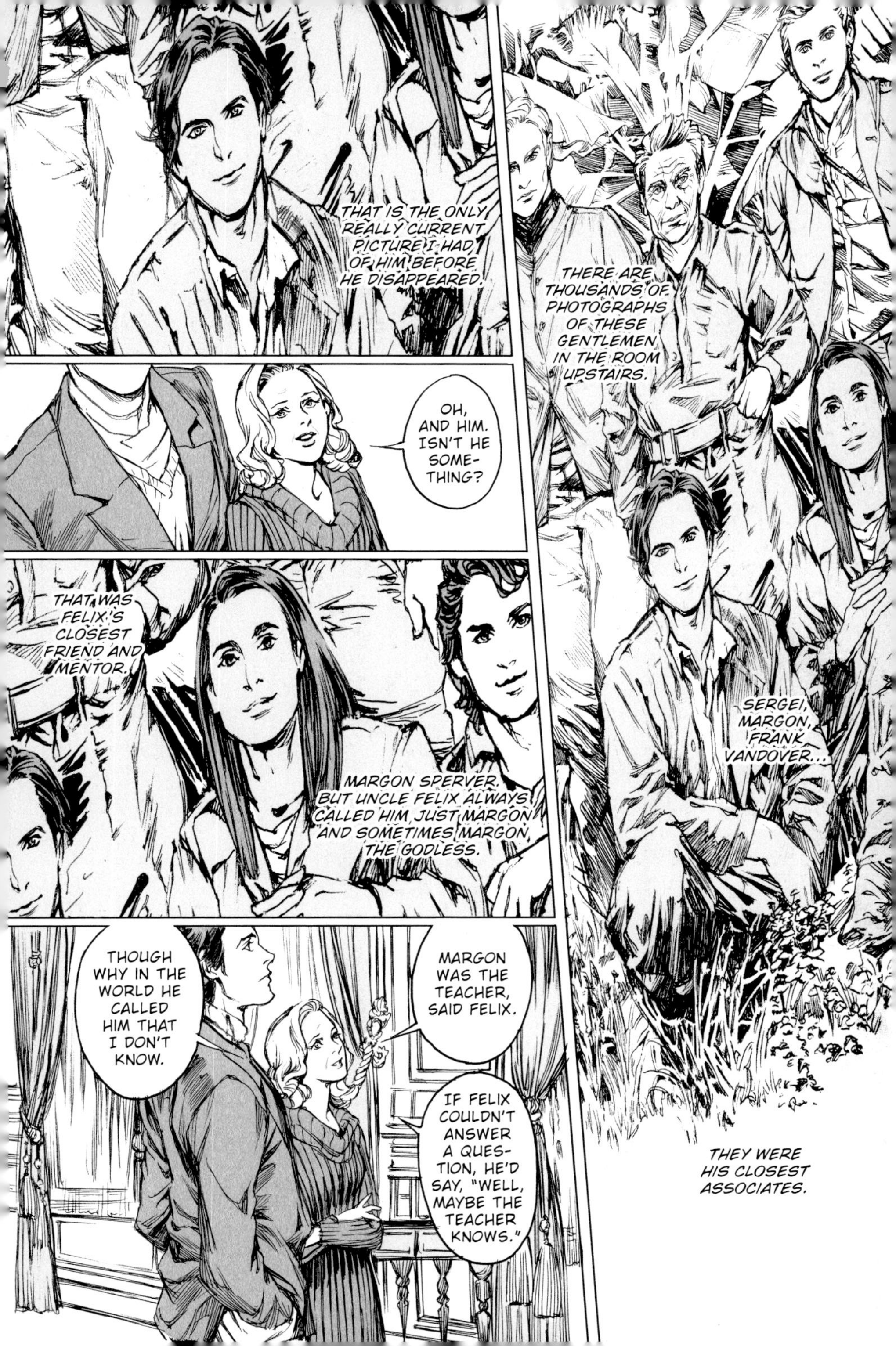
THAT IS THE ONLY REALLY CURRENT PICTURE I HAD OF HIM BEFORE HE DISAPPEARED.
THERE ARE THOUSANDS OF PHOTOGRAPHS OF THESE GENTLEMEN IN THE ROOM UPSTAIRS.
OH, AND HIM. ISN'T HE SOME-THING?
THAT WAS FELIX'S CLOSEST FRIEND AND MENTOR.
MARGON SPERVER, BUT UNCLE FELIX ALWAYS CALLED HIM JUST MARGON AND SOMETIMES MARGON THE GODLESS.
SERGEI, MARGON, FRANK VANDOVER...
THOUGH WHY IN THE WORLD HE CALLED HIM THAT I DON'T KNOW.
MARGON WAS THE TEACHER, SAID FELIX.
IF FELIX COULDN'T ANSWER A QUES-TION, HE'D SAY, "WELL, MAYBE THE TEACHER KNOWS."
THEY WERE HIS CLOSEST ASSOCIATES.

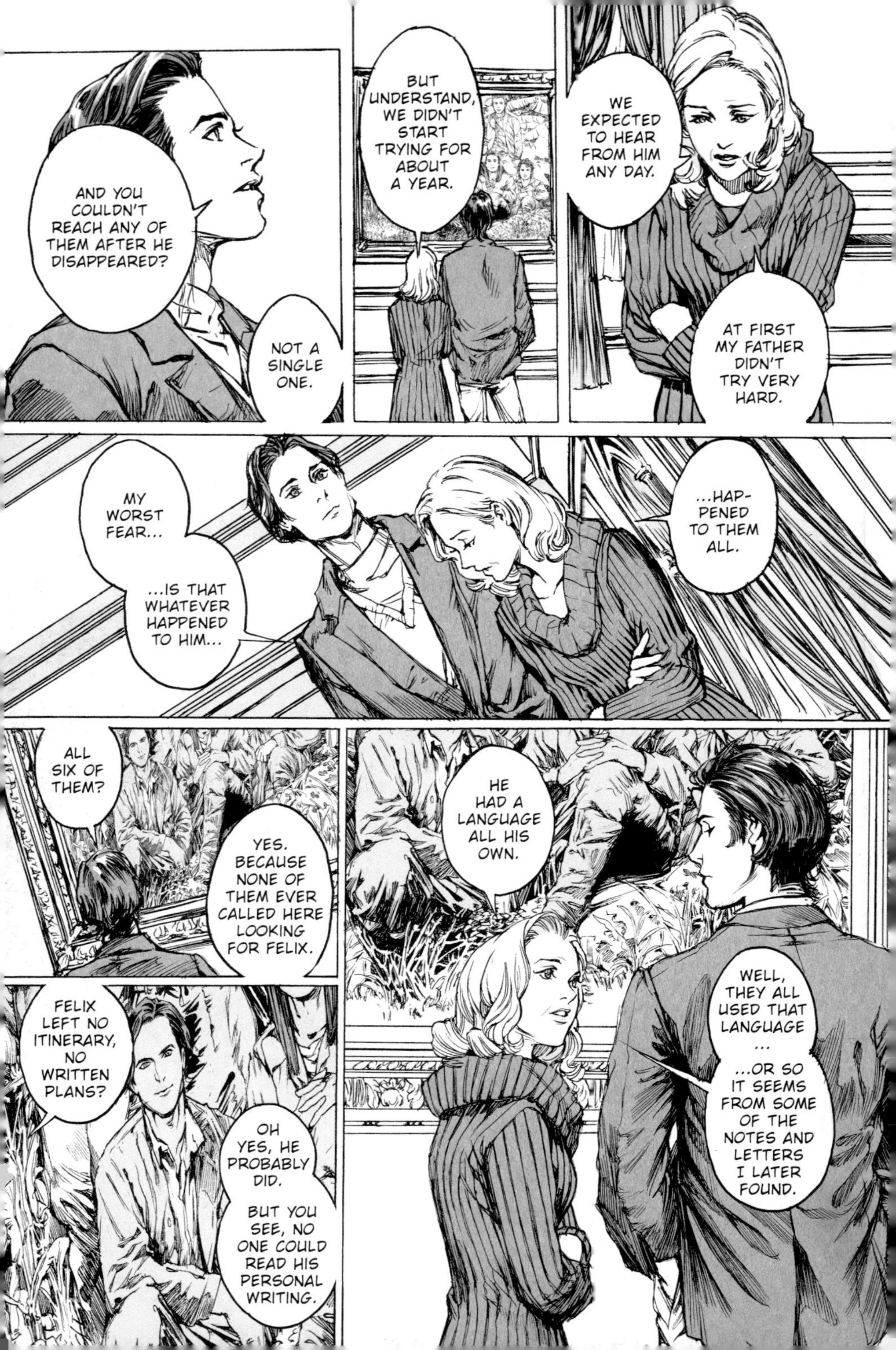
AND YOU COULDN'T REACH ANY OF THEM AFTER HE DISAPPEARED?
NOT A SINGLE ONE.
BUT UNDERSTAND, WE DIDN'T START TRYING FOR ABOUT A YEAR.
WE EXPECTED TO HEAR FROM HIM ANY DAY.
AT FIRST MY FATHER DIDN'T TRY VERY HARD.
MY WORST FEAR...
...IS THAT WHATEVER HAPPENED TO HIM...
...HAP-PENED TO THEM ALL.
ALL SIX OF THEM?
YES. BECAUSE NONE OF THEM EVER CALLED HERE LOOKING FOR FELIX.
HE HAD A LANGUAGE ALL HIS OWN.
FELIX LEFT NO ITINERARY, NO WRITTEN PLANS?
OH YES, HE PROBABLY DID.
BUT YOU SEE, NO ONE COULD READ HIS PERSONAL WRITING.
WELL, THEY ALL USED THAT LANGUAGE ...
...OR SO IT SEEMS FROM SOME OF THE NOTES AND LETTERS I LATER FOUND.

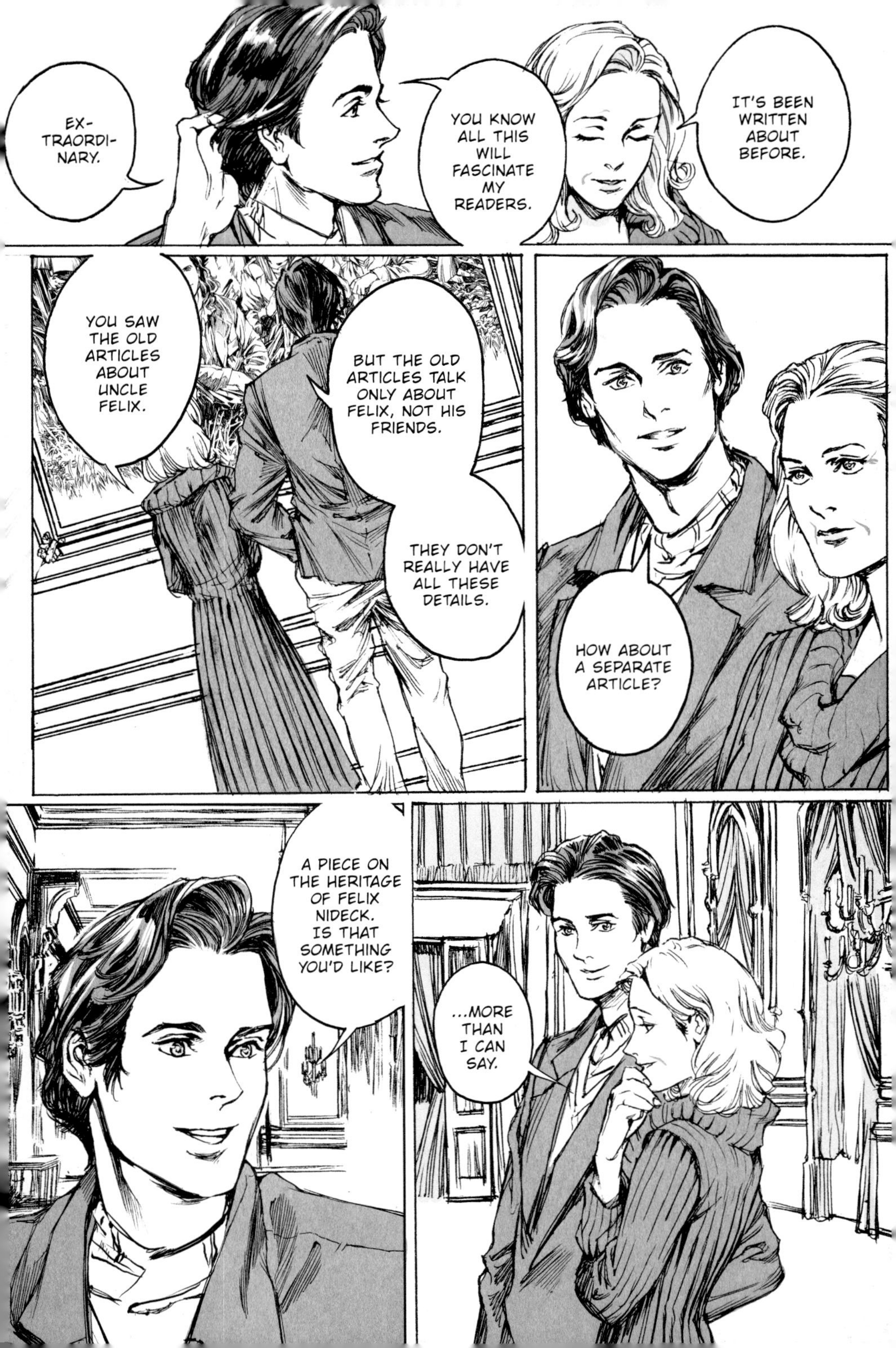
EX-TRAORDI-NARY.
YOU KNOW ALL THIS WILL FASCINATE MY READERS.
IT'S BEEN WRITTEN ABOUT BEFORE.
YOU SAW THE OLD ARTICLES ABOUT UNCLE FELIX.
BUT THE OLD ARTICLES TALK ONLY ABOUT FELIX, NOT HIS FRIENDS.
THEY DON'T REALLY HAVE ALL THESE DETAILS.
HOW ABOUT A SEPARATE ARTICLE?
A PIECE ON THE HERITAGE OF FELIX NIDECK. IS THAT SOMETHING YOU'D LIKE?
...MORE THAN I CAN SAY.

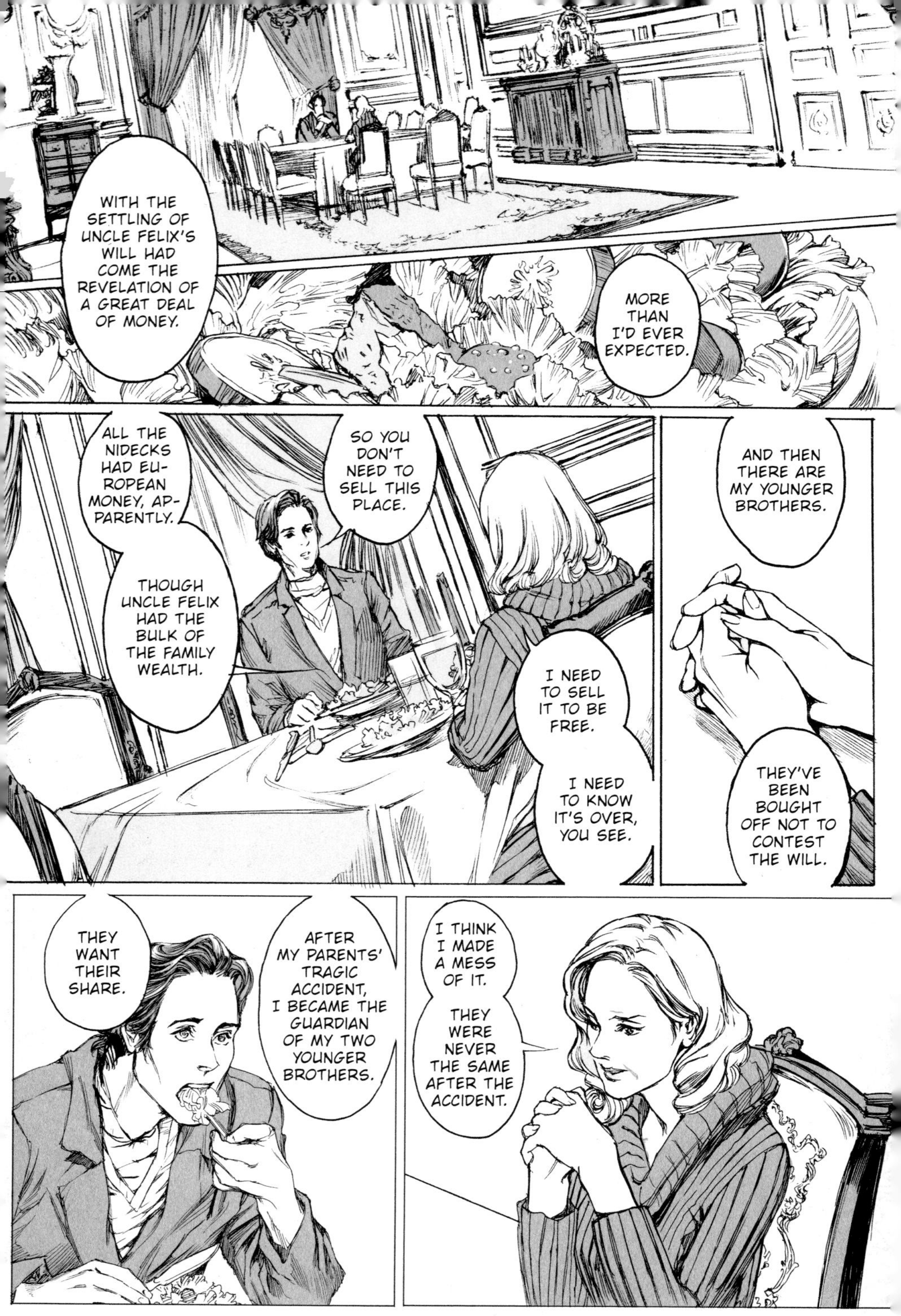
WITH THE SETTLING OF UNCLE FELIX'S WILL HAD COME THE REVELATION OF A GREAT DEAL OF MONEY.
MORE THAN I'D EVER EXPECTED.
ALL THE NIDECKS HAD EU-ROPEAN MONEY, AP-PARENTLY.
THOUGH UNCLE FELIX HAD THE BULK OF THE FAMILY WEALTH.
SO YOU DON'T NEED TO SELL THIS PLACE.
I NEED TO SELL IT TO BE FREE.
I NEED TO KNOW IT'S OVER, YOU SEE.
AND THEN THERE ARE MY YOUNGER BROTHERS.
THEY'VE BEEN BOUGHT OFF NOT TO CONTEST THE WILL.
THEY WANT THEIR SHARE.
AFTER MY PARENTS' TRAGIC ACCIDENT, I BECAME THE GUARDIAN OF MY TWO YOUNGER BROTHERS.
I THINK I MADE A MESS OF IT.
THEY WERE NEVER THE SAME AFTER THE ACCIDENT.

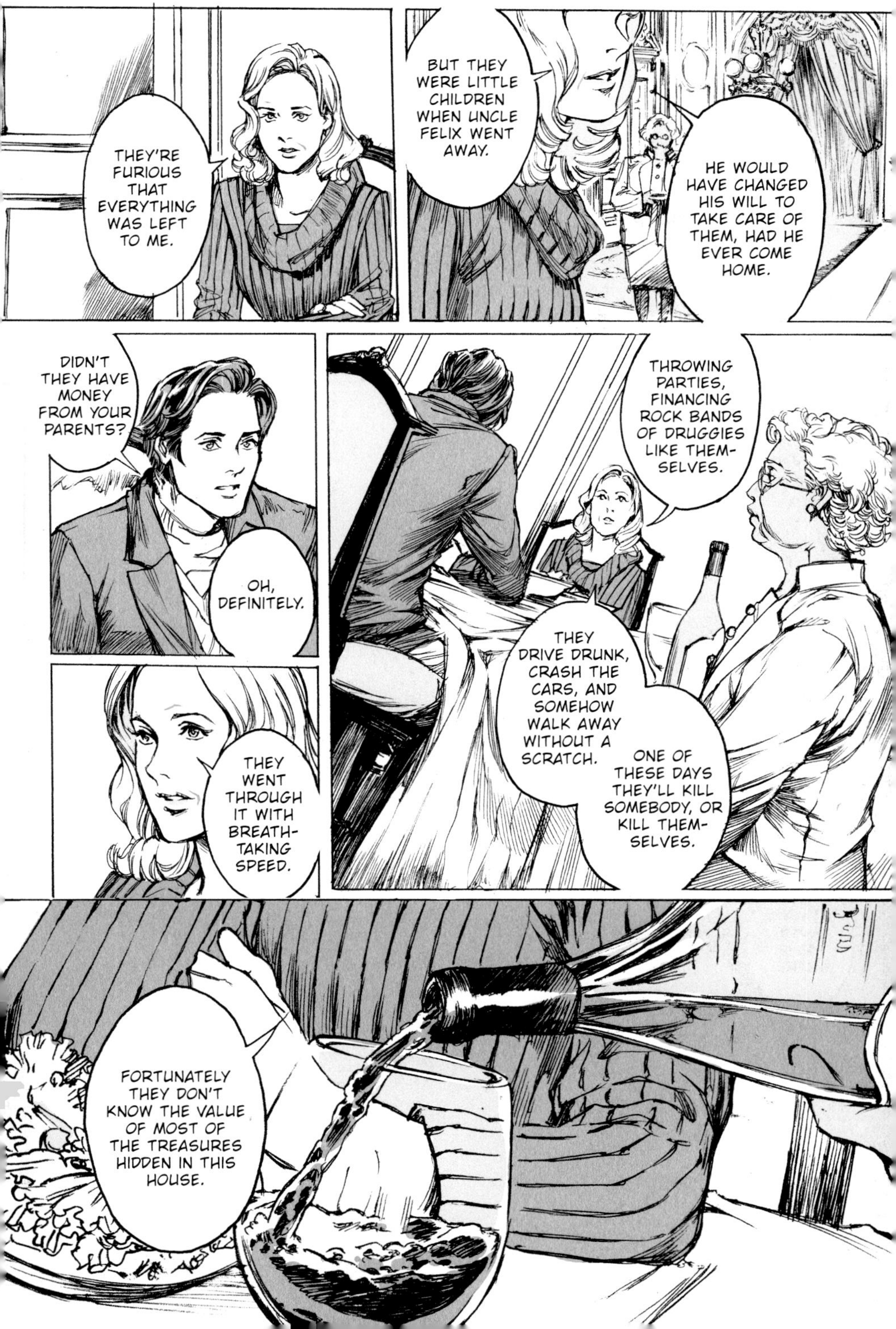
THEY'RE FURIOUS THAT EVERYTHING WAS LEFT TO ME.
BUT THEY WERE LITTLE CHILDREN WHEN UNCLE FELIX WENT AWAY.
HE WOULD HAVE CHANGED HIS WILL TO TAKE CARE OF THEM, HAD HE EVER COME HOME.
DIDN'T THEY HAVE MONEY FROM YOUR PARENTS?
OH, DEFINITELY.
THEY WENT THROUGH IT WITH BREATH-TAKING SPEED.
THROWING PARTIES, FINANCING ROCK BANDS OF DRUGGIES LIKE THEM-SELVES.
THEY DRIVE DRUNK, CRASH THE CARS, AND SOMEHOW WALK AWAY WITHOUT A SCRATCH.
ONE OF THESE DAYS THEY'LL KILL SOMEBODY, OR KILL THEM-SELVES.
FORTUNATELY THEY DON'T KNOW THE VALUE OF MOST OF THE TREASURES HIDDEN IN THIS HOUSE.

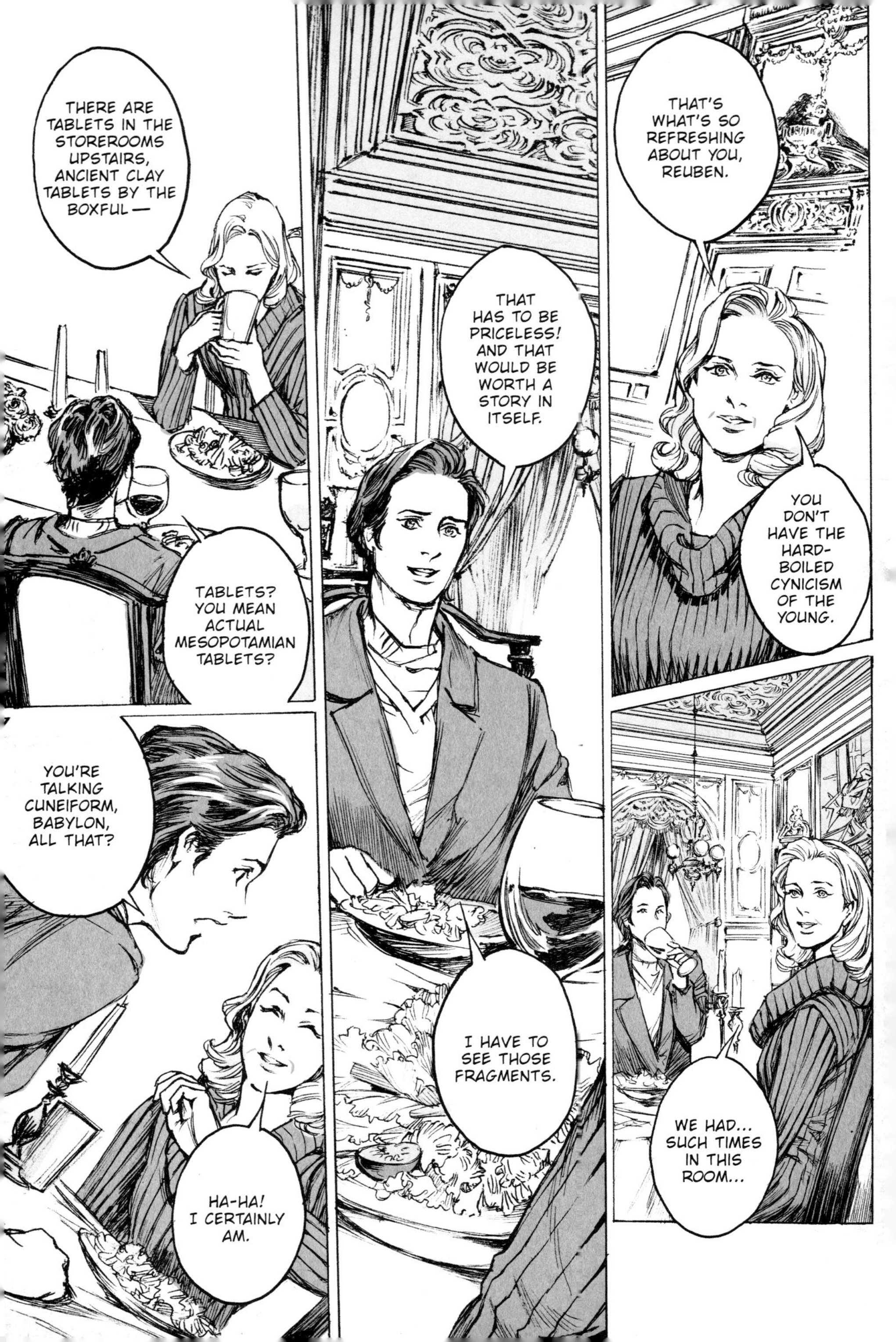
THERE ARE TABLETS IN THE STOREROOMS UPSTAIRS, ANCIENT CLAY TABLETS BY THE BOXFUL—
TABLETS? YOU MEAN ACTUAL MESOPOTAMIAN TABLETS?
YOU'RE TALKING CUNEIFORM, BABYLON, ALL THAT?
HA-HA! I CERTAINLY AM.
THAT HAS TO BE PRICELESS! AND THAT WOULD BE WORTH A STORY IN ITSELF.
I HAVE TO SEE THOSE FRAGMENTS.
THAT'S WHAT'S SO REFRESHING ABOUT YOU, REUBEN.
YOU DON'T HAVE THE HARD-BOILED CYNICISM OF THE YOUNG.
WE HAD... SUCH TIMES IN THIS ROOM...

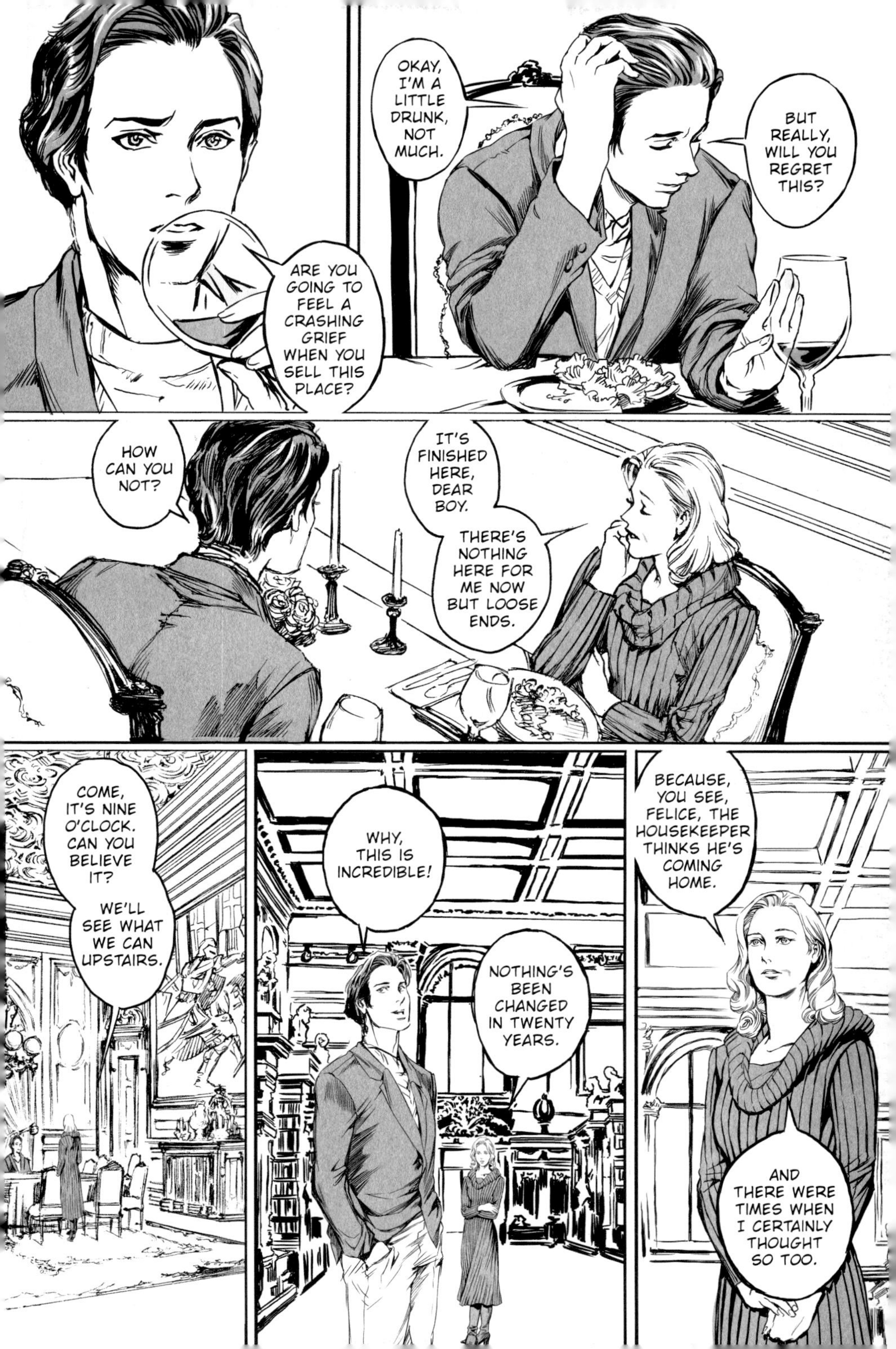
ARE YOU GOING TO FEEL A CRASHING GRIEF WHEN YOU SELL THIS PLACE?
OKAY, I'M A LITTLE DRUNK, NOT MUCH.
BUT REALLY, WILL YOU REGRET THIS?
HOW CAN YOU NOT?
IT'S FINISHED HERE, DEAR BOY.
THERE'S NOTHING HERE FOR ME NOW BUT LOOSE ENDS.
COME, IT'S NINE O'CLOCK. CAN YOU BELIEVE IT?
WE'LL SEE WHAT WE CAN UPSTAIRS.
WHY, THIS IS INCREDIBLE!
NOTHING'S BEEN CHANGED IN TWENTY YEARS.
BECAUSE, YOU SEE, FELICE, THE HOUSEKEEPER THINKS HE'S COMING HOME.
AND THERE WERE TIMES WHEN I CERTAINLY THOUGHT SO TOO.

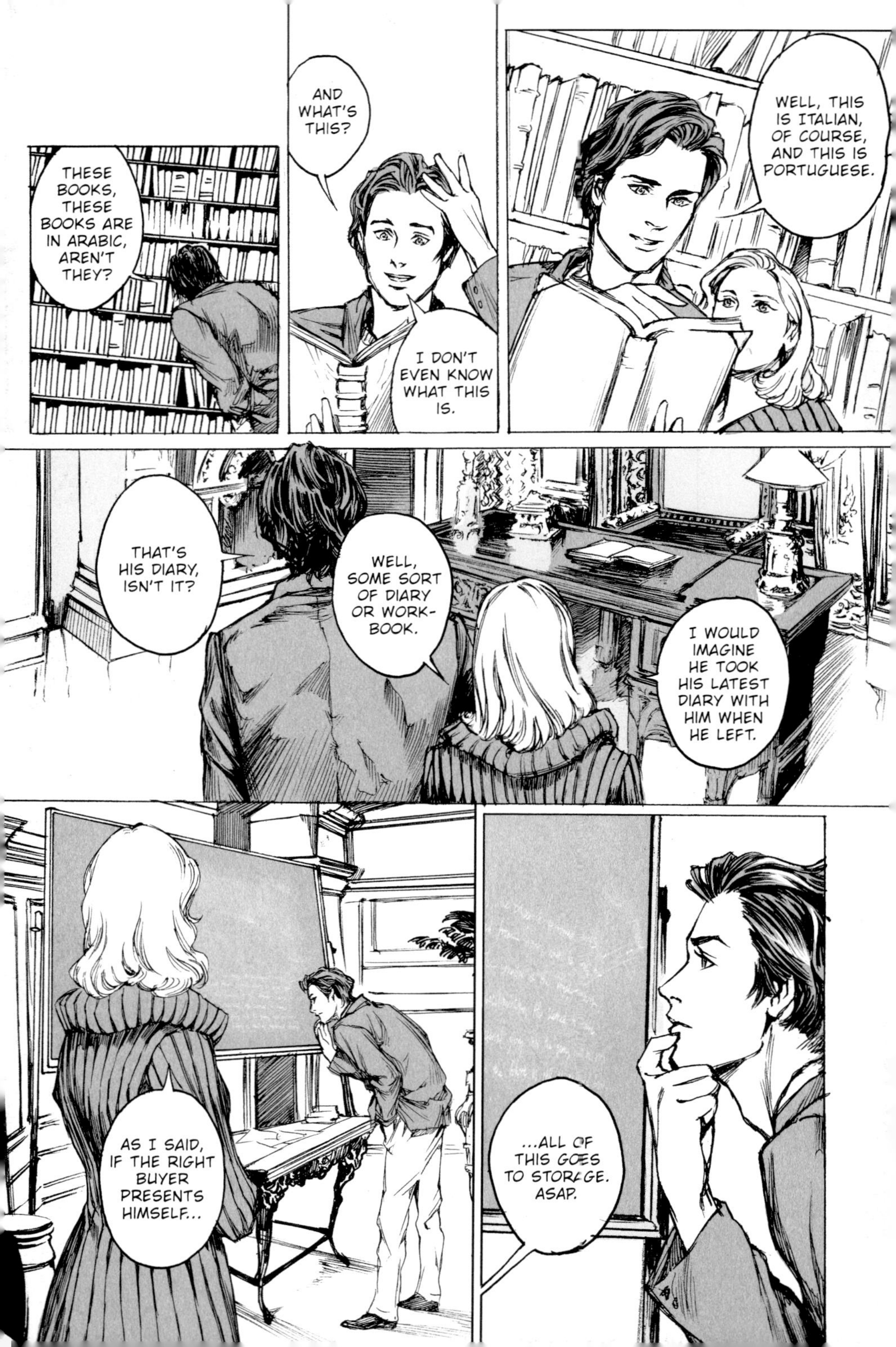

THESE BOOKS, THESE BOOKS ARE IN ARABIC, AREN'T THEY?
AND WHAT'S THIS?
I DON'T EVEN KNOW WHAT THIS IS.
WELL, THIS IS ITALIAN, OF COURSE, AND THIS IS PORTUGUESE.
THAT'S HIS DIARY, ISN'T IT?
WELL, SOME SORT OF DIARY OR WORK-BOOK.
I WOULD IMAGINE HE TOOK HIS LATEST DIARY WITH HIM WHEN HE LEFT.
AS I SAID, IF THE RIGHT BUYER PRESENTS HIMSELF...
...ALL OF THIS GOES TO STORAGE. ASAP.

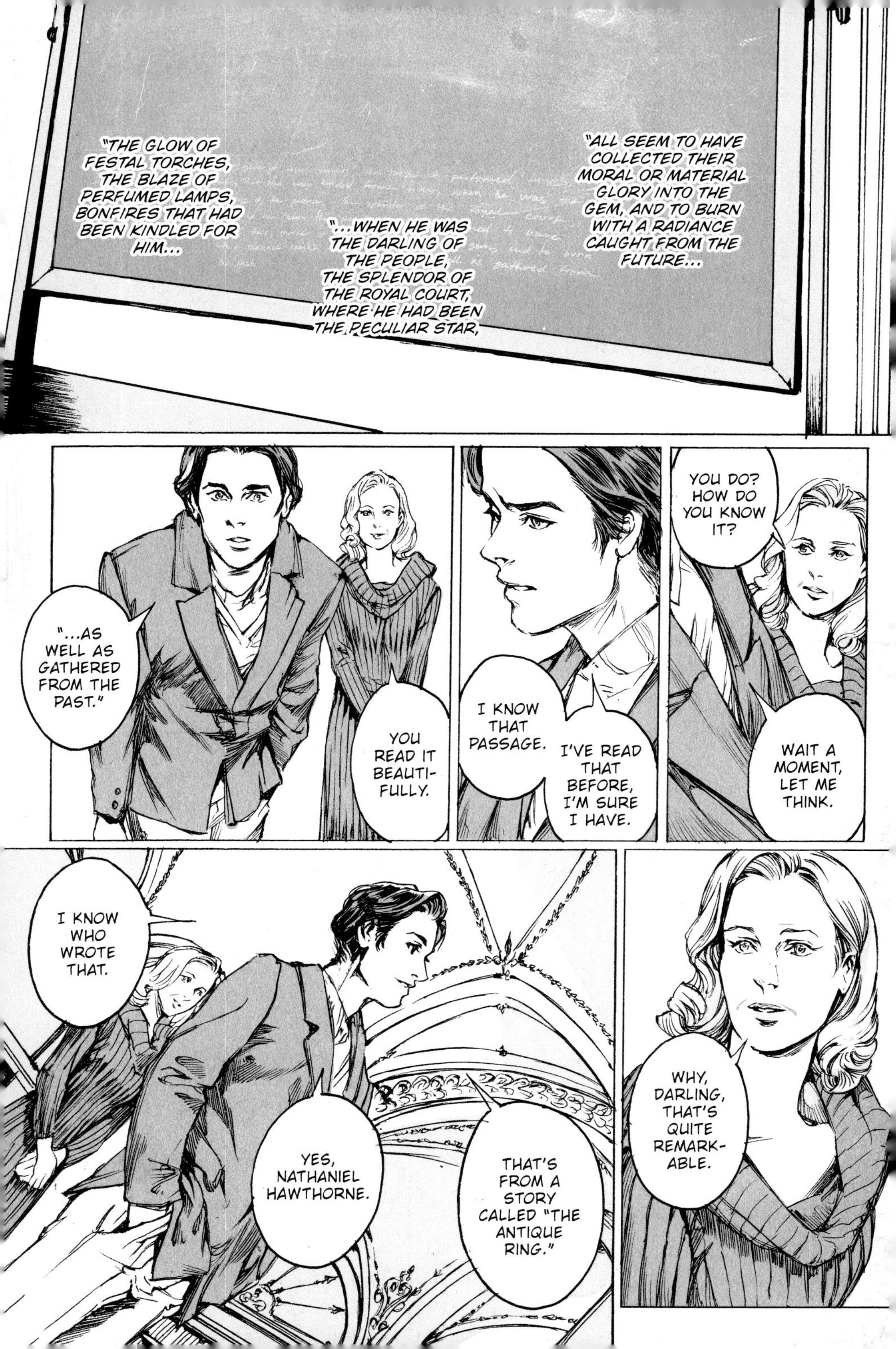
"THE GLOW OF FESTAL TORCHES, THE BLAZE OF PERFUMED LAMPS, BONFIRES THAT HAD BEEN KINDLED FOR HIM...
"...WHEN HE WAS THE DARLING OF THE PEOPLE, THE SPLENDOR OF THE ROYAL COURT, WHERE HE HAD BEEN THE PECULIAR STAR,
"ALL SEEM TO HAVE COLLECTED THEIR MORAL OR MATERIAL GLORY INTO THE GEM, AND TO BURN WITH A RADIANCE CAUGHT FROM THE FUTURE...
"...AS WELL AS GATHERED FROM THE PAST."
YOU READ IT BEAUTI-FULLY.
I KNOW THAT PASSAGE.
I'VE READ THAT BEFORE, I'M SURE I HAVE.
YOU DO? HOW DO YOU KNOW IT?
WAIT A MOMENT, LET ME THINK.
I KNOW WHO WROTE THAT.
YES, NATHANIEL HAWTHORNE.
THAT'S FROM A STORY CALLED "THE ANTIQUE RING."
WHY, DARLING, THAT'S QUITE REMARK-ABLE.

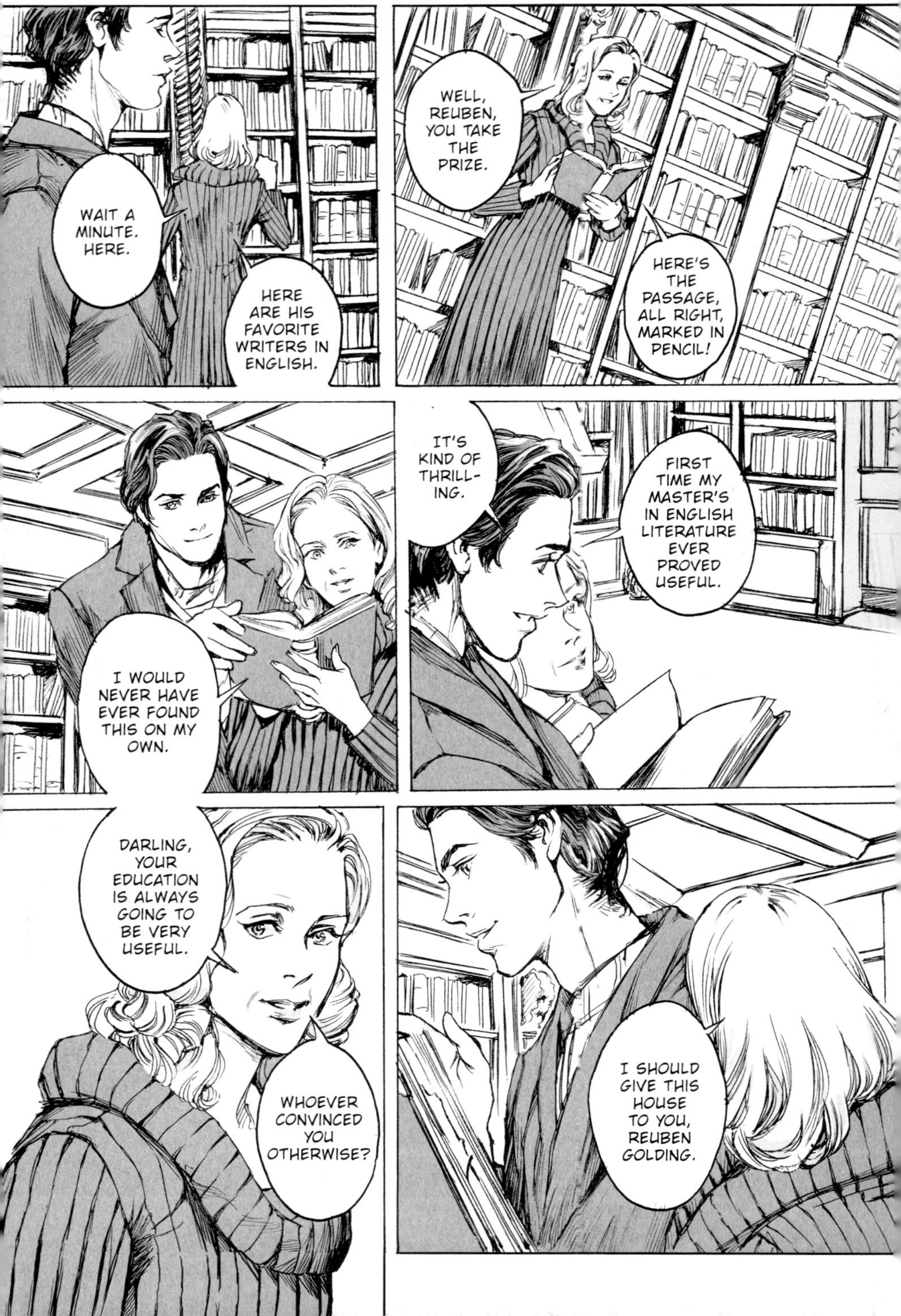
WAIT A MINUTE. HERE.
HERE ARE HIS FAVORITE WRITERS IN ENGLISH.
WELL, REUBEN, YOU TAKE THE PRIZE.
HERE'S THE PASSAGE, ALL RIGHT, MARKED IN PENCIL!
I WOULD NEVER HAVE EVER FOUND THIS ON MY OWN.
IT'S KIND OF THRILL-ING.
FIRST TIME MY MASTER'S IN ENGLISH LITERATURE EVER PROVED USEFUL.
DARLING, YOUR EDUCATION IS ALWAYS GOING TO BE VERY USEFUL.
WHOEVER CONVINCED YOU OTHERWISE?
I SHOULD GIVE THIS HOUSE TO YOU, REUBEN GOLDING.

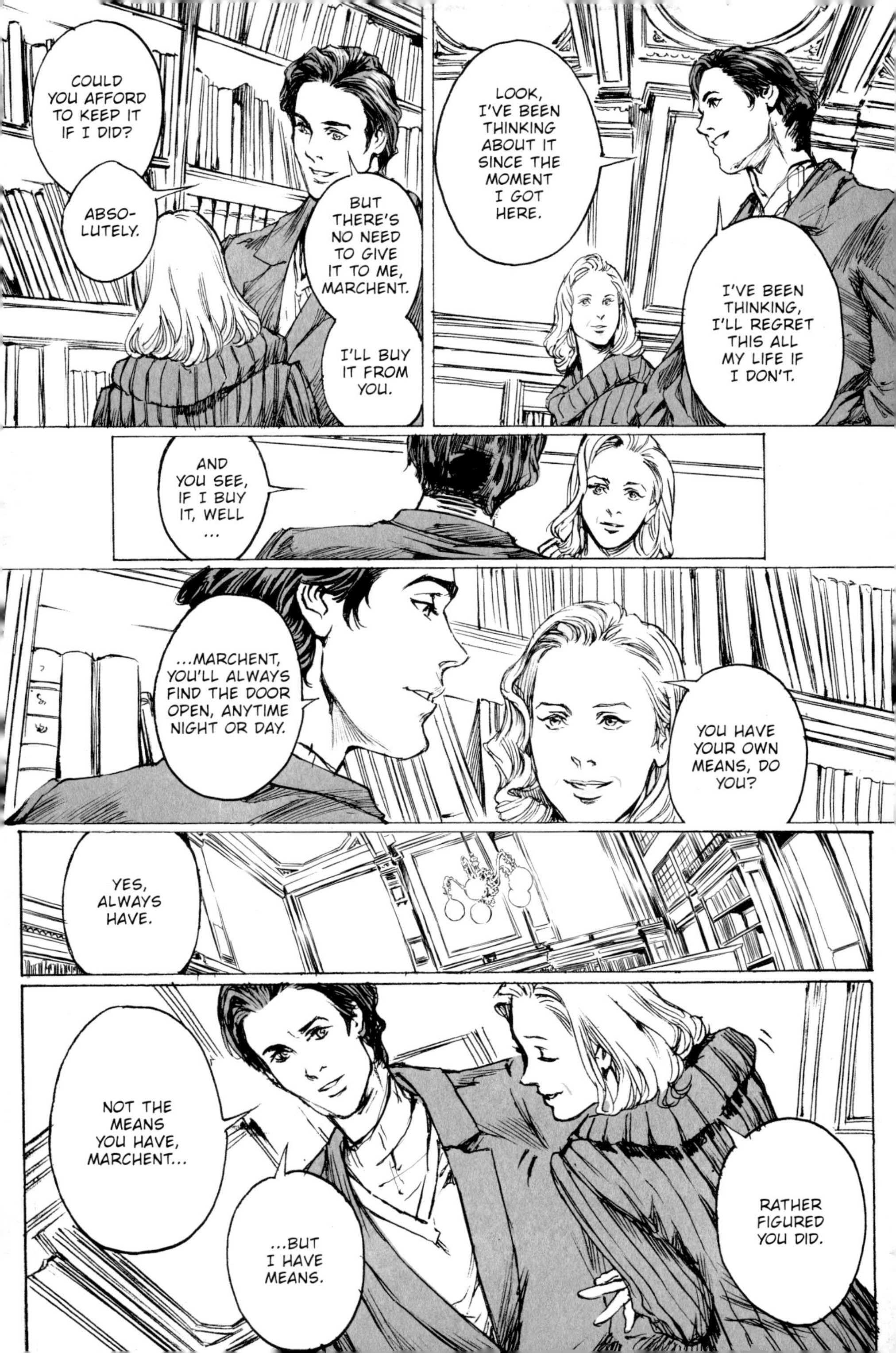
COULD YOU AFFORD TO KEEP IT IF I DID?
ABSO-LUTELY.
BUT THERE'S NO NEED TO GIVE IT TO ME, MARCHENT.
I'LL BUY IT FROM YOU.
LOOK, I'VE BEEN THINKING ABOUT IT SINCE THE MOMENT I GOT HERE.
I'VE BEEN THINKING, I'LL REGRET THIS ALL MY LIFE IF I DON'T.
AND YOU SEE, IF I BUY IT, WELL ...
...MARCHENT, YOU'LL ALWAYS FIND THE DOOR OPEN, ANYTIME NIGHT OR DAY.
YOU HAVE YOUR OWN MEANS, DO YOU?
YES, ALWAYS HAVE.
NOT THE MEANS YOU HAVE, MARCHENT...
...BUT I HAVE MEANS.
RATHER FIGURED YOU DID.

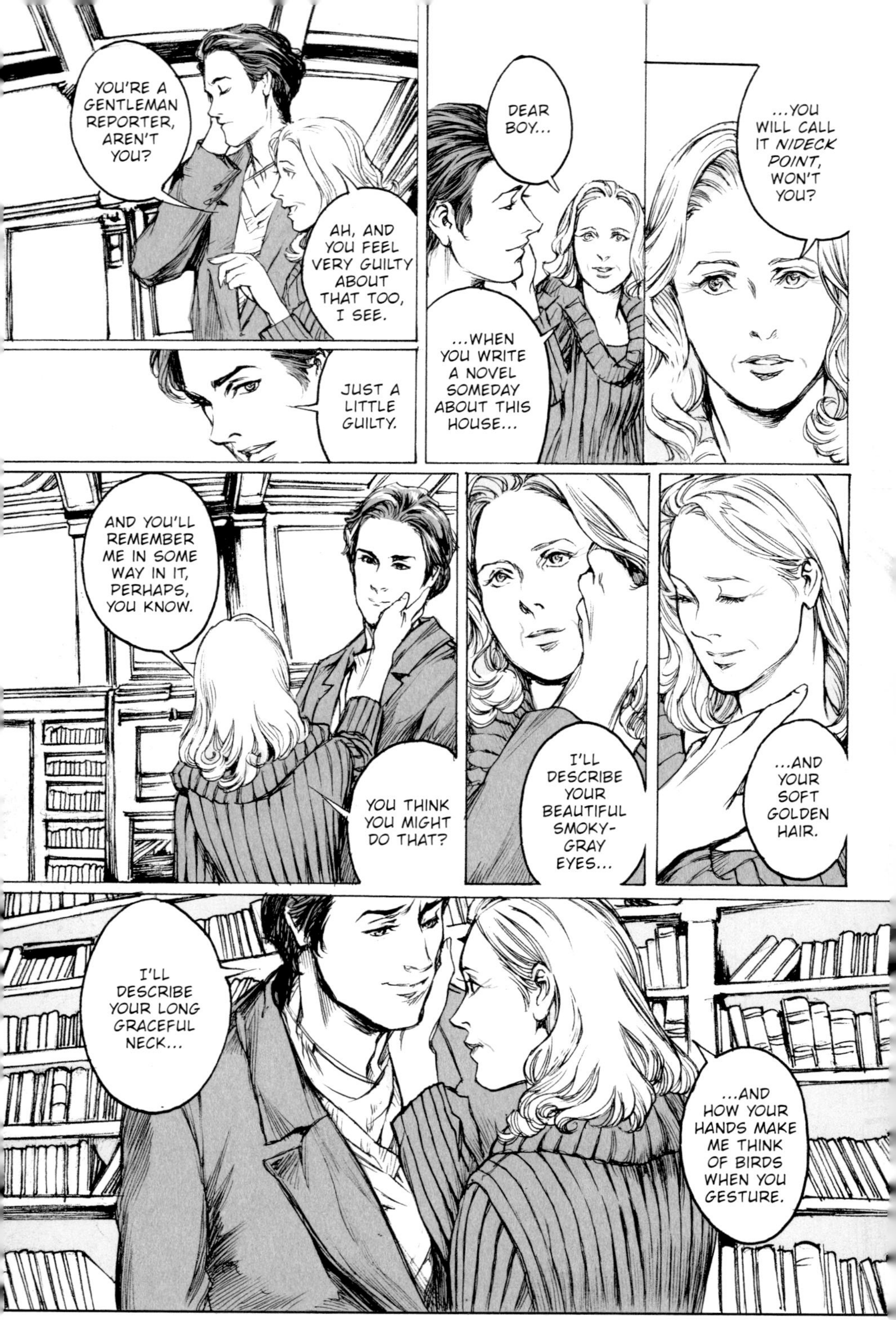
YOU'RE A GENTLEMAN REPORTER, AREN'T YOU?
AH, AND YOU FEEL VERY GUILTY ABOUT THAT TOO, I SEE.
JUST A LITTLE GUILTY.
DEAR BOY...
...WHEN YOU WRITE A NOVEL SOMEDAY ABOUT THIS HOUSE...
...YOU WILL CALL IT *NIDECK POINT*, WON'T YOU?
AND YOU'LL REMEMBER ME IN SOME WAY IN IT, PERHAPS, YOU KNOW.
YOU THINK YOU MIGHT DO THAT?
I'LL DESCRIBE YOUR BEAUTIFUL SMOKY-GRAY EYES...
...AND YOUR SOFT GOLDEN HAIR.
I'LL DESCRIBE YOUR LONG GRACEFUL NECK...
...AND HOW YOUR HANDS MAKE ME THINK OF BIRDS WHEN YOU GESTURE.

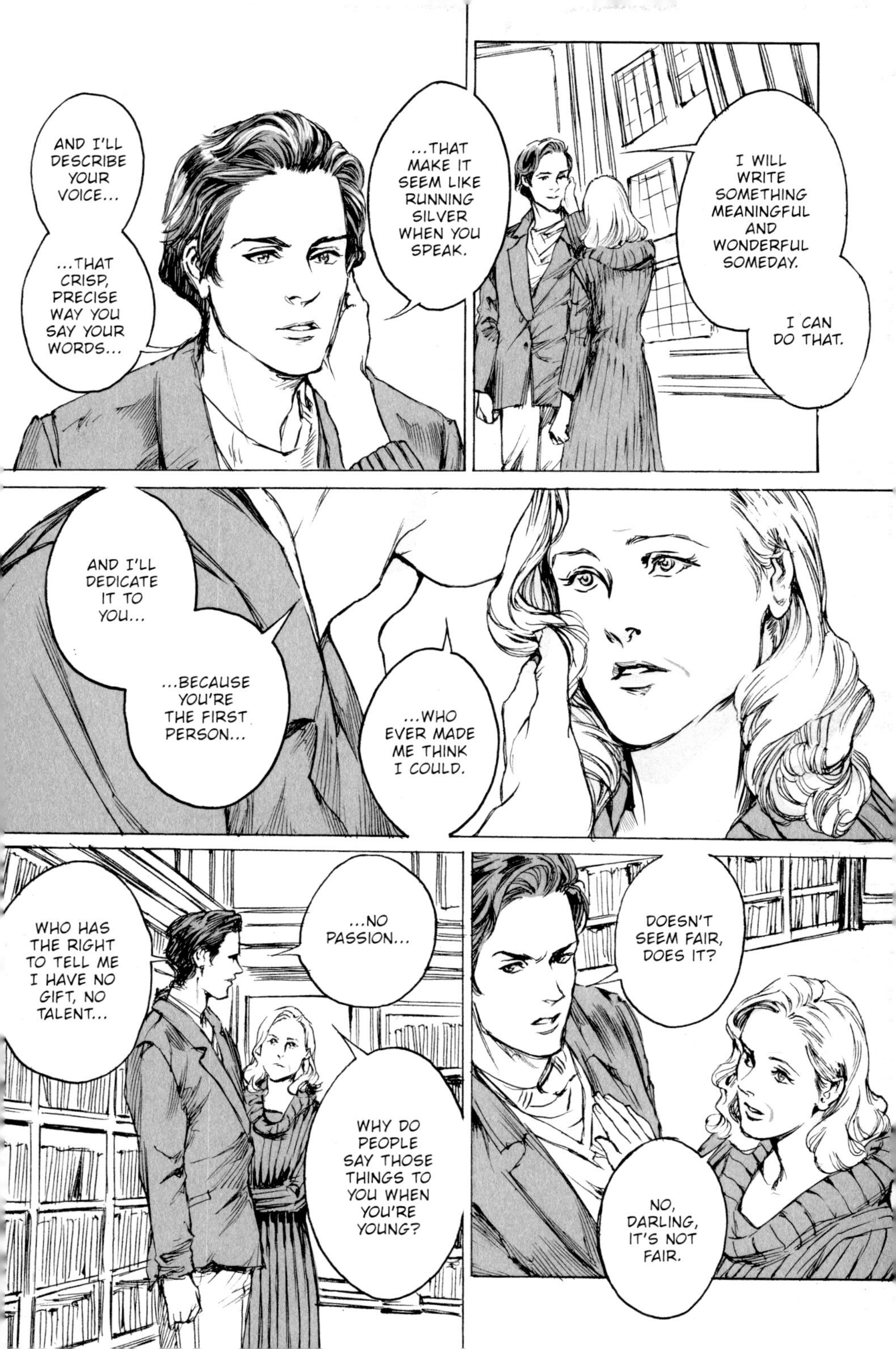
AND I'LL DESCRIBE YOUR VOICE...
...THAT CRISP, PRECISE WAY YOU SAY YOUR WORDS...
...THAT MAKE IT SEEM LIKE RUNNING SILVER WHEN YOU SPEAK.
I WILL WRITE SOMETHING MEANINGFUL AND WONDERFUL SOMEDAY.
I CAN DO THAT.
AND I'LL DEDICATE IT TO YOU...
...BECAUSE YOU'RE THE FIRST PERSON...
...WHO EVER MADE ME THINK I COULD.
WHO HAS THE RIGHT TO TELL ME I HAVE NO GIFT, NO TALENT...
...NO PASSION...
WHY DO PEOPLE SAY THOSE THINGS TO YOU WHEN YOU'RE YOUNG?
DOESN'T SEEM FAIR, DOES IT?
NO, DARLING, IT'S NOT FAIR.

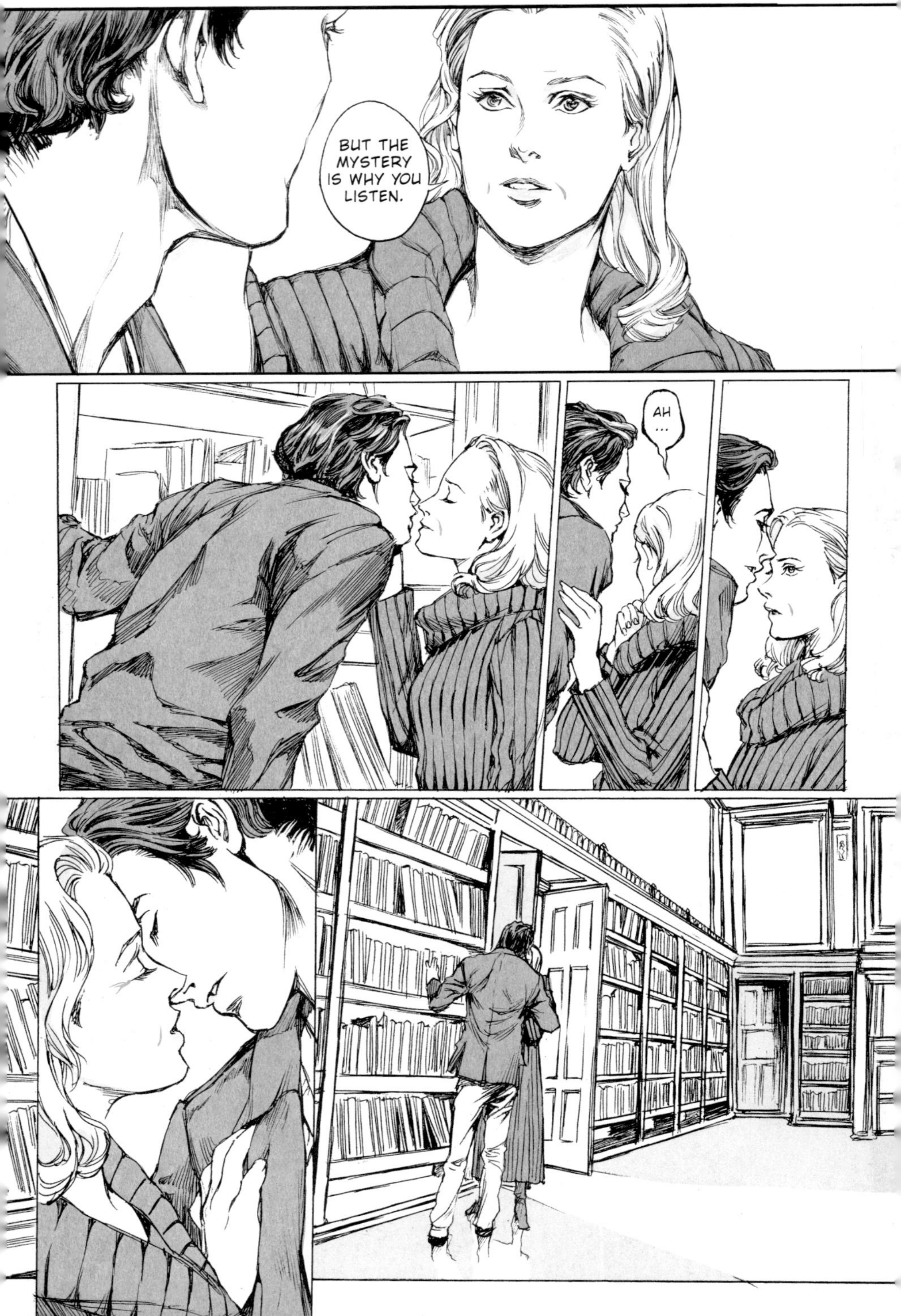
BUT THE MYSTERY IS WHY YOU LISTEN.
AH ...

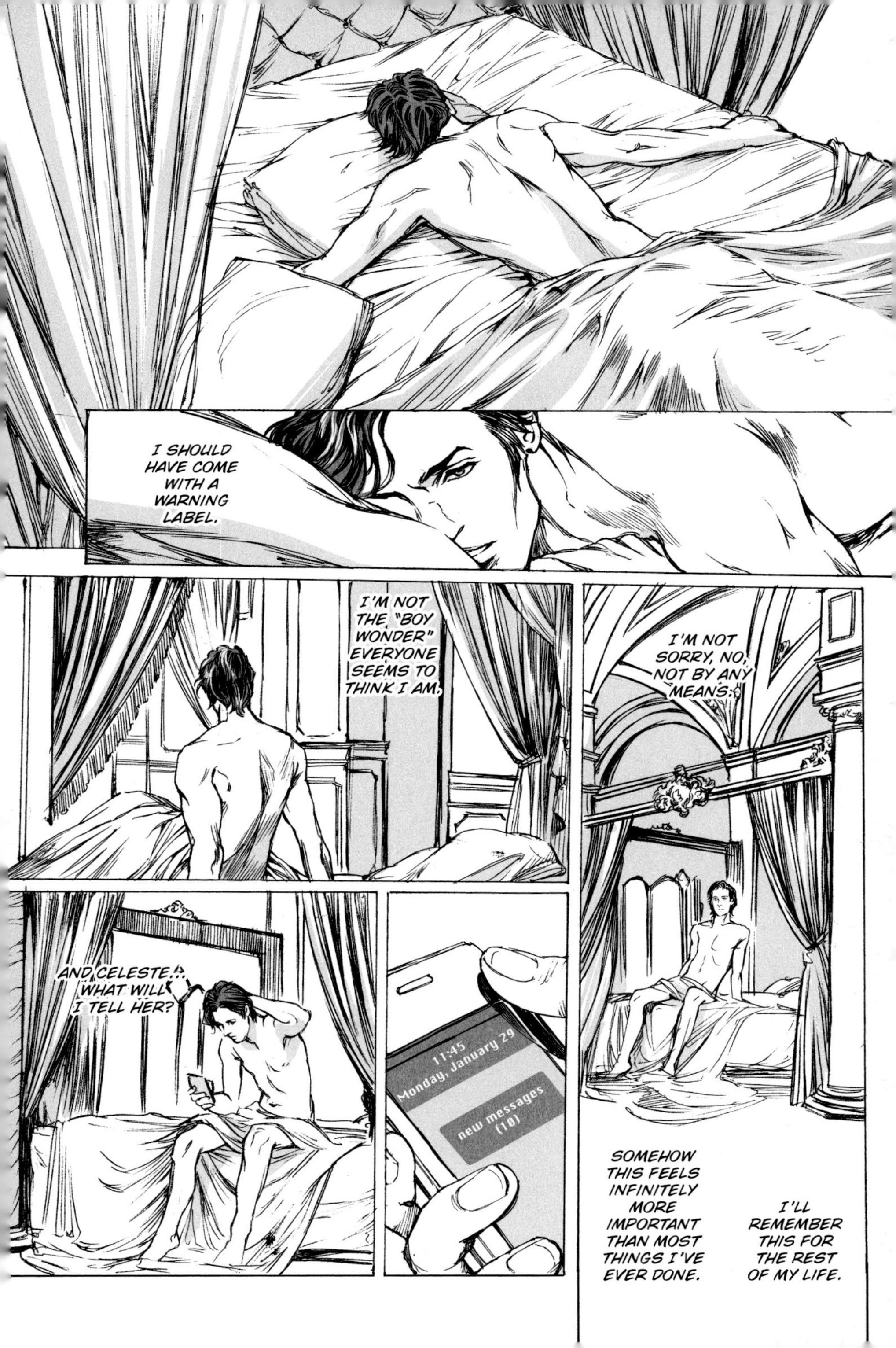
I SHOULD HAVE COME WITH A WARNING LABEL.
I'M NOT THE "BOY WONDER" EVERYONE SEEMS TO THINK I AM.
AND CELESTE... WHAT WILL I TELL HER?
11:45
Monday, January 29
new messages (10)
I'M NOT SORRY, NO, NOT BY ANY MEANS.
SOMEHOW THIS FEELS INFINITELY MORE IMPORTANT THAN MOST THINGS I'VE EVER DONE.
I'LL REMEMBER THIS FOR THE REST OF MY LIFE.

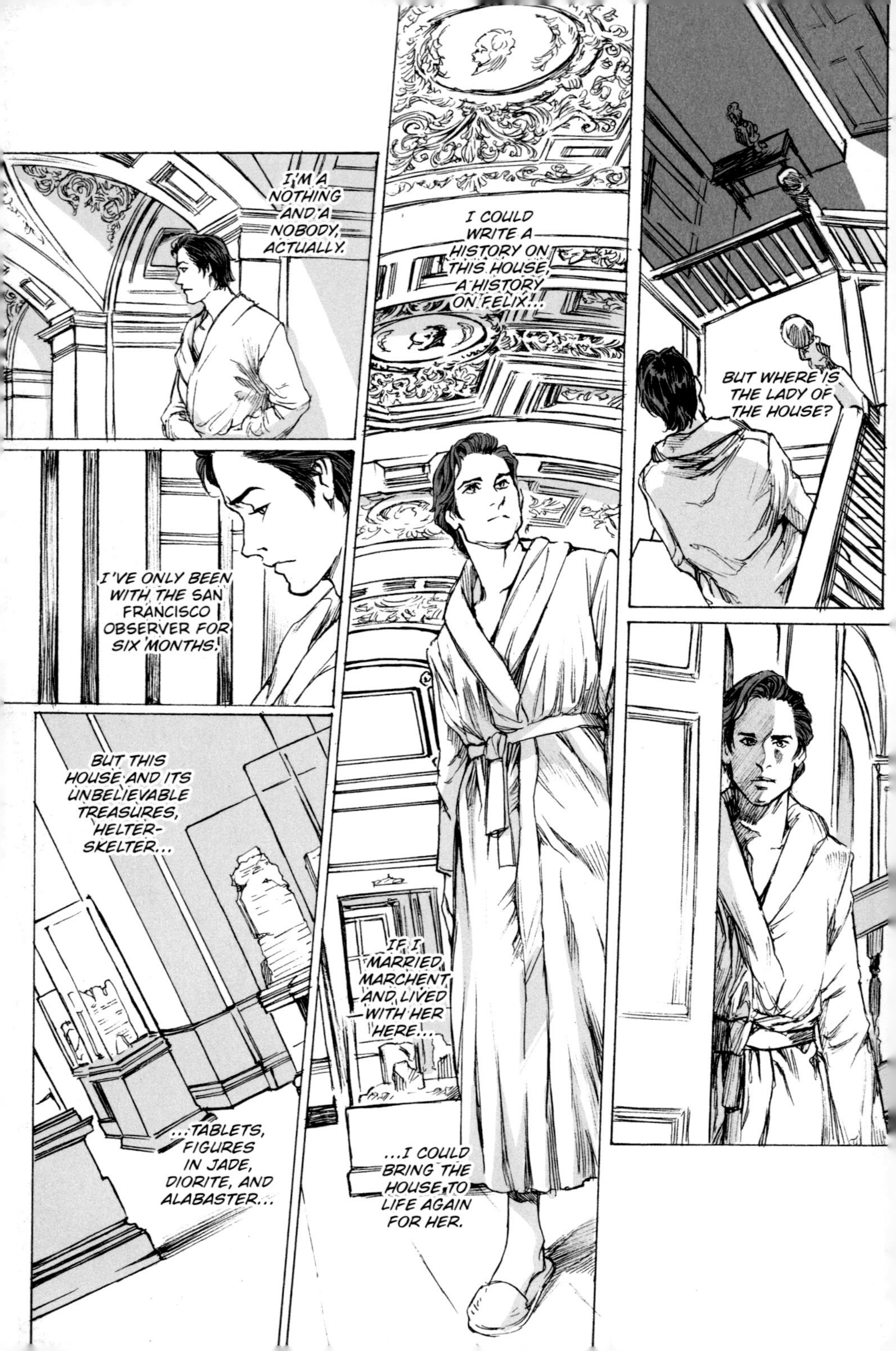
I'M A NOTHING AND A NOBODY, ACTUALLY.
I'VE ONLY BEEN WITH THE SAN FRANCISCO OBSERVER FOR SIX MONTHS.
BUT THIS HOUSE AND ITS UNBELIEVABLE TREASURES, HELTER-SKELTER...
...TABLETS, FIGURES IN JADE, DIORITE, AND ALABASTER...
I COULD WRITE A HISTORY ON THIS HOUSE, A HISTORY ON FELIX...
IF I MARRIED MARCHENT AND LIVED WITH HER HERE...
...I COULD BRING THE HOUSE TO LIFE AGAIN FOR HER.
BUT WHERE IS THE LADY OF THE HOUSE?

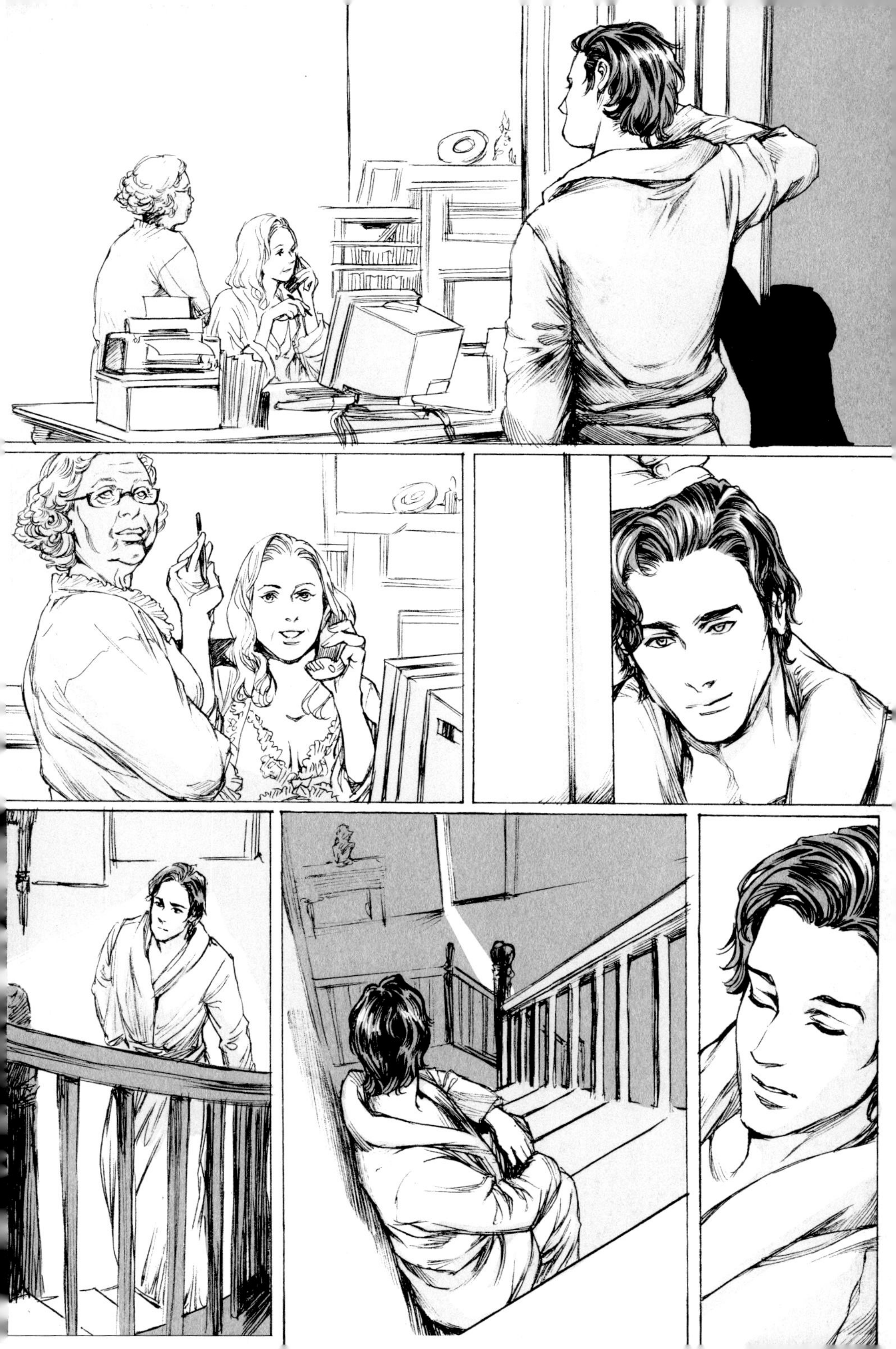

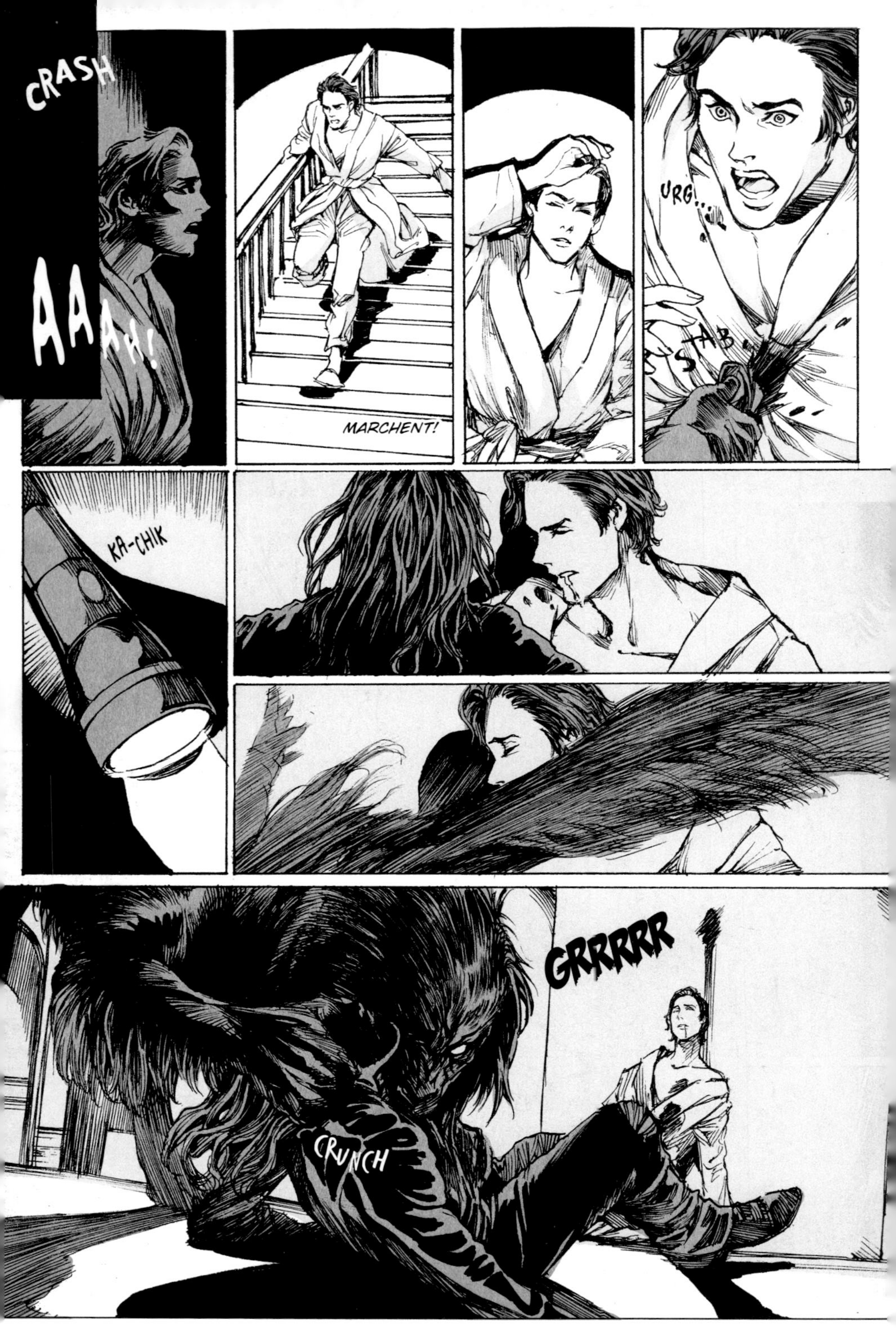
CRASH
AAAAH!
MARCHENT!
URG...
STAB
KA-CHIK
GRRRRR
CRUNCH

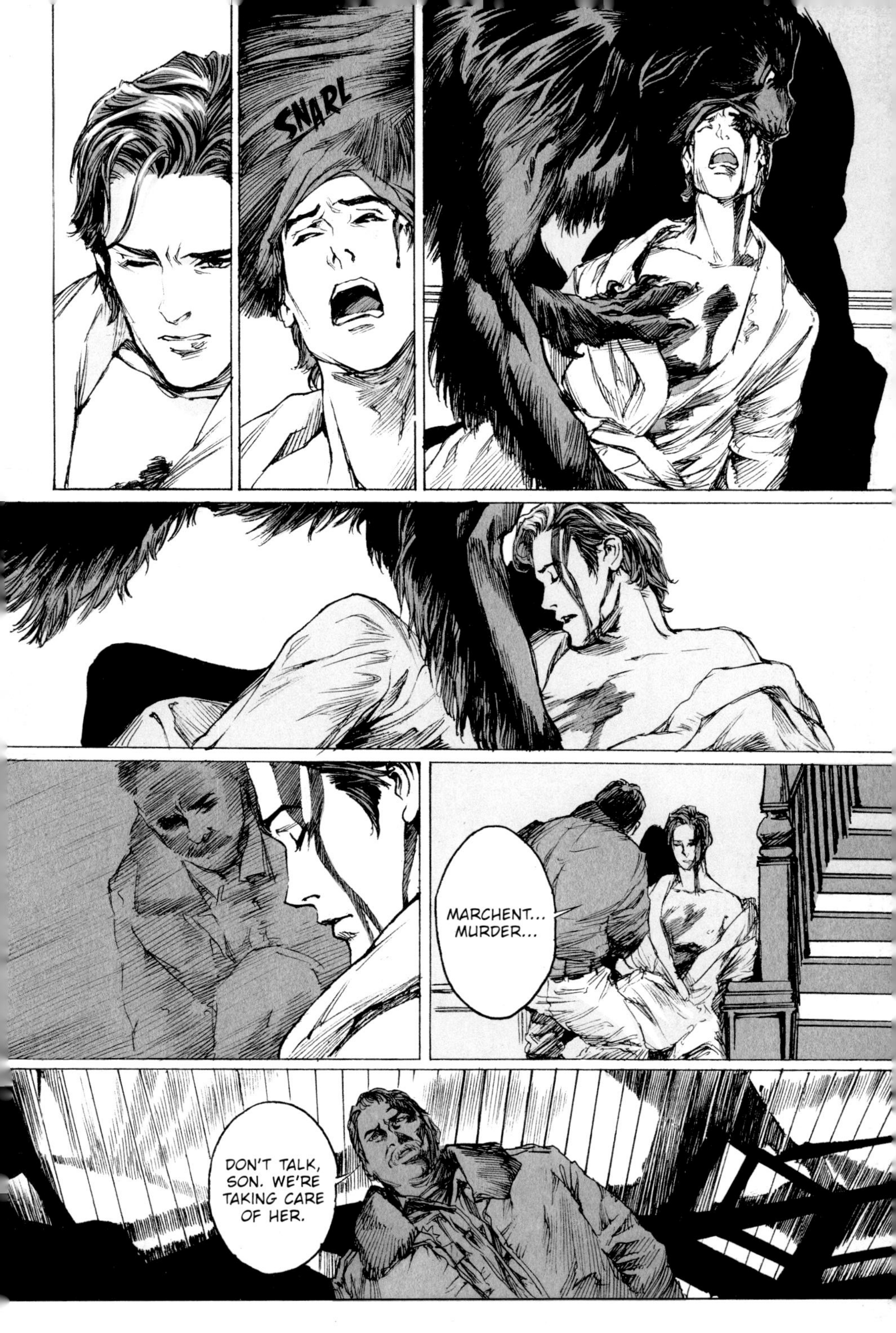
SNARL
MARCHENT... MURDER...
DON'T TALK, SON. WE'RE TAKING CARE OF HER.

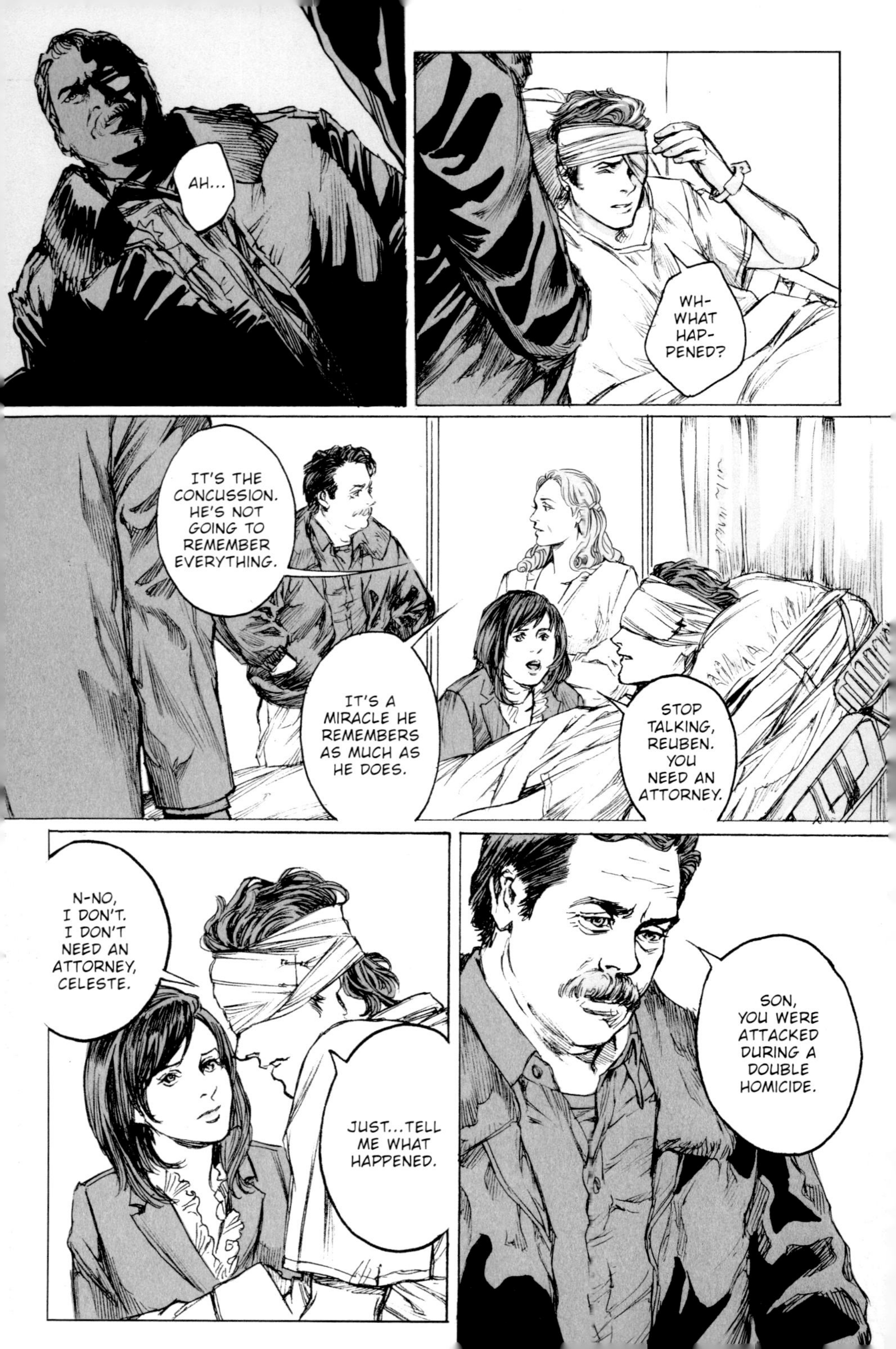
AH...
WH-WHAT HAP-PENED?
IT'S THE CONCUSSION. HE'S NOT GOING TO REMEMBER EVERYTHING.
IT'S A MIRACLE HE REMEMBERS AS MUCH AS HE DOES.
STOP TALKING, REUBEN. YOU NEED AN ATTORNEY.
N-NO, I DON'T. I DON'T NEED AN ATTORNEY, CELESTE.
JUST...TELL ME WHAT HAPPENED.
SON, YOU WERE ATTACKED DURING A DOUBLE HOMICIDE.

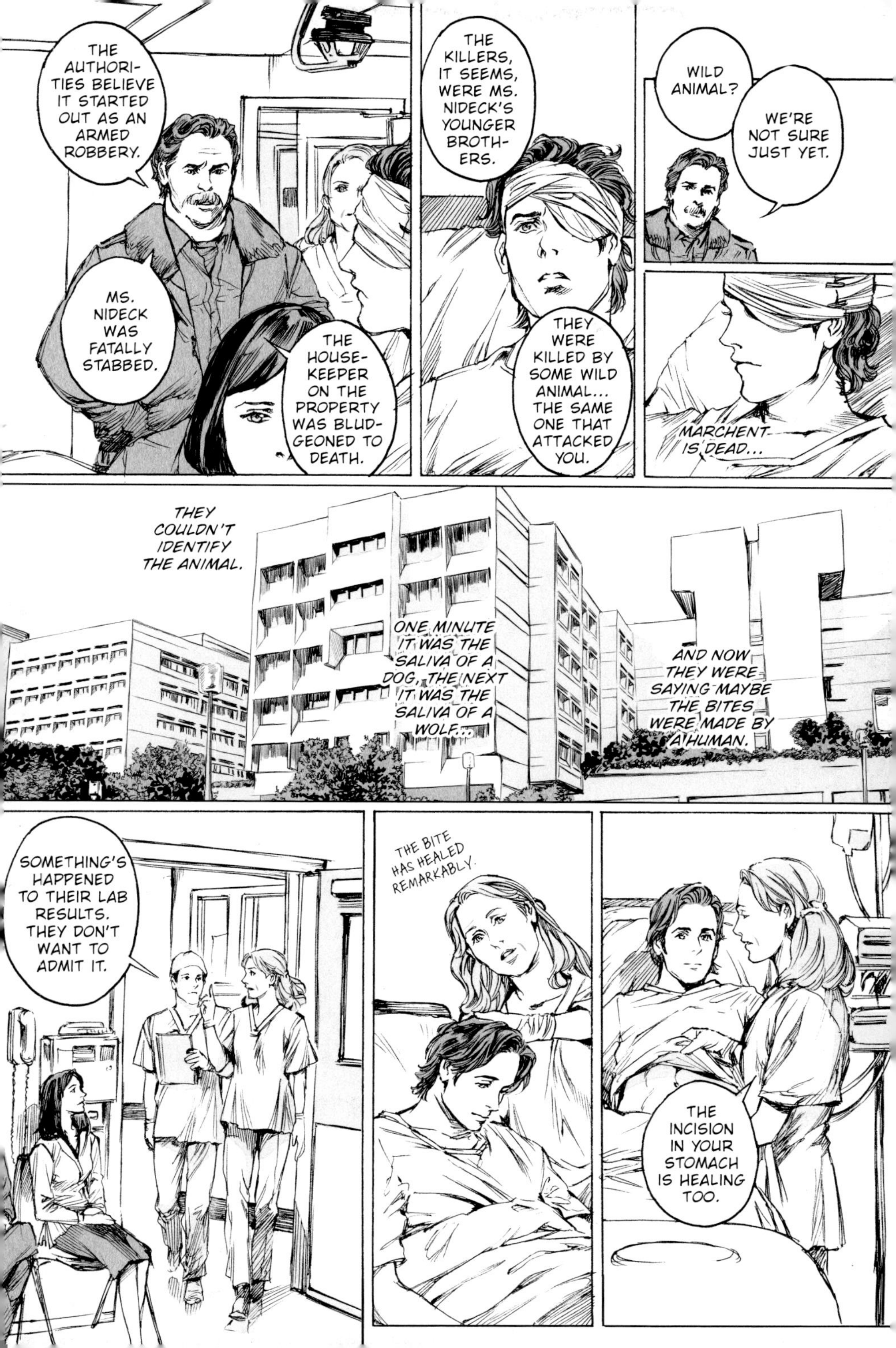
THE AUTHORITIES BELIEVE IT STARTED OUT AS AN ARMED ROBBERY.
MS. NIDECK WAS FATALLY STABBED.
THE HOUSEKEEPER ON THE PROPERTY WAS BLUDGEONED TO DEATH.
THE KILLERS, IT SEEMS, WERE MS. NIDECK'S YOUNGER BROTHERS.
THEY WERE KILLED BY SOME WILD ANIMAL... THE SAME ONE THAT ATTACKED YOU.
WILD ANIMAL?
WE'RE NOT SURE JUST YET.
MARCHENT IS DEAD...
THEY COULDN'T IDENTIFY THE ANIMAL.
ONE MINUTE IT WAS THE SALIVA OF A DOG, THE NEXT IT WAS THE SALIVA OF A WOLF...
AND NOW THEY WERE SAYING MAYBE THE BITES WERE MADE BY A HUMAN.
SOMETHING'S HAPPENED TO THEIR LAB RESULTS. THEY DON'T WANT TO ADMIT IT.
THE BITE HAS HEALED REMARKABLY.
THE INCISION IN YOUR STOMACH IS HEALING TOO.

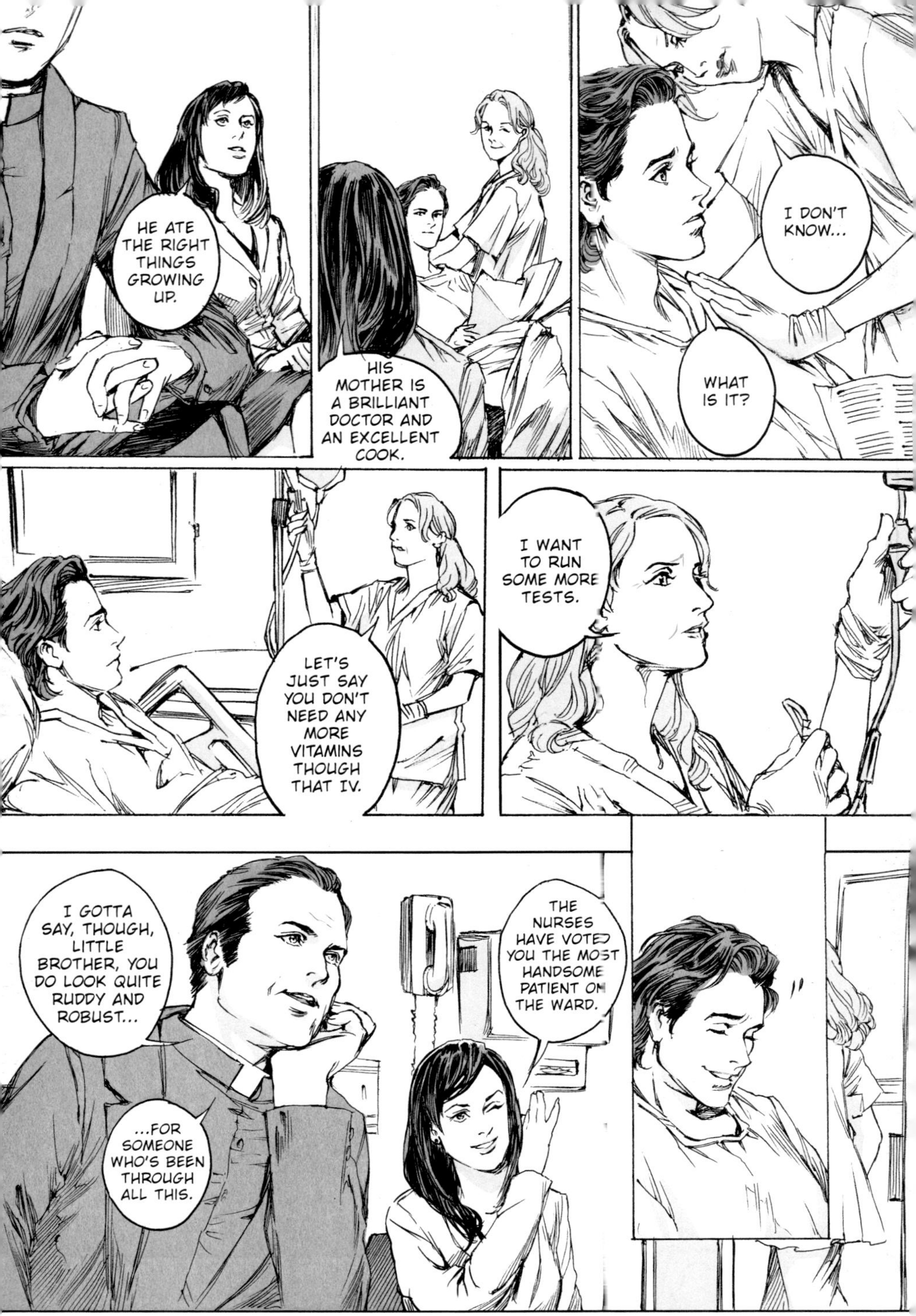
HE ATE THE RIGHT THINGS GROWING UP.
HIS MOTHER IS A BRILLIANT DOCTOR AND AN EXCELLENT COOK.
I DON'T KNOW...
WHAT IS IT?
LET'S JUST SAY YOU DON'T NEED ANY MORE VITAMINS THOUGH THAT IV.
I WANT TO RUN SOME MORE TESTS.
I GOTTA SAY, THOUGH, LITTLE BROTHER, YOU DO LOOK QUITE RUDDY AND ROBUST...
...FOR SOMEONE WHO'S BEEN THROUGH ALL THIS.
THE NURSES HAVE VOTED YOU THE MOST HANDSOME PATIENT ON THE WARD.

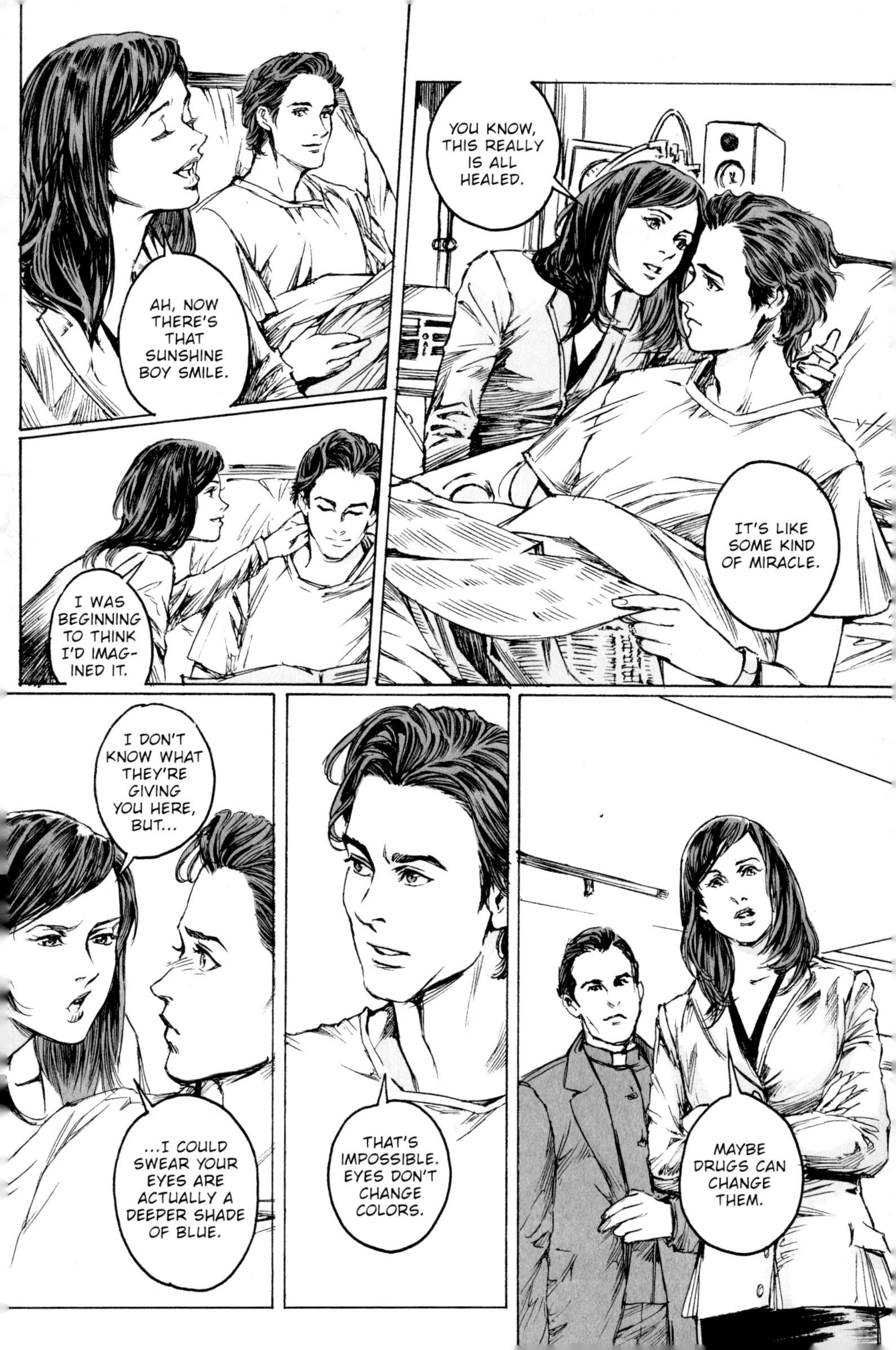
AH, NOW THERE'S THAT SUNSHINE BOY SMILE.
I WAS BEGINNING TO THINK I'D IMAG-INED IT.
YOU KNOW, THIS REALLY IS ALL HEALED.
IT'S LIKE SOME KIND OF MIRACLE.
I DON'T KNOW WHAT THEY'RE GIVING YOU HERE, BUT...
...I COULD SWEAR YOUR EYES ARE ACTUALLY A DEEPER SHADE OF BLUE.
THAT'S IMPOSSIBLE. EYES DON'T CHANGE COLORS.
MAYBE DRUGS CAN CHANGE THEM.

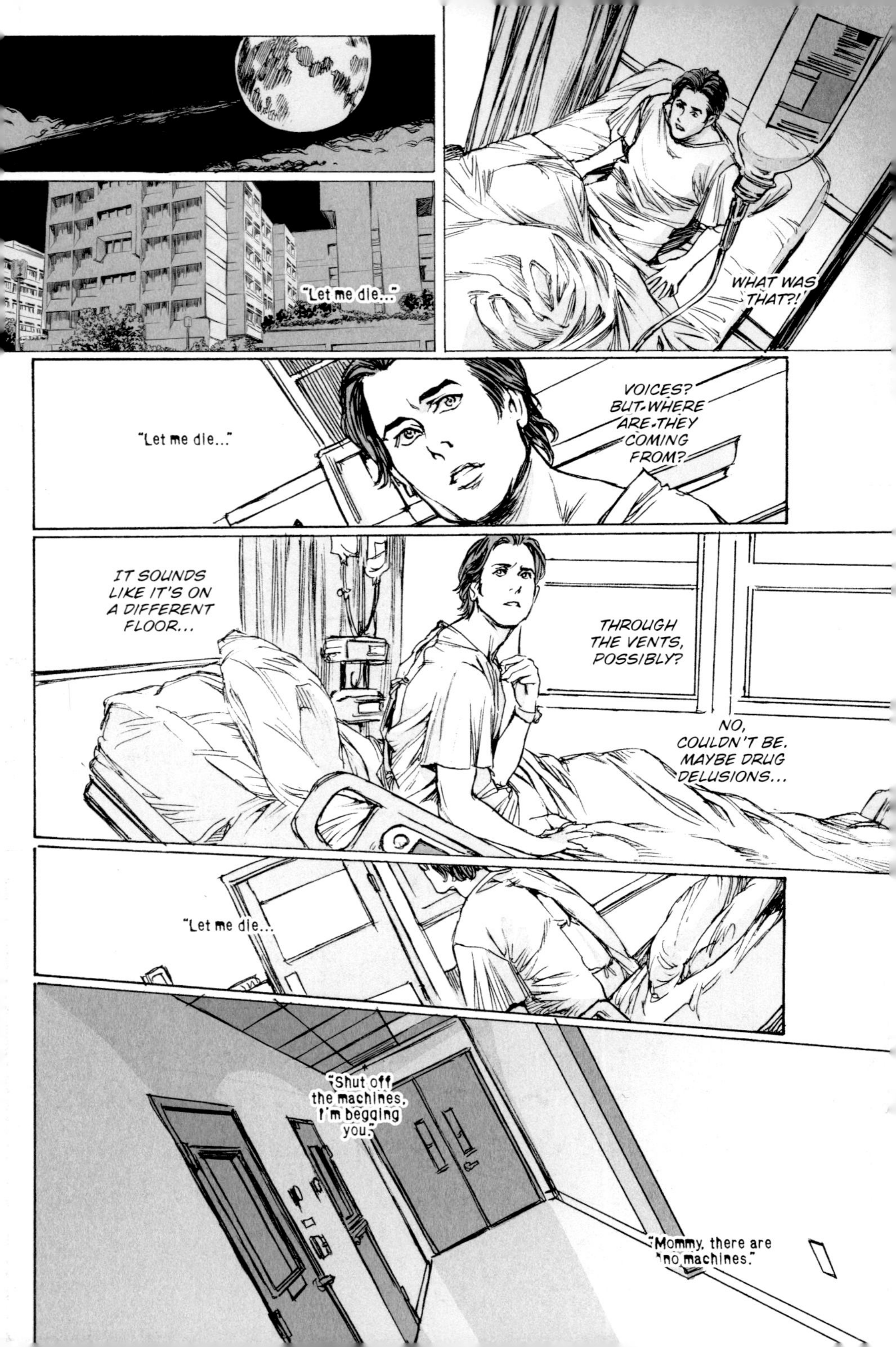
"Let me die..."
WHAT WAS THAT?!
"Let me die..."
VOICES? BUT WHERE ARE THEY COMING FROM?
IT SOUNDS LIKE IT'S ON A DIFFERENT FLOOR...
THROUGH THE VENTS, POSSIBLY?
NO, COULDN'T BE. MAYBE DRUG DELUSIONS...
"Let me die...
"Shut off the machines. I'm begging you."
"Mommy, there are no machines."

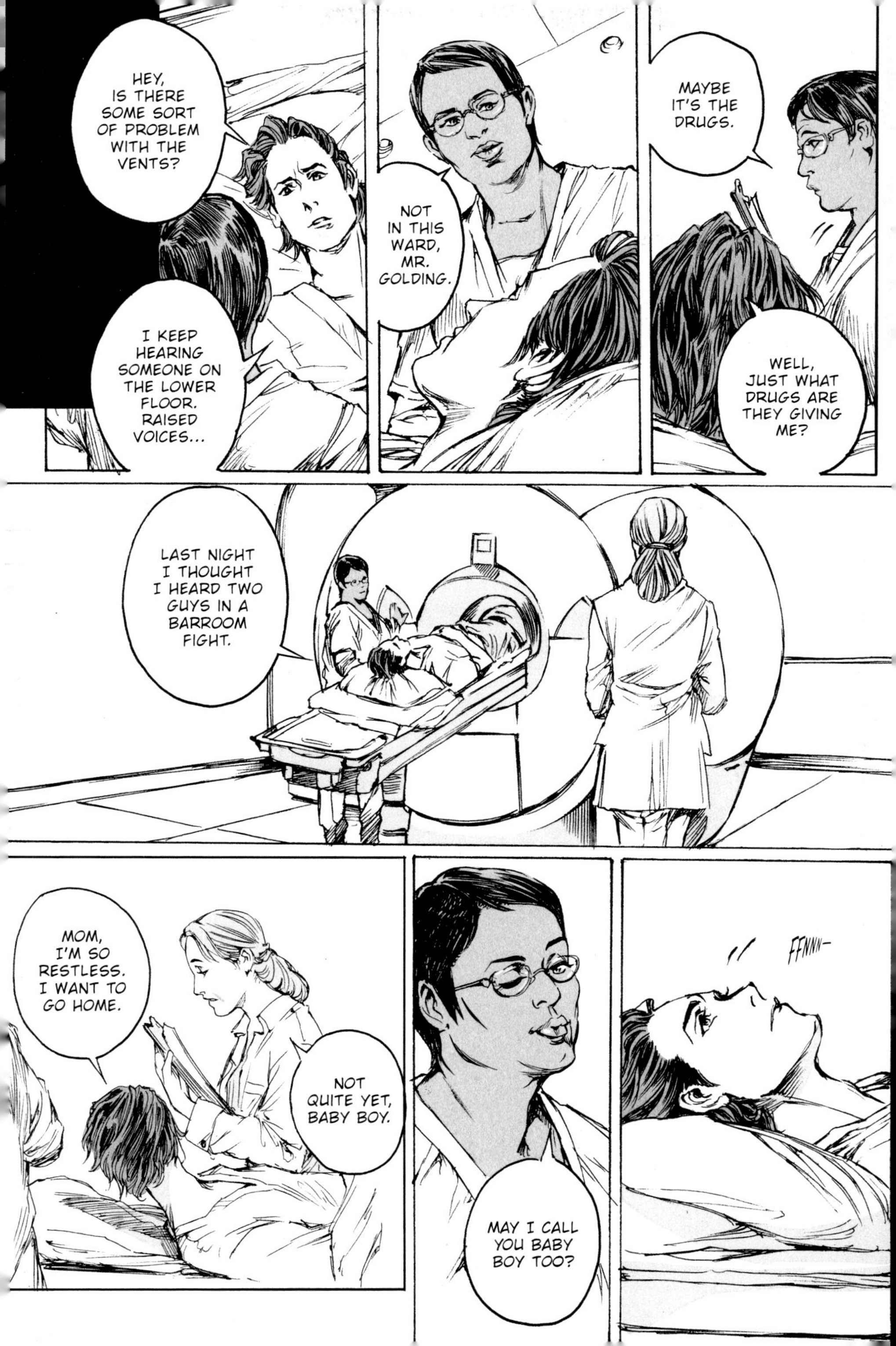
HEY, IS THERE SOME SORT OF PROBLEM WITH THE VENTS?
I KEEP HEARING SOMEONE ON THE LOWER FLOOR. RAISED VOICES...
NOT IN THIS WARD, MR. GOLDING.
MAYBE IT'S THE DRUGS.
WELL, JUST WHAT DRUGS ARE THEY GIVING ME?
LAST NIGHT I THOUGHT I HEARD TWO GUYS IN A BARROOM FIGHT.
MOM, I'M SO RESTLESS. I WANT TO GO HOME.
NOT QUITE YET, BABY BOY.
MAY I CALL YOU BABY BOY TOO?
FFNNN-

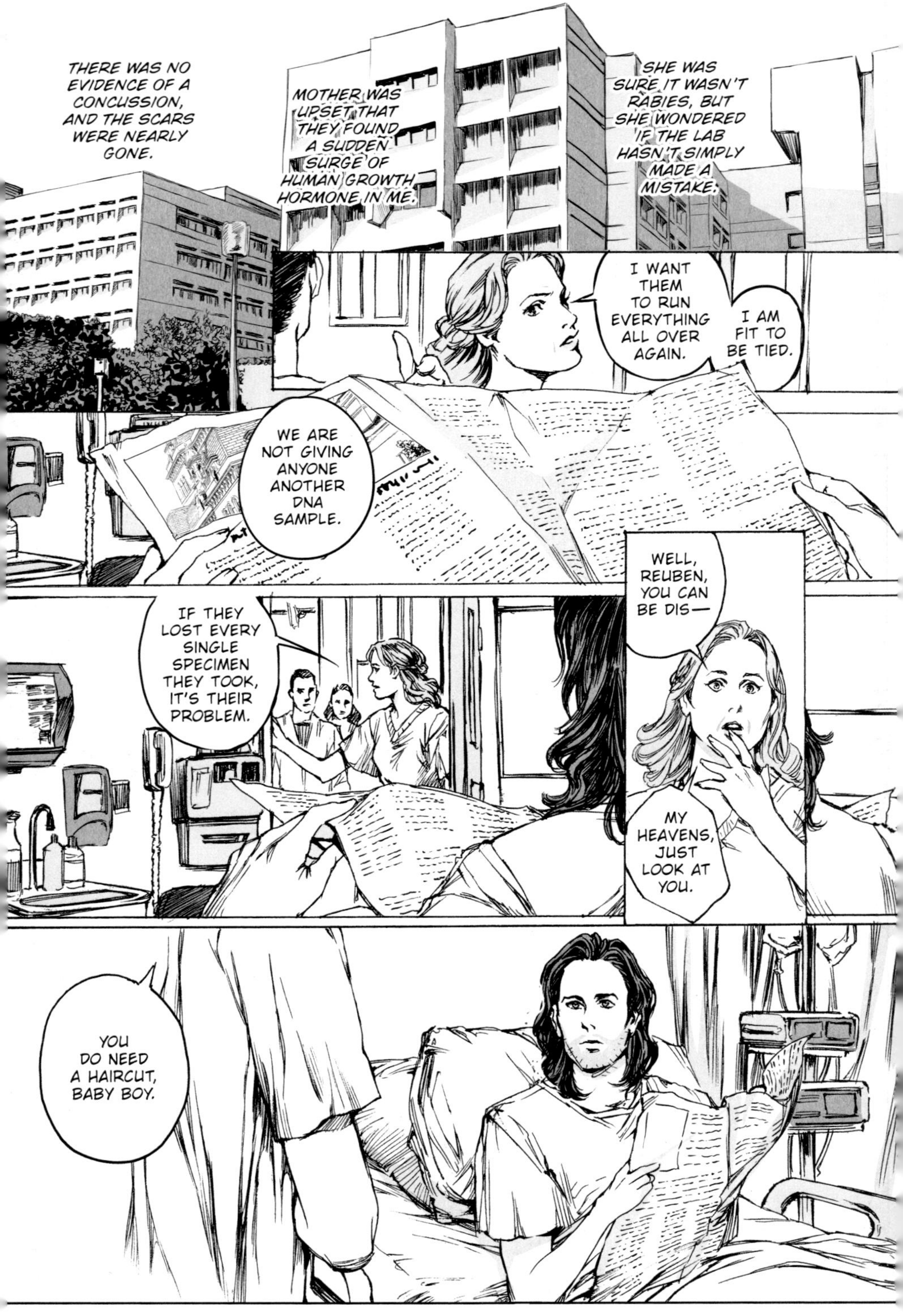
THERE WAS NO EVIDENCE OF A CONCUSSION, AND THE SCARS WERE NEARLY GONE.
MOTHER WAS UPSET THAT THEY FOUND A SUDDEN SURGE OF HUMAN GROWTH HORMONE IN ME.
SHE WAS SURE IT WASN'T RABIES, BUT SHE WONDERED IF THE LAB HASN'T SIMPLY MADE A MISTAKE.
I WANT THEM TO RUN EVERYTHING ALL OVER AGAIN.
I AM FIT TO BE TIED.
WE ARE NOT GIVING ANYONE ANOTHER DNA SAMPLE.
IF THEY LOST EVERY SINGLE SPECIMEN THEY TOOK, IT'S THEIR PROBLEM.
WELL, REUBEN, YOU CAN BE DIS—
MY HEAVENS, JUST LOOK AT YOU.
YOU DO NEED A HAIRCUT, BABY BOY.

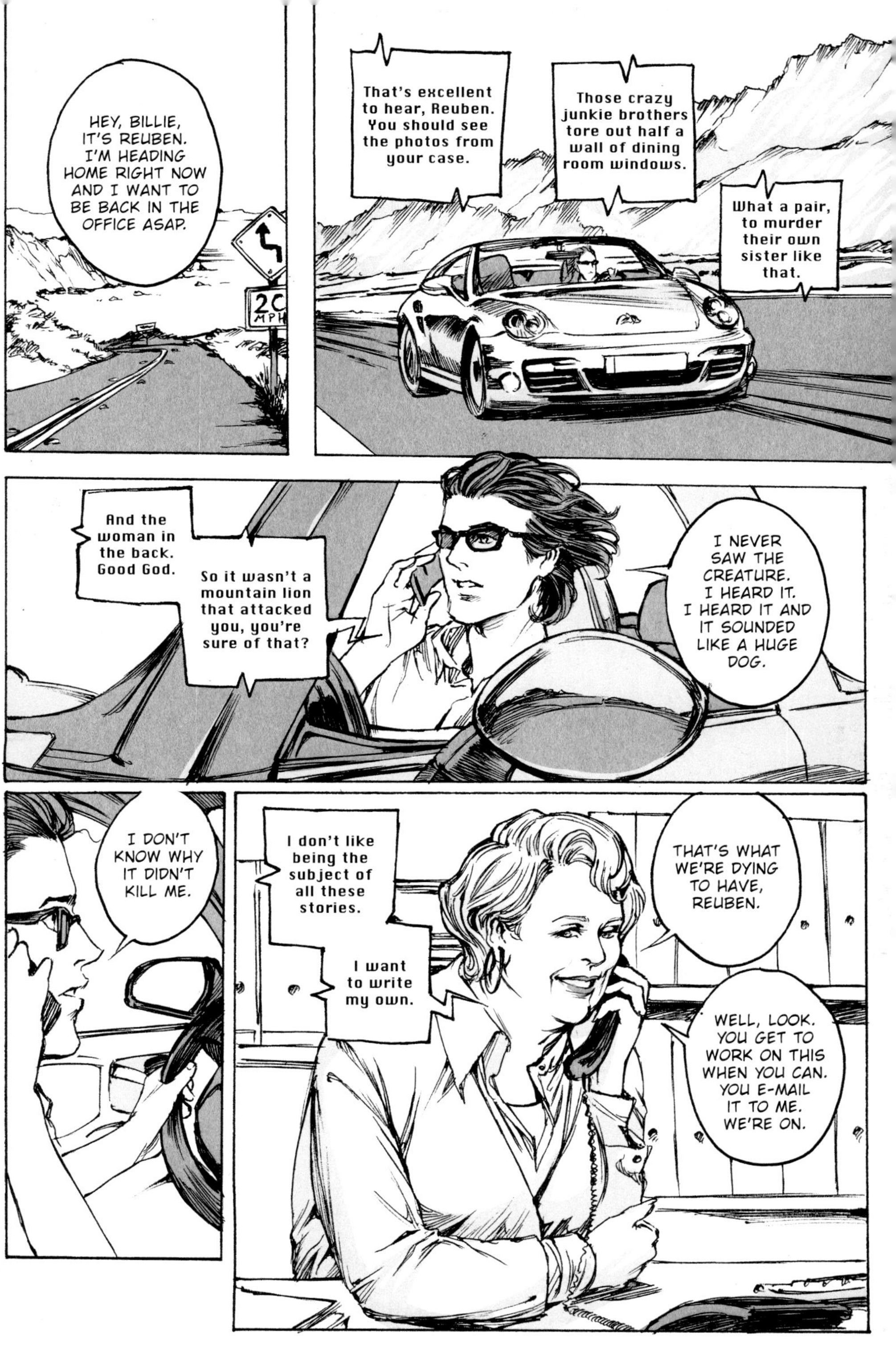
HEY, BILLIE, IT'S REUBEN. I'M HEADING HOME RIGHT NOW AND I WANT TO BE BACK IN THE OFFICE ASAP.
20 MPH
That's excellent to hear, Reuben. You should see the photos from your case.
Those crazy junkie brothers tore out half a wall of dining room windows.
What a pair, to murder their own sister like that.
And the woman in the back. Good God.
So it wasn't a mountain lion that attacked you, you're sure of that?
I NEVER SAW THE CREATURE. I HEARD IT. I HEARD IT AND IT SOUNDED LIKE A HUGE DOG.
I DON'T KNOW WHY IT DIDN'T KILL ME.
I don't like being the subject of all these stories.
I want to write my own.
THAT'S WHAT WE'RE DYING TO HAVE, REUBEN.
WELL, LOOK. YOU GET TO WORK ON THIS WHEN YOU CAN. YOU E-MAIL IT TO ME. WE'RE ON.

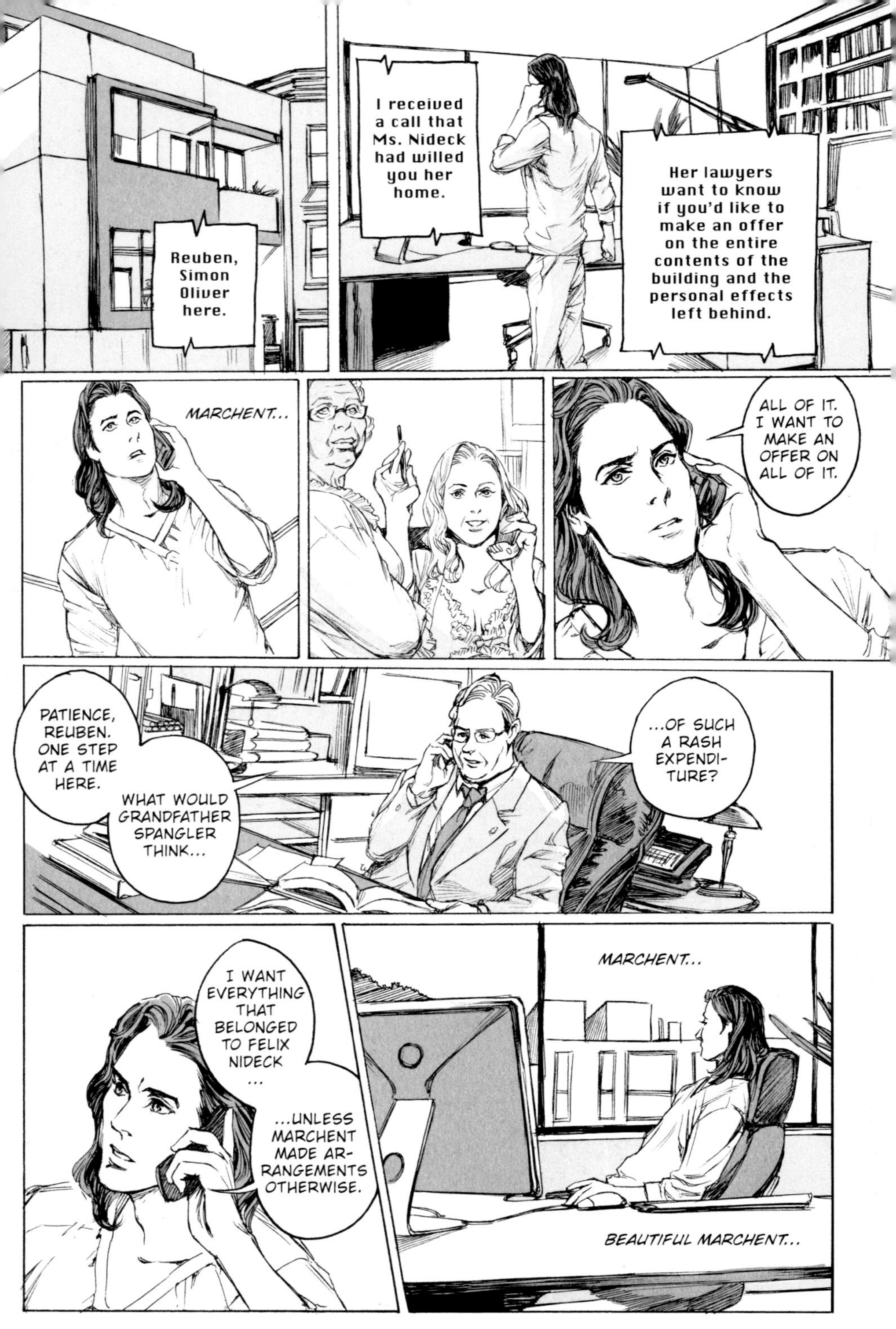
Reuben, Simon Oliver here.
I received a call that Ms. Nideck had willed you her home.
Her lawyers want to know if you'd like to make an offer on the entire contents of the building and the personal effects left behind.
MARCHENT...
ALL OF IT. I WANT TO MAKE AN OFFER ON ALL OF IT.
PATIENCE, REUBEN. ONE STEP AT A TIME HERE.
WHAT WOULD GRANDFATHER SPANGLER THINK...
...OF SUCH A RASH EXPENDI-TURE?
I WANT EVERYTHING THAT BELONGED TO FELIX NIDECK ...
...UNLESS MARCHENT MADE AR-RANGEMENTS OTHERWISE.
MARCHENT...
BEAUTIFUL MARCHENT...

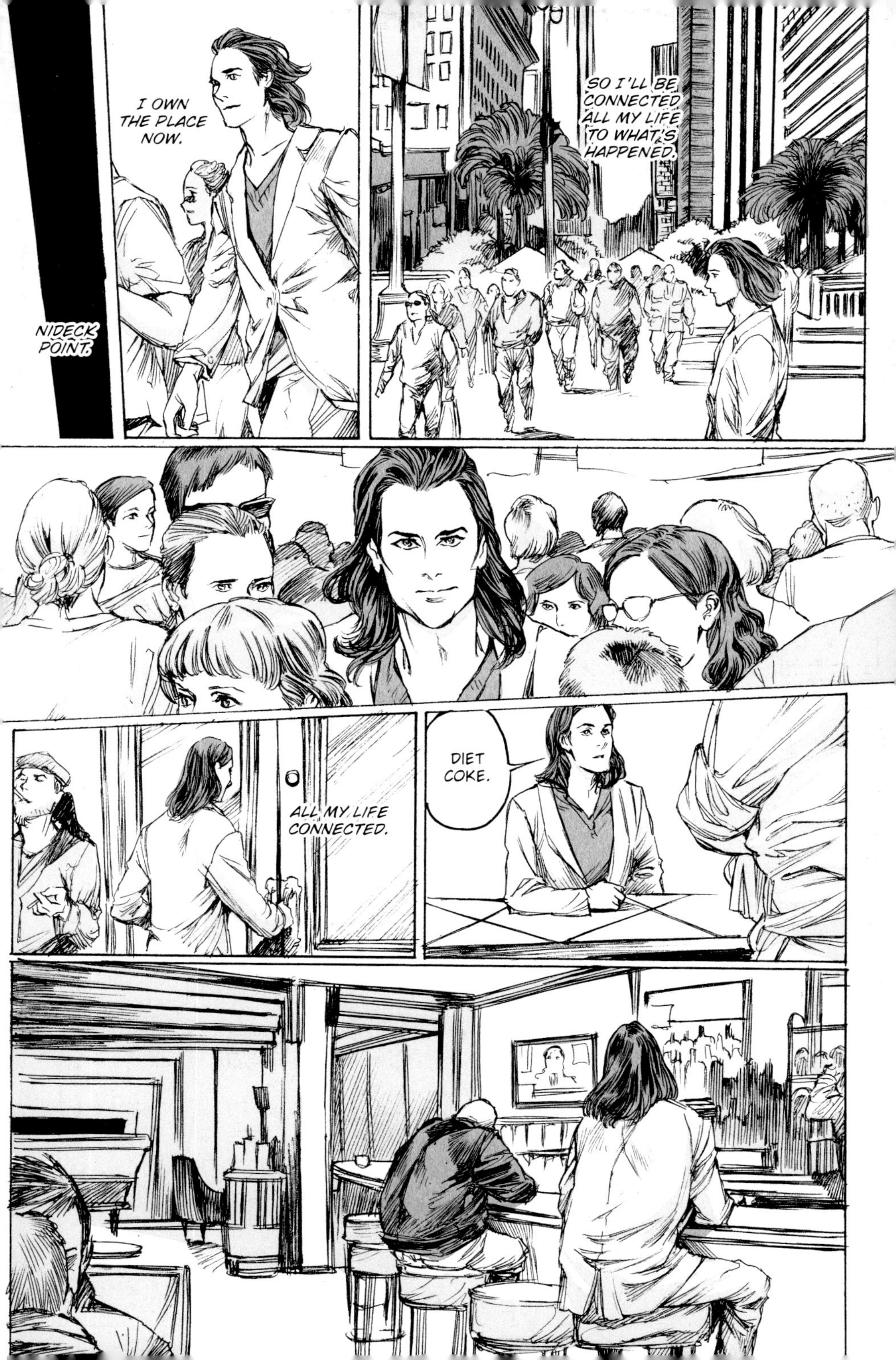
NIDECK POINT.
I OWN THE PLACE NOW.
SO I'LL BE CONNECTED ALL MY LIFE TO WHAT'S HAPPENED.
ALL MY LIFE CONNECTED.
DIET COKE.

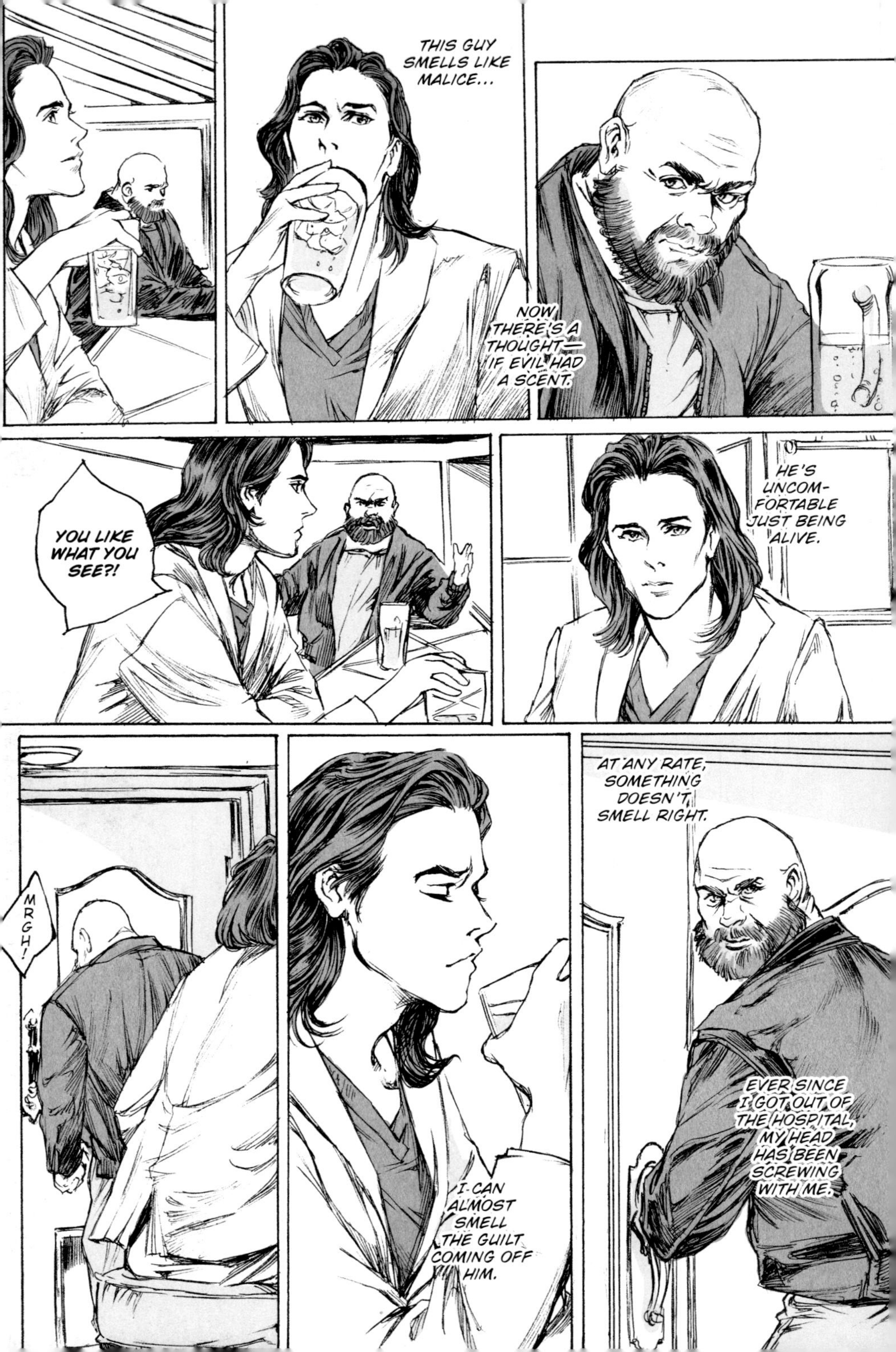
THIS GUY SMELLS LIKE MALICE...
NOW THERE'S A THOUGHT— IF EVIL HAD A SCENT.
YOU LIKE WHAT YOU SEE?!
HE'S UNCOM-FORTABLE JUST BEING ALIVE.
MRGH!
I-CAN ALMOST SMELL THE GUILT COMING OFF HIM.
AT ANY RATE, SOMETHING DOESN'T SMELL RIGHT.
EVER SINCE I GOT OUT OF THE HOSPITAL, MY HEAD HAS BEEN SCREWING WITH ME.

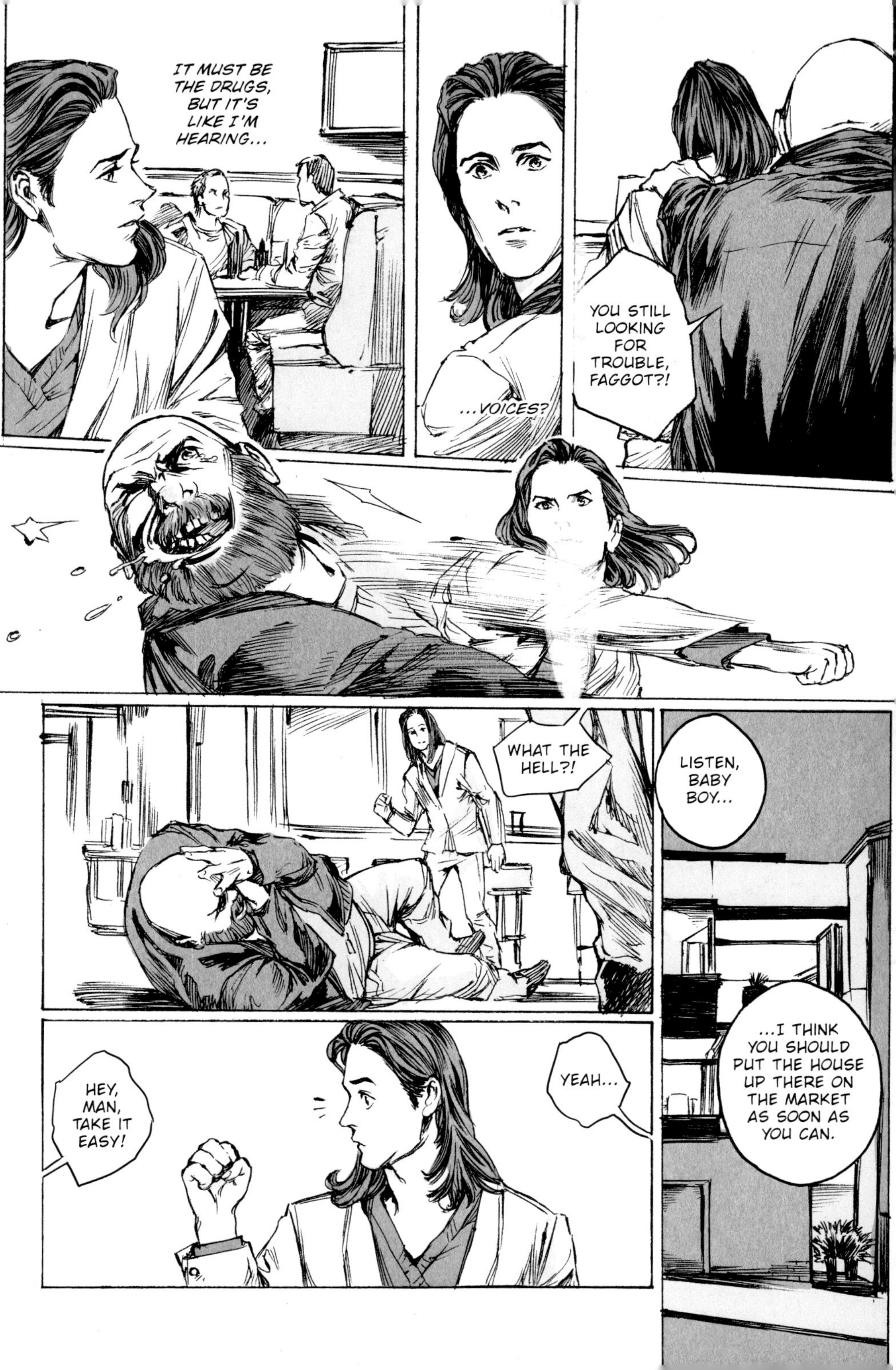
IT MUST BE THE DRUGS, BUT IT'S LIKE I'M HEARING...
...VOICES?
YOU STILL LOOKING FOR TROUBLE, FAGGOT?!
WHAT THE HELL?!
LISTEN, BABY BOY...
...I THINK YOU SHOULD PUT THE HOUSE UP THERE ON THE MARKET AS SOON AS YOU CAN.
HEY, MAN, TAKE IT EASY!
YEAH...

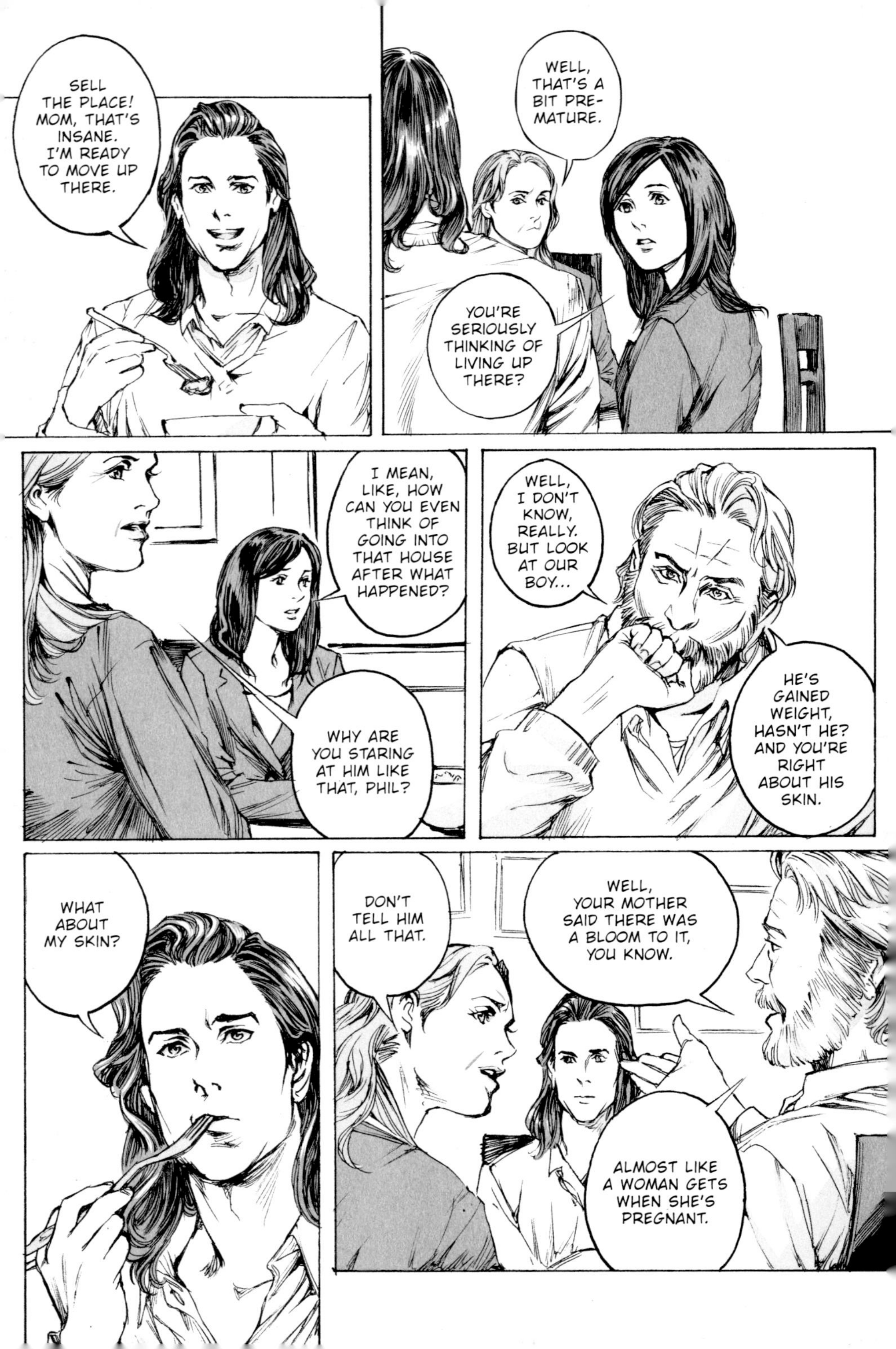
SELL THE PLACE! MOM, THAT'S INSANE. I'M READY TO MOVE UP THERE.
WELL, THAT'S A BIT PRE-MATURE.
YOU'RE SERIOUSLY THINKING OF LIVING UP THERE?
I MEAN, LIKE, HOW CAN YOU EVEN THINK OF GOING INTO THAT HOUSE AFTER WHAT HAPPENED?
WHY ARE YOU STARING AT HIM LIKE THAT, PHIL?
WELL, I DON'T KNOW, REALLY. BUT LOOK AT OUR BOY...
HE'S GAINED WEIGHT, HASN'T HE? AND YOU'RE RIGHT ABOUT HIS SKIN.
WHAT ABOUT MY SKIN?
DON'T TELL HIM ALL THAT.
WELL, YOUR MOTHER SAID THERE WAS A BLOOM TO IT, YOU KNOW.
ALMOST LIKE A WOMAN GETS WHEN SHE'S PREGNANT.

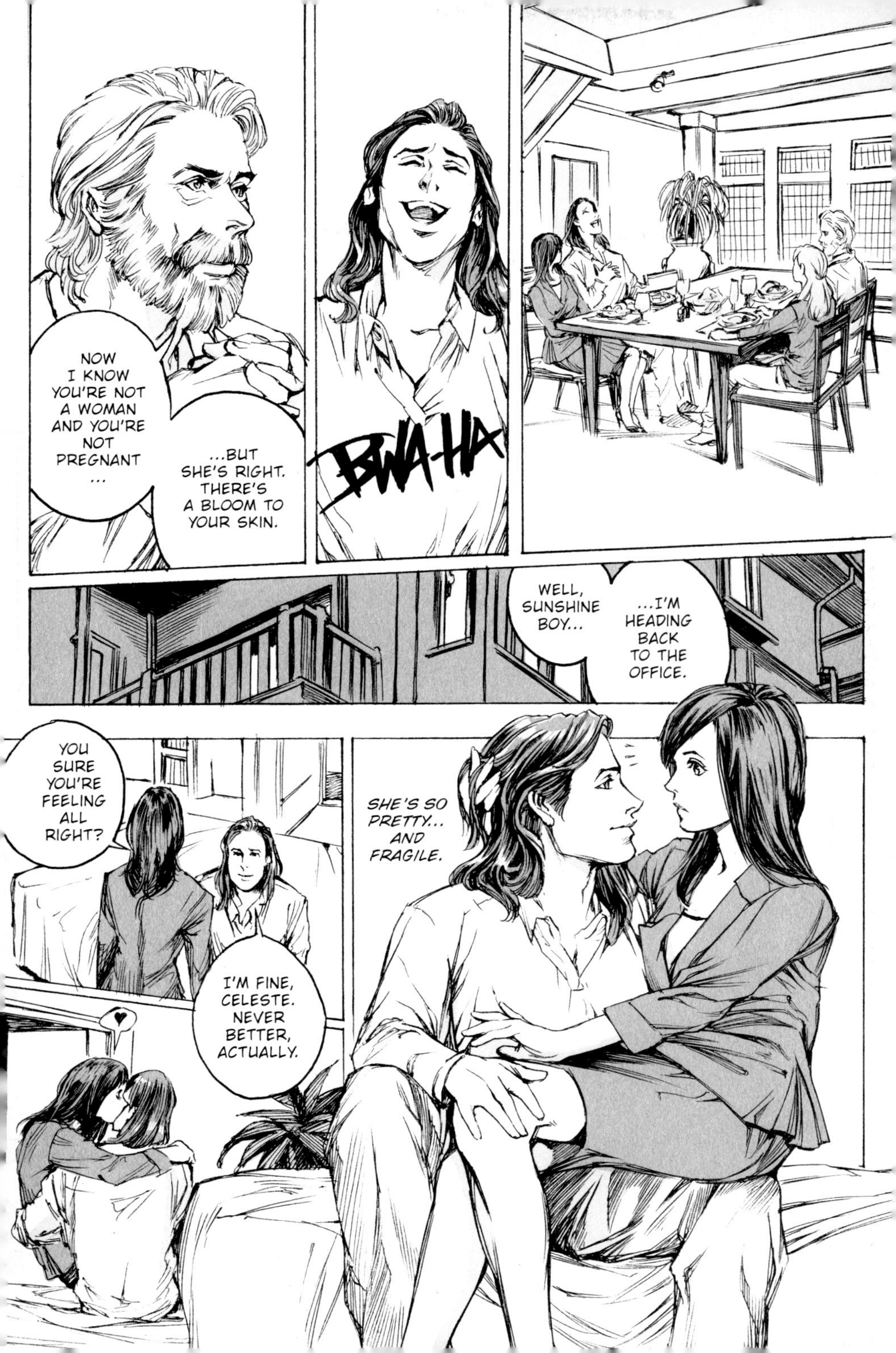
NOW I KNOW YOU'RE NOT A WOMAN AND YOU'RE NOT PREGNANT ...
...BUT SHE'S RIGHT. THERE'S A BLOOM TO YOUR SKIN.
BWA-HA
WELL, SUNSHINE BOY...
...I'M HEADING BACK TO THE OFFICE.
YOU SURE YOU'RE FEELING ALL RIGHT?
I'M FINE, CELESTE. NEVER BETTER, ACTUALLY.
SHE'S SO PRETTY... AND FRAGILE.

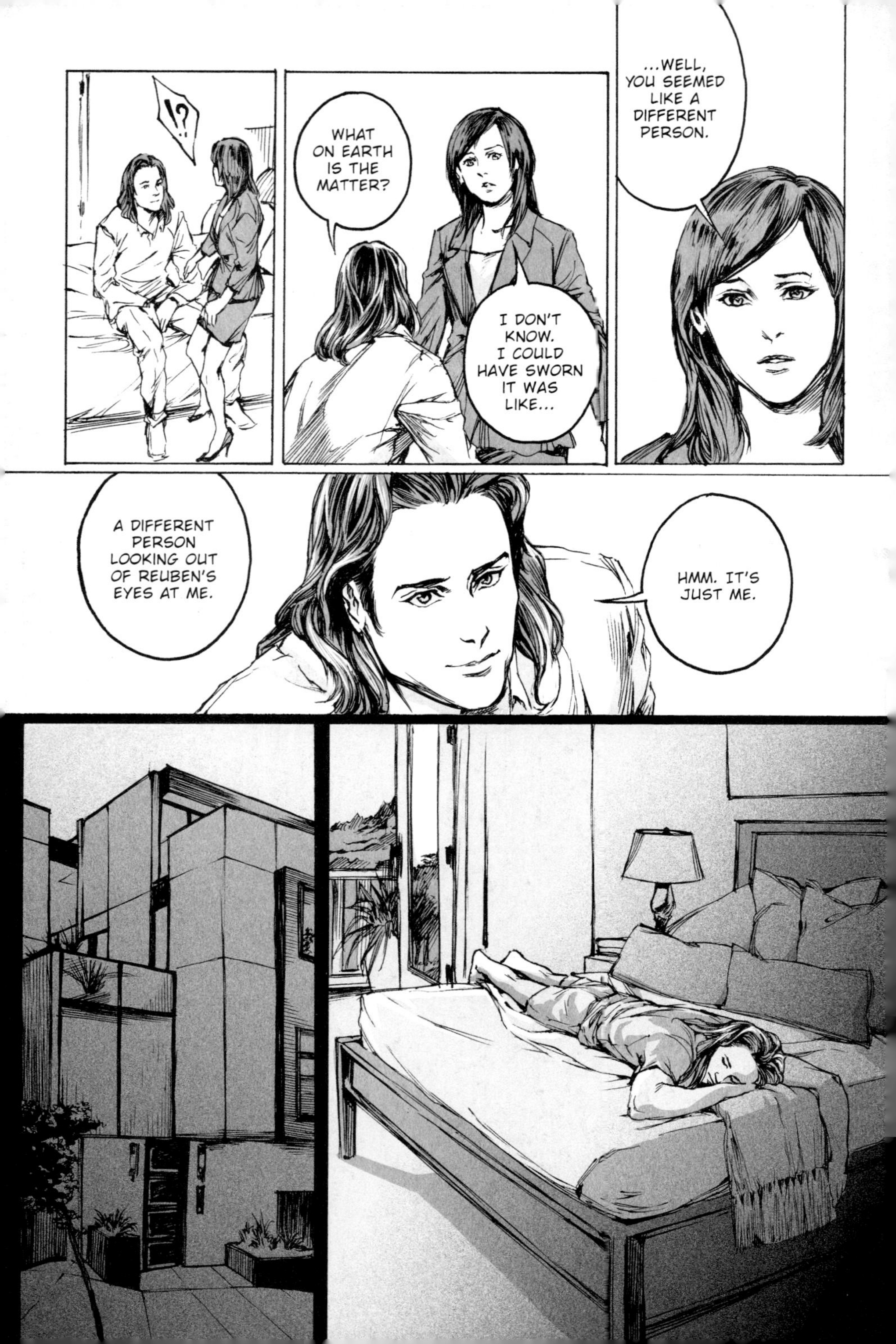
!?
WHAT ON EARTH IS THE MATTER?
I DON'T KNOW. I COULD HAVE SWORN IT WAS LIKE...
...WELL, YOU SEEMED LIKE A DIFFERENT PERSON.
A DIFFERENT PERSON LOOKING OUT OF REUBEN'S EYES AT ME.
HMM. IT'S JUST ME.

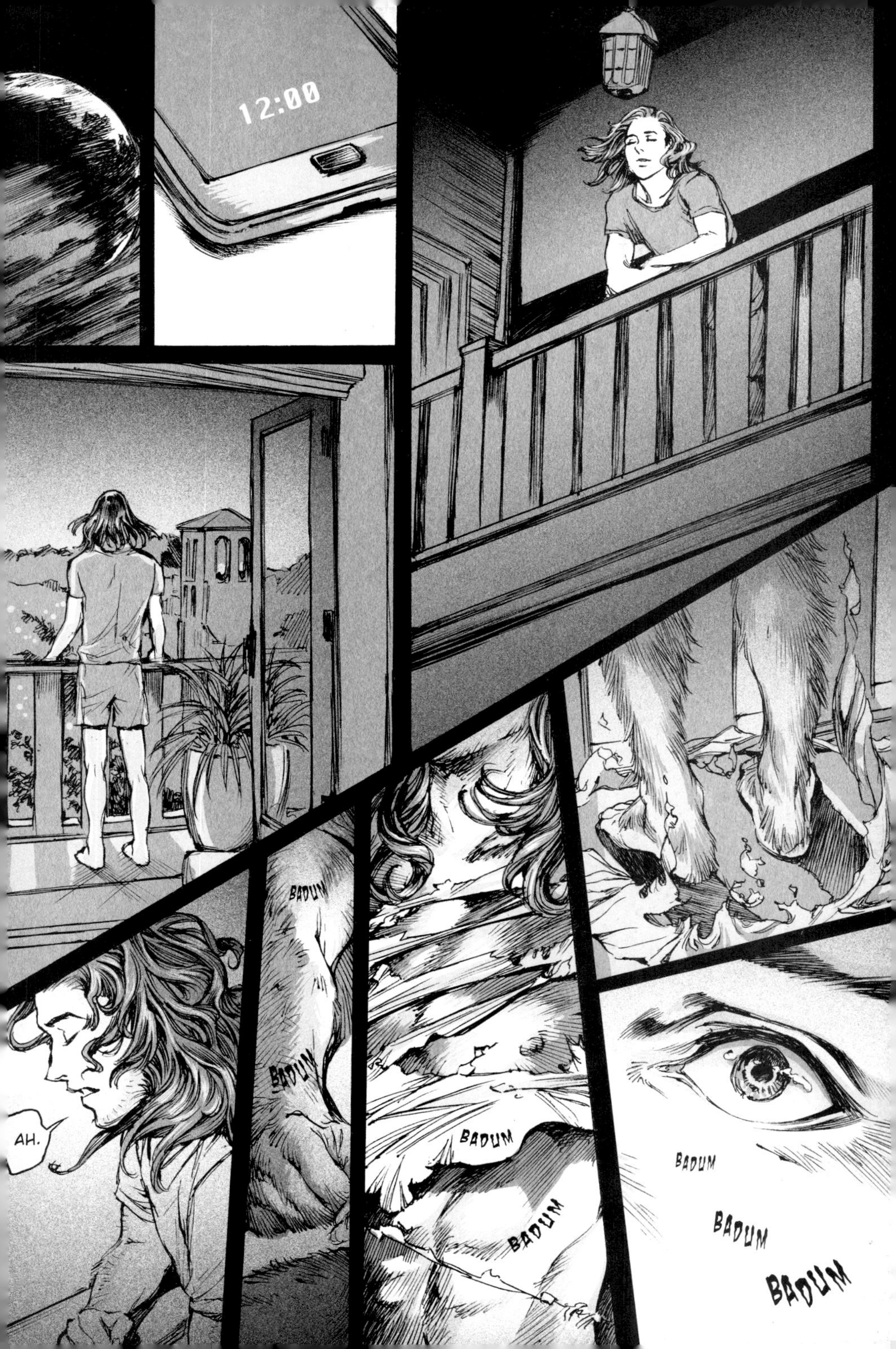
12:00
AH.
BADUM
BADUM
BADUM
BADUM
BADUM
BADUM
BADUM

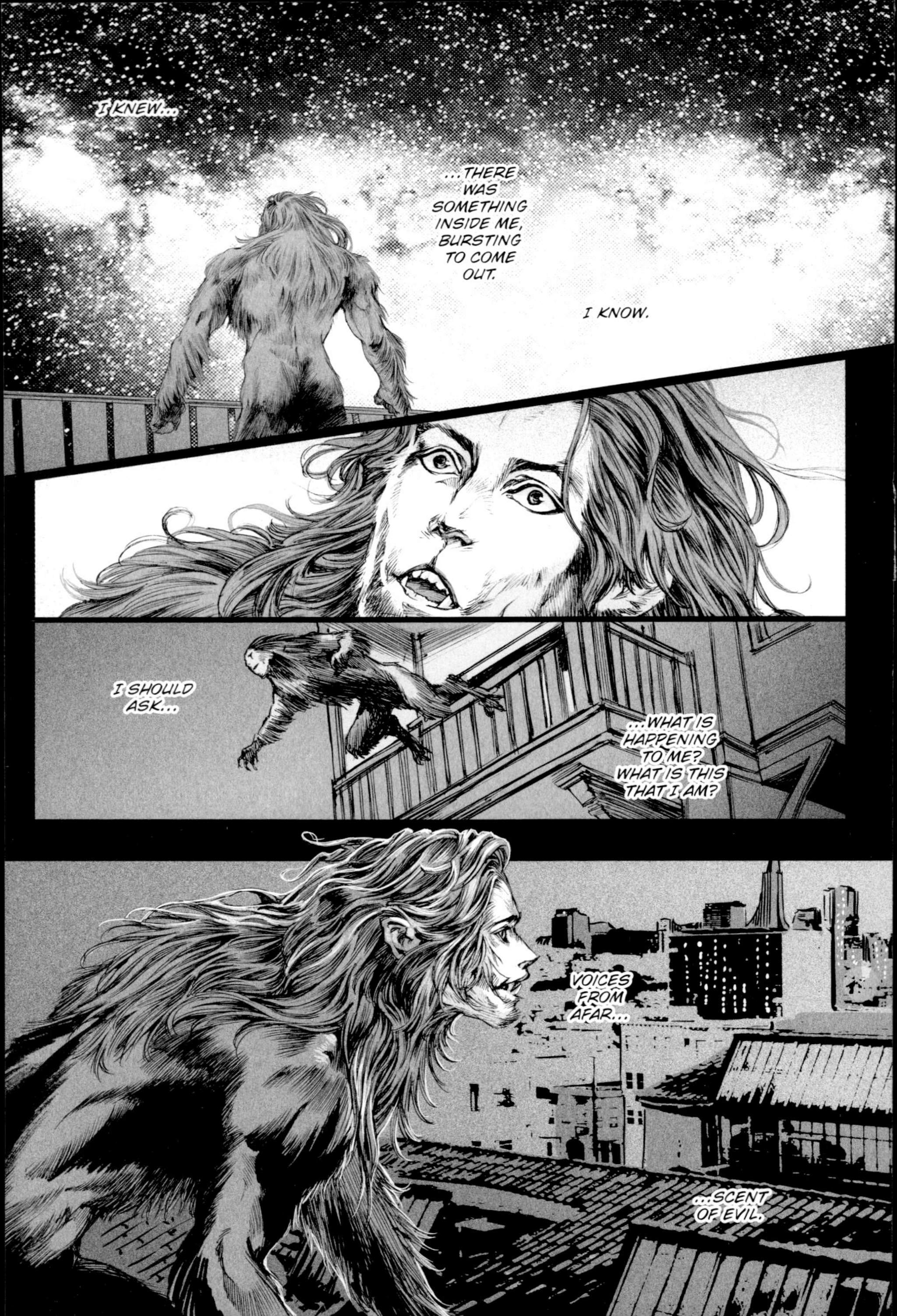
I KNEW...
...THERE WAS SOMETHING INSIDE ME, BURSTING TO COME OUT.
I KNOW.
I SHOULD ASK...
...WHAT IS HAPPENING TO ME? WHAT IS THIS THAT I AM?
VOICES FROM AFAR...
...SCENT OF EVIL.

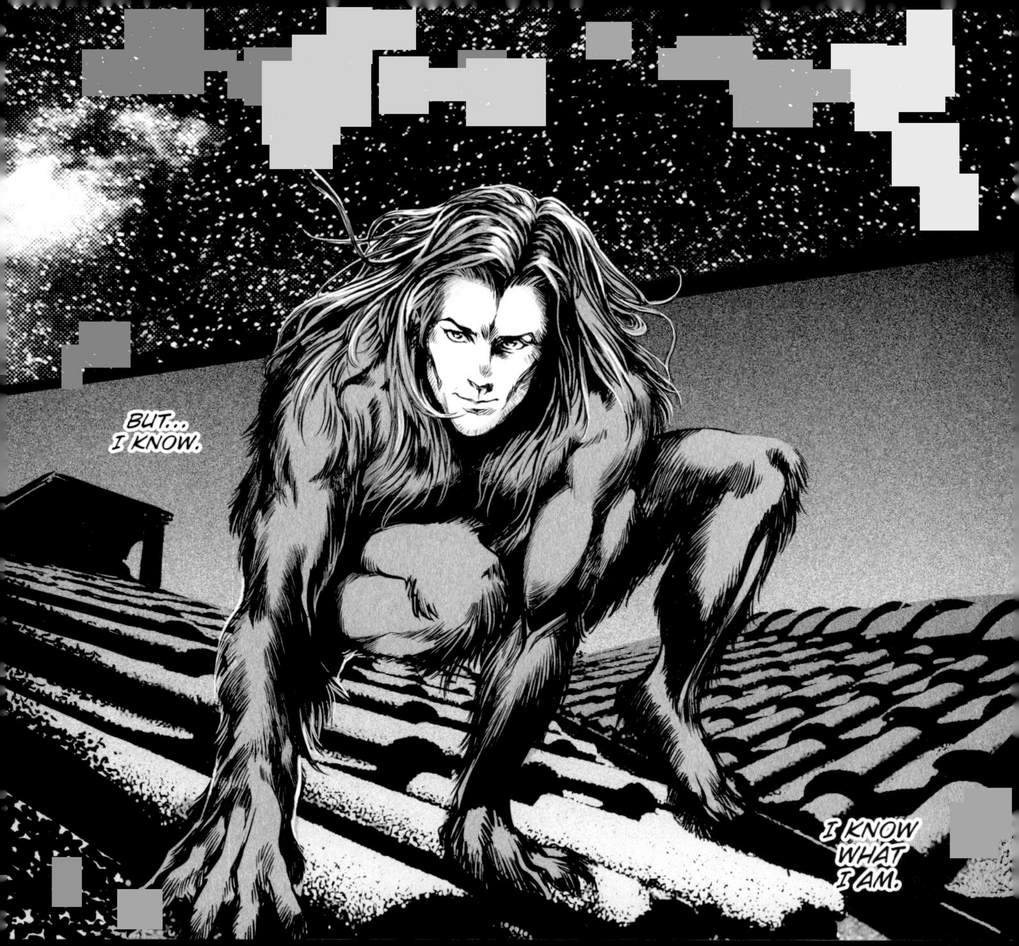
BUT... I KNOW.
I KNOW WHAT I AM.

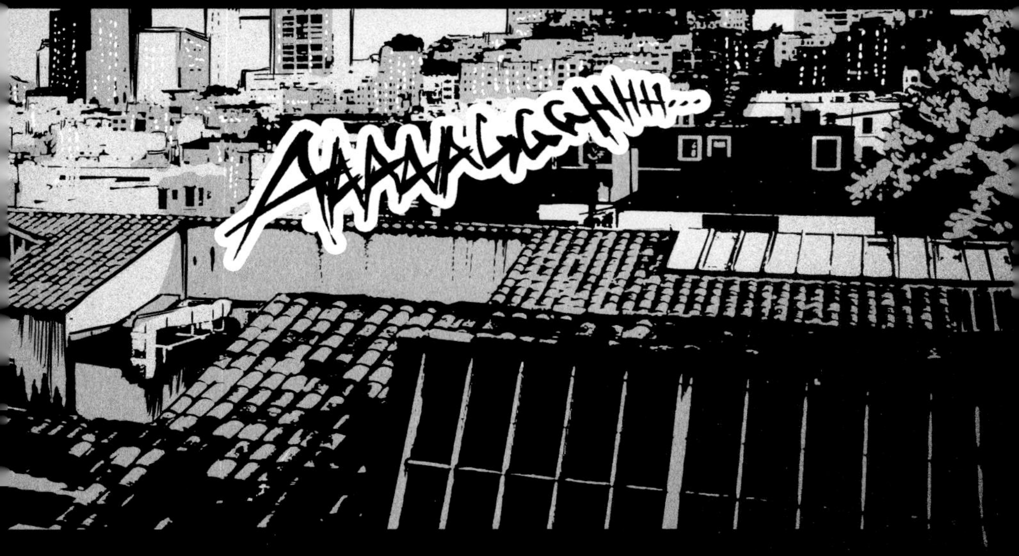
AAAAAGGGHHH...

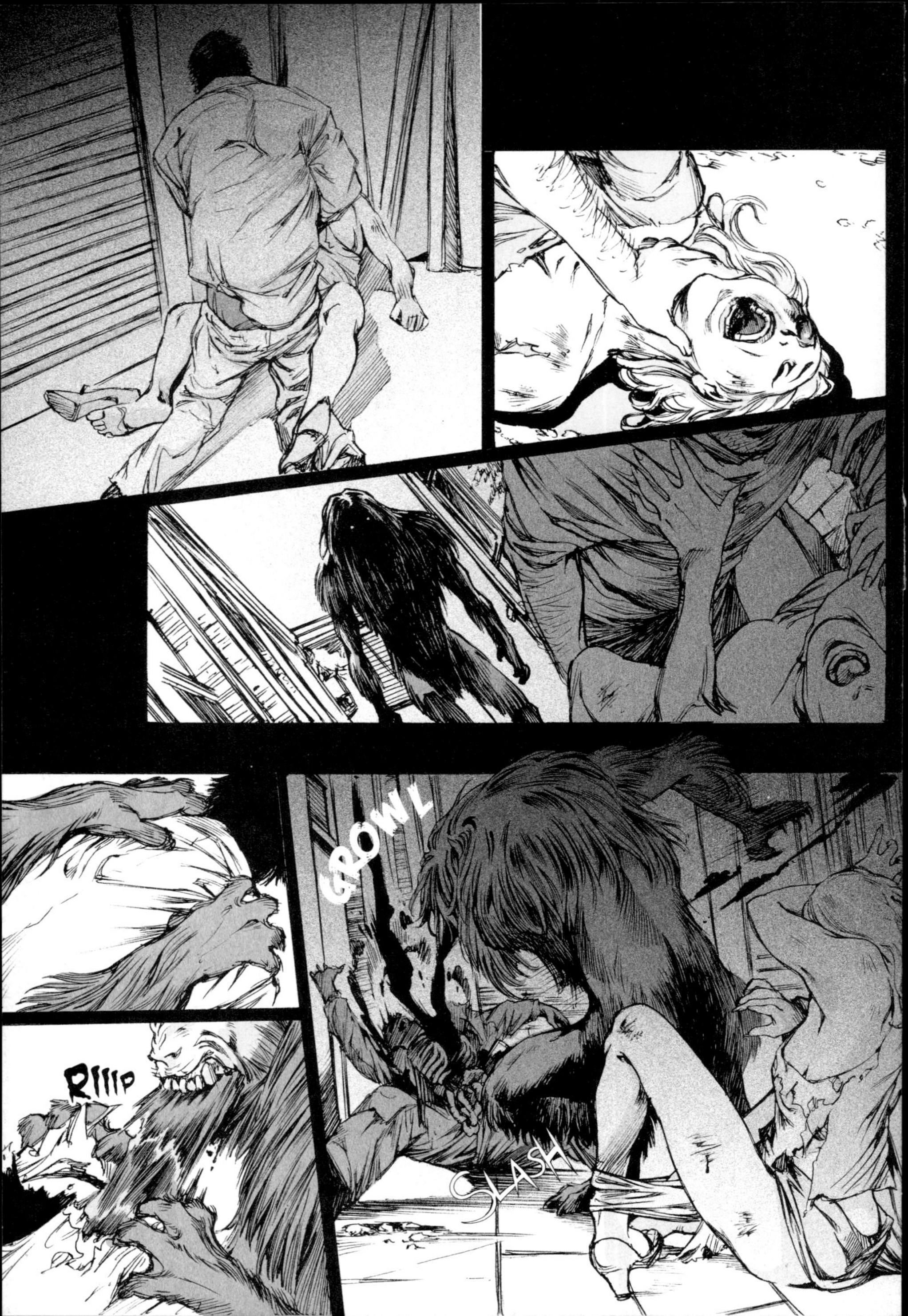
GROWL
RIIIP
SLASH

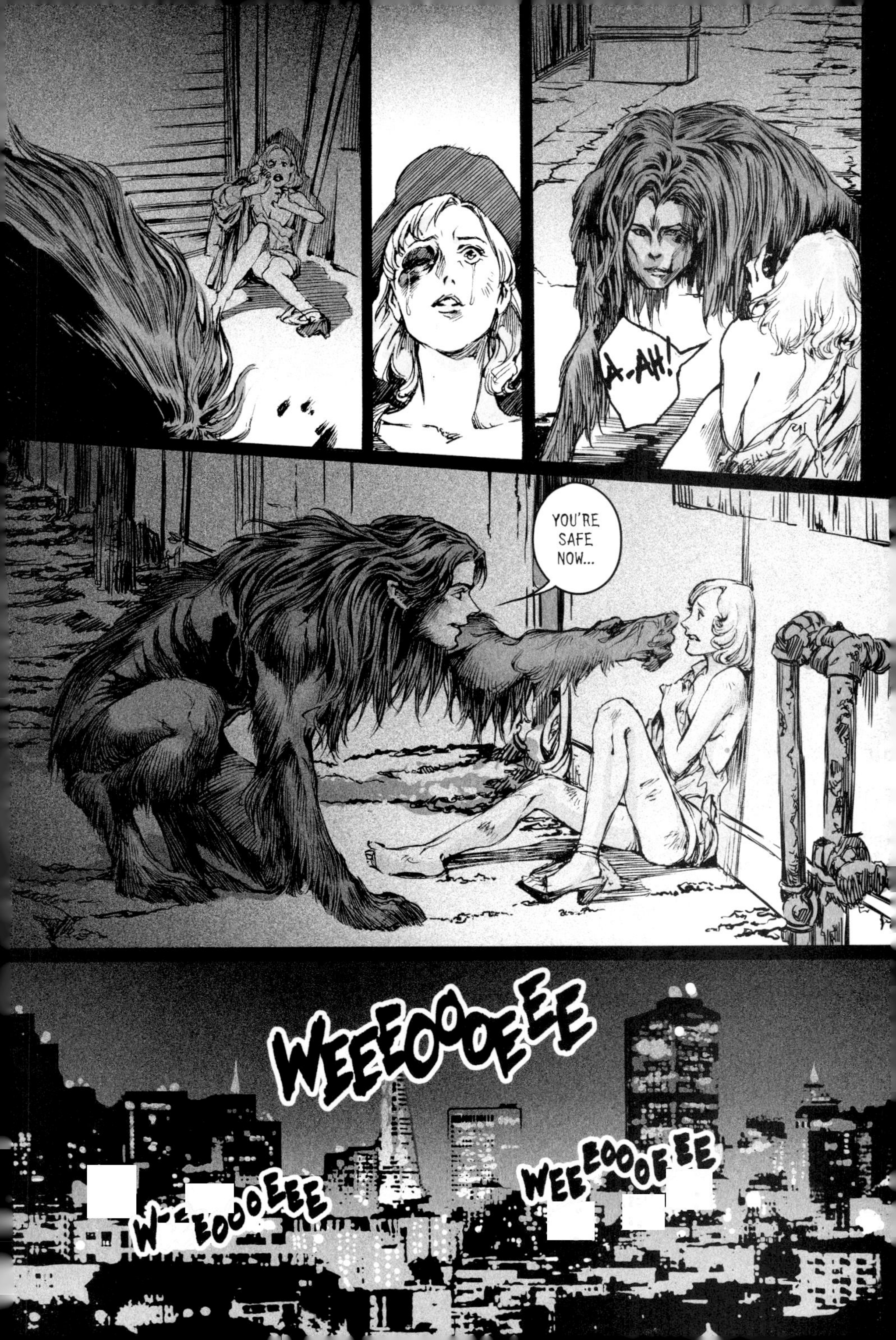
A-AH!
YOU'RE SAFE NOW...
WEEEOOOEEE
WEEEOOOEEE

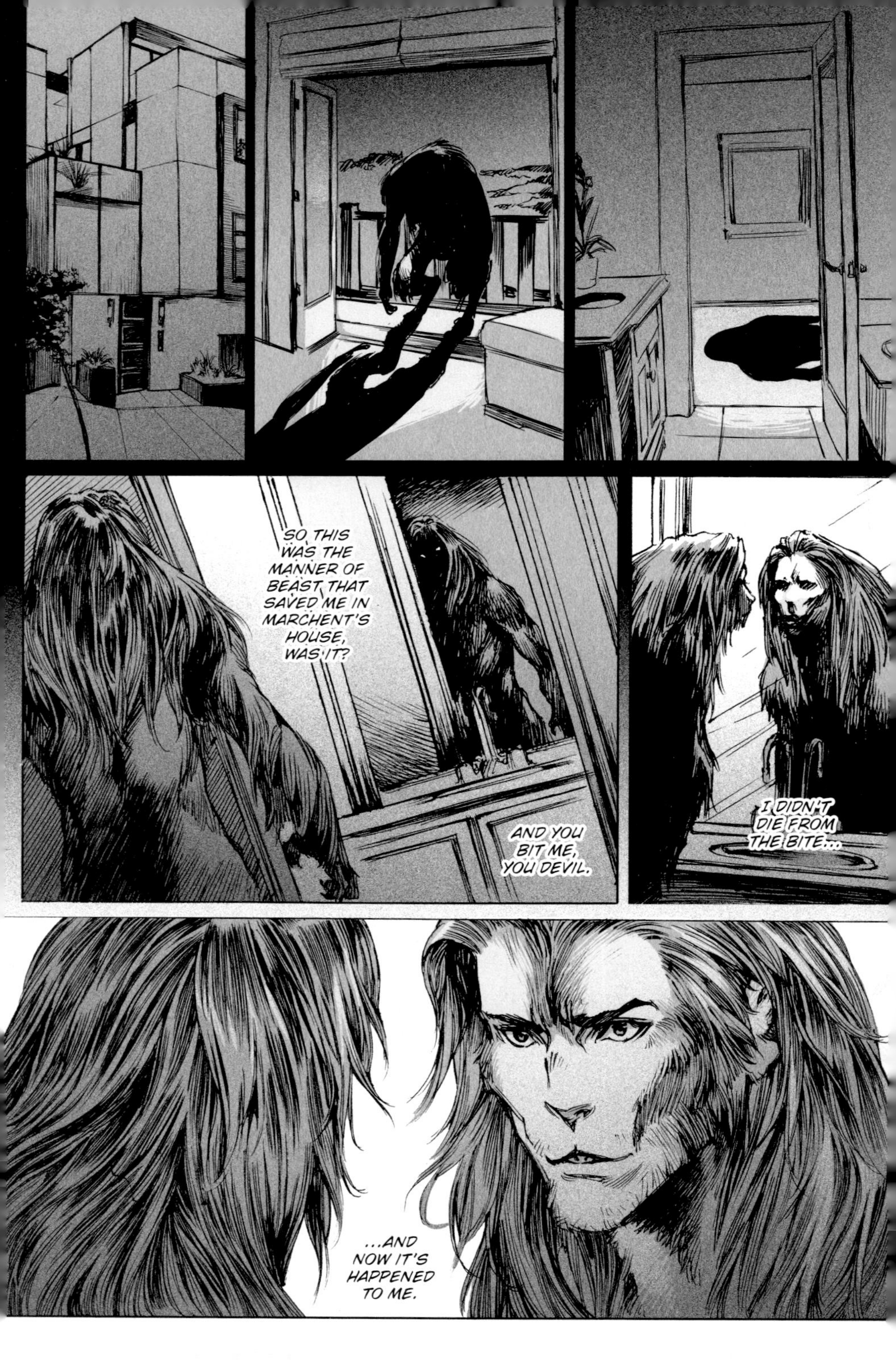
SO THIS WAS THE MANNER OF BEAST THAT SAVED ME IN MARCHENT'S HOUSE, WAS IT?
AND YOU BIT ME, YOU DEVIL.
I DIDN'T DIE FROM THE BITE...
...AND NOW IT'S HAPPENED TO ME.

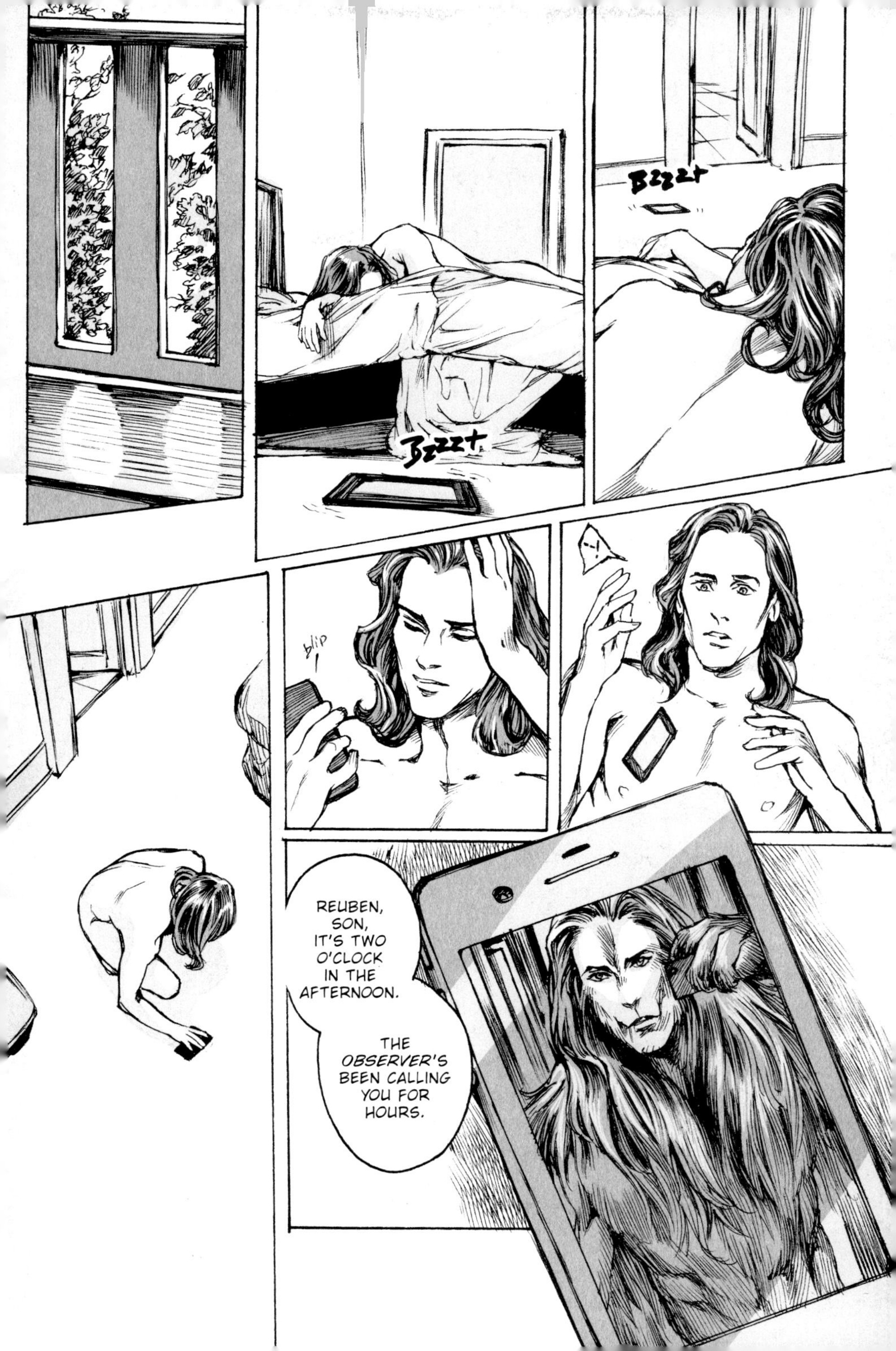
BZZZT
BZZZT
blip
!
REUBEN, SON, IT'S TWO O'CLOCK IN THE AFTERNOON.
THE *OBSERVER'S* BEEN CALLING YOU FOR HOURS.

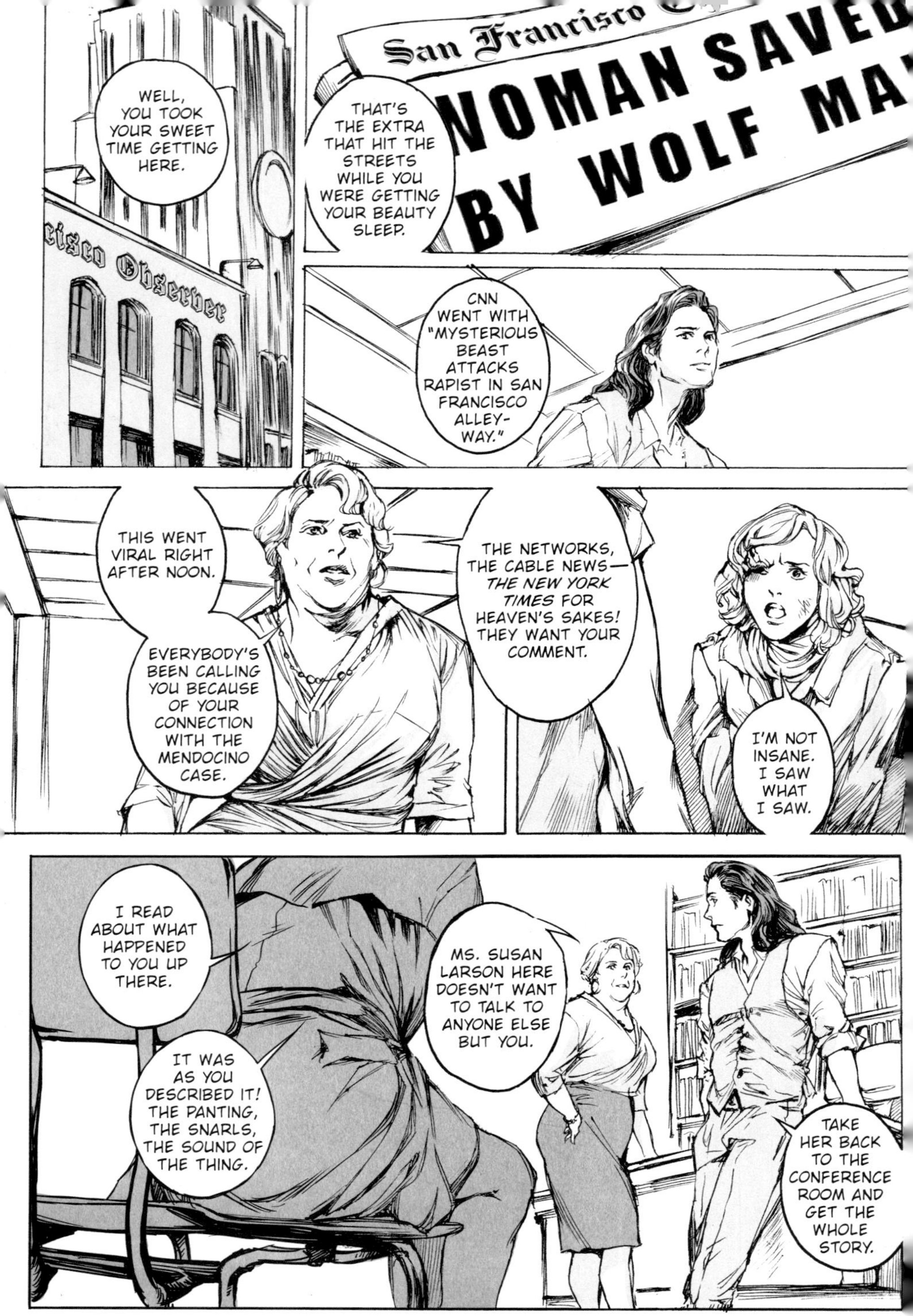

WELL, YOU TOOK YOUR SWEET TIME GETTING HERE.
San Francisco
WOMAN SAVED BY WOLF MA
THAT'S THE EXTRA THAT HIT THE STREETS WHILE YOU WERE GETTING YOUR BEAUTY SLEEP.
CNN WENT WITH "MYSTERIOUS BEAST ATTACKS RAPIST IN SAN FRANCISCO ALLEY-WAY."
THIS WENT VIRAL RIGHT AFTER NOON.
EVERYBODY'S BEEN CALLING YOU BECAUSE OF YOUR CONNECTION WITH THE MENDOCINO CASE.
THE NETWORKS, THE CABLE NEWS— *THE NEW YORK TIMES* FOR HEAVEN'S SAKES! THEY WANT YOUR COMMENT.
I'M NOT INSANE. I SAW WHAT I SAW.
I READ ABOUT WHAT HAPPENED TO YOU UP THERE.
IT WAS AS YOU DESCRIBED IT! THE PANTING, THE SNARLS, THE SOUND OF THE THING.
MS. SUSAN LARSON HERE DOESN'T WANT TO TALK TO ANYONE ELSE BUT YOU.
TAKE HER BACK TO THE CONFERENCE ROOM AND GET THE WHOLE STORY.

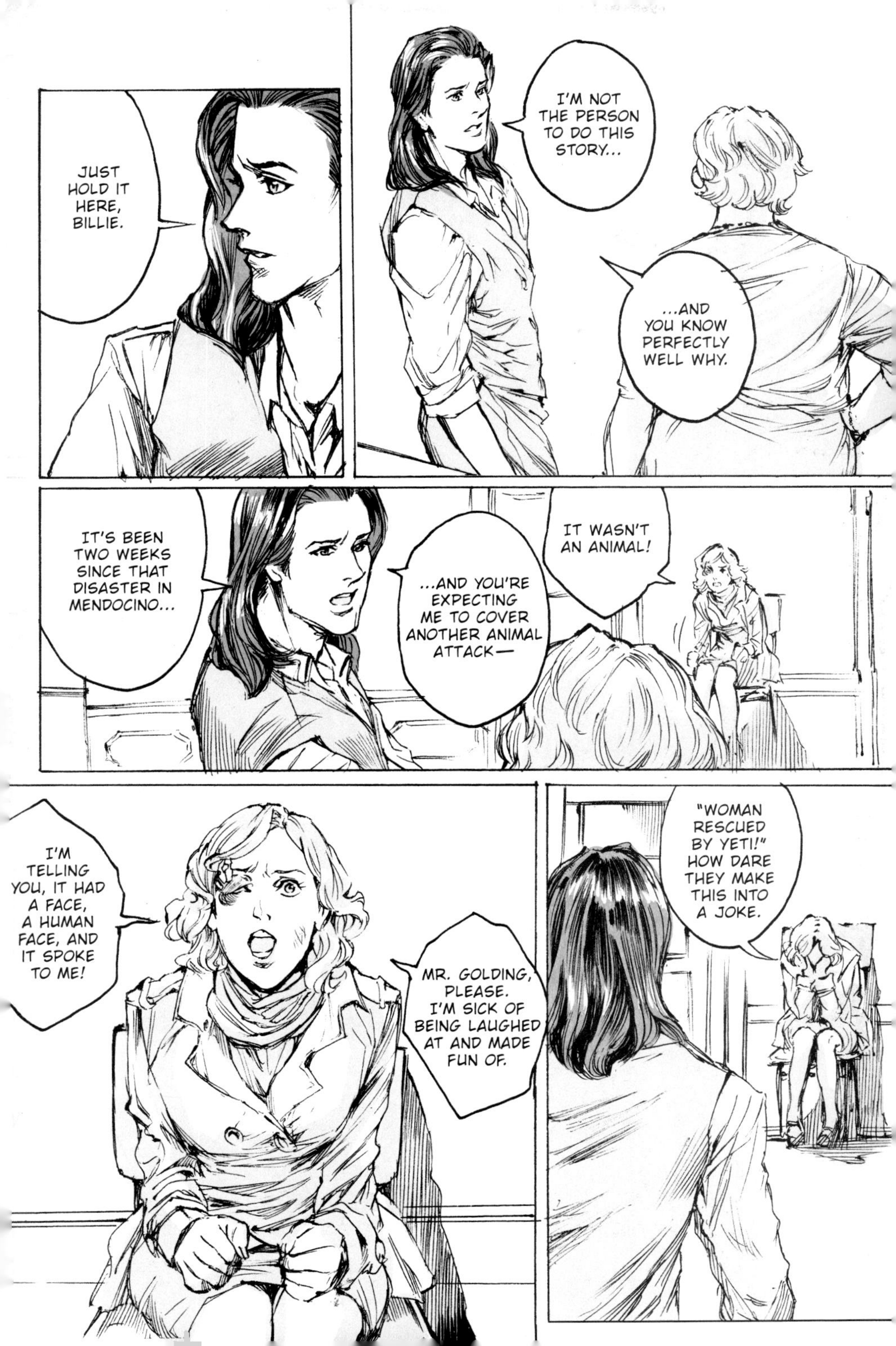
JUST HOLD IT HERE, BILLIE.
I'M NOT THE PERSON TO DO THIS STORY...
...AND YOU KNOW PERFECTLY WELL WHY.
IT'S BEEN TWO WEEKS SINCE THAT DISASTER IN MENDOCINO...
...AND YOU'RE EXPECTING ME TO COVER ANOTHER ANIMAL ATTACK—
IT WASN'T AN ANIMAL!
I'M TELLING YOU, IT HAD A FACE, A HUMAN FACE, AND IT SPOKE TO ME!
MR. GOLDING, PLEASE. I'M SICK OF BEING LAUGHED AT AND MADE FUN OF.
"WOMAN RESCUED BY YETI!" HOW DARE THEY MAKE THIS INTO A JOKE.

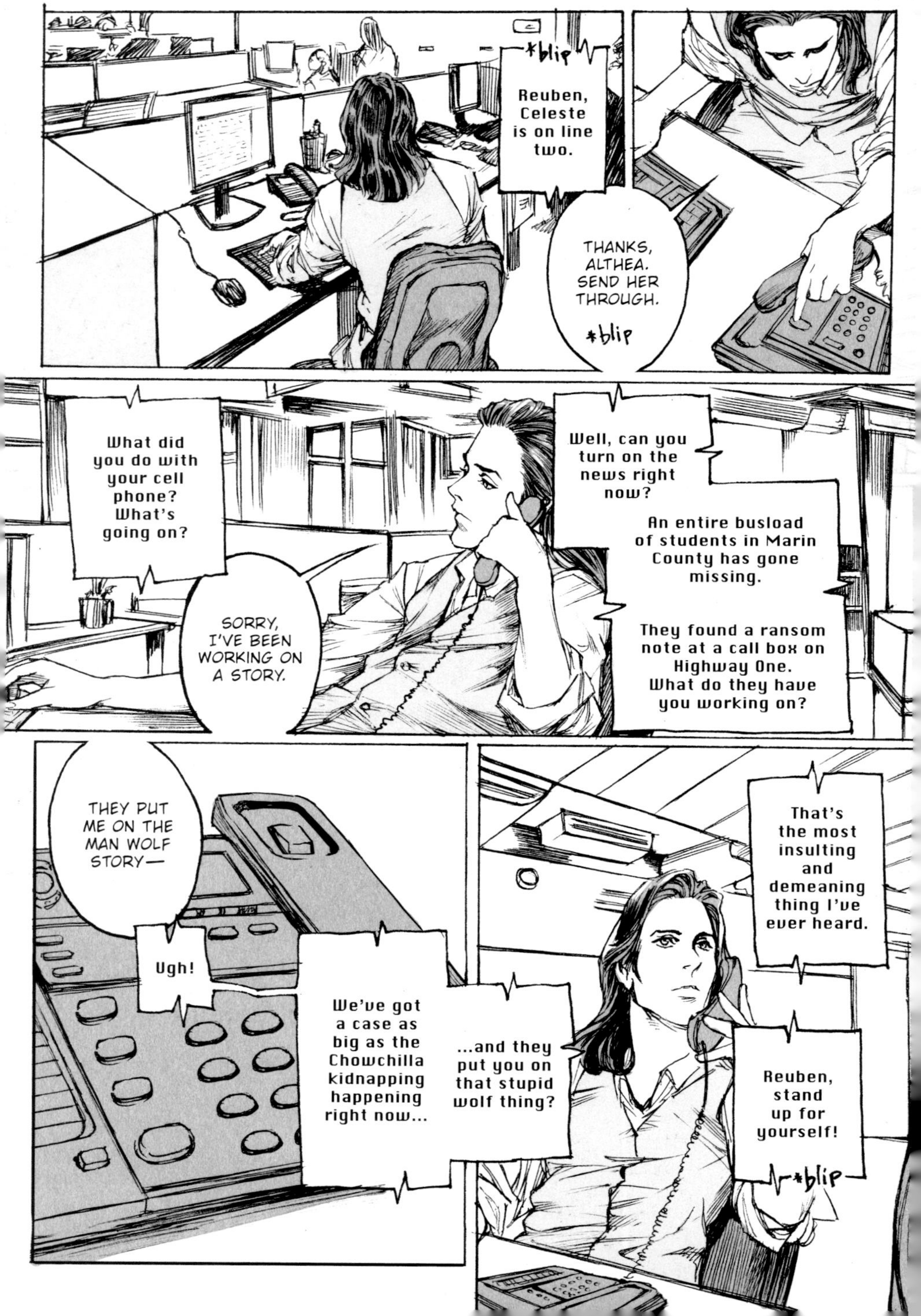
*blip
Reuben, Celeste is on line two.
THANKS, ALTHEA. SEND HER THROUGH.
*blip
What did you do with your cell phone? What's going on?
SORRY, I'VE BEEN WORKING ON A STORY.
Well, can you turn on the news right now?
An entire busload of students in Marin County has gone missing.
They found a ransom note at a call box on Highway One. What do they have you working on?
THEY PUT ME ON THE MAN WOLF STORY—
Ugh!
We've got a case as big as the Chowchilla kidnapping happening right now...
...and they put you on that stupid wolf thing?
That's the most insulting and demeaning thing I've ever heard.
Reuben, stand up for yourself!
*blip

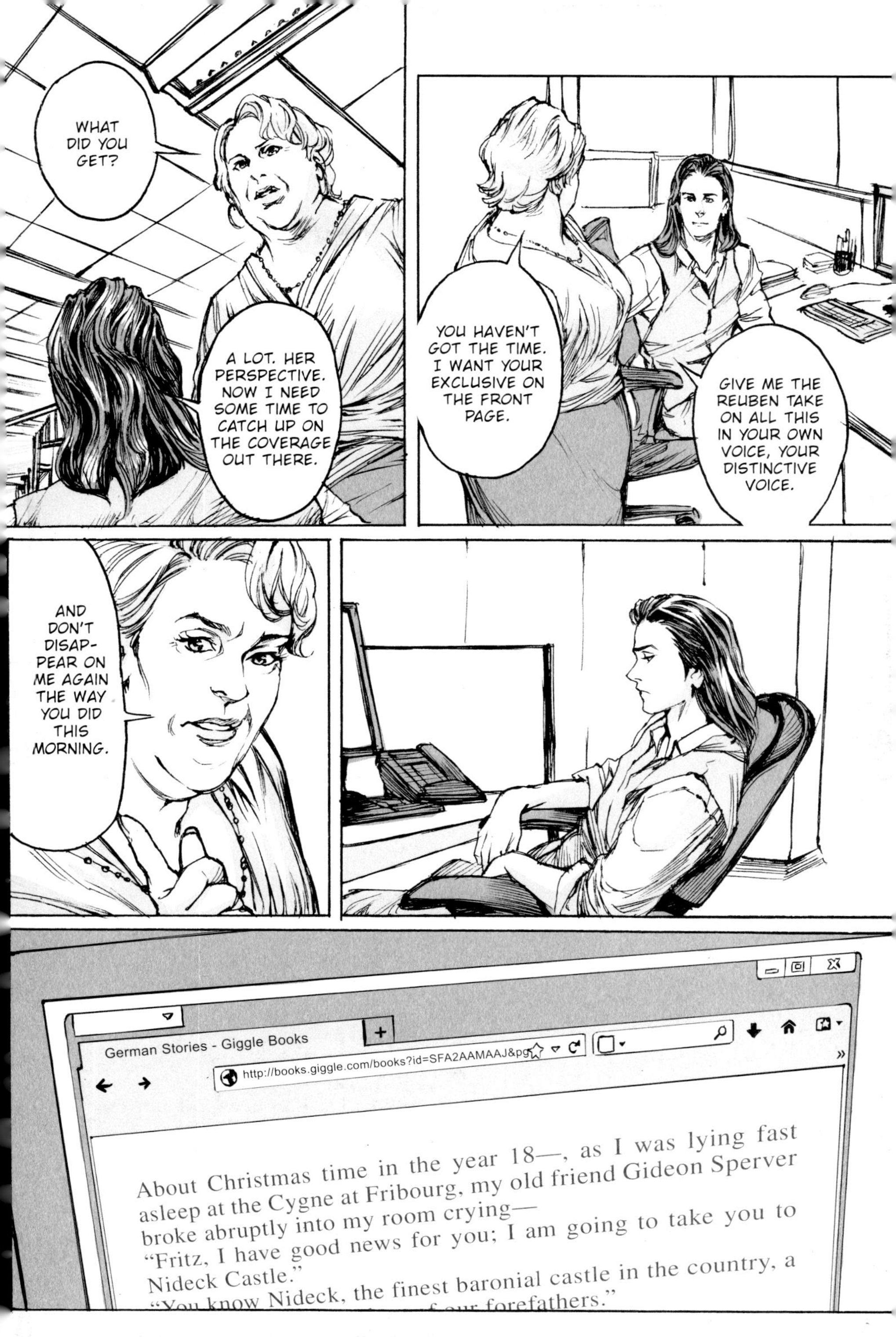

WHAT DID YOU GET?
A LOT. HER PERSPECTIVE. NOW I NEED SOME TIME TO CATCH UP ON THE COVERAGE OUT THERE.
YOU HAVEN'T GOT THE TIME. I WANT YOUR EXCLUSIVE ON THE FRONT PAGE.
GIVE ME THE REUBEN TAKE ON ALL THIS IN YOUR OWN VOICE, YOUR DISTINCTIVE VOICE.
AND DON'T DISAP-PEAR ON ME AGAIN THE WAY YOU DID THIS MORNING.
German Stories - Giggle Books
http://books.giggle.com/books?id=SFA2AAMAAJ&pg
About Christmas time in the year 18—, as I was lying fast asleep at the Cygne at Fribourg, my old friend Gideon Sperver broke abruptly into my room crying—
“Fritz, I have good news for you; I am going to take you to Nideck Castle.”
“You know Nideck, the finest baronial castle in the country, a

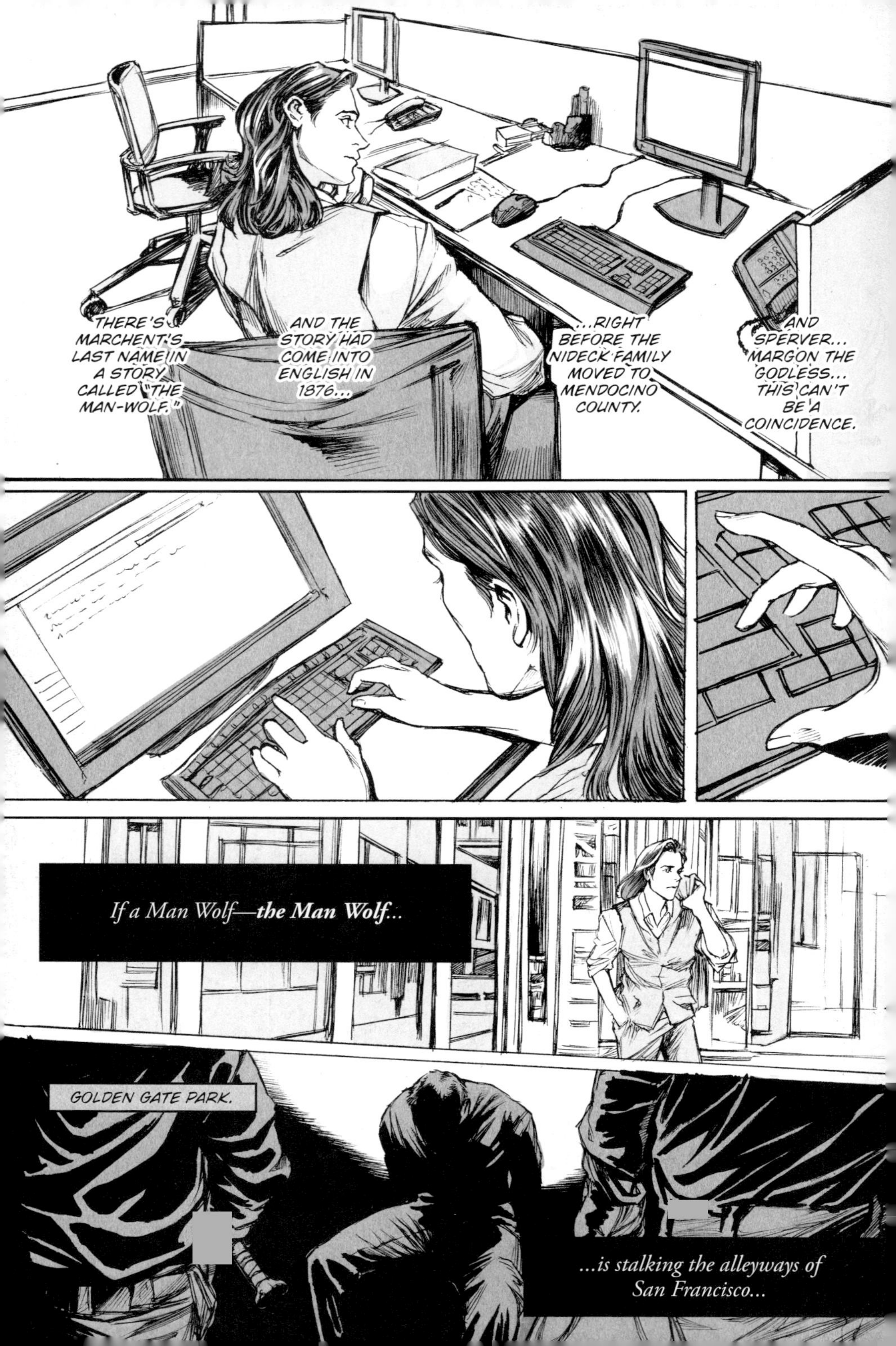
THERE'S MARCHENT'S LAST NAME IN A STORY CALLED "THE MAN-WOLF."
AND THE STORY HAD COME INTO ENGLISH IN 1876...
...RIGHT BEFORE THE NIDECK FAMILY MOVED TO MENDOCINO COUNTY.
AND SPERVER... MARGON THE GODLESS... THIS CAN'T BE A COINCIDENCE.
If a Man Wolf—**the Man Wolf**...
GOLDEN GATE PARK.
...is stalking the alleyways of San Francisco...

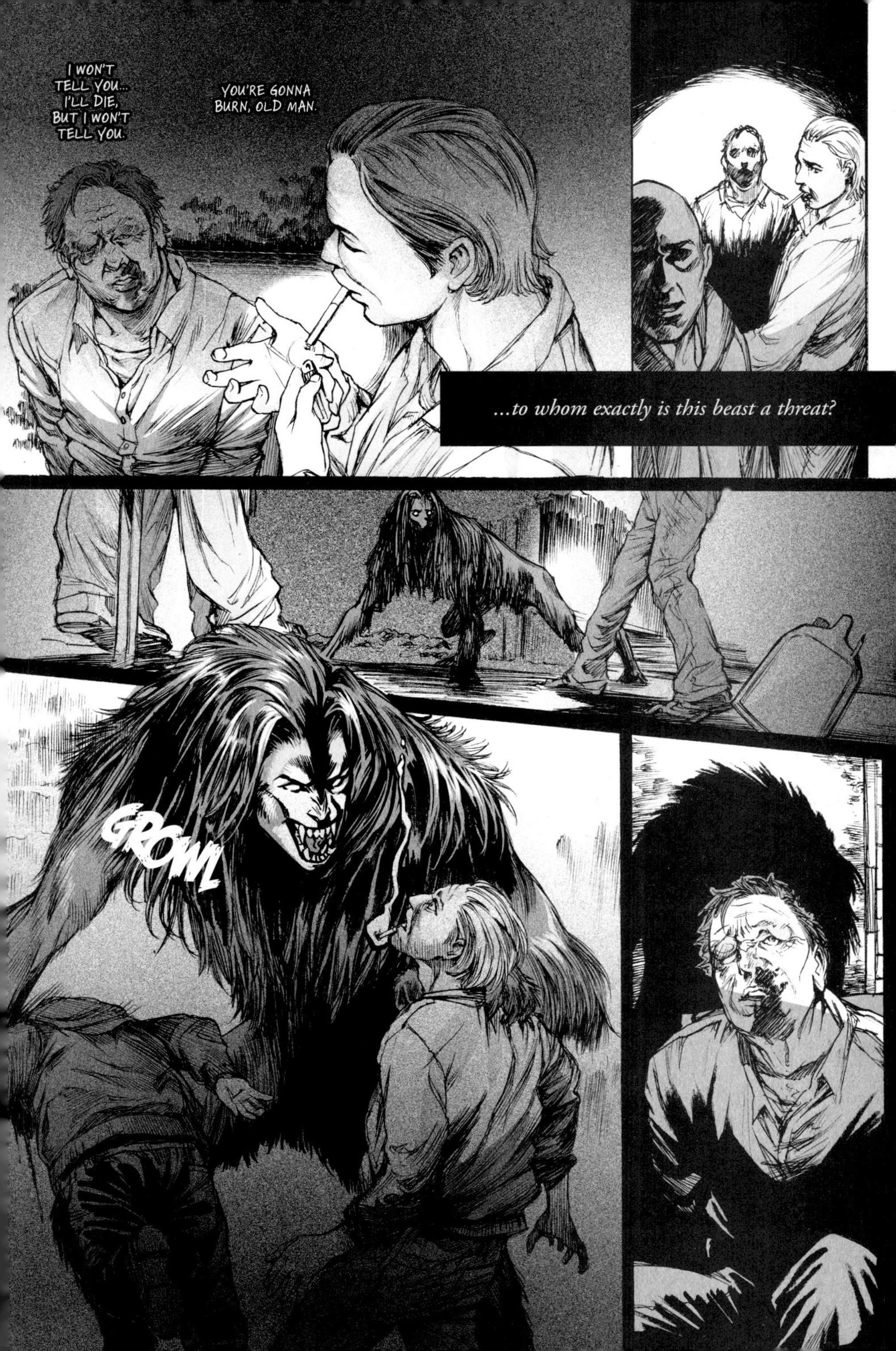
I WON'T TELL YOU... I'LL DIE, BUT I WON'T TELL YOU.
YOU'RE GONNA BURN, OLD MAN.
...to whom exactly is this beast a threat?
GROWL

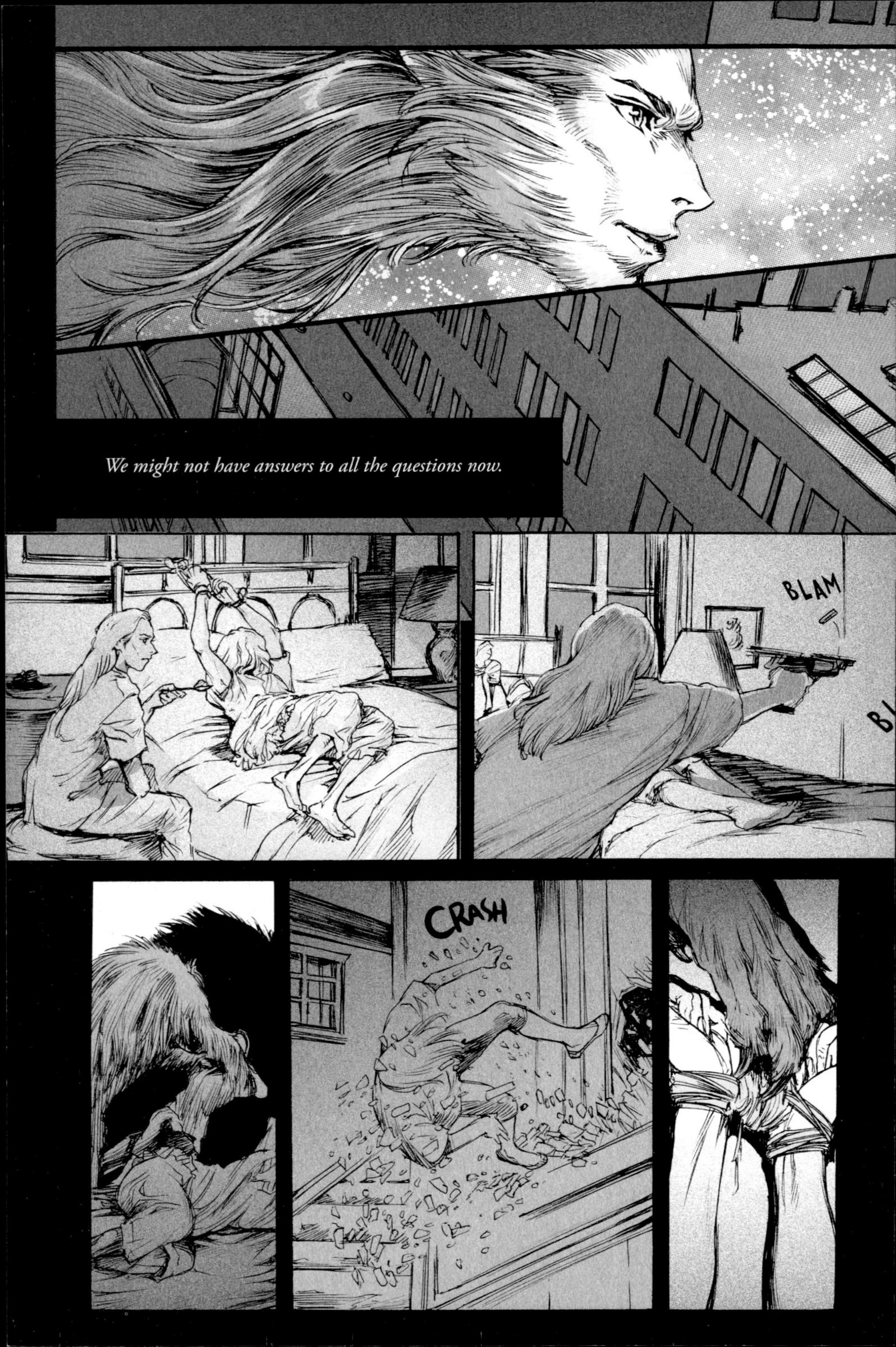

We might not have answers to all the questions now.
BLAM
CRASH

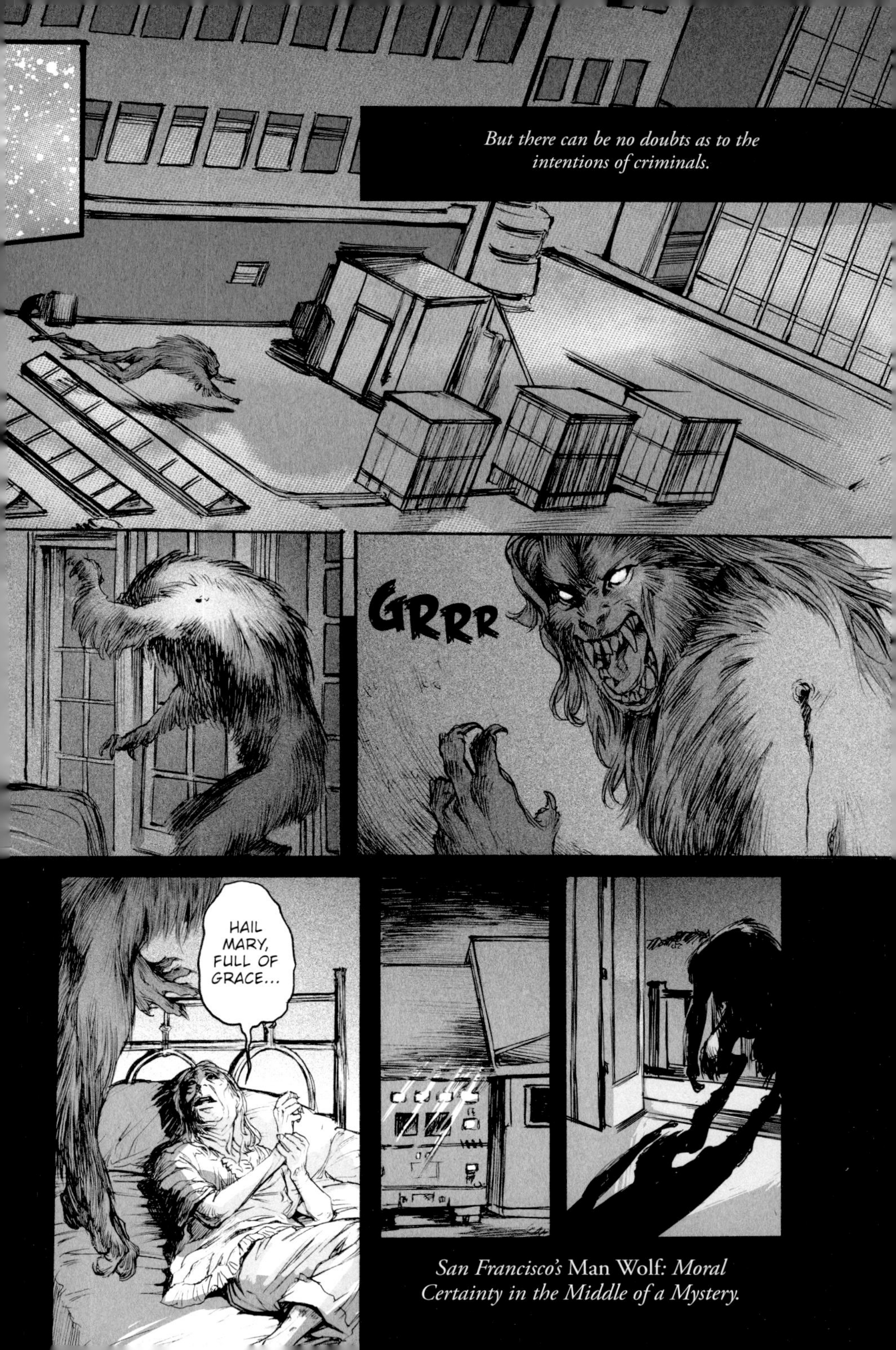
But there can be no doubts as to the intentions of criminals.
GRRR
HAIL MARY, FULL OF GRACE...
San Francisco's Man Wolf: *Moral Certainty in the Middle of a Mystery.*

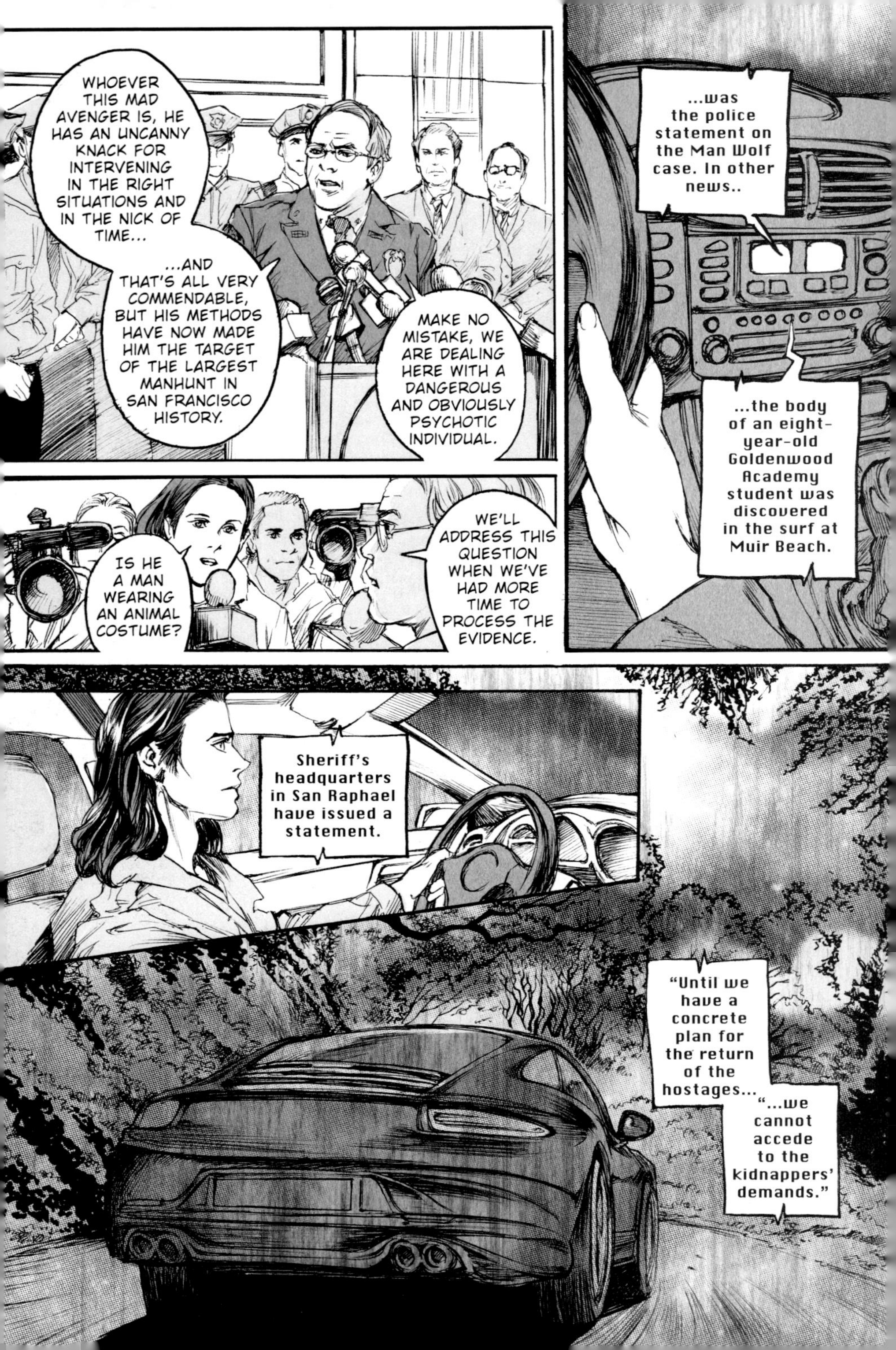
WHOEVER THIS MAD AVENGER IS, HE HAS AN UNCANNY KNACK FOR INTERVENING IN THE RIGHT SITUATIONS AND IN THE NICK OF TIME...
...AND THAT'S ALL VERY COMMENDABLE, BUT HIS METHODS HAVE NOW MADE HIM THE TARGET OF THE LARGEST MANHUNT IN SAN FRANCISCO HISTORY.
MAKE NO MISTAKE, WE ARE DEALING HERE WITH A DANGEROUS AND OBVIOUSLY PSYCHOTIC INDIVIDUAL.
IS HE A MAN WEARING AN ANIMAL COSTUME?
WE'LL ADDRESS THIS QUESTION WHEN WE'VE HAD MORE TIME TO PROCESS THE EVIDENCE.
...was the police statement on the Man Wolf case. In other news..
...the body of an eight-year-old Goldenwood Academy student was discovered in the surf at Muir Beach.
Sheriff's headquarters in San Raphael have issued a statement.
"Until we have a concrete plan for the return of the hostages...
"...we cannot accede to the kidnappers' demands."

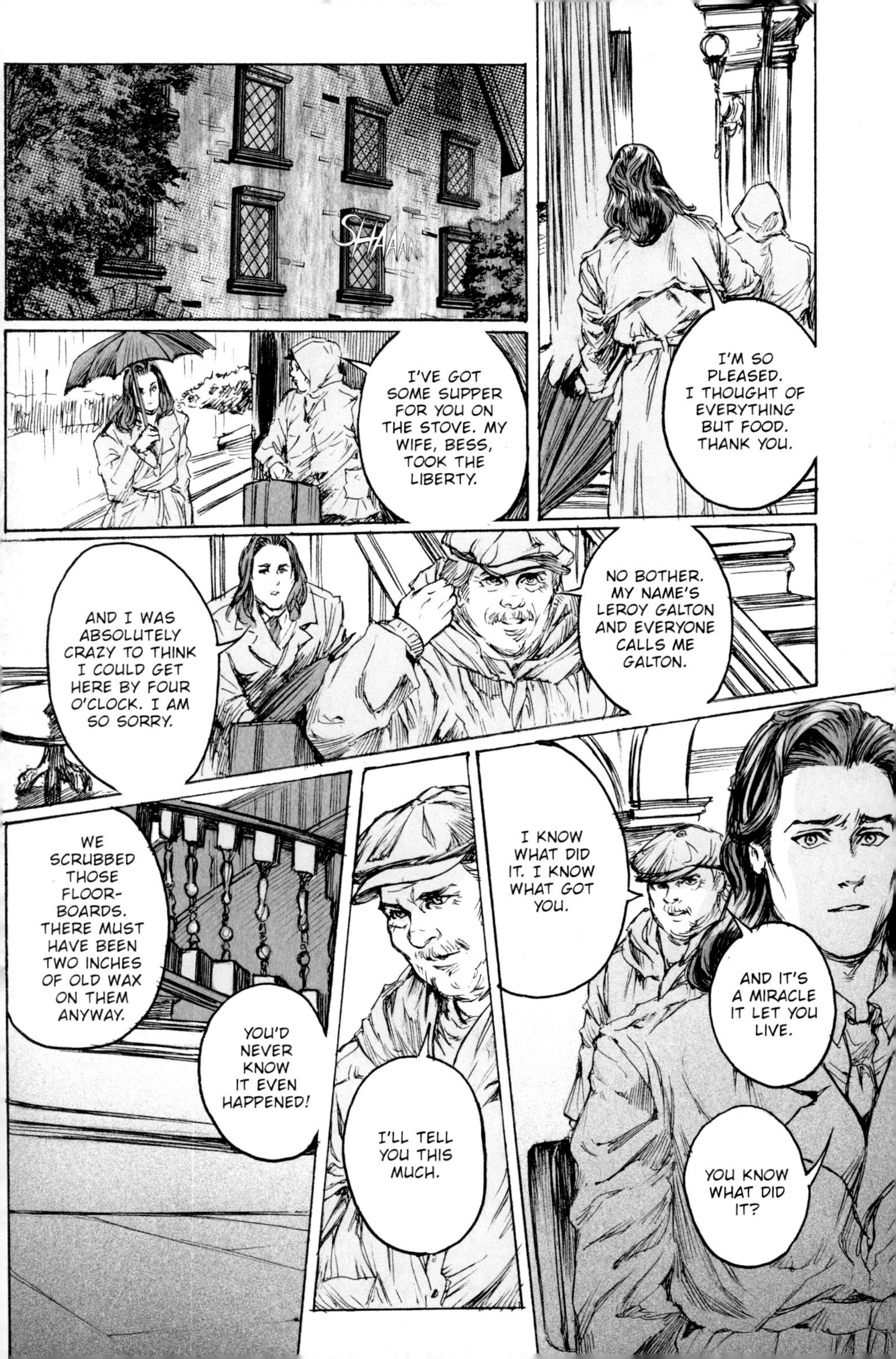
SHAAAAA
I'VE GOT SOME SUPPER FOR YOU ON THE STOVE. MY WIFE, BESS, TOOK THE LIBERTY.
I'M SO PLEASED. I THOUGHT OF EVERYTHING BUT FOOD. THANK YOU.
AND I WAS ABSOLUTELY CRAZY TO THINK I COULD GET HERE BY FOUR O'CLOCK. I AM SO SORRY.
NO BOTHER. MY NAME'S LEROY GALTON AND EVERYONE CALLS ME GALTON.
WE SCRUBBED THOSE FLOOR-BOARDS. THERE MUST HAVE BEEN TWO INCHES OF OLD WAX ON THEM ANYWAY.
YOU'D NEVER KNOW IT EVEN HAPPENED!
I'LL TELL YOU THIS MUCH.
I KNOW WHAT DID IT. I KNOW WHAT GOT YOU.
AND IT'S A MIRACLE IT LET YOU LIVE.
YOU KNOW WHAT DID IT?

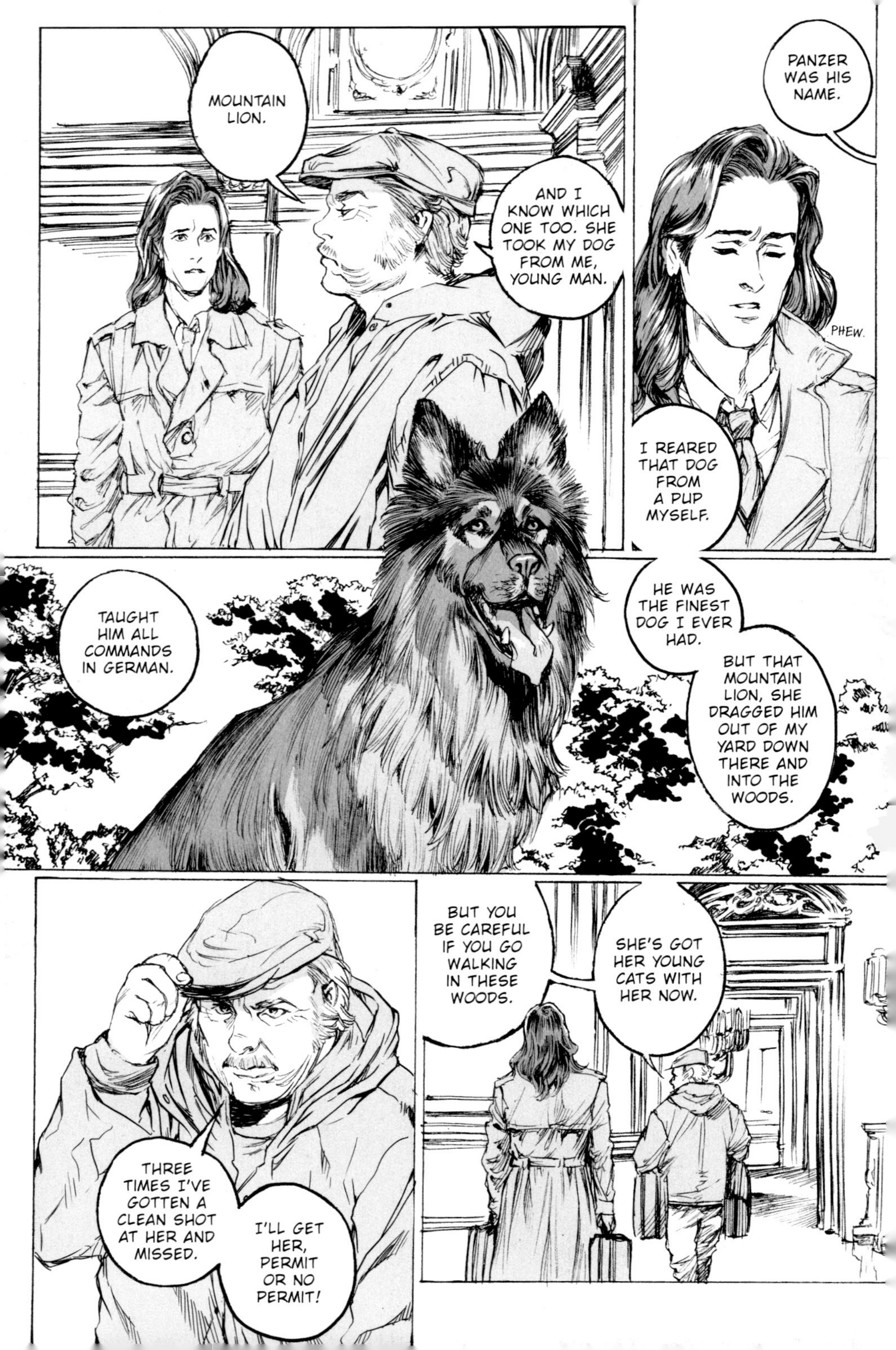
MOUNTAIN LION.
AND I KNOW WHICH ONE TOO. SHE TOOK MY DOG FROM ME, YOUNG MAN.
PANZER WAS HIS NAME.
PHEW.
I REARED THAT DOG FROM A PUP MYSELF.
TAUGHT HIM ALL COMMANDS IN GERMAN.
HE WAS THE FINEST DOG I EVER HAD.
BUT THAT MOUNTAIN LION, SHE DRAGGED HIM OUT OF MY YARD DOWN THERE AND INTO THE WOODS.
THREE TIMES I'VE GOTTEN A CLEAN SHOT AT HER AND MISSED.
I'LL GET HER, PERMIT OR NO PERMIT!
BUT YOU BE CAREFUL IF YOU GO WALKING IN THESE WOODS.
SHE'S GOT HER YOUNG CATS WITH HER NOW.

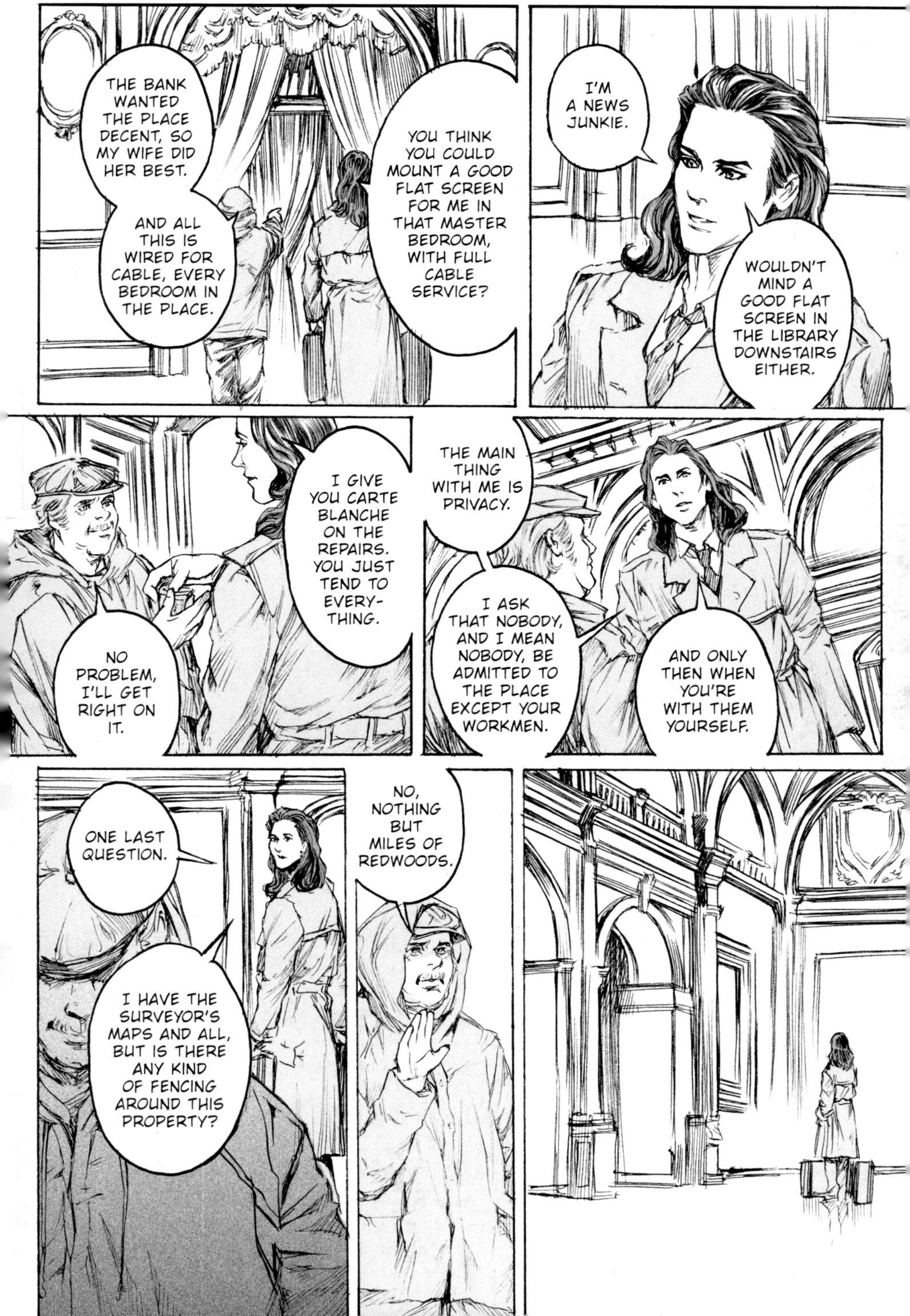
THE BANK WANTED THE PLACE DECENT, SO MY WIFE DID HER BEST.
AND ALL THIS IS WIRED FOR CABLE, EVERY BEDROOM IN THE PLACE.
YOU THINK YOU COULD MOUNT A GOOD FLAT SCREEN FOR ME IN THAT MASTER BEDROOM, WITH FULL CABLE SERVICE?
I'M A NEWS JUNKIE.
WOULDN'T MIND A GOOD FLAT SCREEN IN THE LIBRARY DOWNSTAIRS EITHER.
I GIVE YOU CARTE BLANCHE ON THE REPAIRS. YOU JUST TEND TO EVERY-THING.
NO PROBLEM, I'LL GET RIGHT ON IT.
THE MAIN THING WITH ME IS PRIVACY.
I ASK THAT NOBODY, AND I MEAN NOBODY, BE ADMITTED TO THE PLACE EXCEPT YOUR WORKMEN.
AND ONLY THEN WHEN YOU'RE WITH THEM YOURSELF.
ONE LAST QUESTION.
I HAVE THE SURVEYOR'S MAPS AND ALL, BUT IS THERE ANY KIND OF FENCING AROUND THIS PROPERTY?
NO, NOTHING BUT MILES OF REDWOODS.

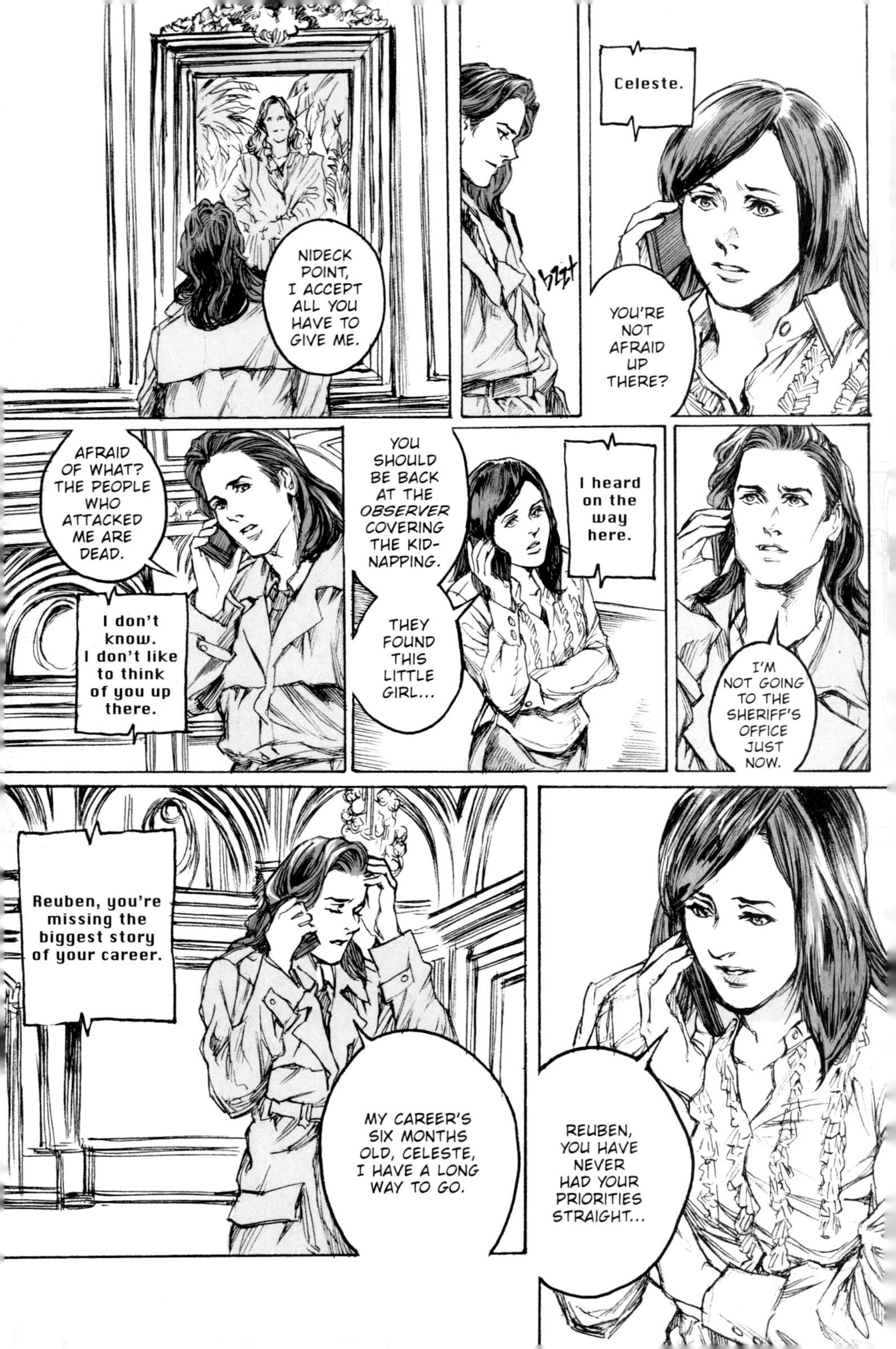
NIDECK POINT, I ACCEPT ALL YOU HAVE TO GIVE ME.
BZZT
Celeste.
YOU'RE NOT AFRAID UP THERE?
AFRAID OF WHAT? THE PEOPLE WHO ATTACKED ME ARE DEAD.
I don't know. I don't like to think of you up there.
YOU SHOULD BE BACK AT THE *OBSERVER* COVERING THE KID-NAPPING.
THEY FOUND THIS LITTLE GIRL...
I heard on the way here.
I'M NOT GOING TO THE SHERIFF'S OFFICE JUST NOW.
Reuben, you're missing the biggest story of your career.
MY CAREER'S SIX MONTHS OLD, CELESTE, I HAVE A LONG WAY TO GO.
REUBEN, YOU HAVE NEVER HAD YOUR PRIORITIES STRAIGHT...

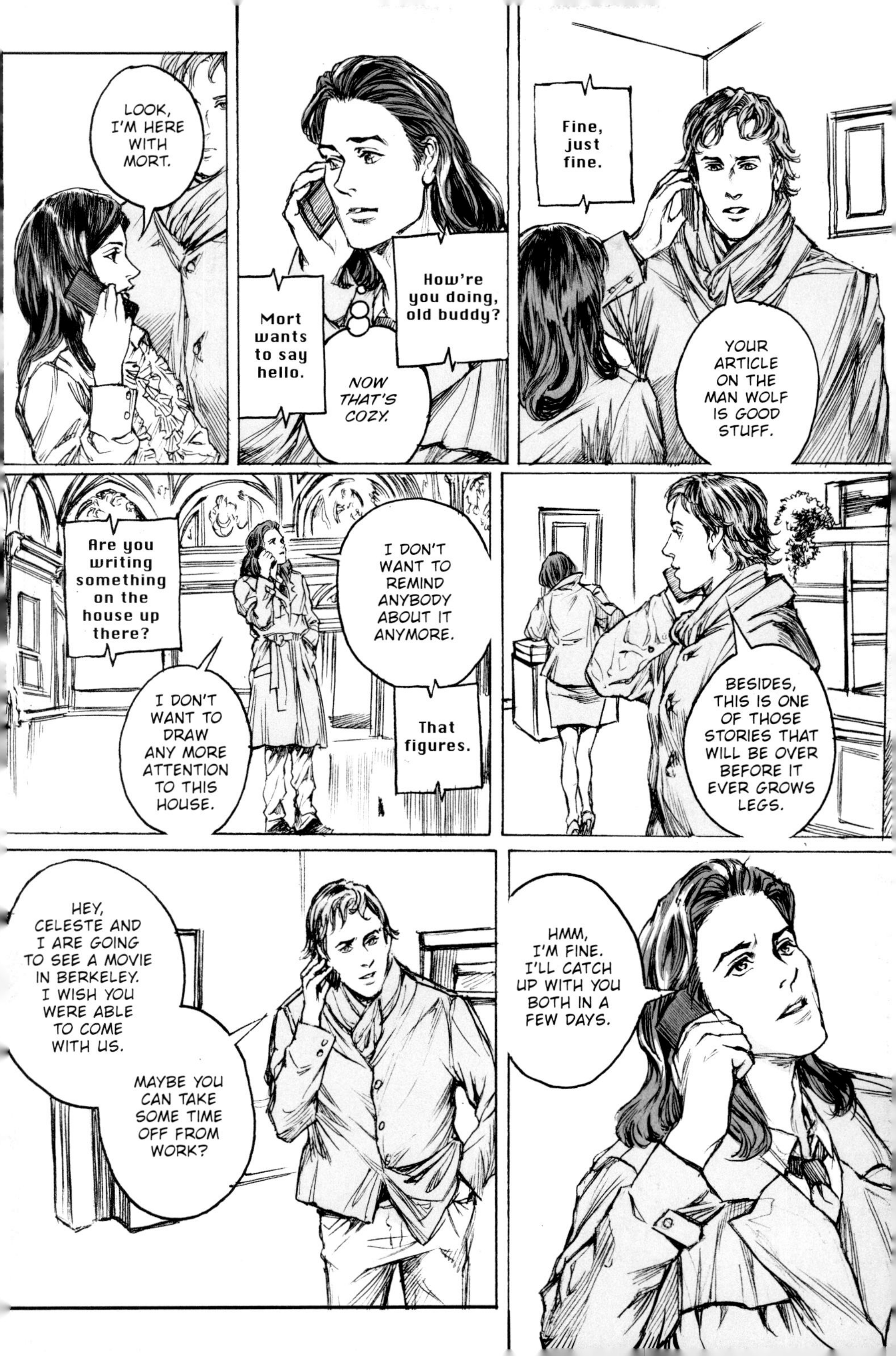
LOOK, I'M HERE WITH MORT.
Mort wants to say hello.
How're you doing, old buddy?
NOW THAT'S COZY.
Fine, just fine.
YOUR ARTICLE ON THE MAN WOLF IS GOOD STUFF.
Are you writing something on the house up there?
I DON'T WANT TO DRAW ANY MORE ATTENTION TO THIS HOUSE.
I DON'T WANT TO REMIND ANYBODY ABOUT IT ANYMORE.
That figures.
BESIDES, THIS IS ONE OF THOSE STORIES THAT WILL BE OVER BEFORE IT EVER GROWS LEGS.
HEY, CELESTE AND I ARE GOING TO SEE A MOVIE IN BERKELEY. I WISH YOU WERE ABLE TO COME WITH US.
MAYBE YOU CAN TAKE SOME TIME OFF FROM WORK?
HMM, I'M FINE. I'LL CATCH UP WITH YOU BOTH IN A FEW DAYS.

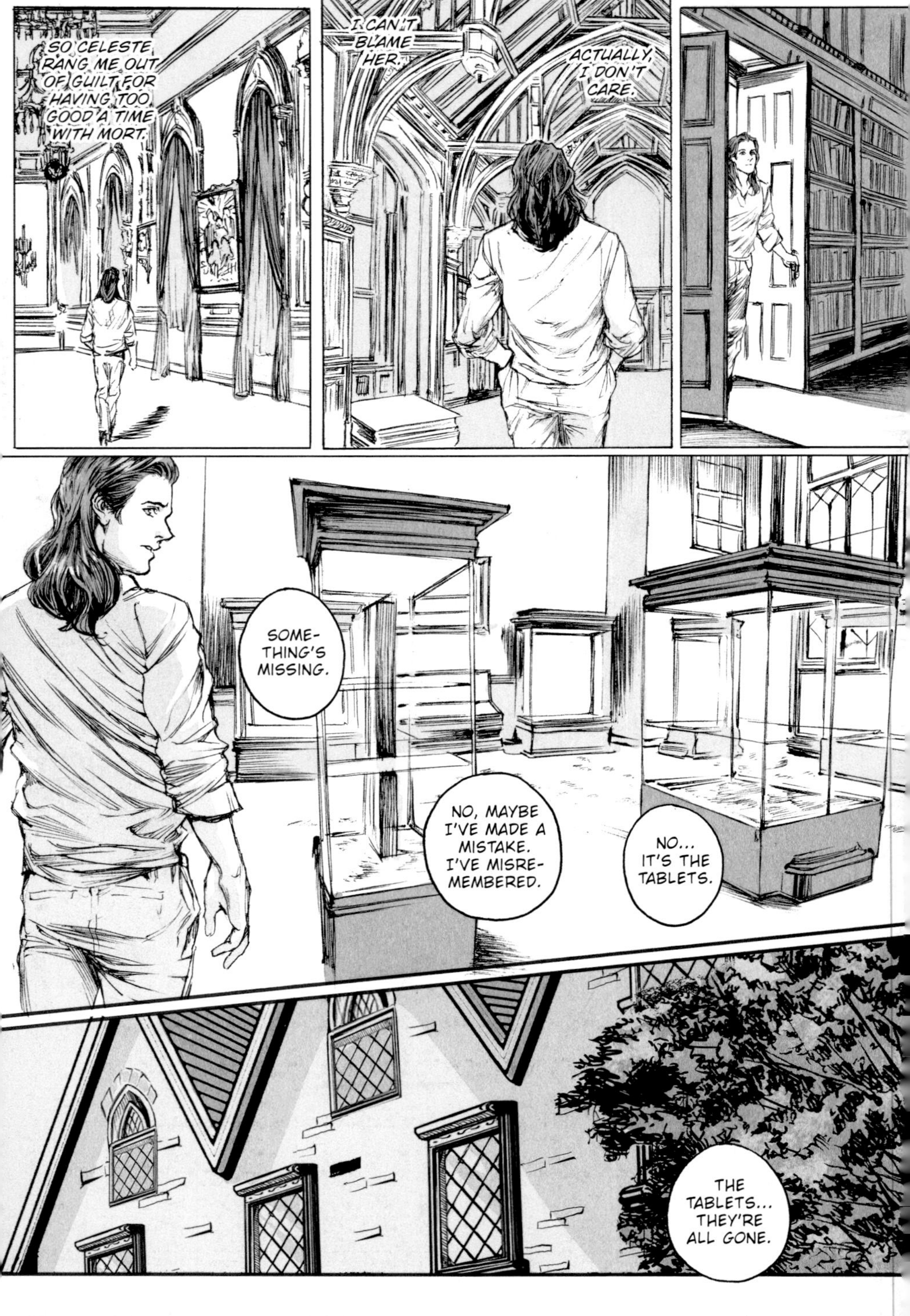
SO CELESTE RANG ME OUT OF GUILT FOR HAVING TOO GOOD A TIME WITH MORT.
I CAN'T BLAME HER.
ACTUALLY, I DON'T CARE.
SOMETHING'S MISSING.
NO, MAYBE I'VE MADE A MISTAKE. I'VE MISREMEMBERED.
NO... IT'S THE TABLETS.
THE TABLETS... THEY'RE ALL GONE.

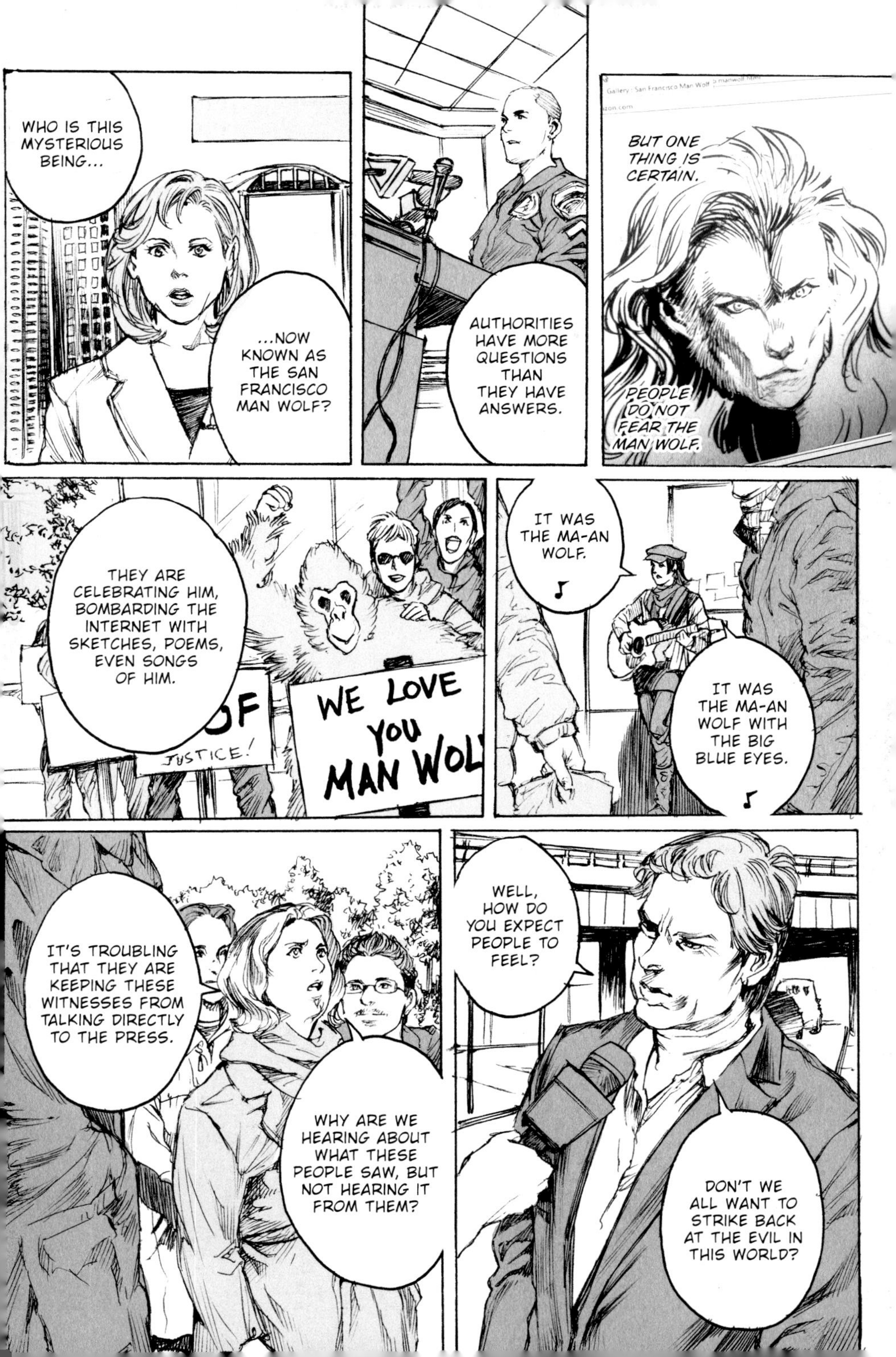
WHO IS THIS MYSTERIOUS BEING...
...NOW KNOWN AS THE SAN FRANCISCO MAN WOLF?
AUTHORITIES HAVE MORE QUESTIONS THAN THEY HAVE ANSWERS.
BUT ONE THING IS CERTAIN.
PEOPLE DO NOT FEAR THE MAN WOLF.
THEY ARE CELEBRATING HIM, BOMBARDING THE INTERNET WITH SKETCHES, POEMS, EVEN SONGS OF HIM.
OF
JUSTICE!
WE LOVE YOU MAN WOL
IT WAS THE MA-AN WOLF.
IT WAS THE MA-AN WOLF WITH THE BIG BLUE EYES.
IT'S TROUBLING THAT THEY ARE KEEPING THESE WITNESSES FROM TALKING DIRECTLY TO THE PRESS.
WHY ARE WE HEARING ABOUT WHAT THESE PEOPLE SAW, BUT NOT HEARING IT FROM THEM?
WELL, HOW DO YOU EXPECT PEOPLE TO FEEL?
DON'T WE ALL WANT TO STRIKE BACK AT THE EVIL IN THIS WORLD?

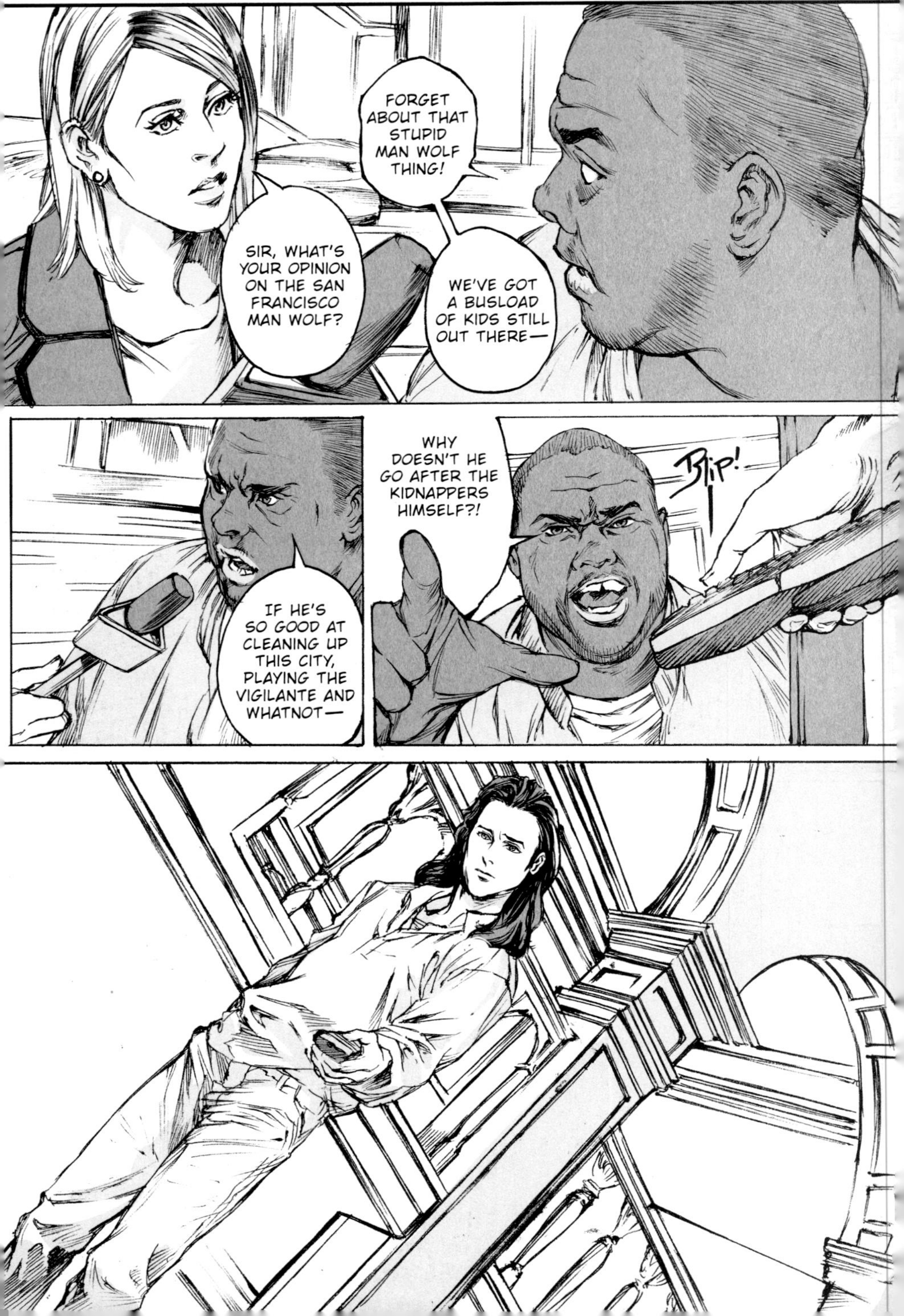
SIR, WHAT'S YOUR OPINION ON THE SAN FRANCISCO MAN WOLF?
FORGET ABOUT THAT STUPID MAN WOLF THING!
WE'VE GOT A BUSLOAD OF KIDS STILL OUT THERE—
IF HE'S SO GOOD AT CLEANING UP THIS CITY, PLAYING THE VIGILANTE AND WHATNOT—
WHY DOESN'T HE GO AFTER THE KIDNAPPERS HIMSELF?!
BLIP!

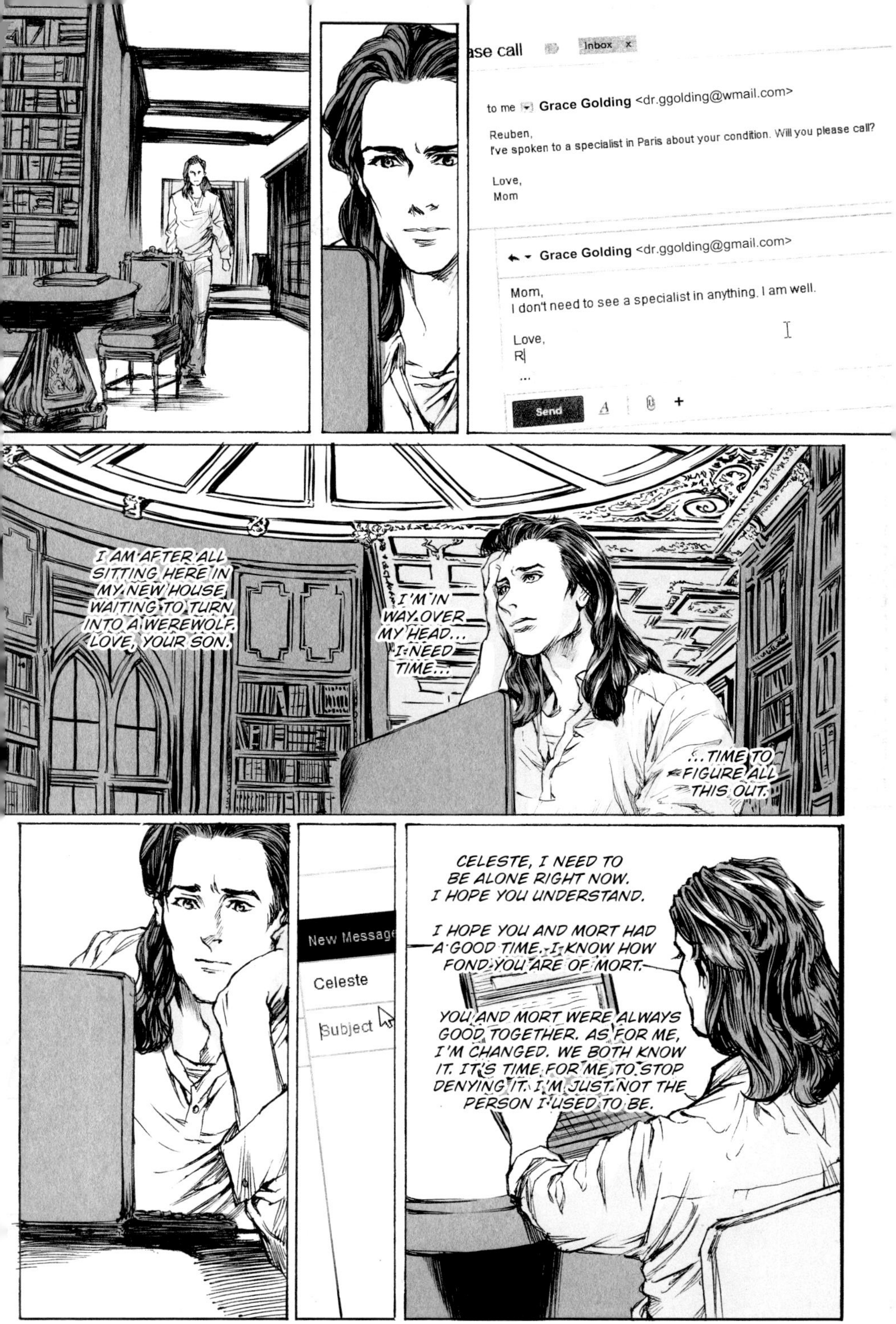

...ase call
Inbox x
to me Grace Golding <dr.ggolding@wmail.com>
Reuben,
I've spoken to a specialist in Paris about your condition. Will you please call?
Love,
Mom
Grace Golding <dr.ggolding@gmail.com>
Mom,
I don't need to see a specialist in anything. I am well.
Love,
R
Send
I AM AFTER ALL SITTING HERE IN MY NEW HOUSE WAITING TO TURN INTO A WEREWOLF. LOVE, YOUR SON.
I'M IN WAY OVER MY HEAD... I NEED TIME...
...TIME TO FIGURE ALL THIS OUT.
New Message
Celeste
Subject
CELESTE, I NEED TO BE ALONE RIGHT NOW. I HOPE YOU UNDERSTAND.
I HOPE YOU AND MORT HAD A GOOD TIME. I KNOW HOW FOND YOU ARE OF MORT.
YOU AND MORT WERE ALWAYS GOOD TOGETHER. AS FOR ME, I'M CHANGED. WE BOTH KNOW IT. IT'S TIME FOR ME TO STOP DENYING IT. I'M JUST NOT THE PERSON I USED TO BE.

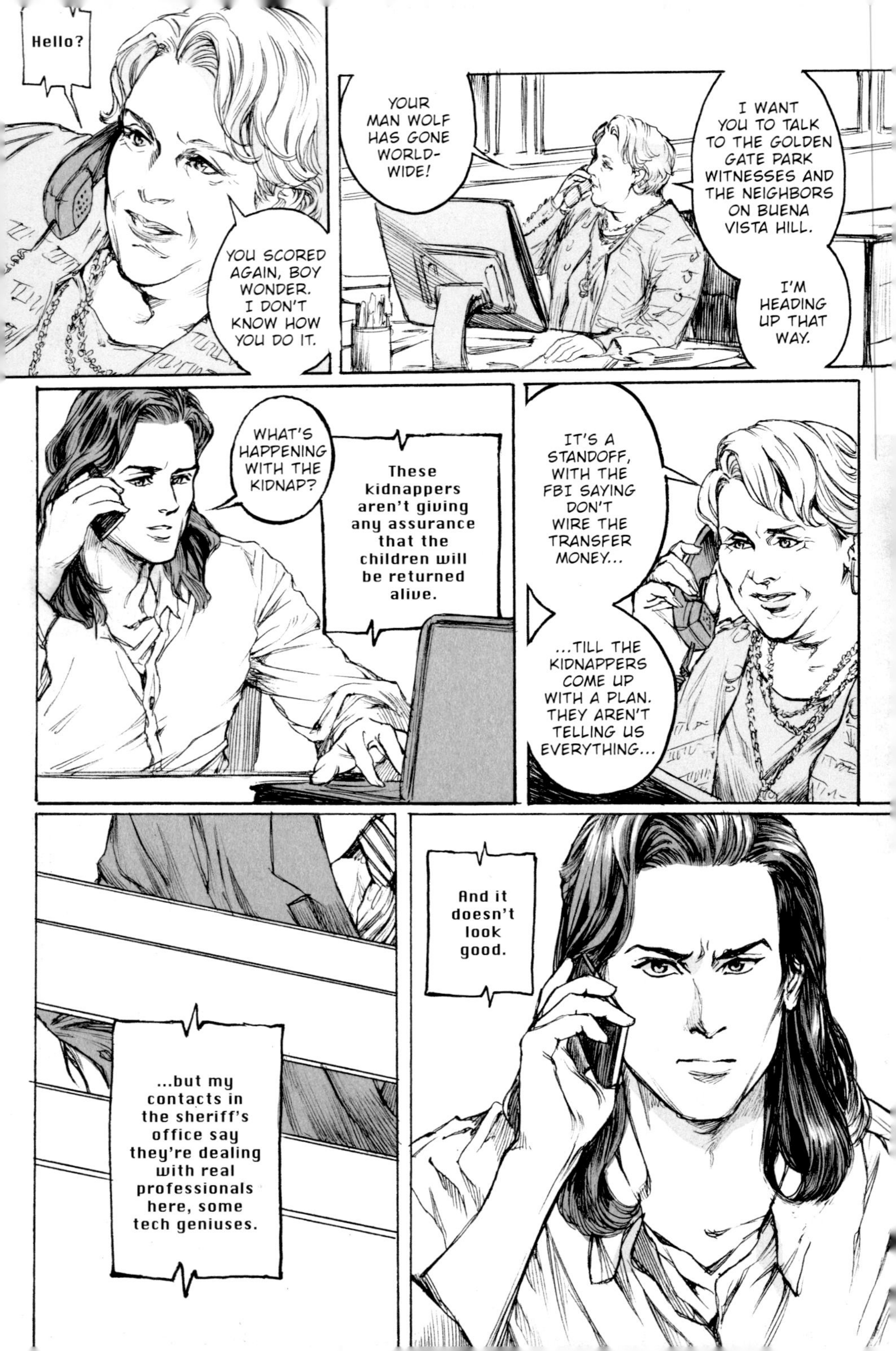
Hello?
YOU SCORED AGAIN, BOY WONDER. I DON'T KNOW HOW YOU DO IT.
YOUR MAN WOLF HAS GONE WORLD-WIDE!
I WANT YOU TO TALK TO THE GOLDEN GATE PARK WITNESSES AND THE NEIGHBORS ON BUENA VISTA HILL.
I'M HEADING UP THAT WAY.
WHAT'S HAPPENING WITH THE KIDNAP?
These kidnappers aren't giving any assurance that the children will be returned alive.
IT'S A STANDOFF, WITH THE FBI SAYING DON'T WIRE THE TRANSFER MONEY...
...TILL THE KIDNAPPERS COME UP WITH A PLAN. THEY AREN'T TELLING US EVERYTHING...
...but my contacts in the sheriff's office say they're dealing with real professionals here, some tech geniuses.
And it doesn't look good.

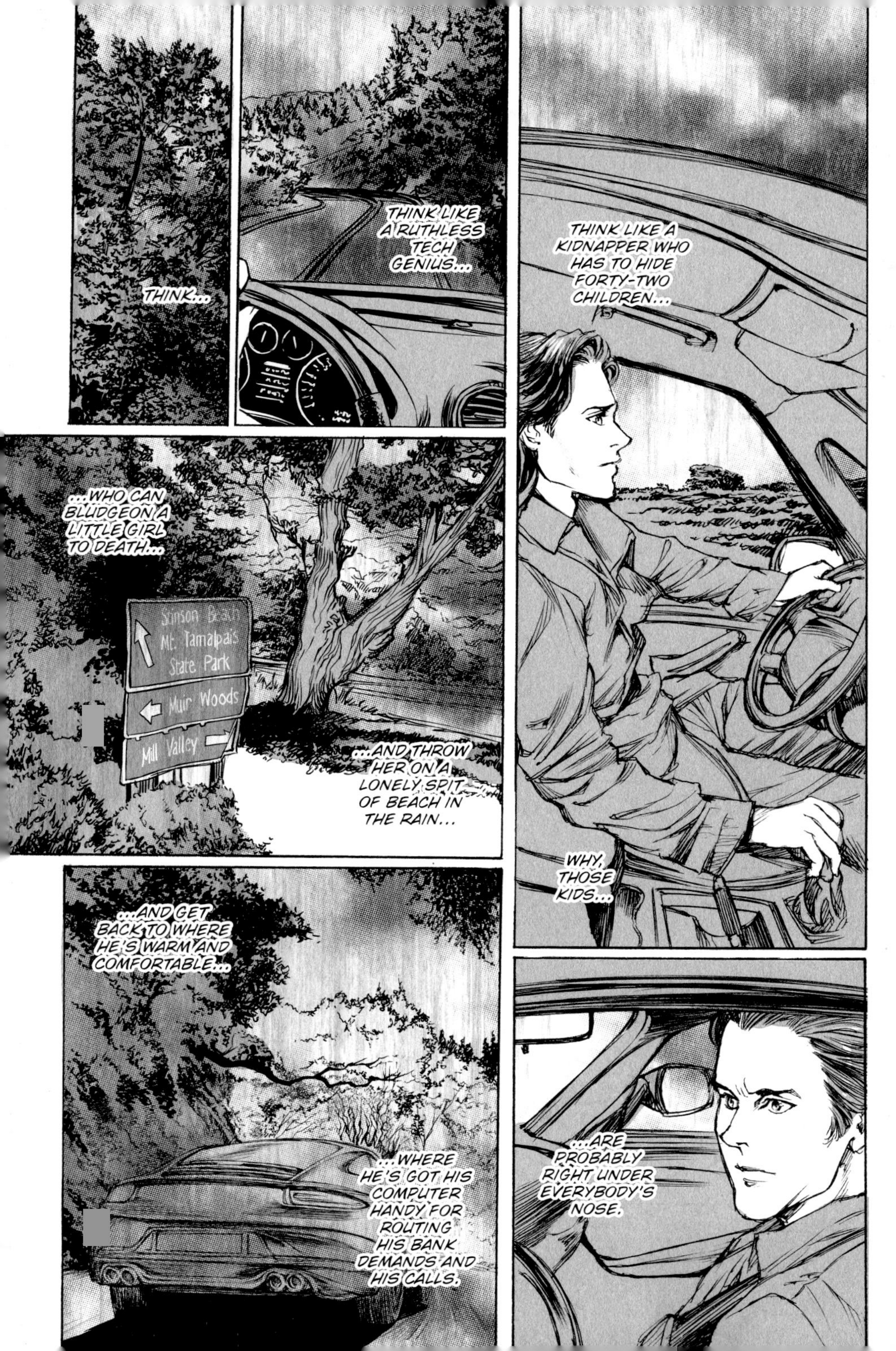
THINK...
THINK LIKE A RUTHLESS TECH GENIUS...
THINK LIKE A KIDNAPPER WHO HAS TO HIDE FORTY-TWO CHILDREN...
...WHO CAN BLUDGEON A LITTLE GIRL TO DEATH...
Stinson Beach
Mt. Tamalpais State Park
Muir Woods
Mill Valley
...AND THROW HER ON A LONELY SPIT OF BEACH IN THE RAIN...
...AND GET BACK TO WHERE HE'S WARM AND COMFORTABLE...
...WHERE HE'S GOT HIS COMPUTER HANDY FOR ROUTING HIS BANK DEMANDS AND HIS CALLS.
WHY, THOSE KIDS...
...ARE PROBABLY RIGHT UNDER EVERYBODY'S NOSE.

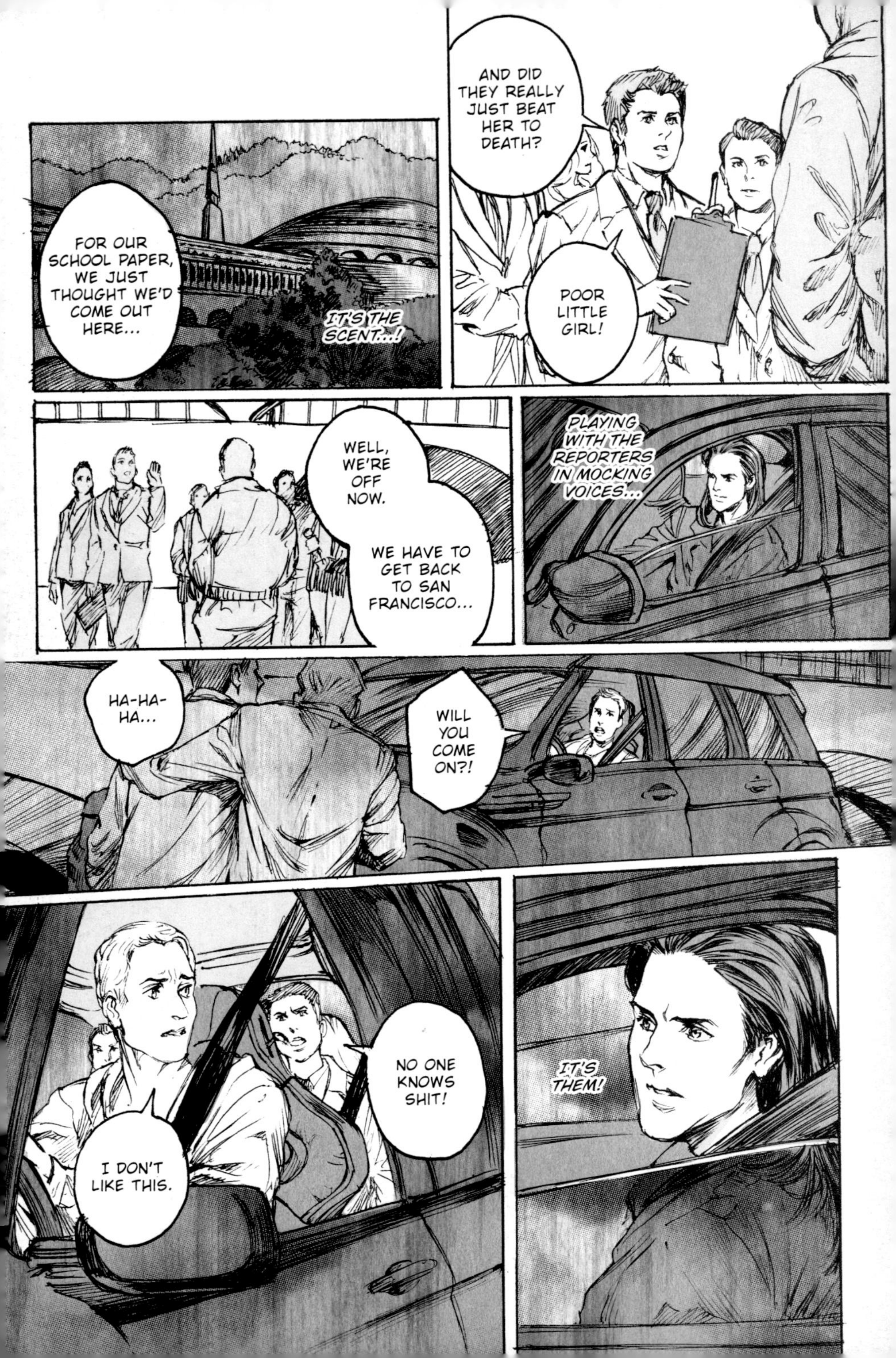
FOR OUR SCHOOL PAPER, WE JUST THOUGHT WE'D COME OUT HERE...
IT'S THE SCENT...!
AND DID THEY REALLY JUST BEAT HER TO DEATH?
POOR LITTLE GIRL!
WELL, WE'RE OFF NOW.
WE HAVE TO GET BACK TO SAN FRANCISCO...
PLAYING WITH THE REPORTERS IN MOCKING VOICES...
HA-HA-HA...
WILL YOU COME ON?!
NO ONE KNOWS SHIT!
I DON'T LIKE THIS.
IT'S THEM!

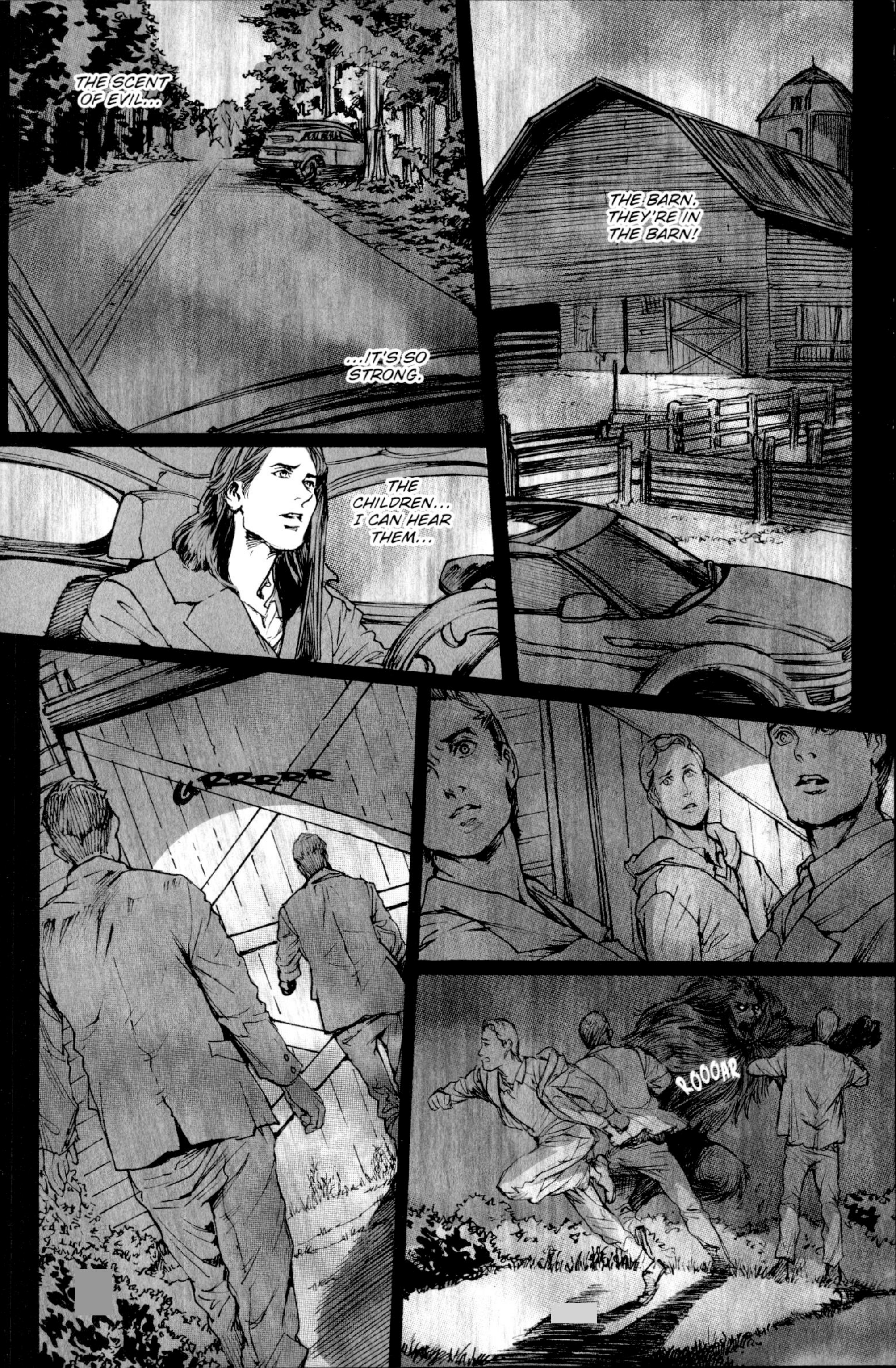
THE SCENT OF EVIL...
...IT'S SO STRONG.
THE BARN. THEY'RE IN THE BARN!
THE CHILDREN... I CAN HEAR THEM...
GRRRRRR
ROOOAR

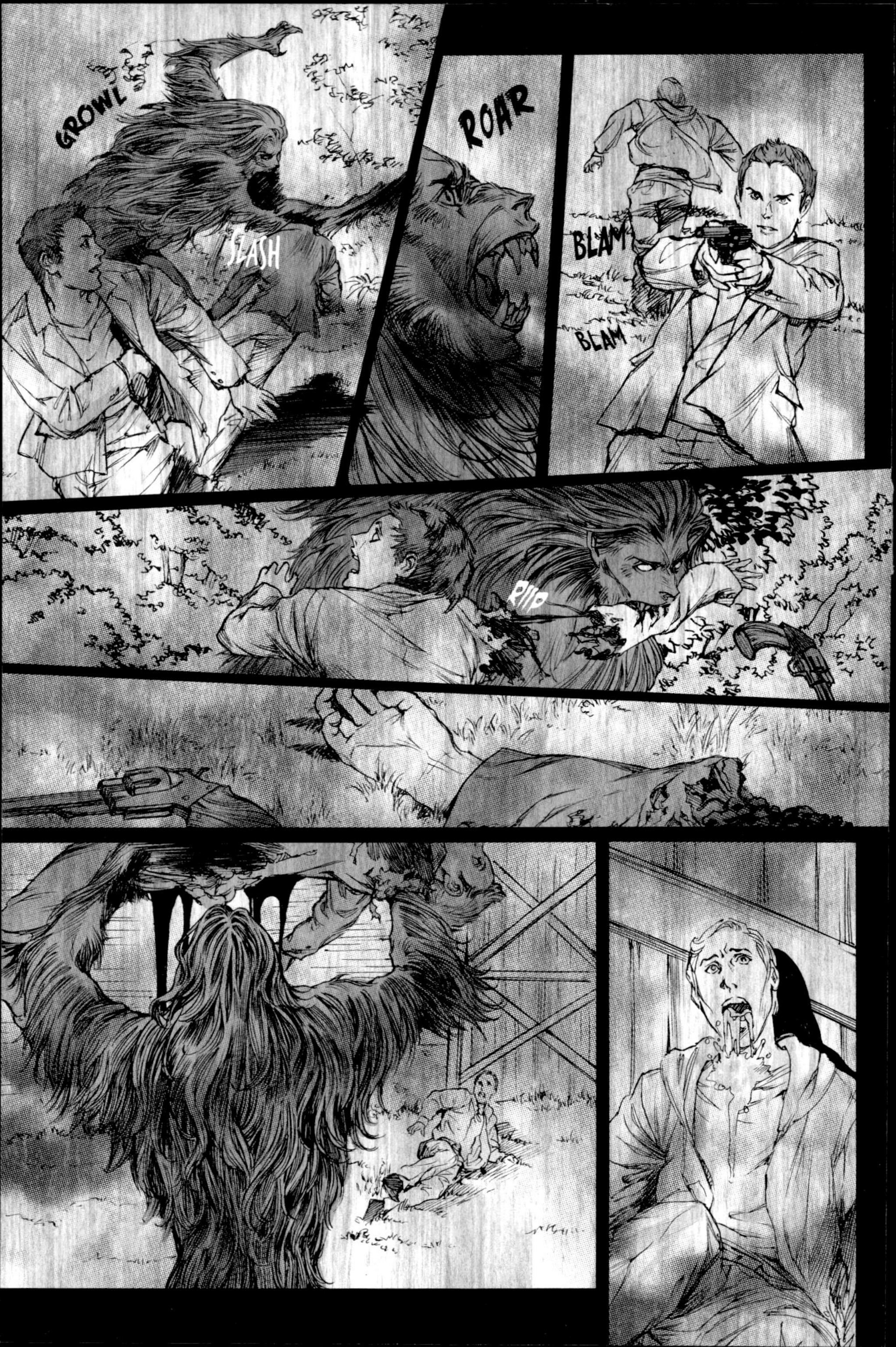
GROWL
SLASH
ROAR
BLAM
BLAM
RIIP

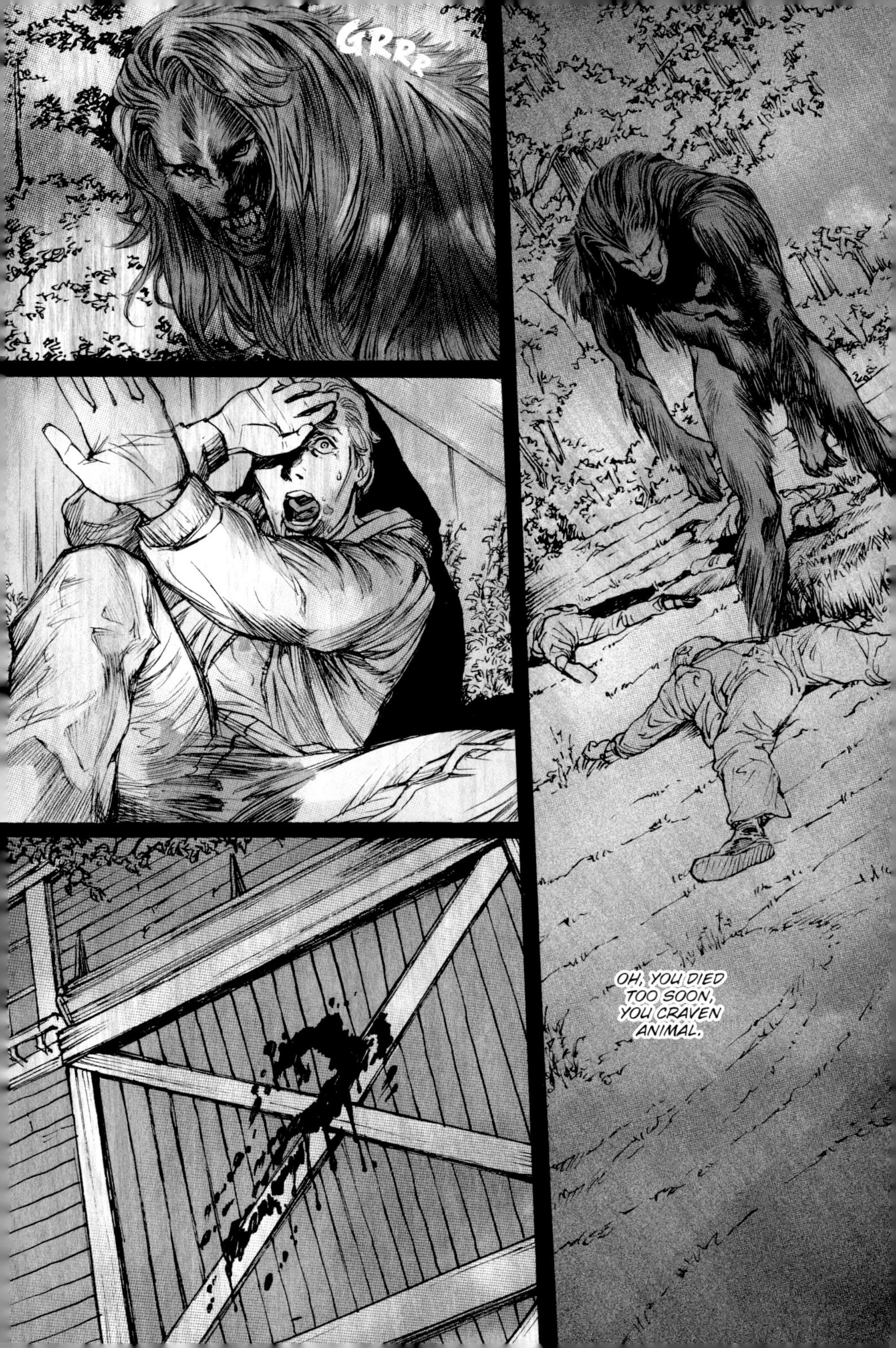
GRRR
OH, YOU DIED TOO SOON, YOU CRAVEN ANIMAL.

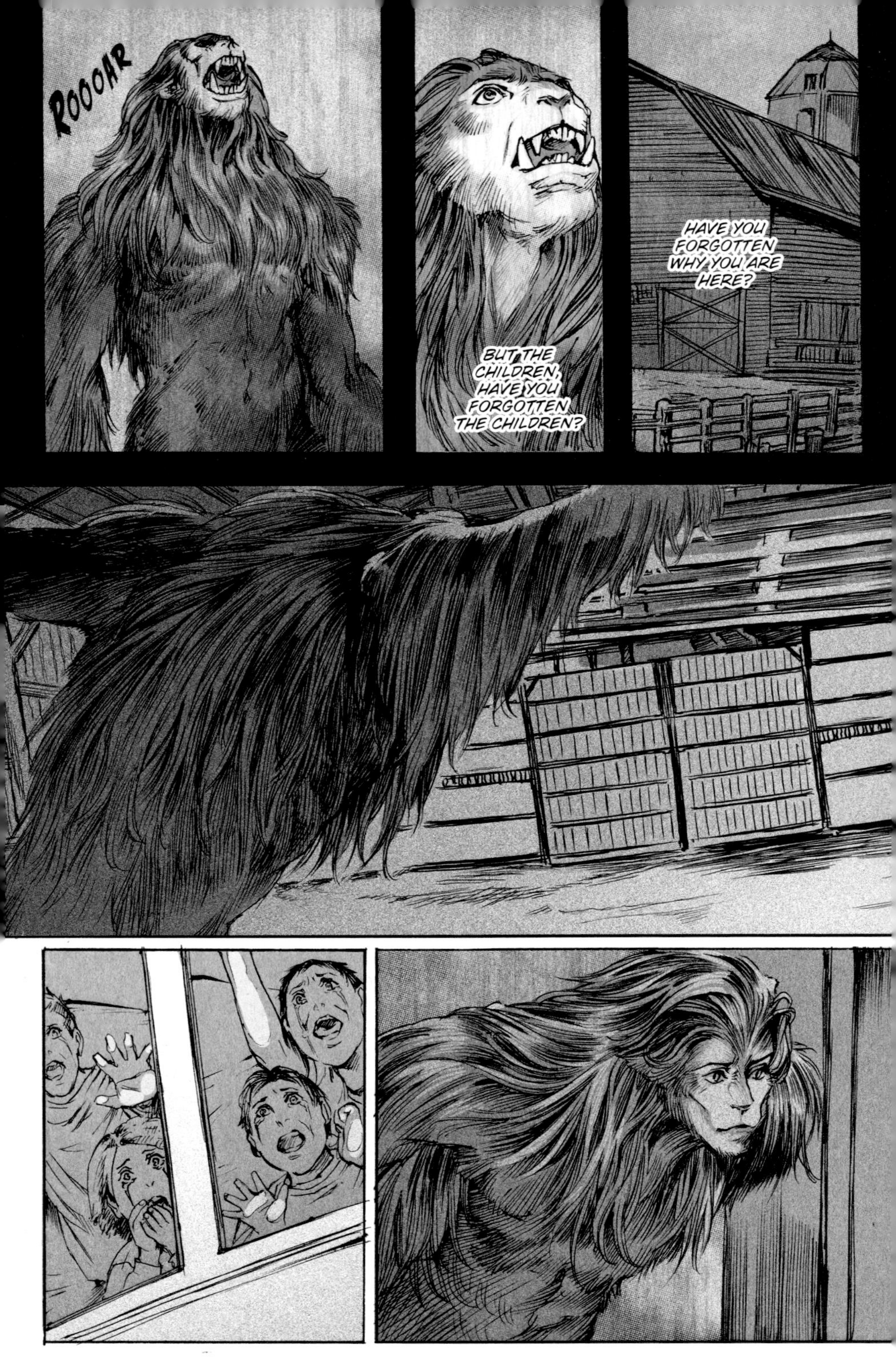
ROOOAR
BUT THE CHILDREN, HAVE YOU FORGOTTEN THE CHILDREN?
HAVE YOU FORGOTTEN WHY YOU ARE HERE?

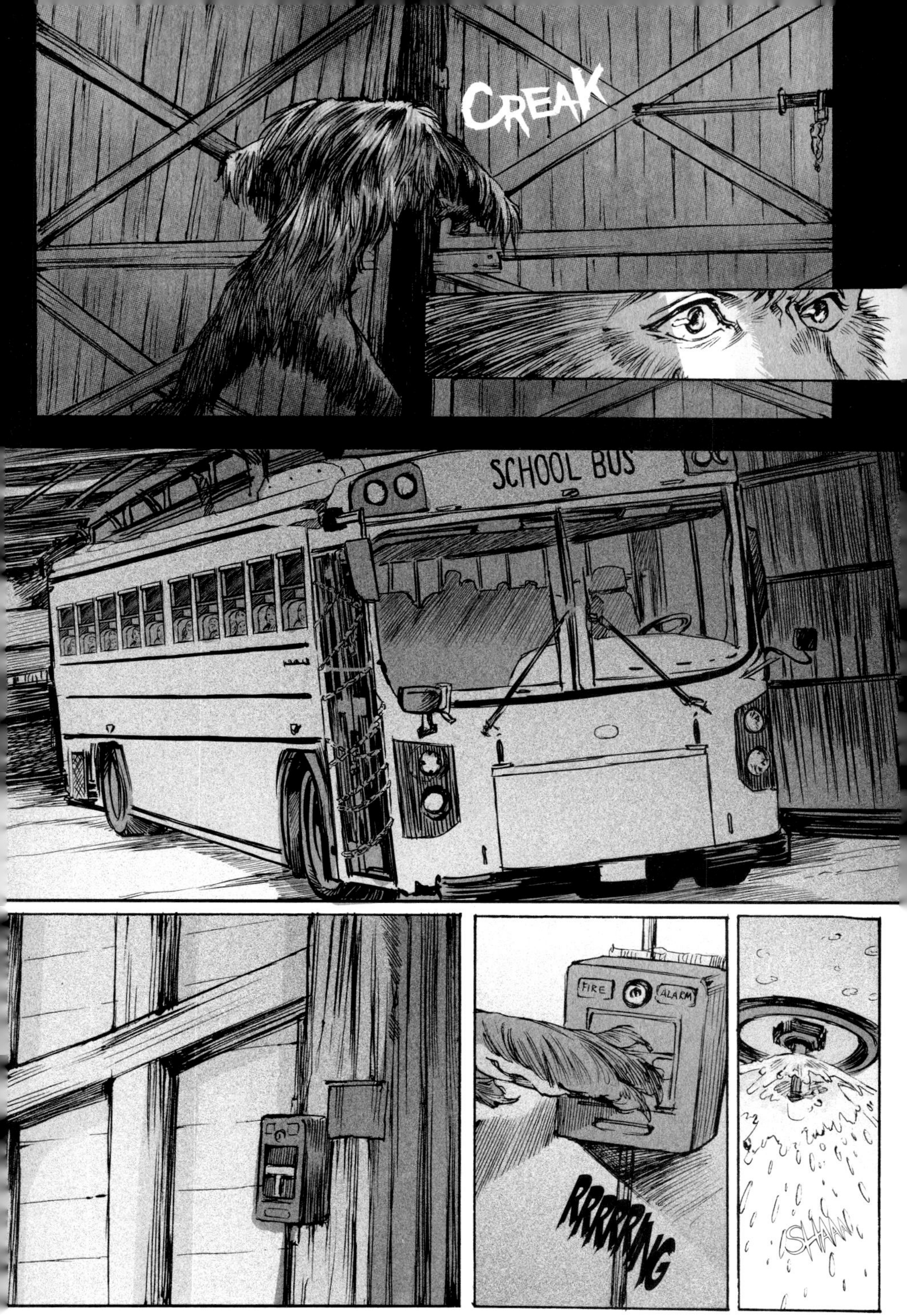
CREAK
SCHOOL BUS
FIRE
ALARM
RRRRRING
SHAAAA

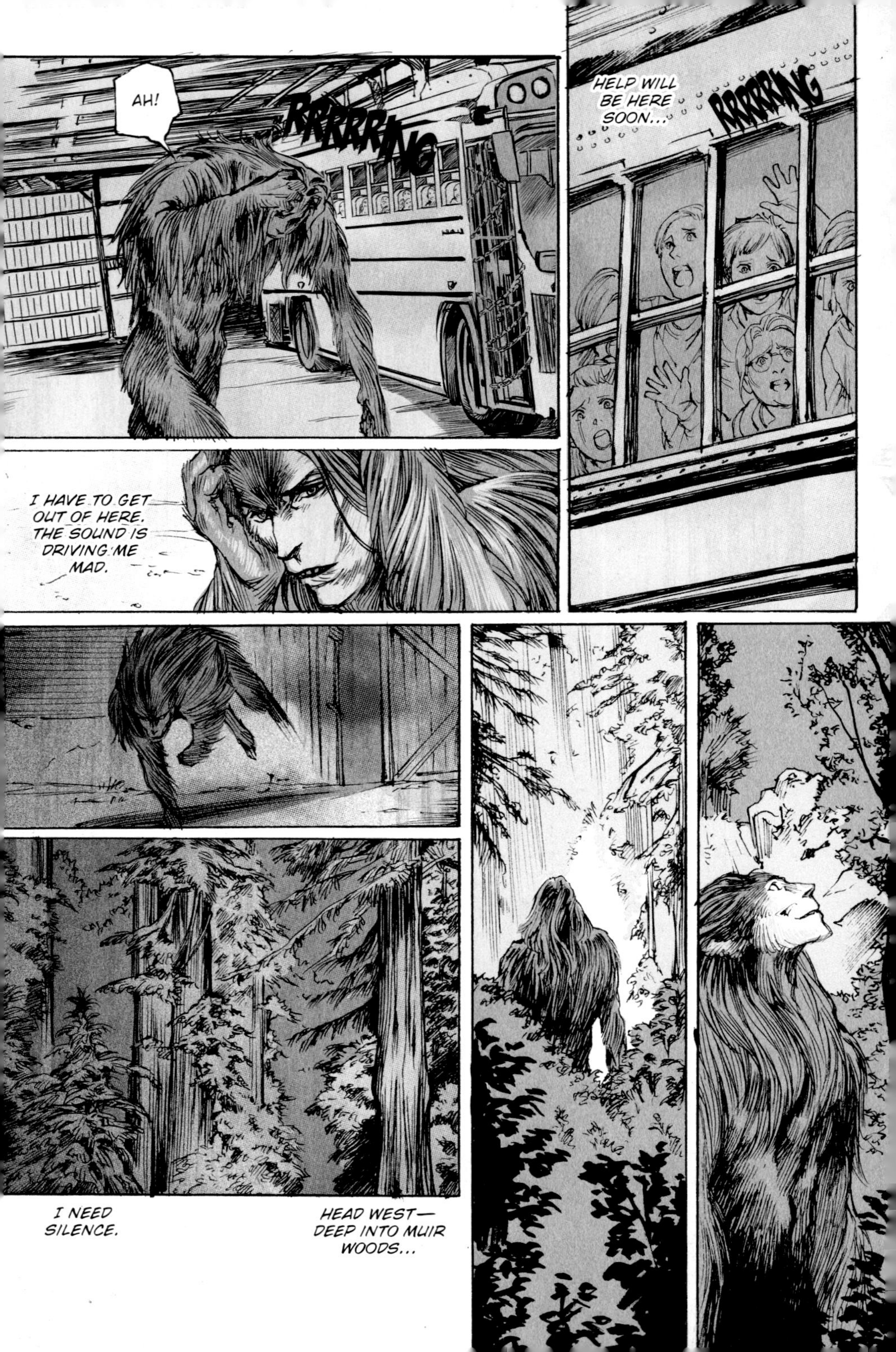
AH!
RRRRRING
HELP WILL BE HERE SOON...
RRRRRING
I HAVE TO GET OUT OF HERE. THE SOUND IS DRIVING ME MAD.
I NEED SILENCE.
HEAD WEST— DEEP INTO MUIR WOODS...

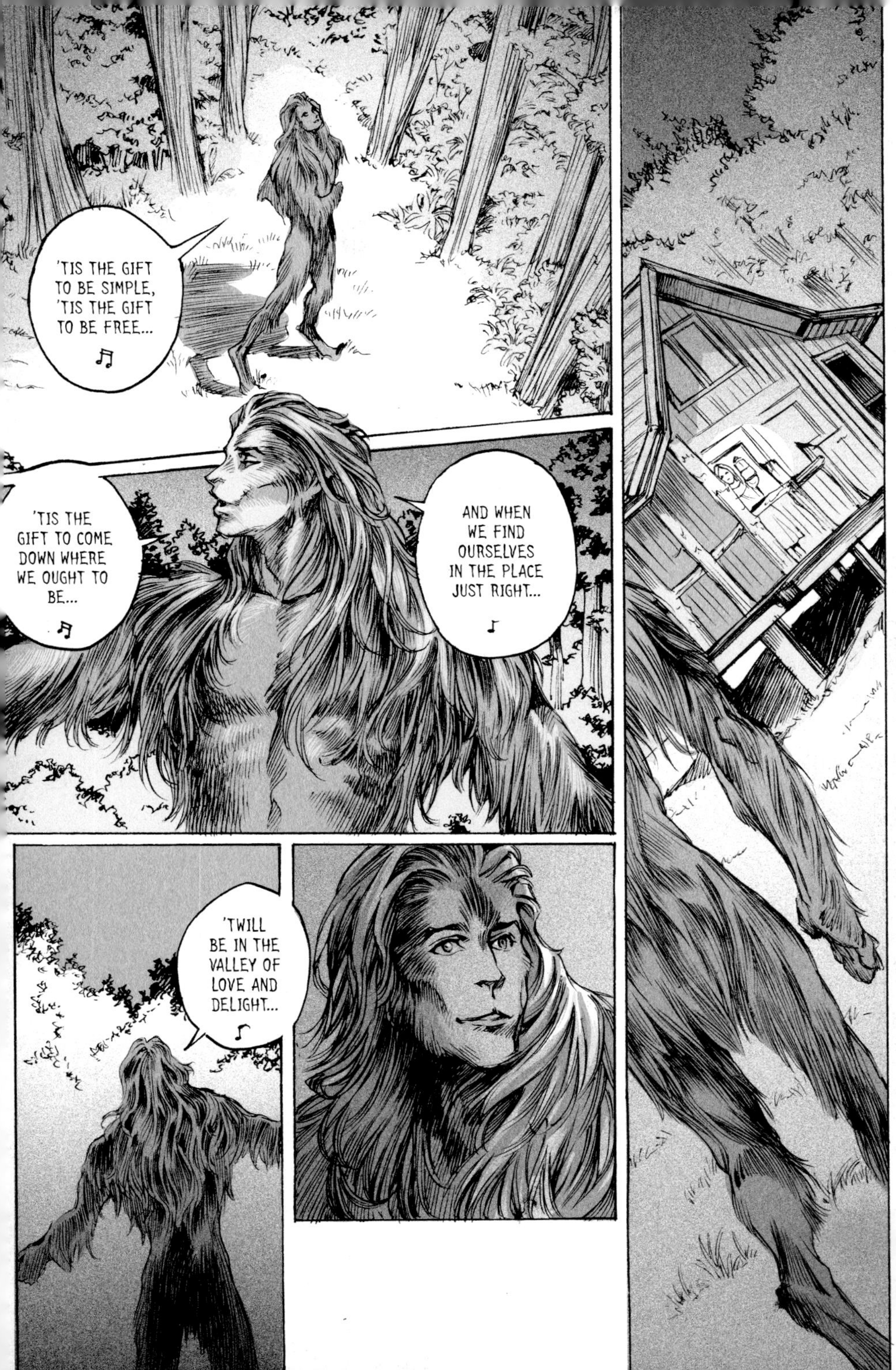
'TIS THE GIFT TO BE SIMPLE, 'TIS THE GIFT TO BE FREE...
'TIS THE GIFT TO COME DOWN WHERE WE OUGHT TO BE...
AND WHEN WE FIND OURSELVES IN THE PLACE JUST RIGHT...
'TWILL BE IN THE VALLEY OF LOVE AND DELIGHT...

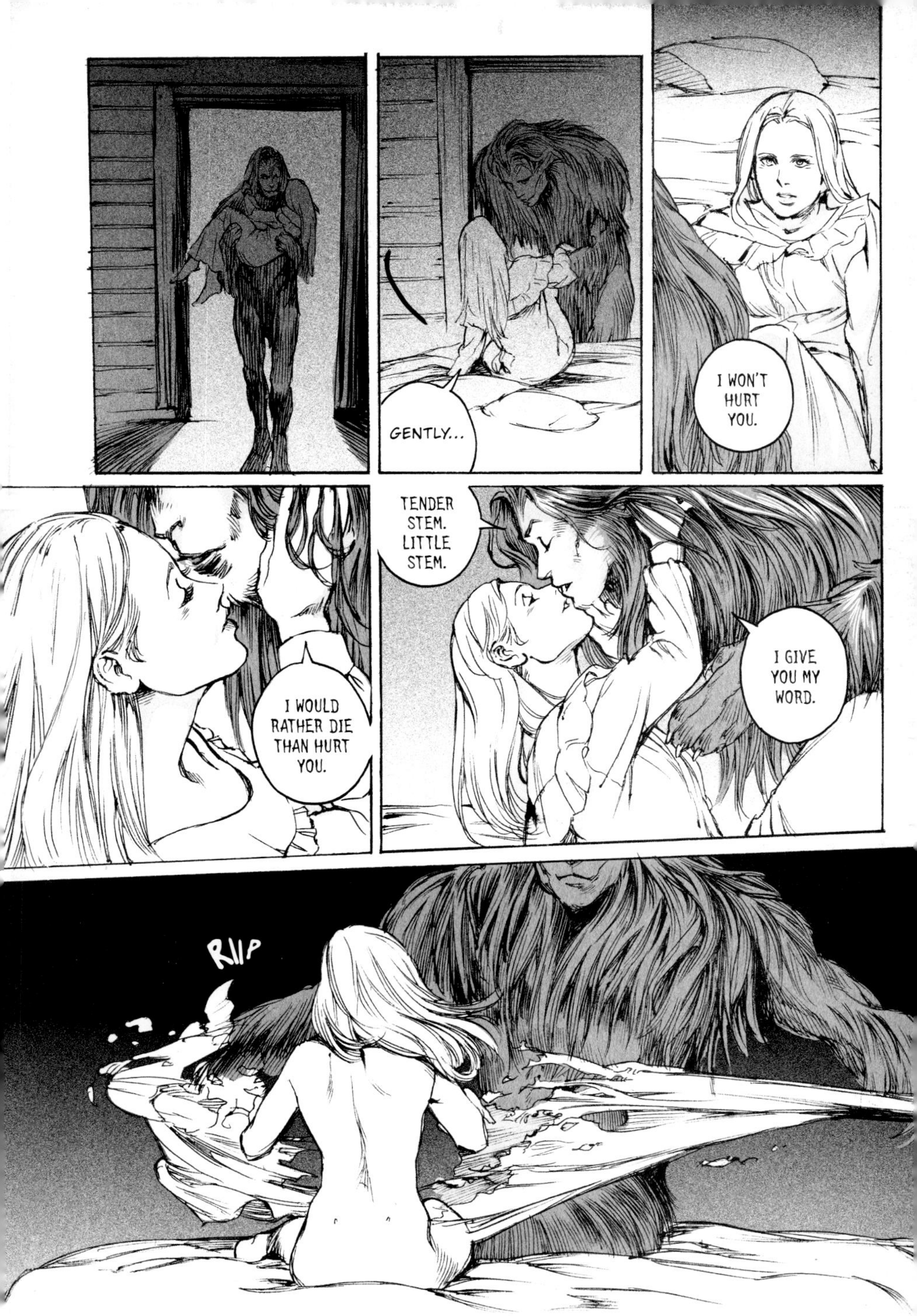
GENTLY...
I WON'T HURT YOU.
TENDER STEM. LITTLE STEM.
I WOULD RATHER DIE THAN HURT YOU.
I GIVE YOU MY WORD.
RIIP

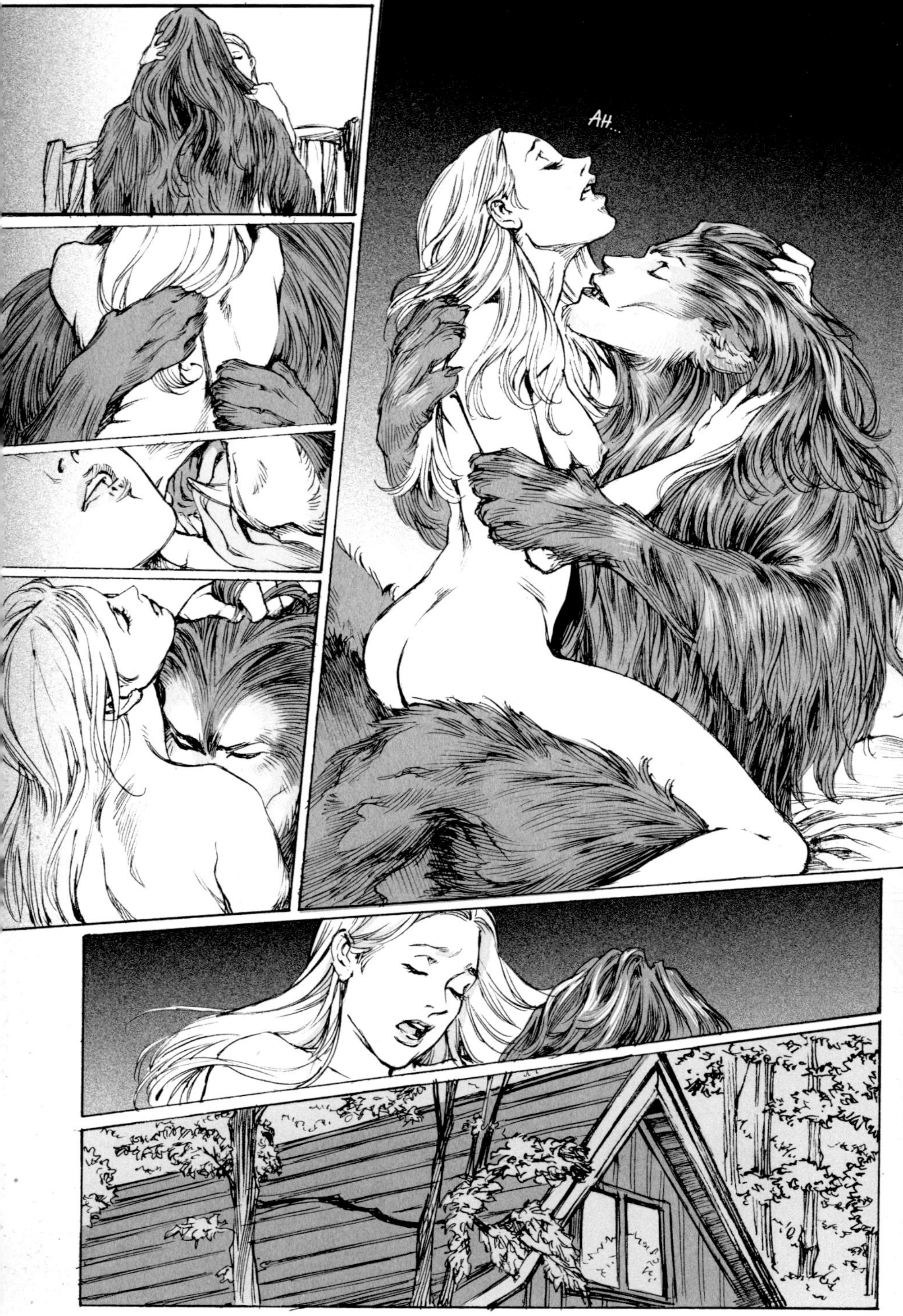
AH...

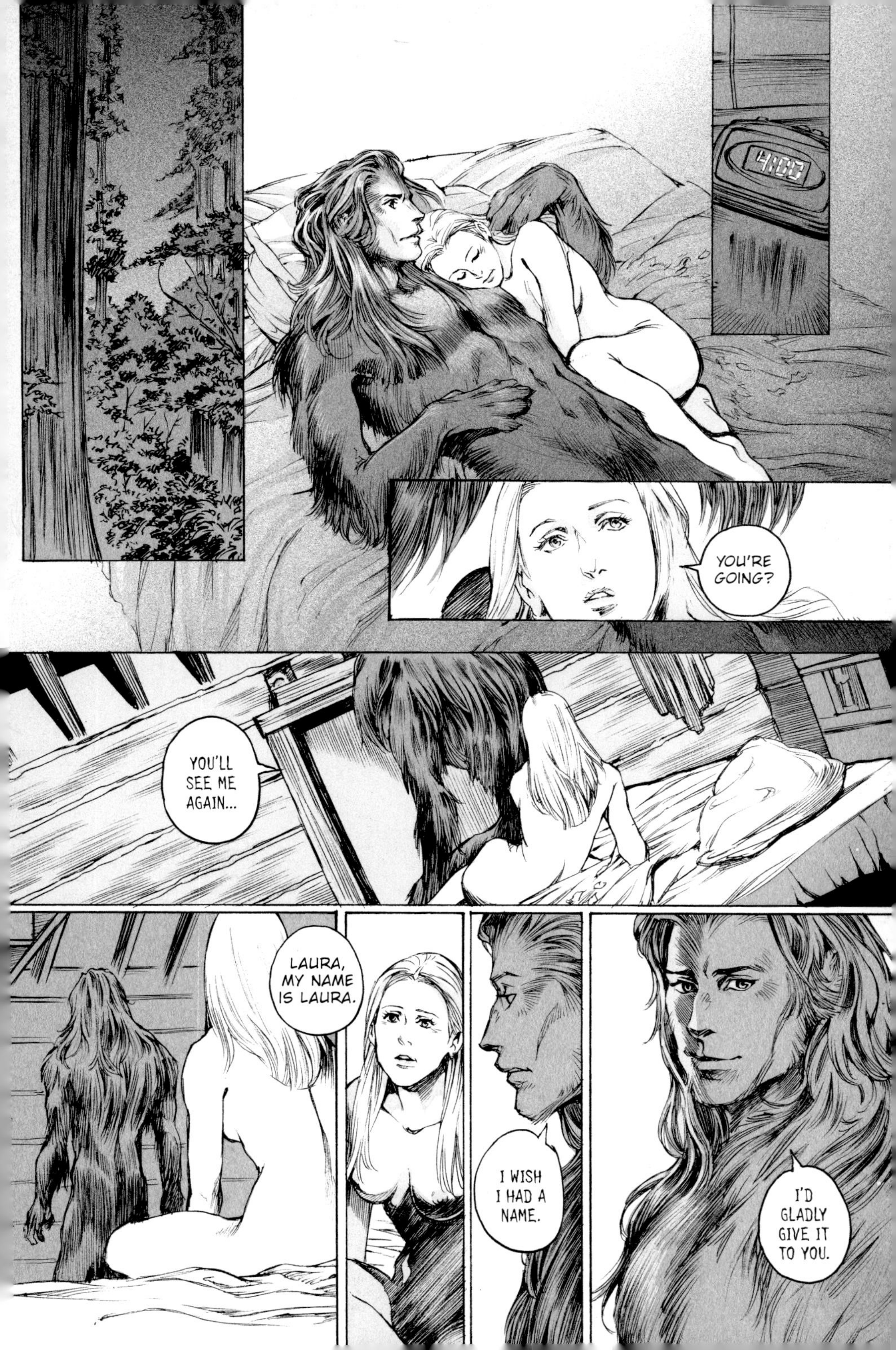
4:00
YOU'RE GOING?
YOU'LL SEE ME AGAIN...
LAURA, MY NAME IS LAURA.
I WISH I HAD A NAME.
I'D GLADLY GIVE IT TO YOU.

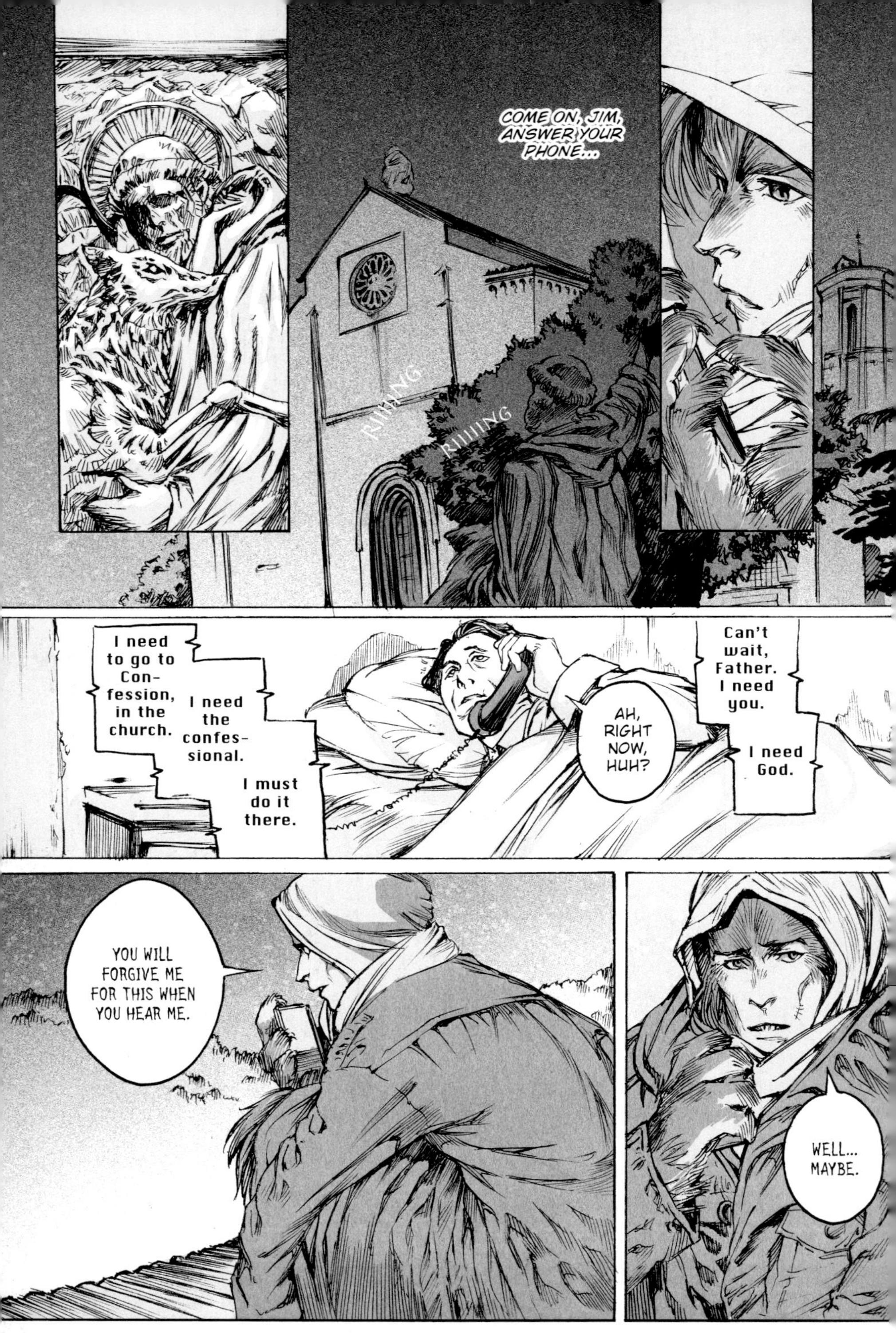
COME ON, JIM, ANSWER YOUR PHONE...
RIIIIING
RIIIIING
I need to go to Con-fession, in the church.
I need the confes-sional.
I must do it there.
AH, RIGHT NOW, HUH?
Can't wait, Father. I need you.
I need God.
YOU WILL FORGIVE ME FOR THIS WHEN YOU HEAR ME.
WELL... MAYBE.

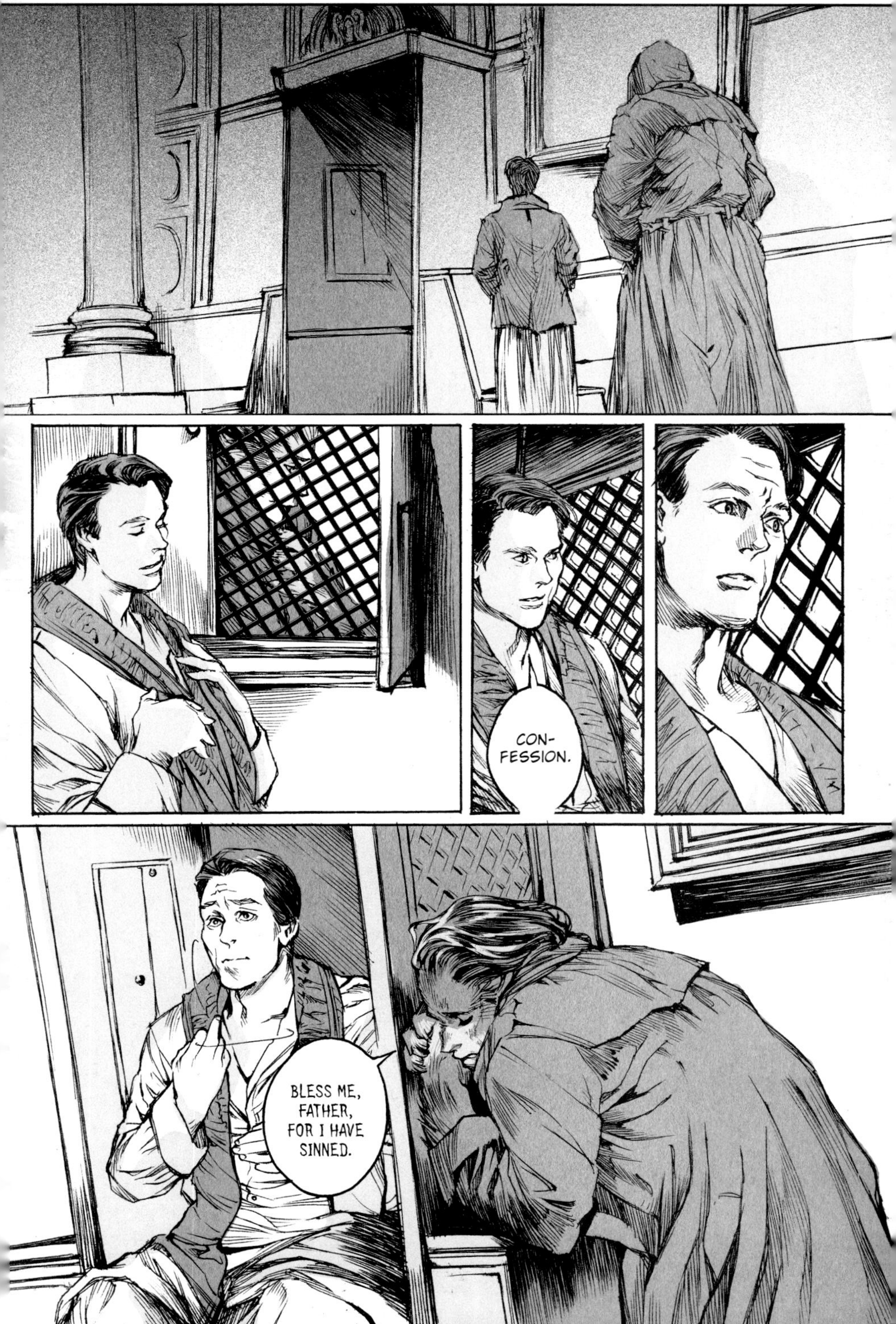
CON-
FESSION.
BLESS ME, FATHER, FOR I HAVE SINNED.

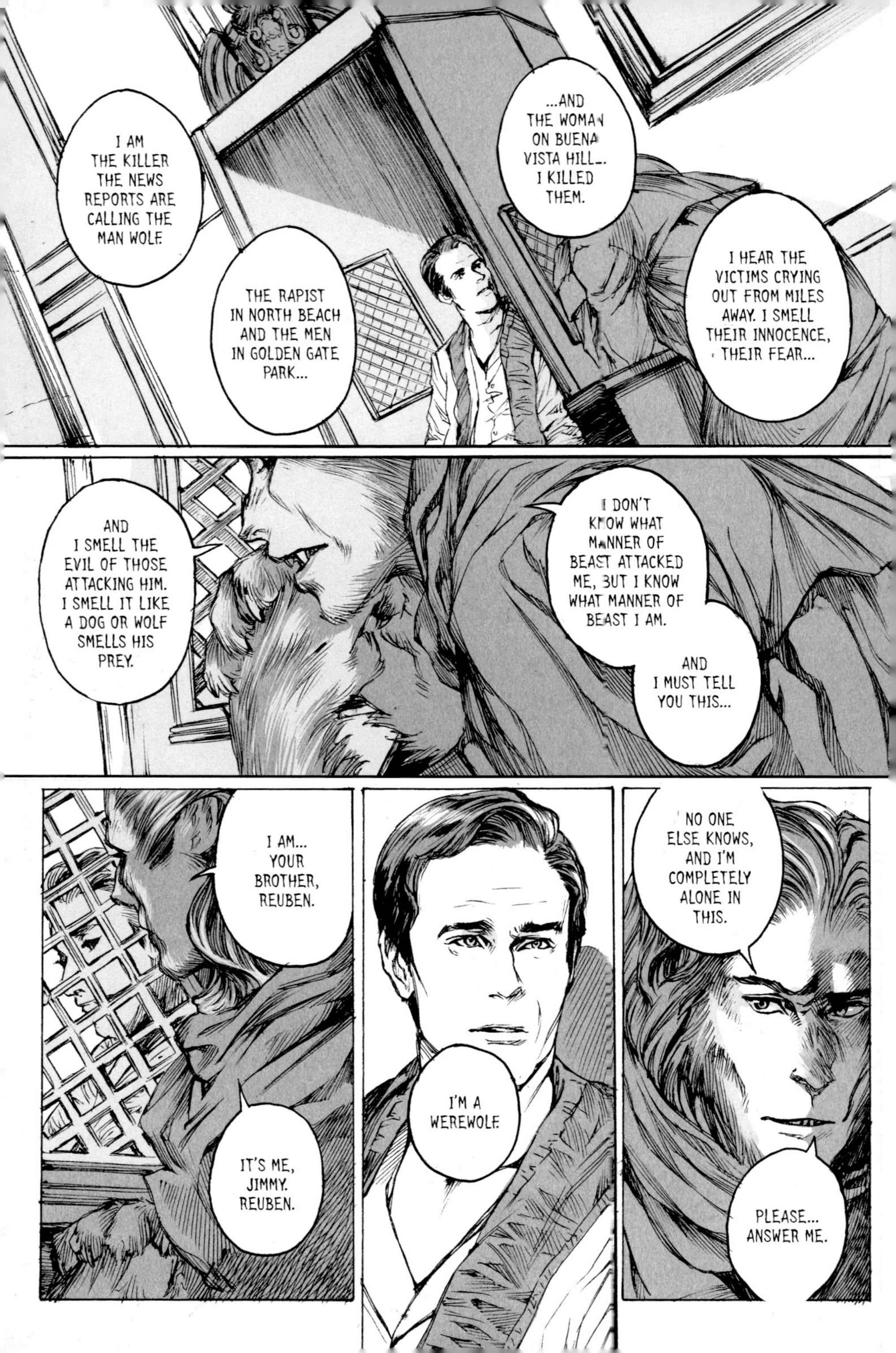
I AM THE KILLER THE NEWS REPORTS ARE CALLING THE MAN WOLF.
THE RAPIST IN NORTH BEACH AND THE MEN IN GOLDEN GATE PARK...
...AND THE WOMAN ON BUENA VISTA HILL... I KILLED THEM.
I HEAR THE VICTIMS CRYING OUT FROM MILES AWAY. I SMELL THEIR INNOCENCE, THEIR FEAR...
AND I SMELL THE EVIL OF THOSE ATTACKING HIM. I SMELL IT LIKE A DOG OR WOLF SMELLS HIS PREY.
I DON'T KNOW WHAT MANNER OF BEAST ATTACKED ME, BUT I KNOW WHAT MANNER OF BEAST I AM.
AND I MUST TELL YOU THIS...
I AM... YOUR BROTHER, REUBEN.
IT'S ME, JIMMY. REUBEN.
I'M A WEREWOLF.
NO ONE ELSE KNOWS, AND I'M COMPLETELY ALONE IN THIS.
PLEASE... ANSWER ME.

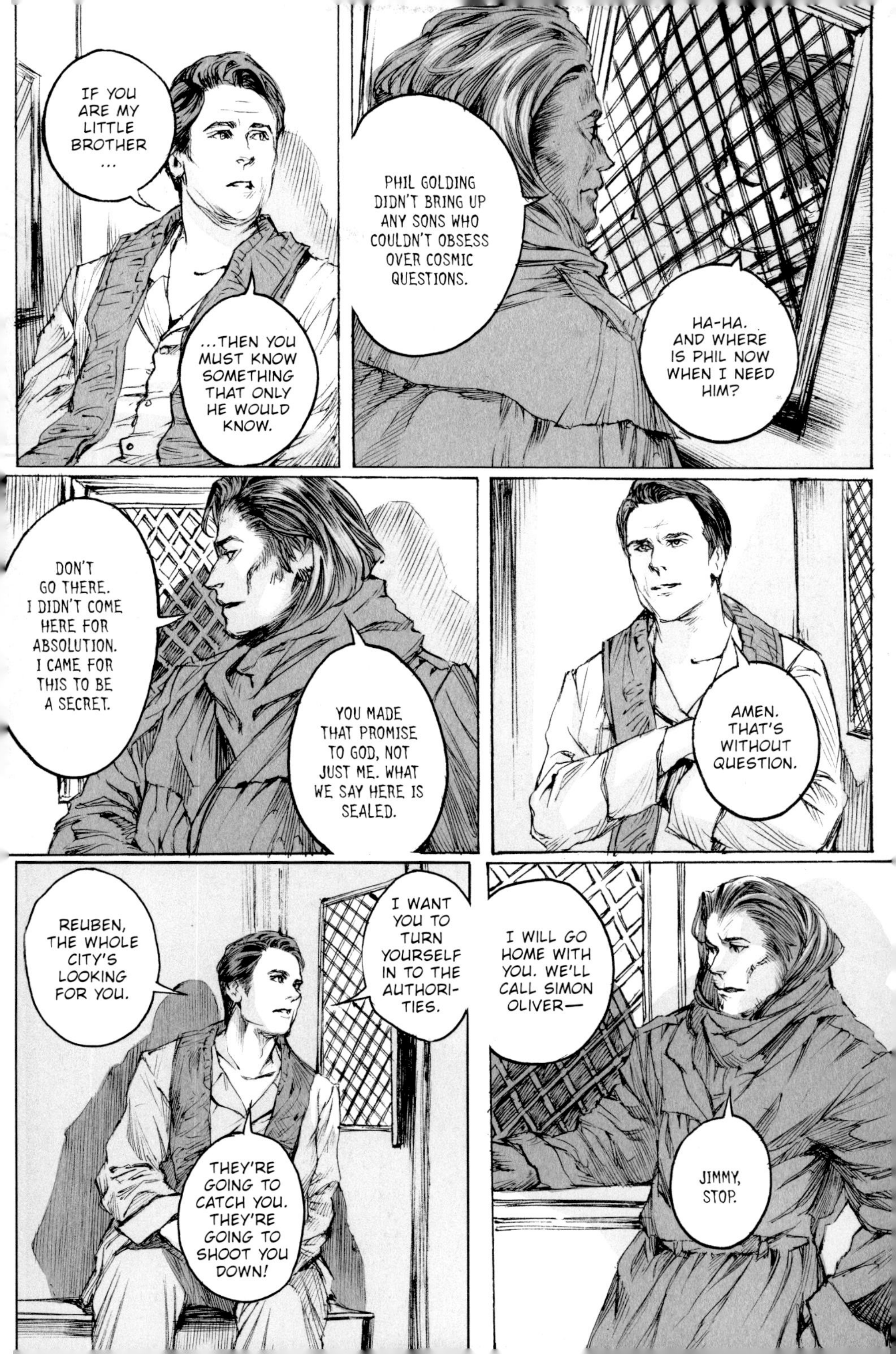
IF YOU ARE MY LITTLE BROTHER ...
...THEN YOU MUST KNOW SOMETHING THAT ONLY HE WOULD KNOW.
PHIL GOLDING DIDN'T BRING UP ANY SONS WHO COULDN'T OBSESS OVER COSMIC QUESTIONS.
HA-HA. AND WHERE IS PHIL NOW WHEN I NEED HIM?
DON'T GO THERE. I DIDN'T COME HERE FOR ABSOLUTION. I CAME FOR THIS TO BE A SECRET.
YOU MADE THAT PROMISE TO GOD, NOT JUST ME. WHAT WE SAY HERE IS SEALED.
AMEN. THAT'S WITHOUT QUESTION.
REUBEN, THE WHOLE CITY'S LOOKING FOR YOU.
I WANT YOU TO TURN YOURSELF IN TO THE AUTHORI-TIES.
THEY'RE GOING TO CATCH YOU. THEY'RE GOING TO SHOOT YOU DOWN!
I WILL GO HOME WITH YOU. WE'LL CALL SIMON OLIVER—
JIMMY, STOP.

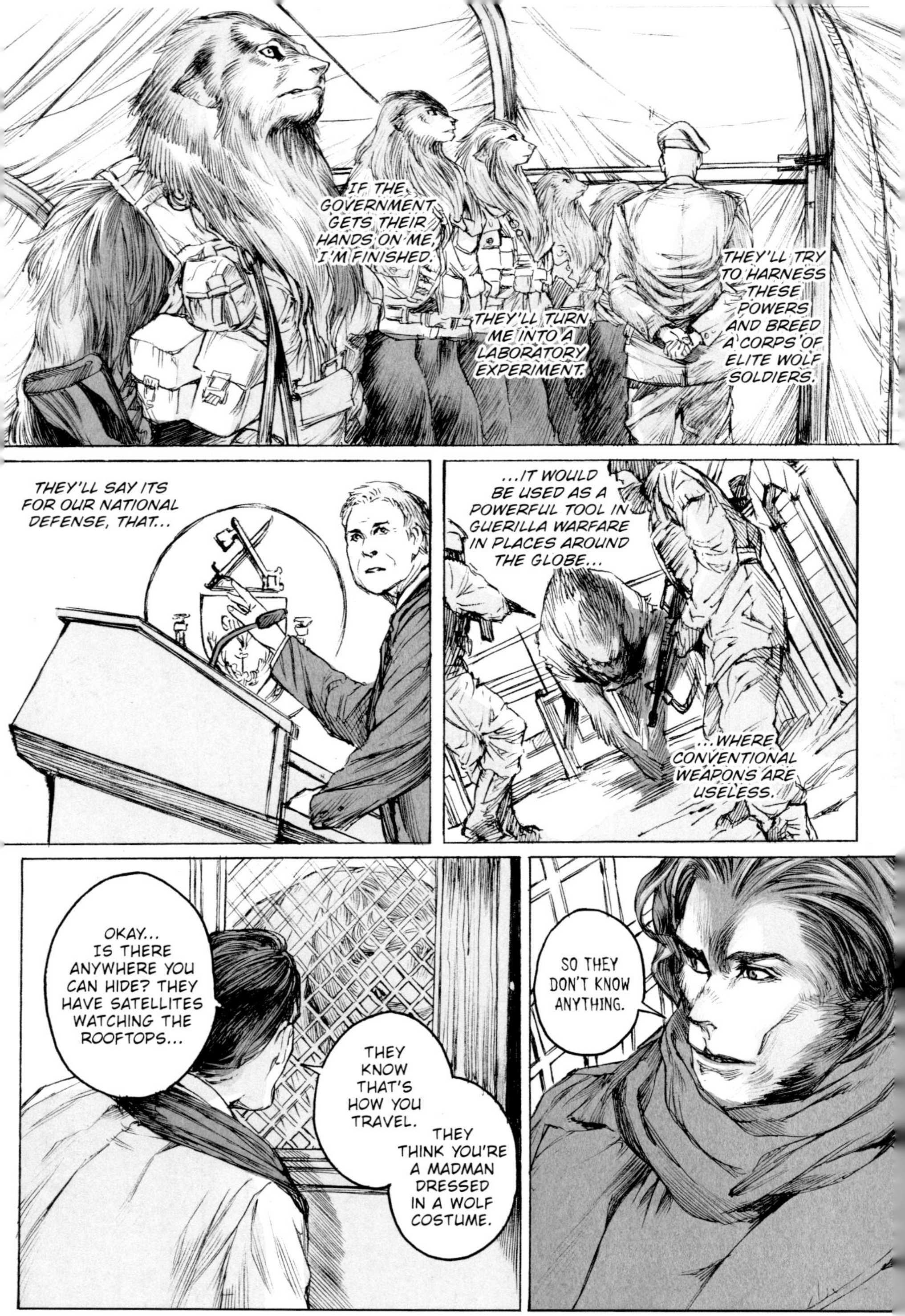
IF THE GOVERNMENT GETS THEIR HANDS ON ME, I'M FINISHED.
THEY'LL TURN ME INTO A LABORATORY EXPERIMENT.
THEY'LL TRY TO HARNESS THESE POWERS AND BREED A CORPS OF ELITE WOLF SOLDIERS.
THEY'LL SAY ITS FOR OUR NATIONAL DEFENSE, THAT...
...IT WOULD BE USED AS A POWERFUL TOOL IN GUERILLA WARFARE IN PLACES AROUND THE GLOBE...
...WHERE CONVENTIONAL WEAPONS ARE USELESS.
OKAY... IS THERE ANYWHERE YOU CAN HIDE? THEY HAVE SATELLITES WATCHING THE ROOFTOPS...
THEY KNOW THAT'S HOW YOU TRAVEL.
THEY THINK YOU'RE A MADMAN DRESSED IN A WOLF COSTUME.
SO THEY DON'T KNOW ANYTHING.

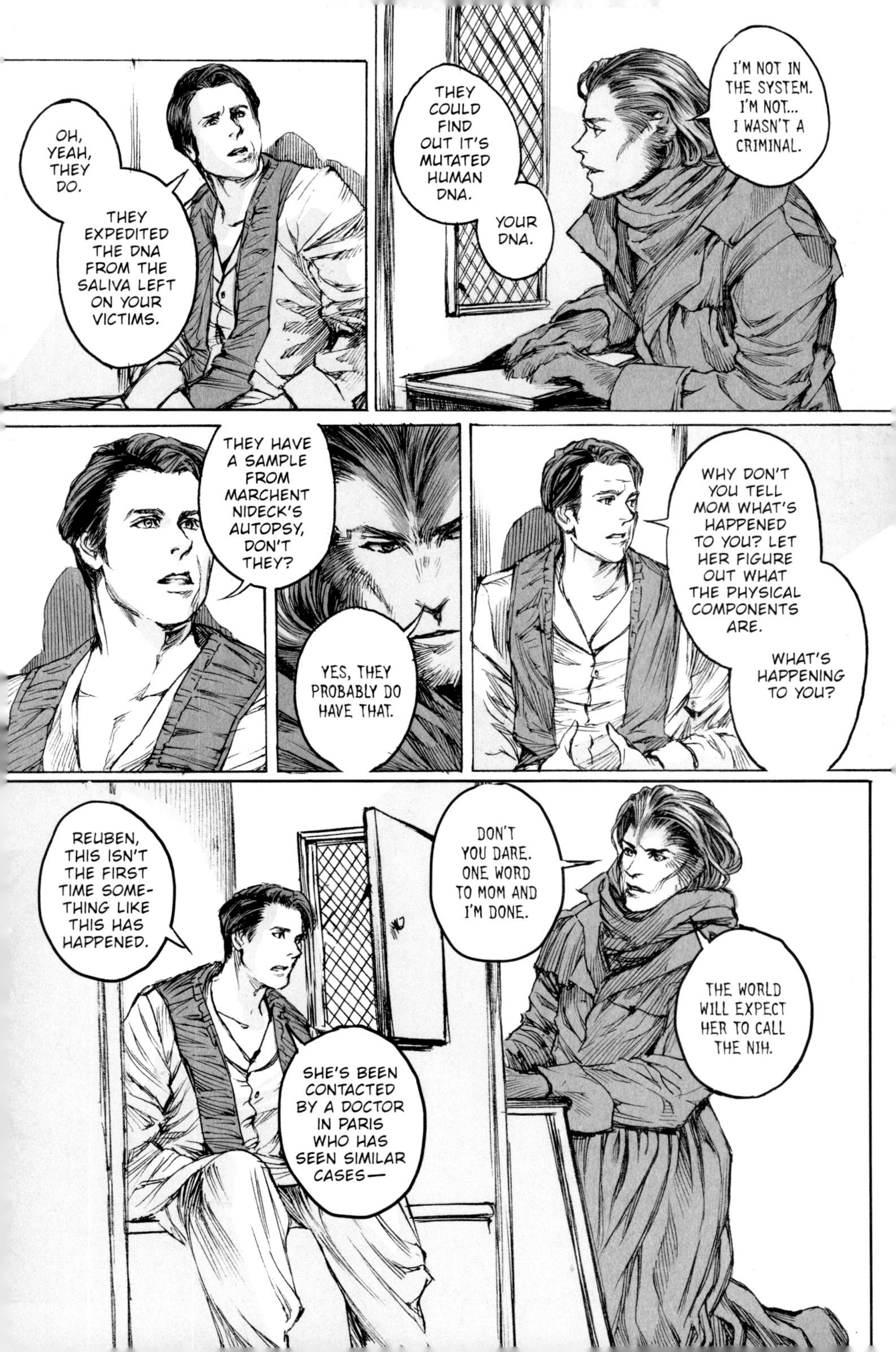
OH, YEAH, THEY DO.
THEY EXPEDITED THE DNA FROM THE SALIVA LEFT ON YOUR VICTIMS.
THEY COULD FIND OUT IT'S MUTATED HUMAN DNA.
YOUR DNA.
I'M NOT IN THE SYSTEM. I'M NOT... I WASN'T A CRIMINAL.
THEY HAVE A SAMPLE FROM MARCHENT NIDECK'S AUTOPSY, DON'T THEY?
YES, THEY PROBABLY DO HAVE THAT.
WHY DON'T YOU TELL MOM WHAT'S HAPPENED TO YOU? LET HER FIGURE OUT WHAT THE PHYSICAL COMPONENTS ARE.
WHAT'S HAPPENING TO YOU?
REUBEN, THIS ISN'T THE FIRST TIME SOME-THING LIKE THIS HAS HAPPENED.
DON'T YOU DARE. ONE WORD TO MOM AND I'M DONE.
SHE'S BEEN CONTACTED BY A DOCTOR IN PARIS WHO HAS SEEN SIMILAR CASES—
THE WORLD WILL EXPECT HER TO CALL THE NIH.

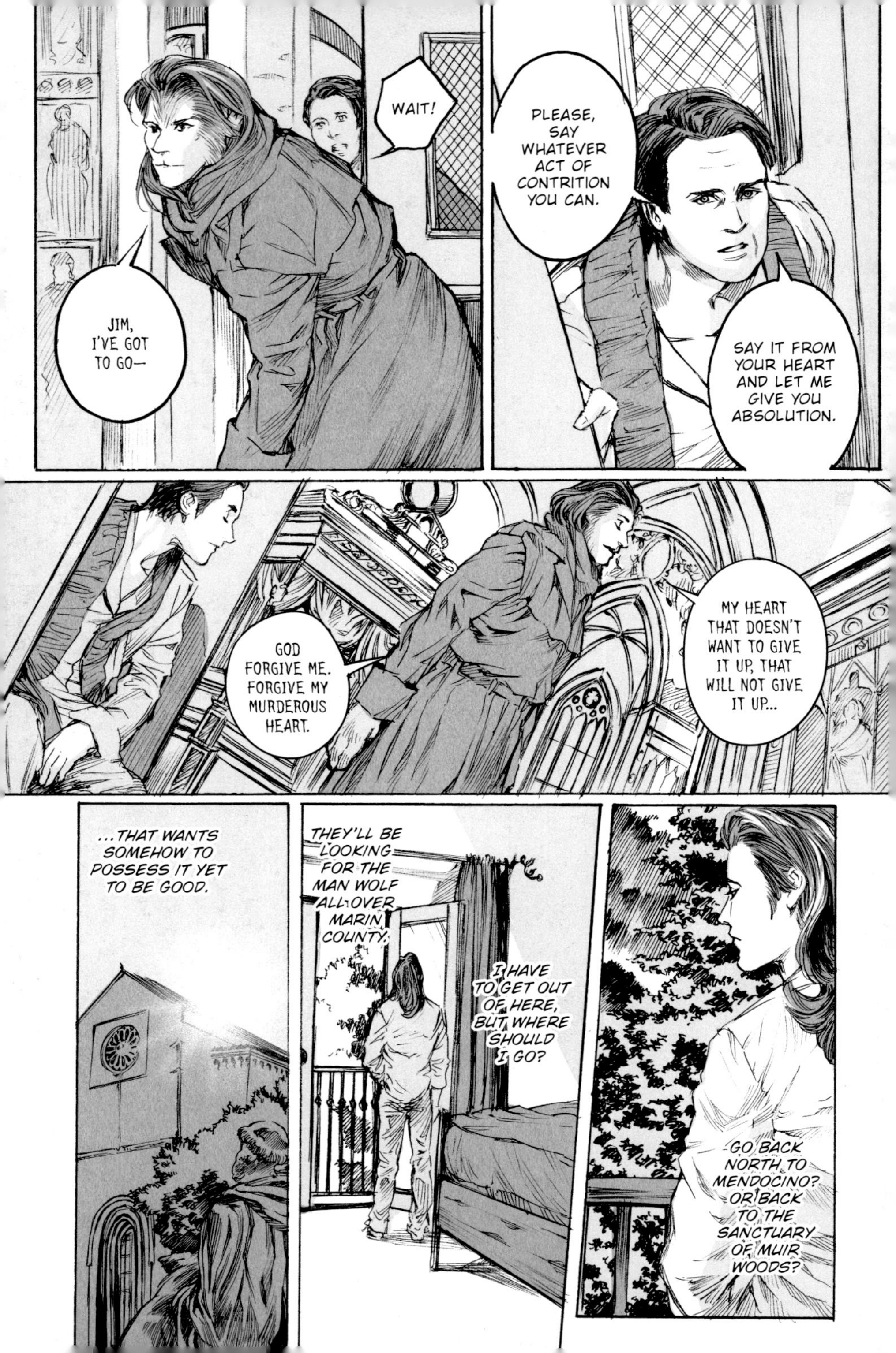

WAIT!
JIM, I'VE GOT TO GO—
PLEASE, SAY WHATEVER ACT OF CONTRITION YOU CAN.
SAY IT FROM YOUR HEART AND LET ME GIVE YOU ABSOLUTION.
GOD FORGIVE ME. FORGIVE MY MURDEROUS HEART.
MY HEART THAT DOESN'T WANT TO GIVE IT UP, THAT WILL NOT GIVE IT UP...
...THAT WANTS SOMEHOW TO POSSESS IT YET TO BE GOOD.
THEY'LL BE LOOKING FOR THE MAN WOLF ALL OVER MARIN COUNTY.
I HAVE TO GET OUT OF HERE, BUT WHERE SHOULD I GO?
GO BACK NORTH TO MENDOCINO? OR BACK TO THE SANCTUARY OF MUIR WOODS?

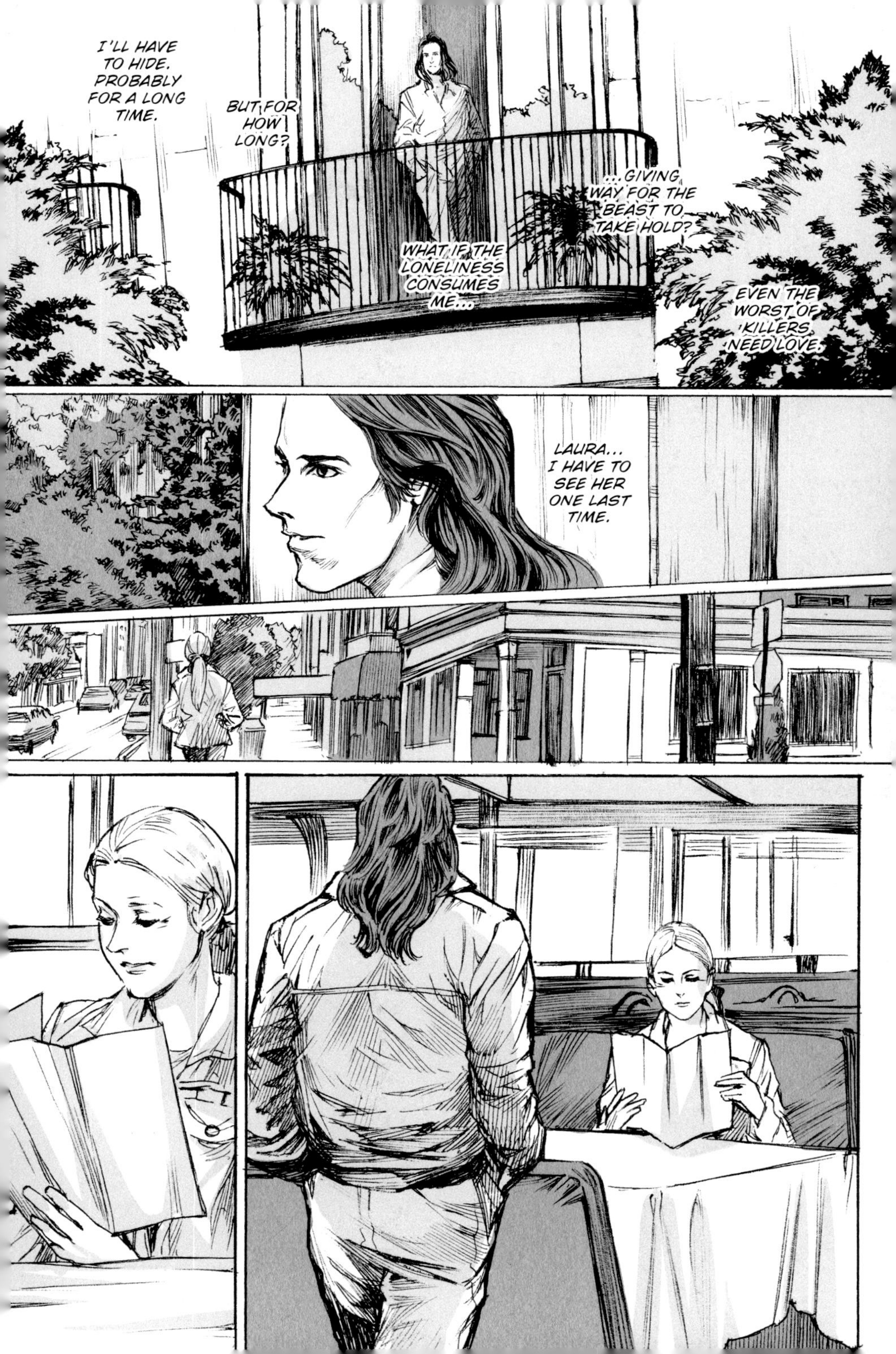
I'LL HAVE TO HIDE. PROBABLY FOR A LONG TIME.
BUT FOR HOW LONG?
WHAT IF THE LONELINESS CONSUMES ME...
...GIVING WAY FOR THE BEAST TO TAKE HOLD?
EVEN THE WORST OF KILLERS NEED LOVE.
LAURA... I HAVE TO SEE HER ONE LAST TIME.

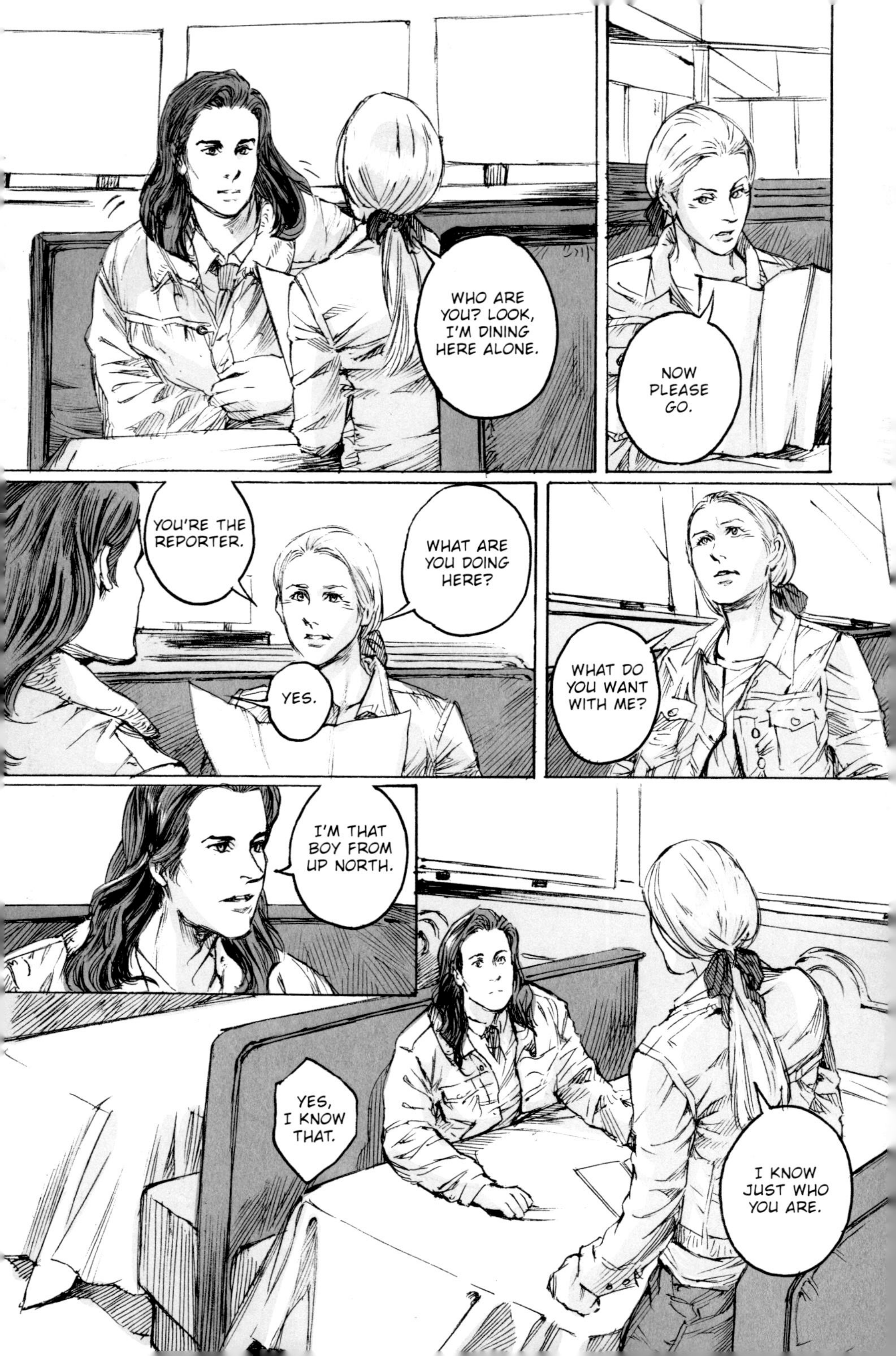
WHO ARE YOU? LOOK, I'M DINING HERE ALONE.
NOW PLEASE GO.
YOU'RE THE REPORTER.
WHAT ARE YOU DOING HERE?
YES.
WHAT DO YOU WANT WITH ME?
I'M THAT BOY FROM UP NORTH.
YES, I KNOW THAT.
I KNOW JUST WHO YOU ARE.

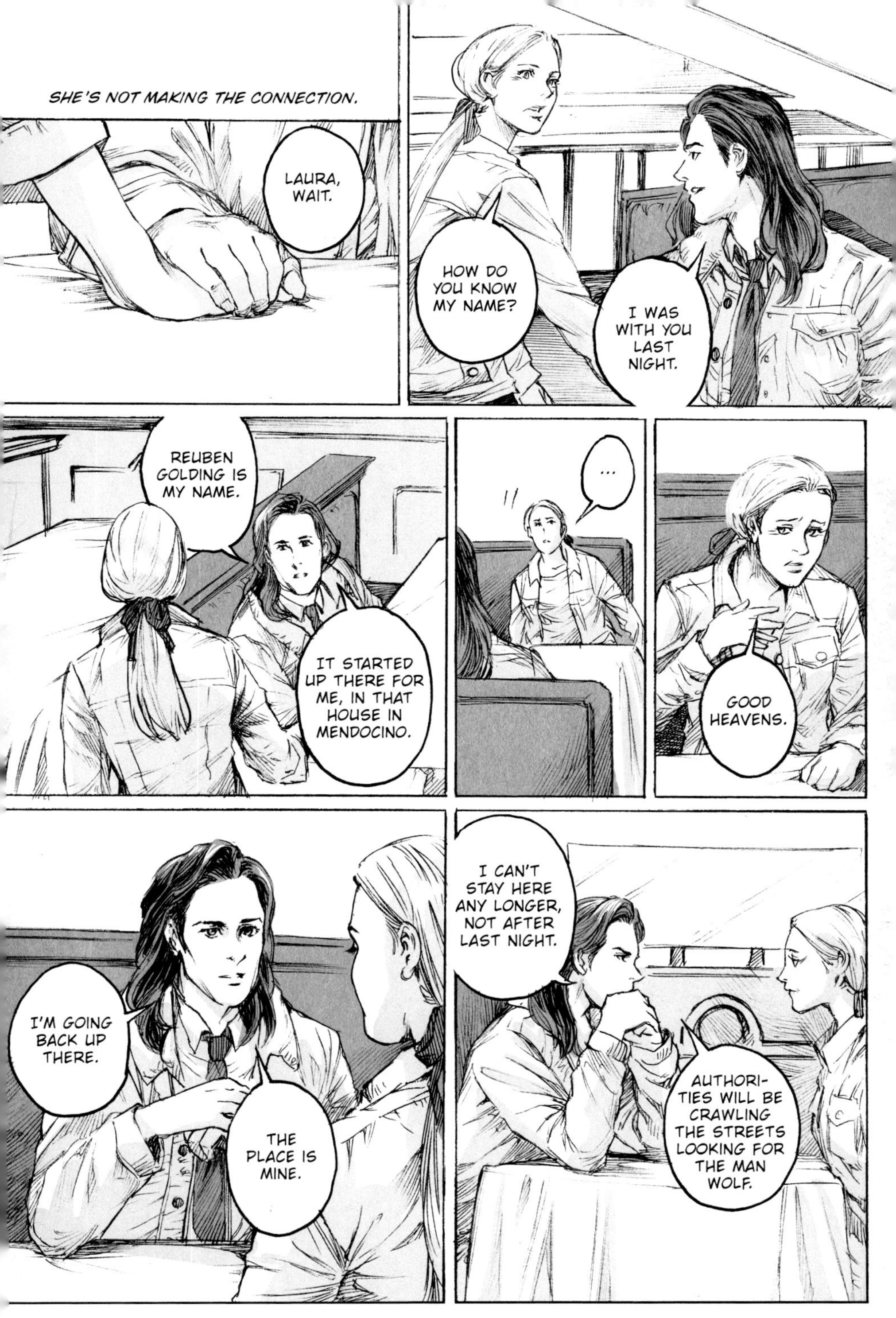
SHE'S NOT MAKING THE CONNECTION.
LAURA, WAIT.
HOW DO YOU KNOW MY NAME?
I WAS WITH YOU LAST NIGHT.
REUBEN GOLDING IS MY NAME.
IT STARTED UP THERE FOR ME, IN THAT HOUSE IN MENDOCINO.
...
GOOD HEAVENS.
I'M GOING BACK UP THERE.
THE PLACE IS MINE.
I CAN'T STAY HERE ANY LONGER, NOT AFTER LAST NIGHT.
AUTHORI-TIES WILL BE CRAWLING THE STREETS LOOKING FOR THE MAN WOLF.

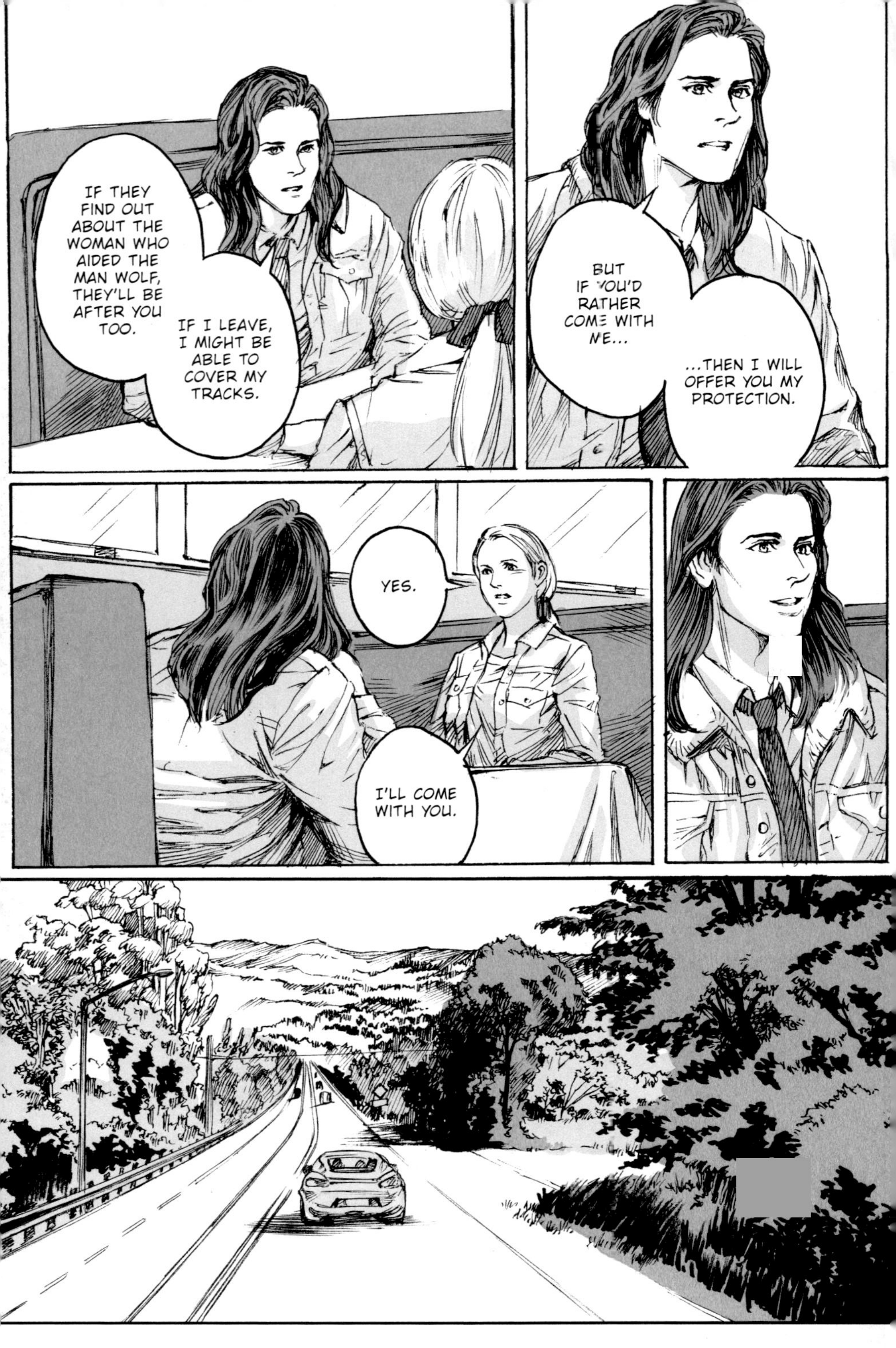
IF THEY FIND OUT ABOUT THE WOMAN WHO AIDED THE MAN WOLF, THEY'LL BE AFTER YOU TOO.
IF I LEAVE, I MIGHT BE ABLE TO COVER MY TRACKS.
BUT IF YOU'D RATHER COME WITH ME...
...THEN I WILL OFFER YOU MY PROTECTION.
YES.
I'LL COME WITH YOU.

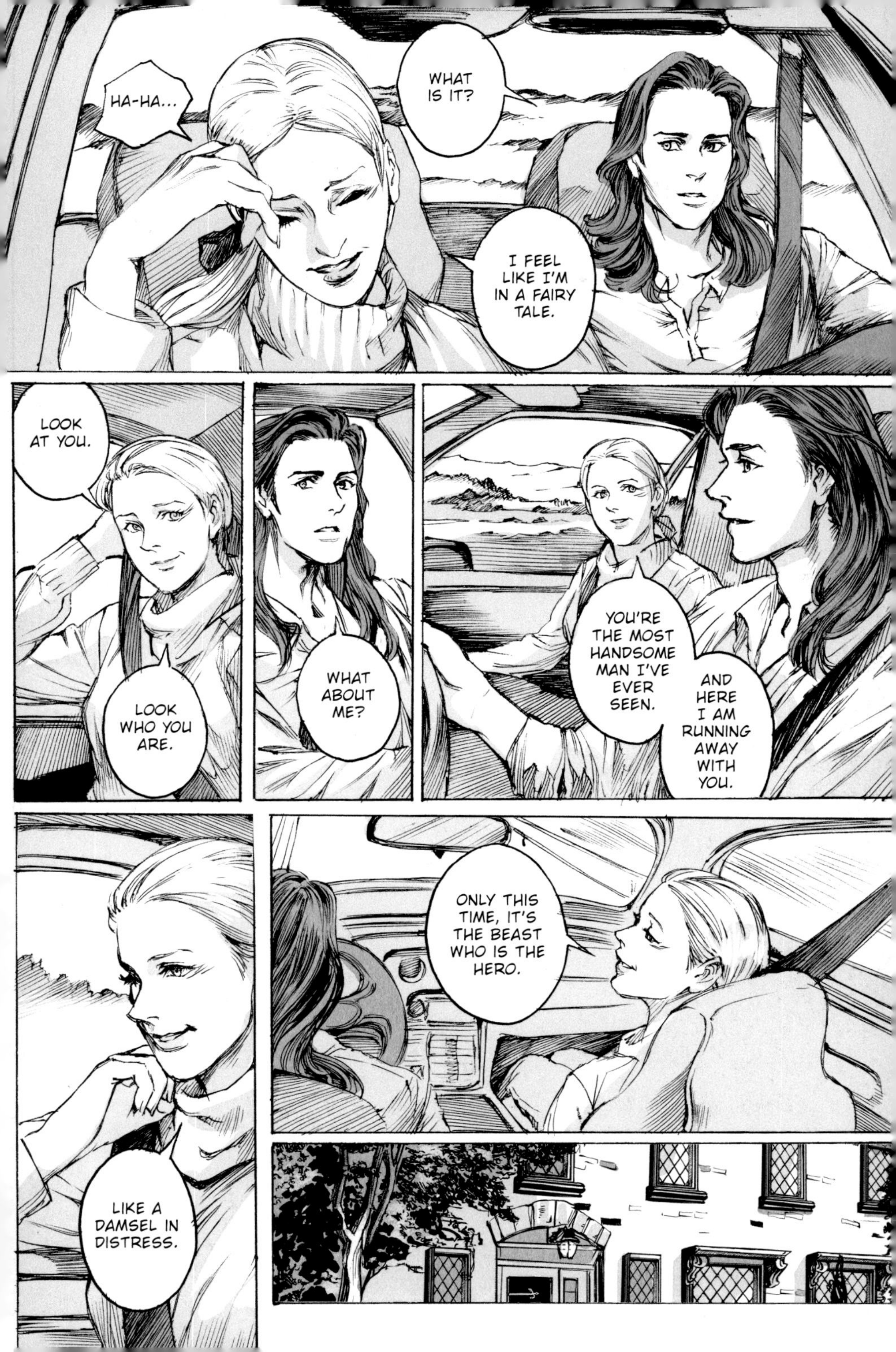
HA-HA...
WHAT IS IT?
I FEEL LIKE I'M IN A FAIRY TALE.
LOOK AT YOU.
LOOK WHO YOU ARE.
WHAT ABOUT ME?
YOU'RE THE MOST HANDSOME MAN I'VE EVER SEEN.
AND HERE I AM RUNNING AWAY WITH YOU.
LIKE A DAMSEL IN DISTRESS.
ONLY THIS TIME, IT'S THE BEAST WHO IS THE HERO.

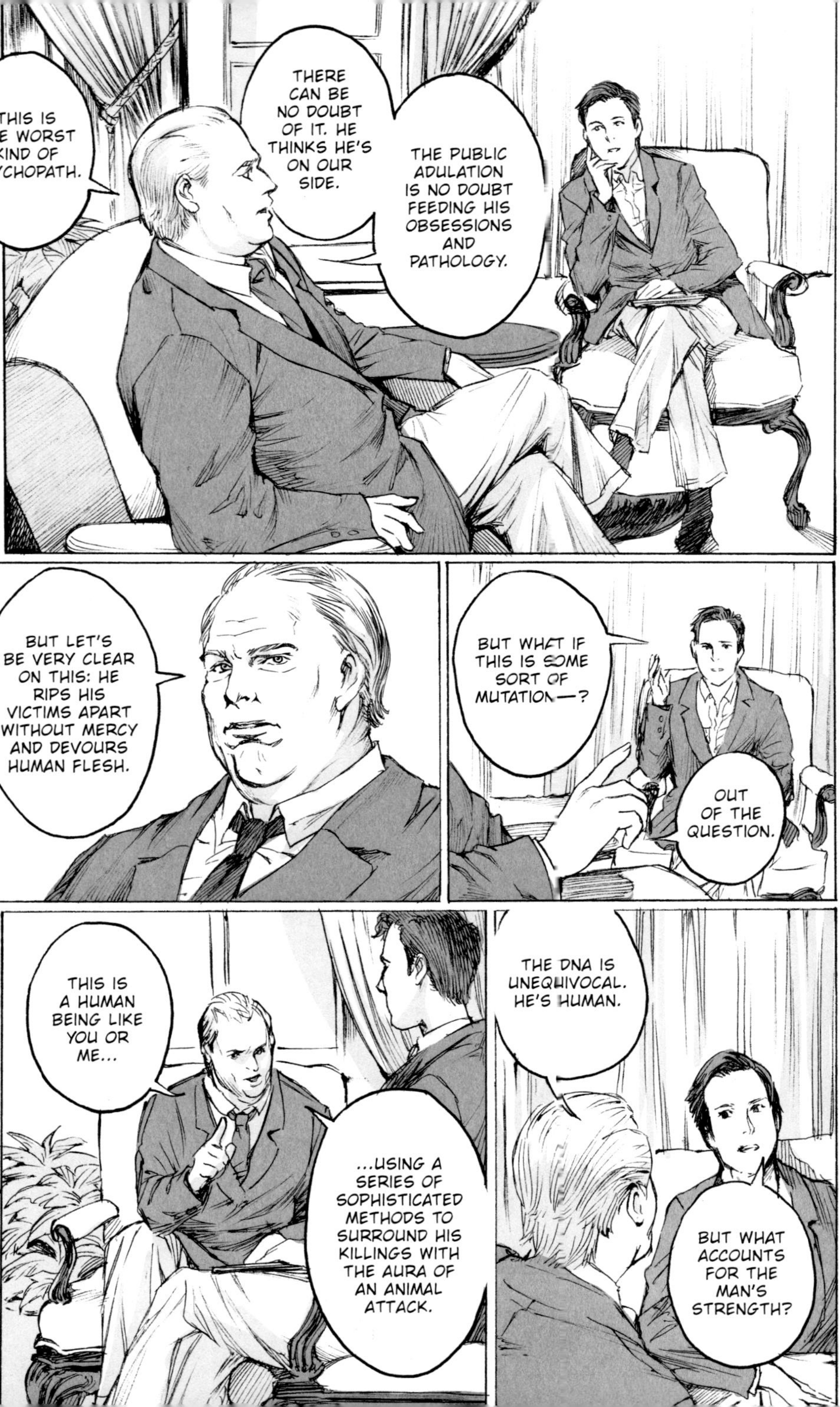
THIS IS THE WORST KIND OF PSYCHOPATH.
THERE CAN BE NO DOUBT OF IT. HE THINKS HE'S ON OUR SIDE.
THE PUBLIC ADULATION IS NO DOUBT FEEDING HIS OBSESSIONS AND PATHOLOGY.
BUT LET'S BE VERY CLEAR ON THIS: HE RIPS HIS VICTIMS APART WITHOUT MERCY AND DEVOURS HUMAN FLESH.
BUT WHAT IF THIS IS SOME SORT OF MUTATION—?
OUT OF THE QUESTION.
THIS IS A HUMAN BEING LIKE YOU OR ME...
...USING A SERIES OF SOPHISTICATED METHODS TO SURROUND HIS KILLINGS WITH THE AURA OF AN ANIMAL ATTACK.
THE DNA IS UNEQUIVOCAL. HE'S HUMAN.
BUT WHAT ACCOUNTS FOR THE MAN'S STRENGTH?

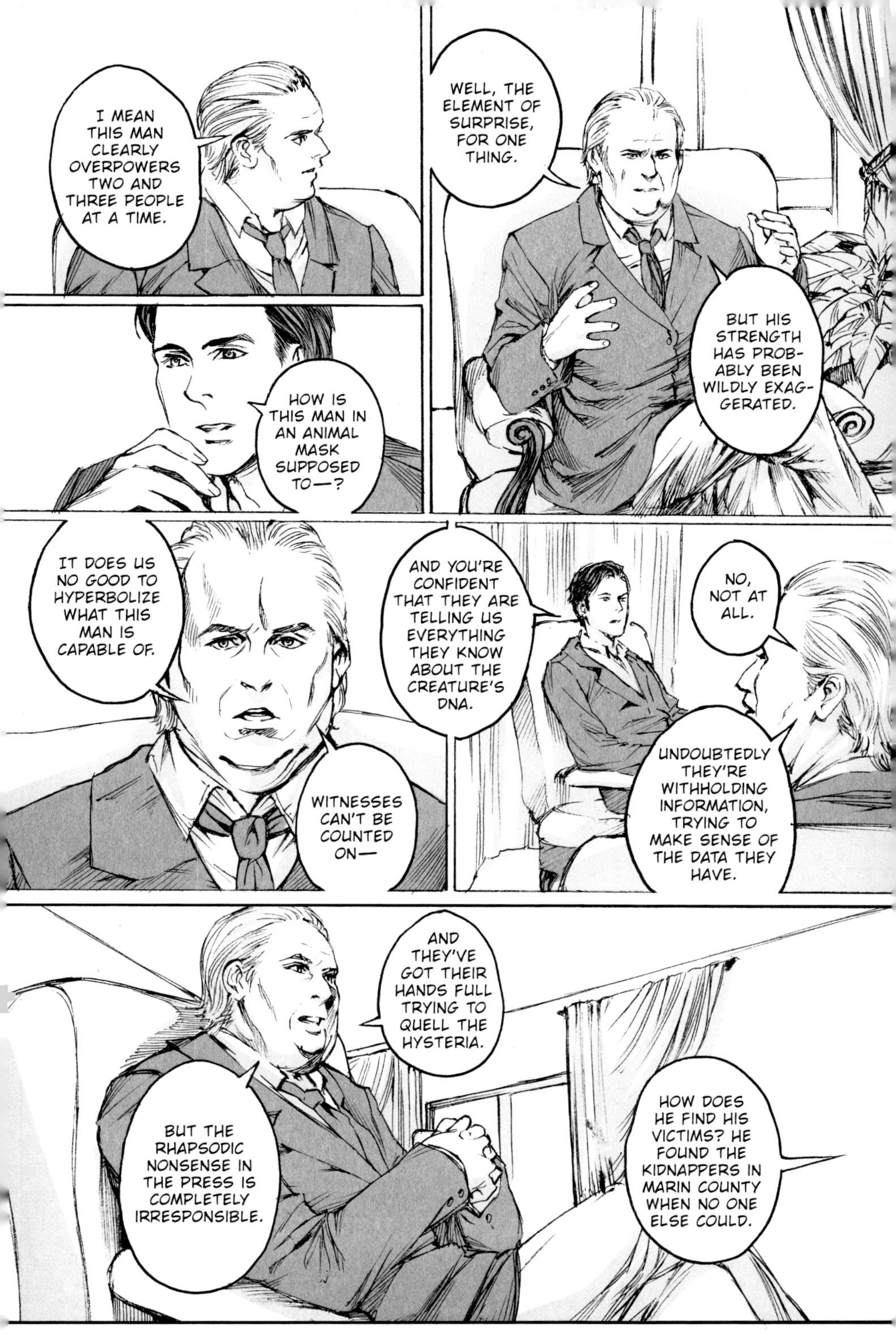
I MEAN THIS MAN CLEARLY OVERPOWERS TWO AND THREE PEOPLE AT A TIME.
WELL, THE ELEMENT OF SURPRISE, FOR ONE THING.
HOW IS THIS MAN IN AN ANIMAL MASK SUPPOSED TO—?
BUT HIS STRENGTH HAS PROB-ABLY BEEN WILDLY EXAG-GERATED.
IT DOES US NO GOOD TO HYPERBOLIZE WHAT THIS MAN IS CAPABLE OF.
WITNESSES CAN'T BE COUNTED ON—
AND YOU'RE CONFIDENT THAT THEY ARE TELLING US EVERYTHING THEY KNOW ABOUT THE CREATURE'S DNA.
NO, NOT AT ALL.
UNDOUBTEDLY THEY'RE WITHHOLDING INFORMATION, TRYING TO MAKE SENSE OF THE DATA THEY HAVE.
AND THEY'VE GOT THEIR HANDS FULL TRYING TO QUELL THE HYSTERIA.
BUT THE RHAPSODIC NONSENSE IN THE PRESS IS COMPLETELY IRRESPONSIBLE.
HOW DOES HE FIND HIS VICTIMS? HE FOUND THE KIDNAPPERS IN MARIN COUNTY WHEN NO ONE ELSE COULD.

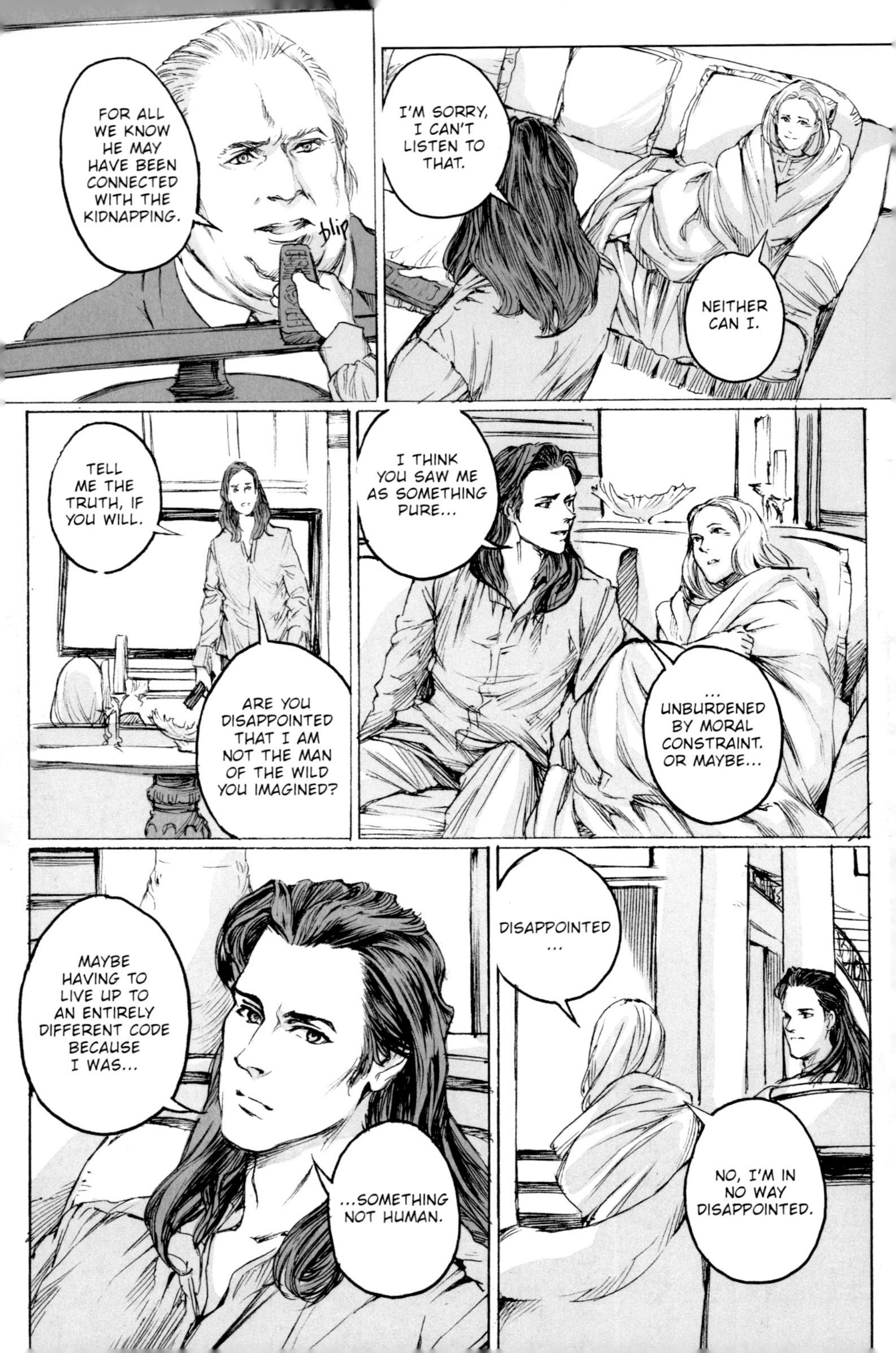
FOR ALL WE KNOW HE MAY HAVE BEEN CONNECTED WITH THE KIDNAPPING.
blip
I'M SORRY, I CAN'T LISTEN TO THAT.
NEITHER CAN I.
TELL ME THE TRUTH, IF YOU WILL.
ARE YOU DISAPPOINTED THAT I AM NOT THE MAN OF THE WILD YOU IMAGINED?
I THINK YOU SAW ME AS SOMETHING PURE...
...UNBURDENED BY MORAL CONSTRAINT. OR MAYBE...
MAYBE HAVING TO LIVE UP TO AN ENTIRELY DIFFERENT CODE BECAUSE I WAS...
...SOMETHING NOT HUMAN.
DISAPPOINTED...
NO, I'M IN NO WAY DISAPPOINTED.

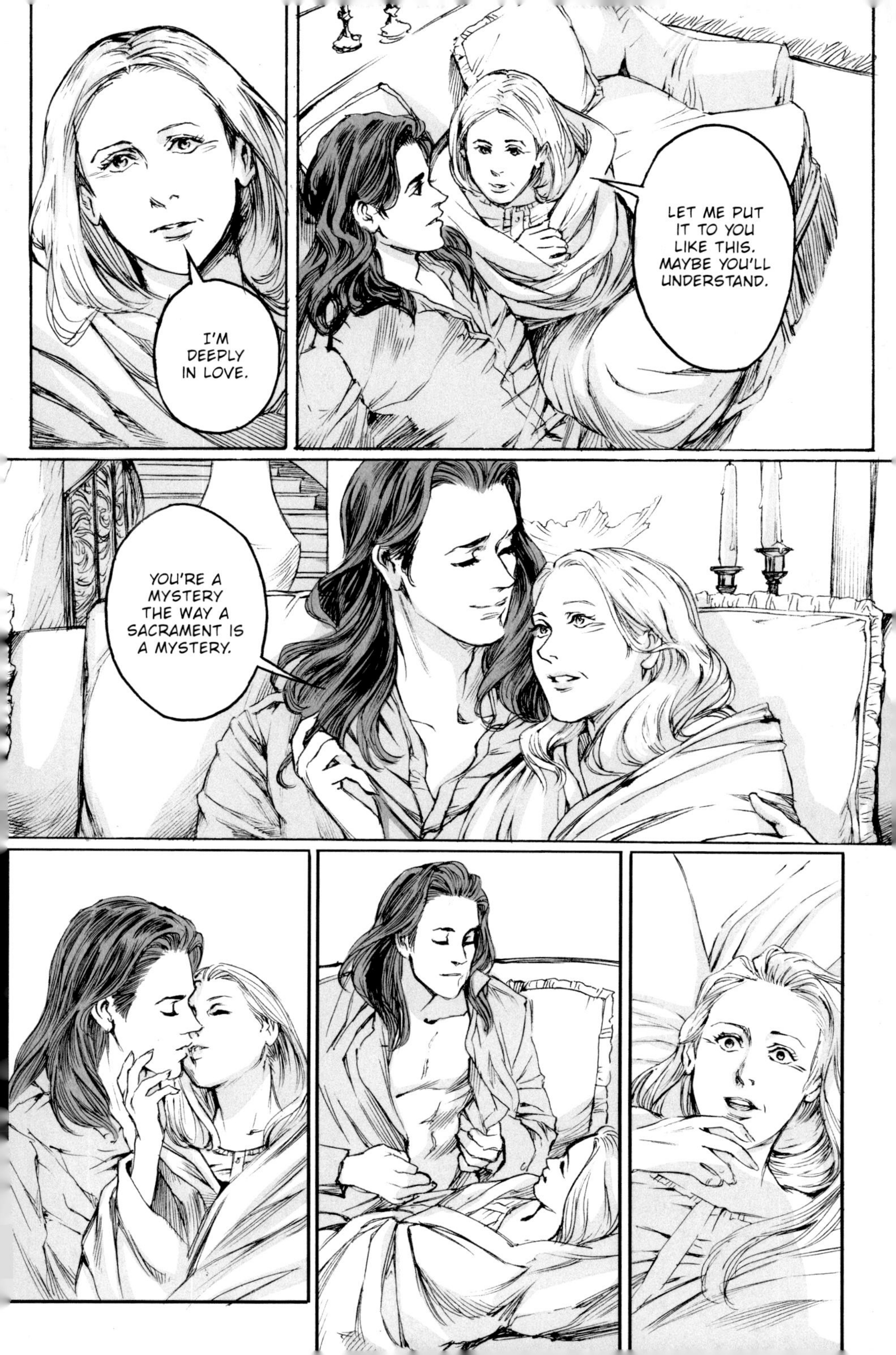
I'M DEEPLY IN LOVE.
LET ME PUT IT TO YOU LIKE THIS. MAYBE YOU'LL UNDERSTAND.
YOU'RE A MYSTERY THE WAY A SACRAMENT IS A MYSTERY.

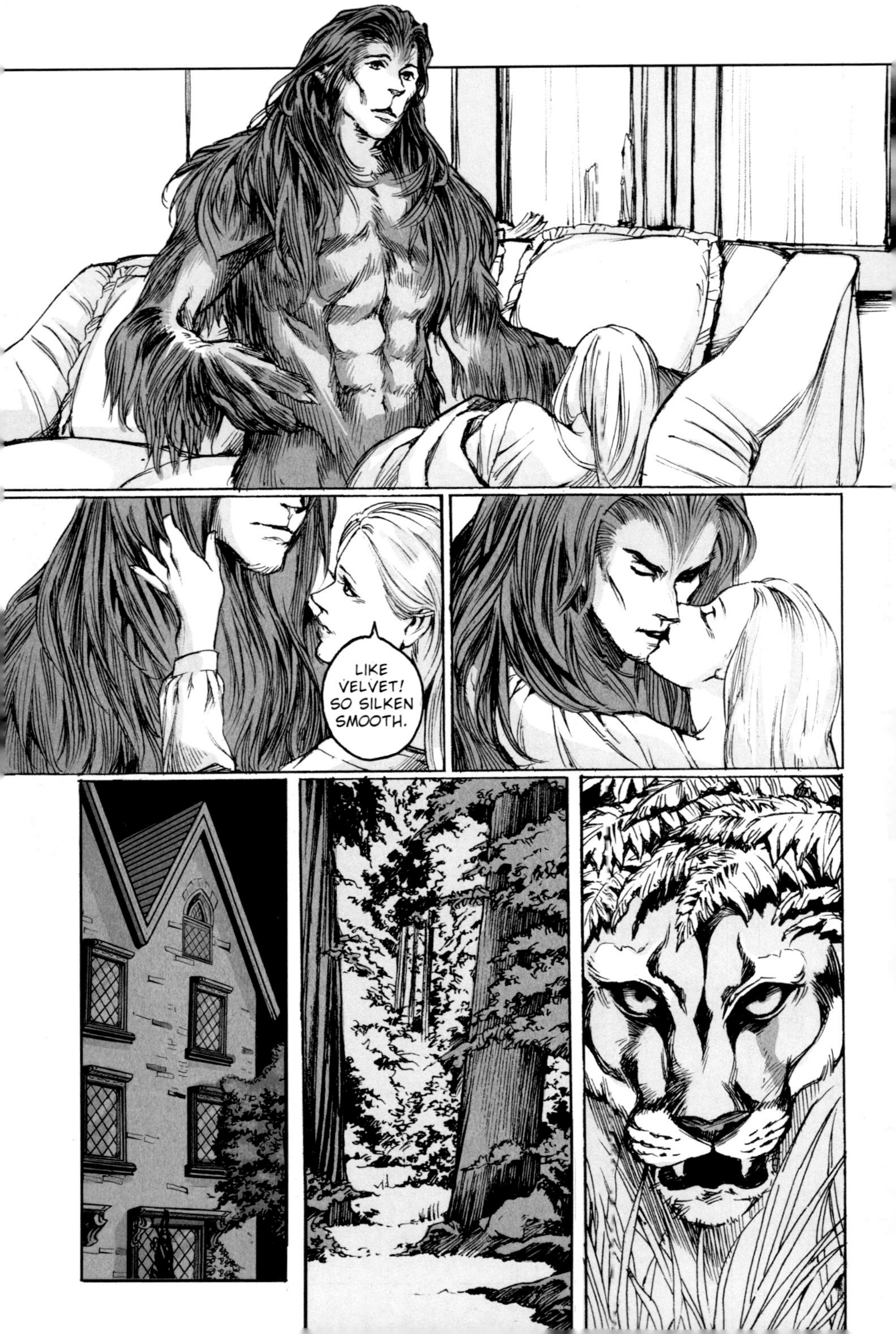
LIKE VELVET! SO SILKEN SMOOTH.

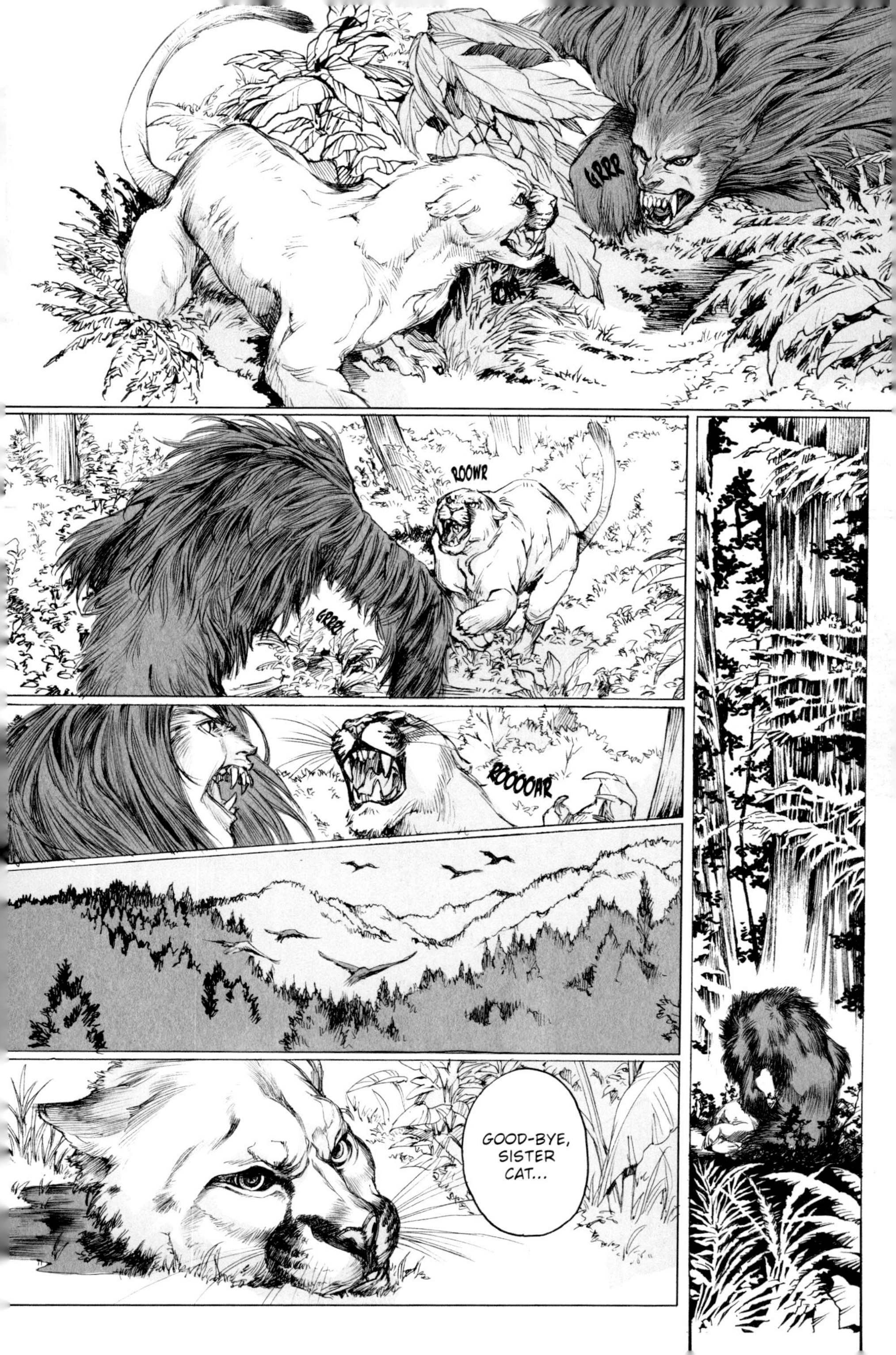
GRRR
ROAR
ROOWR
GRRR
ROOOOAR
GOOD-BYE, SISTER CAT...

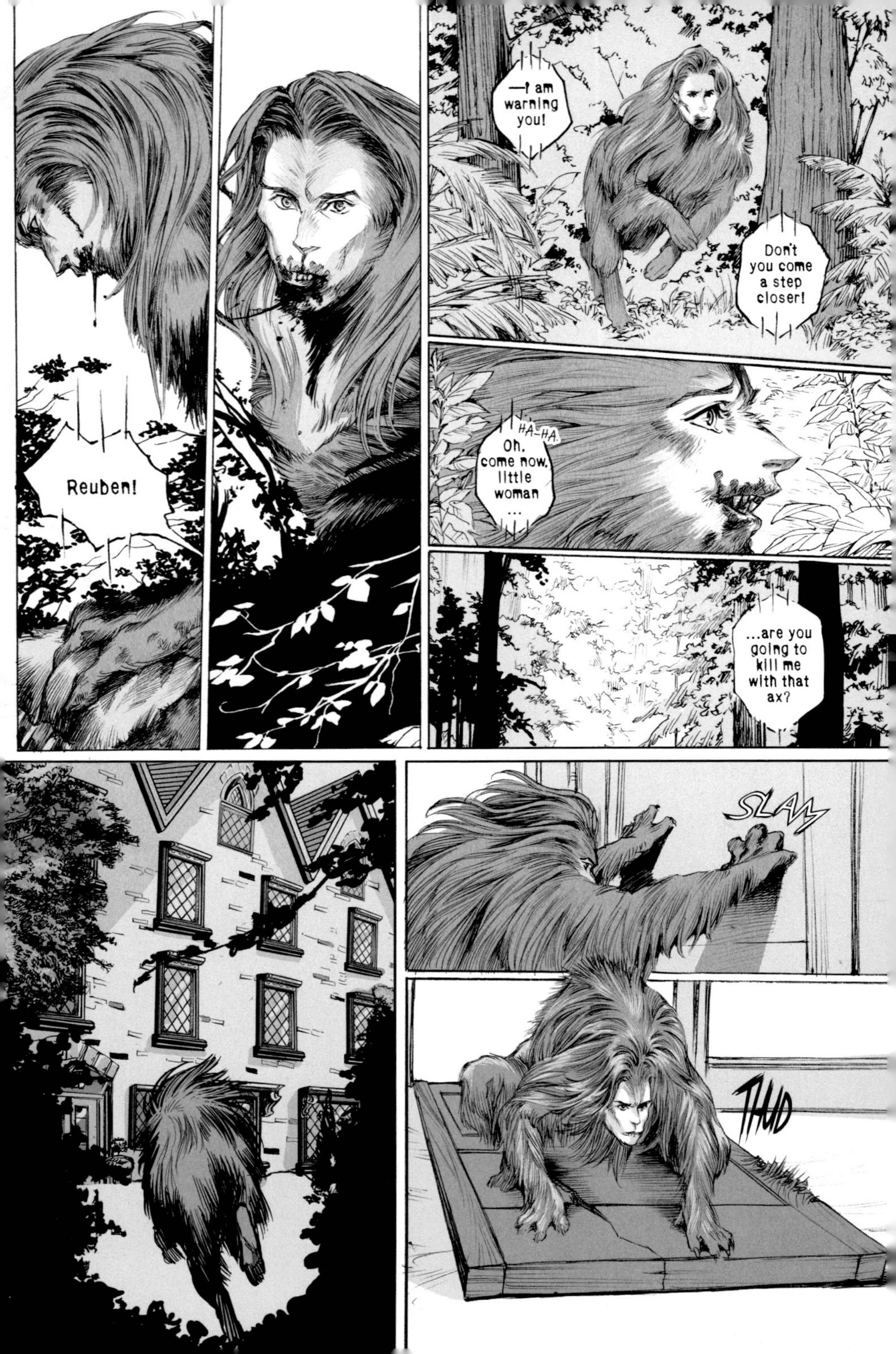
Reuben!
—I am warning you!
Don't you come a step closer!
HA-HA.
Oh, come now, little woman ...
...are you going to kill me with that ax?
SLAM
THUD

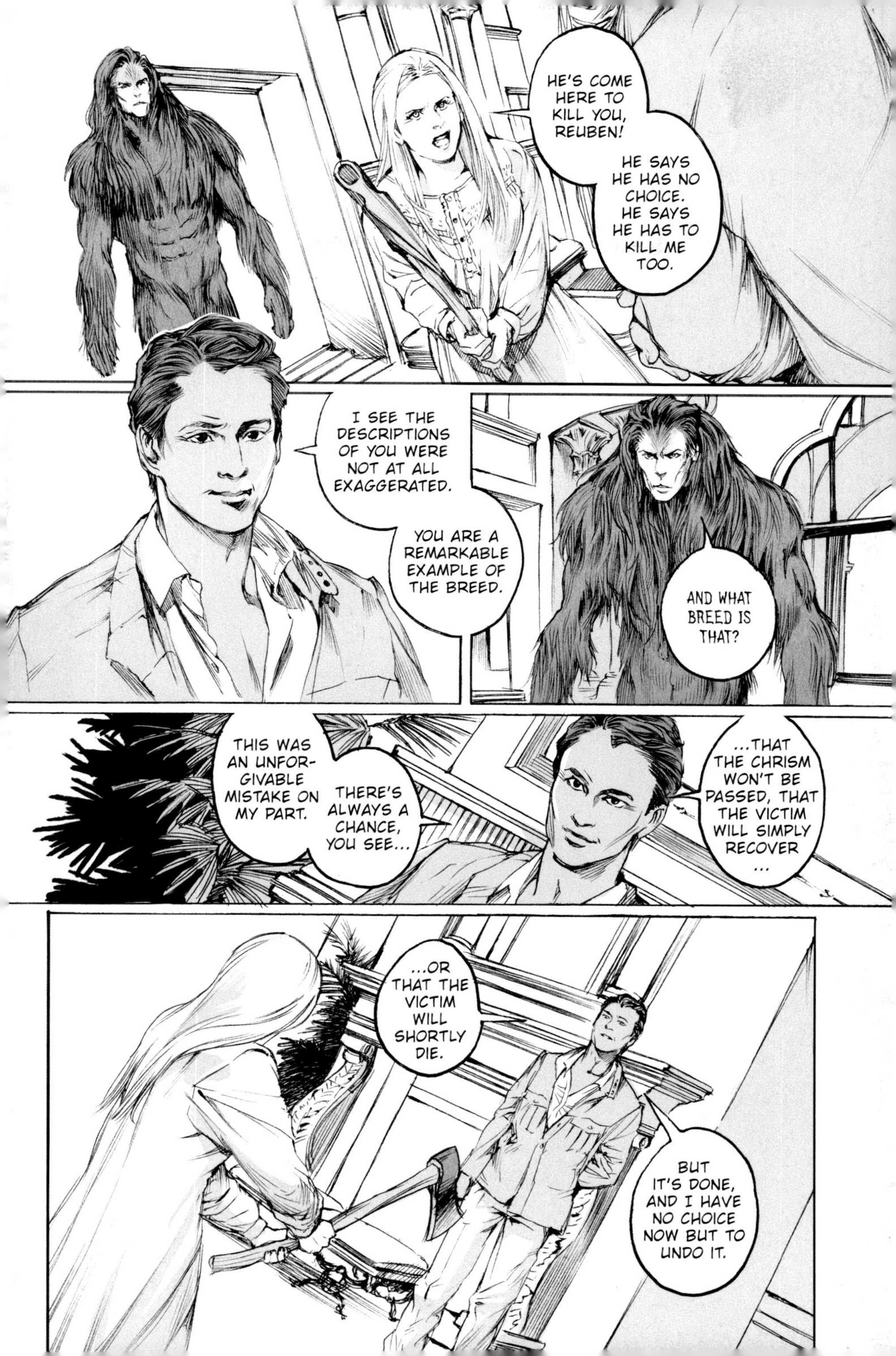
HE'S COME HERE TO KILL YOU, REUBEN!
HE SAYS HE HAS NO CHOICE. HE SAYS HE HAS TO KILL ME TOO.
I SEE THE DESCRIPTIONS OF YOU WERE NOT AT ALL EXAGGERATED.
YOU ARE A REMARKABLE EXAMPLE OF THE BREED.
AND WHAT BREED IS THAT?
THIS WAS AN UNFORGIVABLE MISTAKE ON MY PART.
THERE'S ALWAYS A CHANCE, YOU SEE...
...THAT THE CHRISM WON'T BE PASSED, THAT THE VICTIM WILL SIMPLY RECOVER ...
...OR THAT THE VICTIM WILL SHORTLY DIE.
BUT IT'S DONE, AND I HAVE NO CHOICE NOW BUT TO UNDO IT.

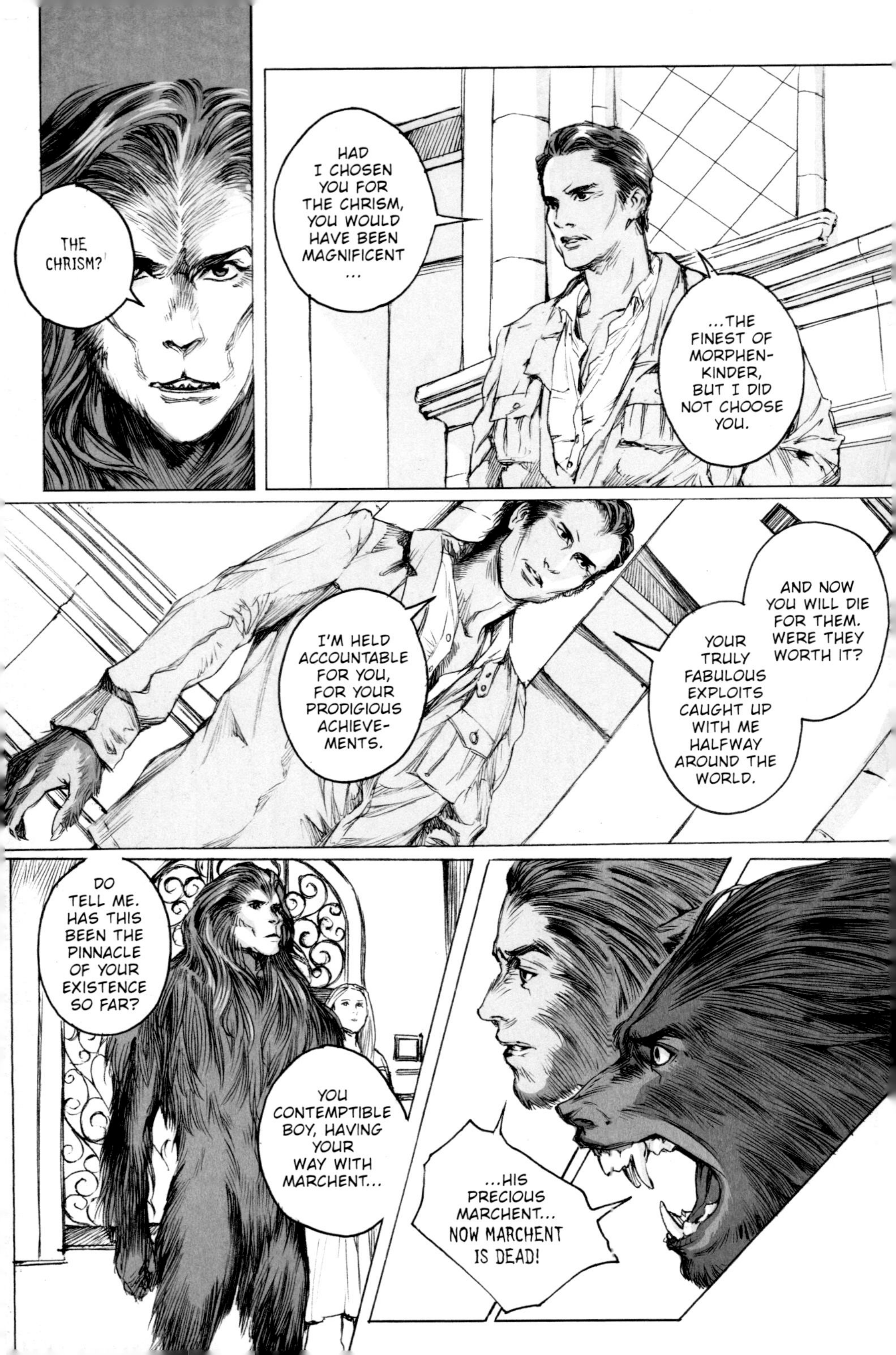
THE CHRISM?
HAD I CHOSEN YOU FOR THE CHRISM, YOU WOULD HAVE BEEN MAGNIFICENT ...
...THE FINEST OF MORPHEN-KINDER, BUT I DID NOT CHOOSE YOU.
I'M HELD ACCOUNTABLE FOR YOU, FOR YOUR PRODIGIOUS ACHIEVE-MENTS.
YOUR TRULY FABULOUS EXPLOITS CAUGHT UP WITH ME HALFWAY AROUND THE WORLD.
AND NOW YOU WILL DIE FOR THEM. WERE THEY WORTH IT?
DO TELL ME. HAS THIS BEEN THE PINNACLE OF YOUR EXISTENCE SO FAR?
YOU CONTEMPTIBLE BOY, HAVING YOUR WAY WITH MARCHENT...
...HIS PRECIOUS MARCHENT... NOW MARCHENT IS DEAD!

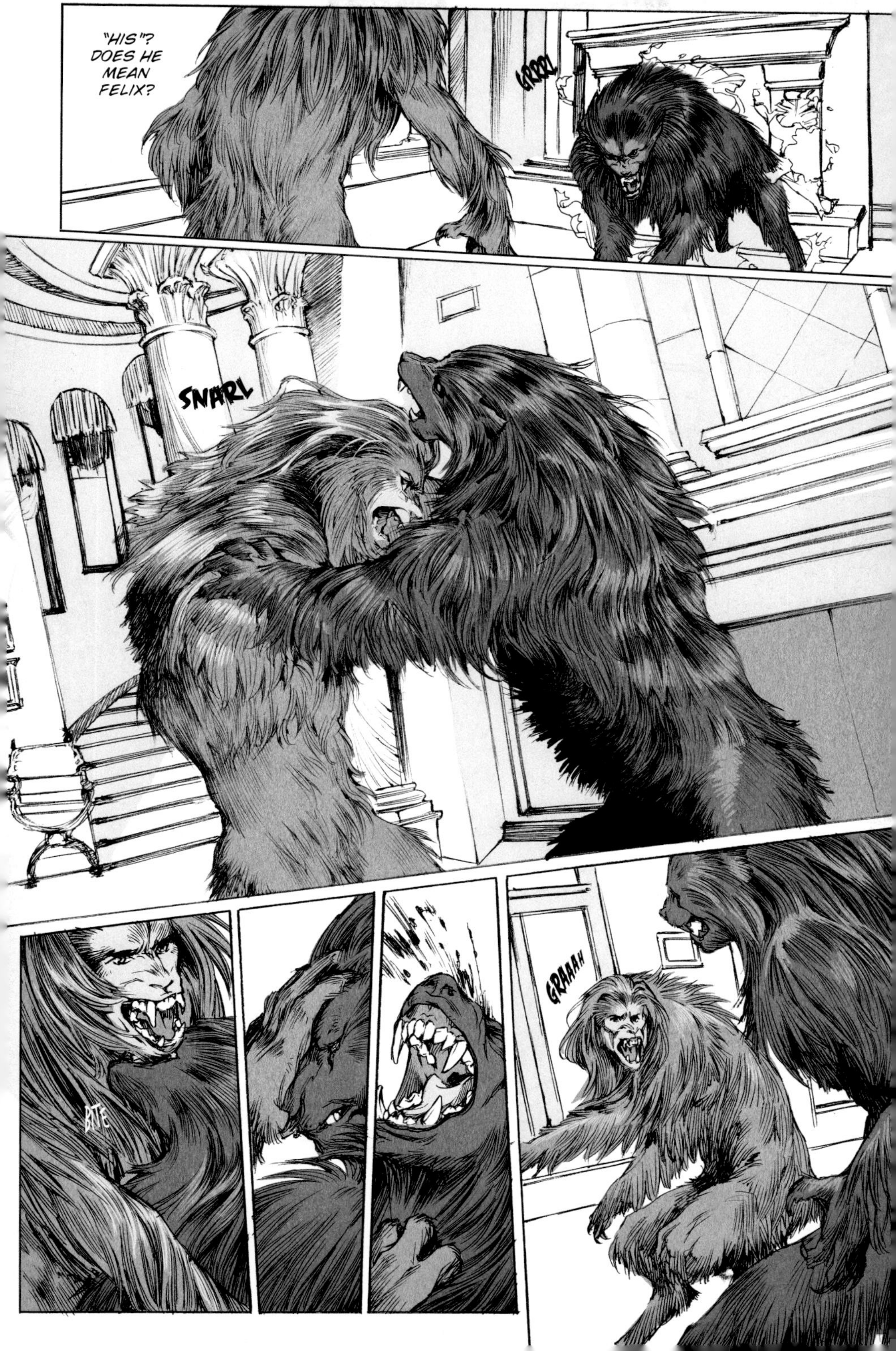
"HIS"? DOES HE MEAN FELIX?
GRRRL
SNARL
BITE
GRAAAH

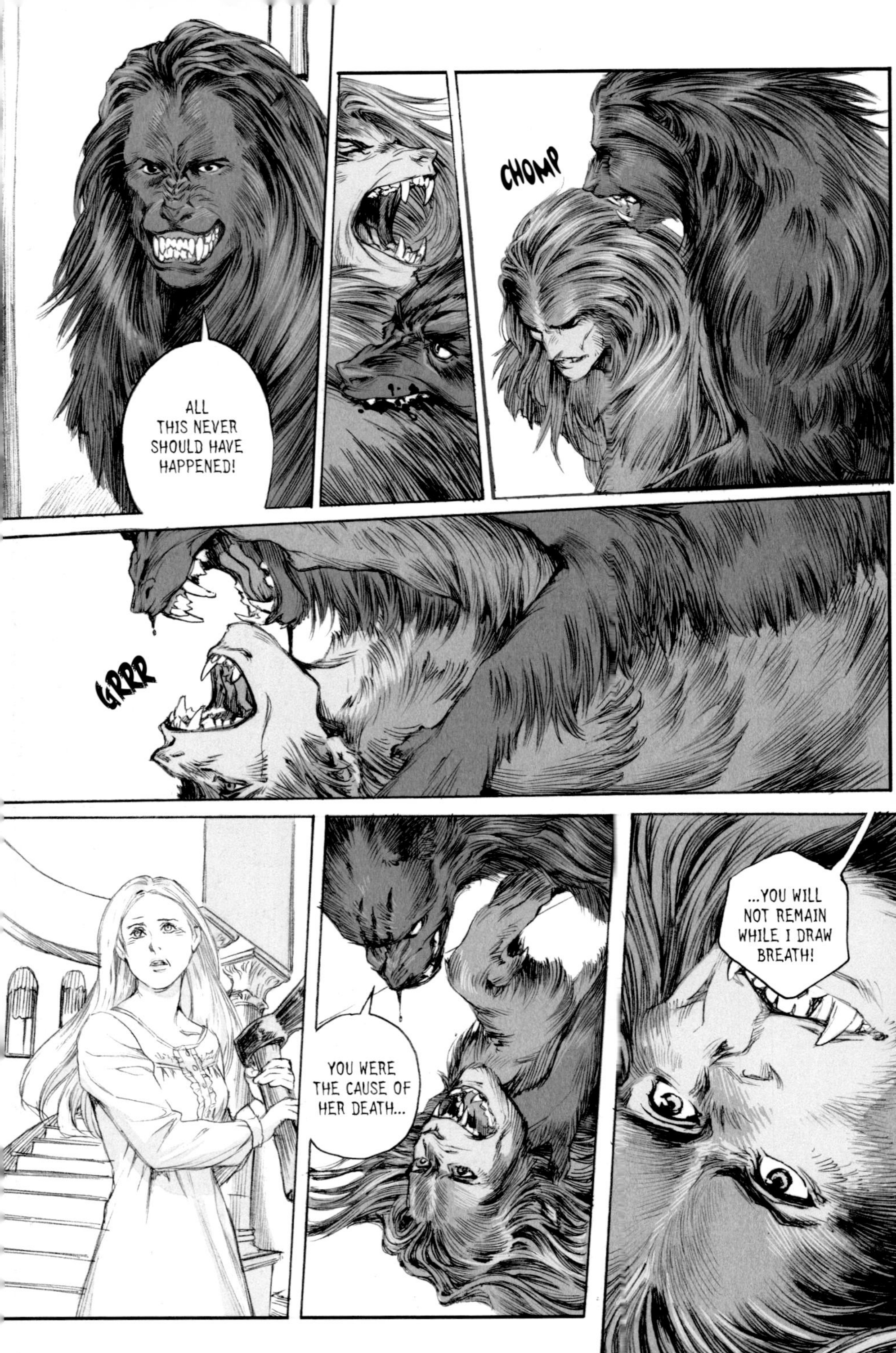
ALL THIS NEVER SHOULD HAVE HAPPENED!
CHOMP
GRRR
YOU WERE THE CAUSE OF HER DEATH...
...YOU WILL NOT REMAIN WHILE I DRAW BREATH!

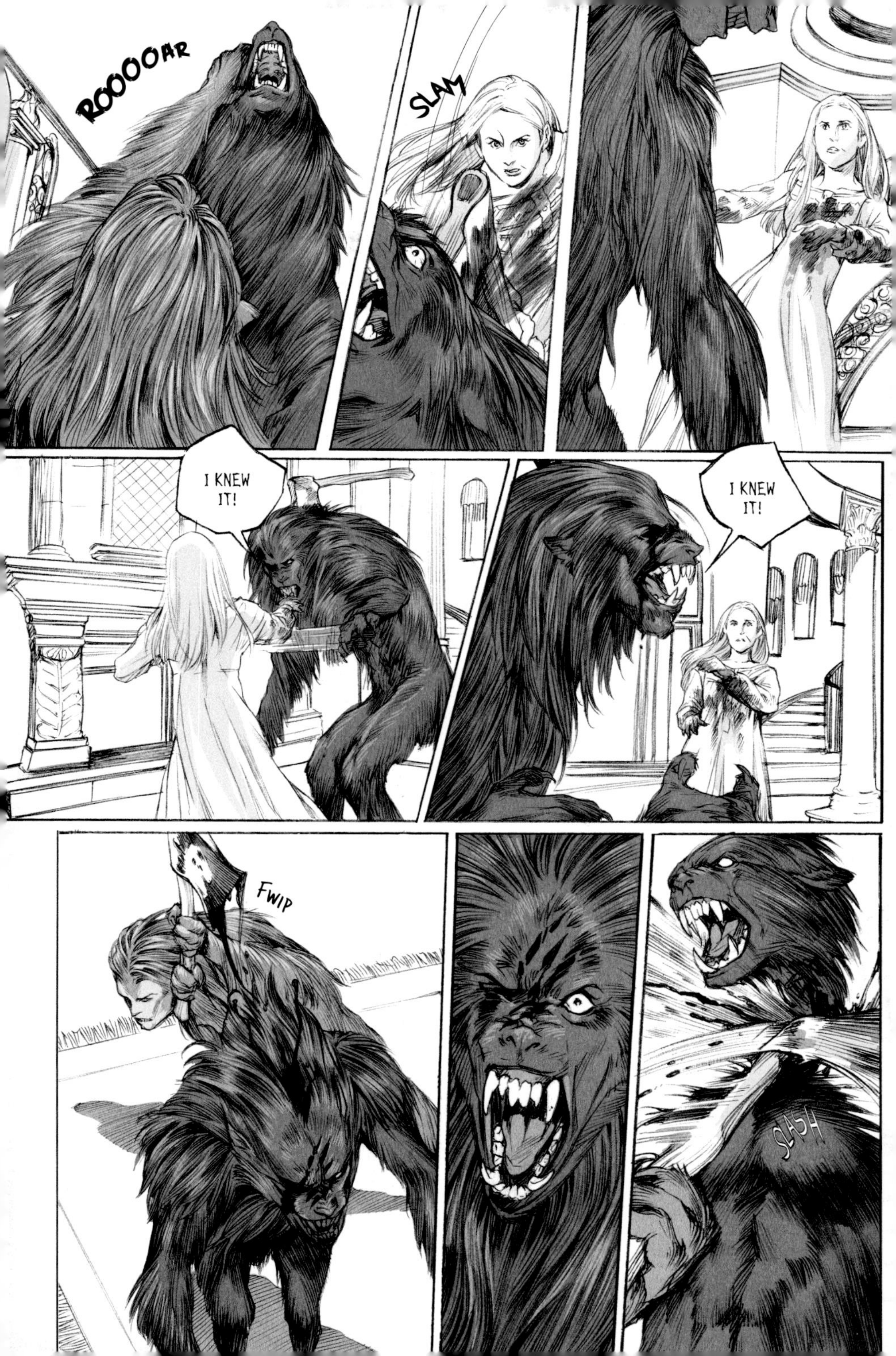
ROOOOAR
SLAM
I KNEW IT!
I KNEW IT!
FWIP
SLASH

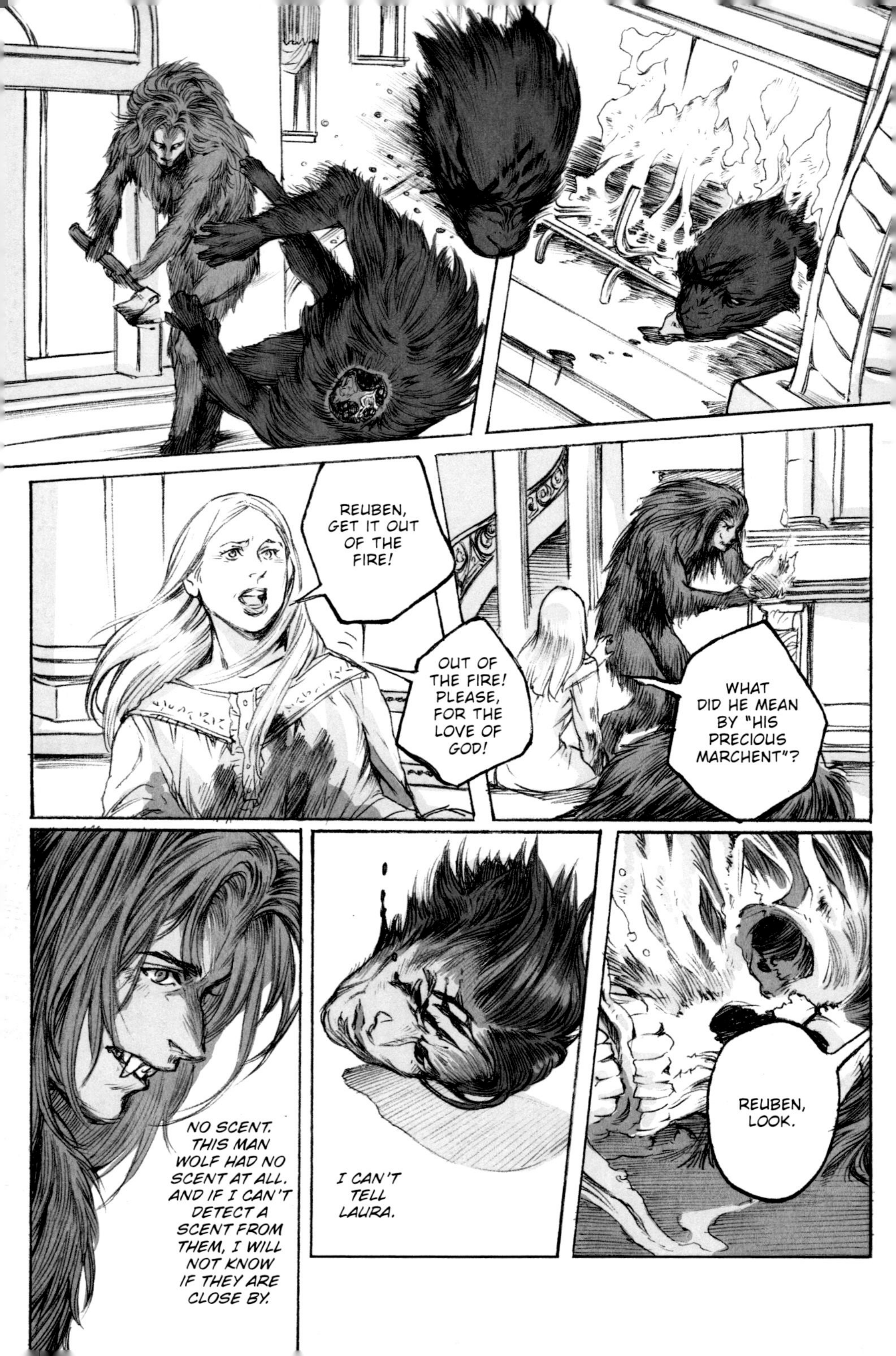
REUBEN, GET IT OUT OF THE FIRE!
OUT OF THE FIRE! PLEASE, FOR THE LOVE OF GOD!
WHAT DID HE MEAN BY "HIS PRECIOUS MARCHENT"?
NO SCENT. THIS MAN WOLF HAD NO SCENT AT ALL. AND IF I CAN'T DETECT A SCENT FROM THEM, I WILL NOT KNOW IF THEY ARE CLOSE BY.
I CAN'T TELL LAURA.
REUBEN, LOOK.

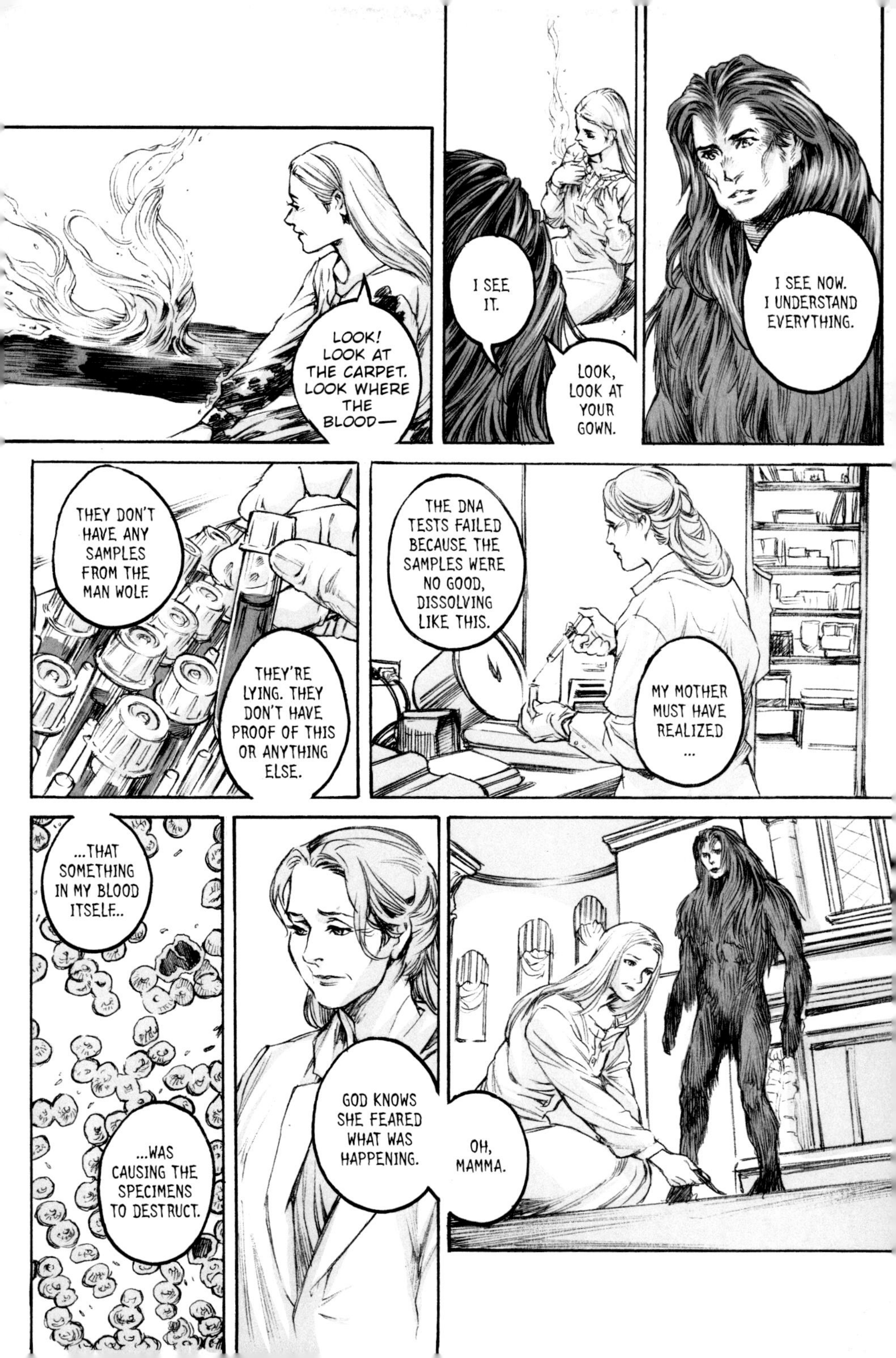
LOOK! LOOK AT THE CARPET. LOOK WHERE THE BLOOD—
I SEE IT.
LOOK, LOOK AT YOUR GOWN.
I SEE NOW. I UNDERSTAND EVERYTHING.
THEY DON'T HAVE ANY SAMPLES FROM THE MAN WOLF.
THEY'RE LYING. THEY DON'T HAVE PROOF OF THIS OR ANYTHING ELSE.
THE DNA TESTS FAILED BECAUSE THE SAMPLES WERE NO GOOD, DISSOLVING LIKE THIS.
MY MOTHER MUST HAVE REALIZED ...
...THAT SOMETHING IN MY BLOOD ITSELF...
...WAS CAUSING THE SPECIMENS TO DESTRUCT.
GOD KNOWS SHE FEARED WHAT WAS HAPPENING.
OH, MAMMA.

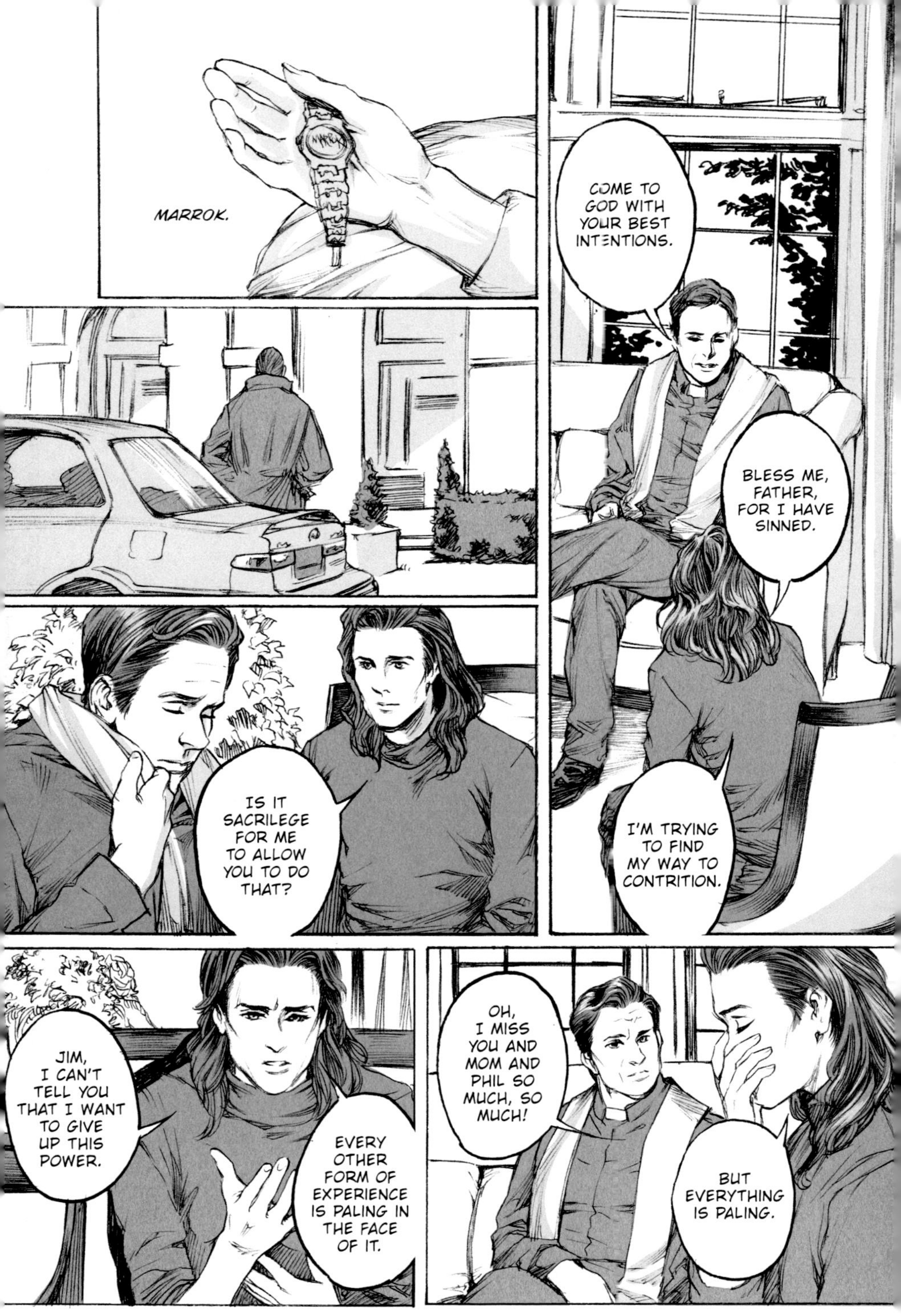
MARROK.
COME TO GOD WITH YOUR BEST INTENTIONS.
BLESS ME, FATHER, FOR I HAVE SINNED.
I'M TRYING TO FIND MY WAY TO CONTRITION.
IS IT SACRILEGE FOR ME TO ALLOW YOU TO DO THAT?
JIM, I CAN'T TELL YOU THAT I WANT TO GIVE UP THIS POWER.
EVERY OTHER FORM OF EXPERIENCE IS PALING IN THE FACE OF IT.
OH, I MISS YOU AND MOM AND PHIL SO MUCH, SO MUCH!
BUT EVERYTHING IS PALING.

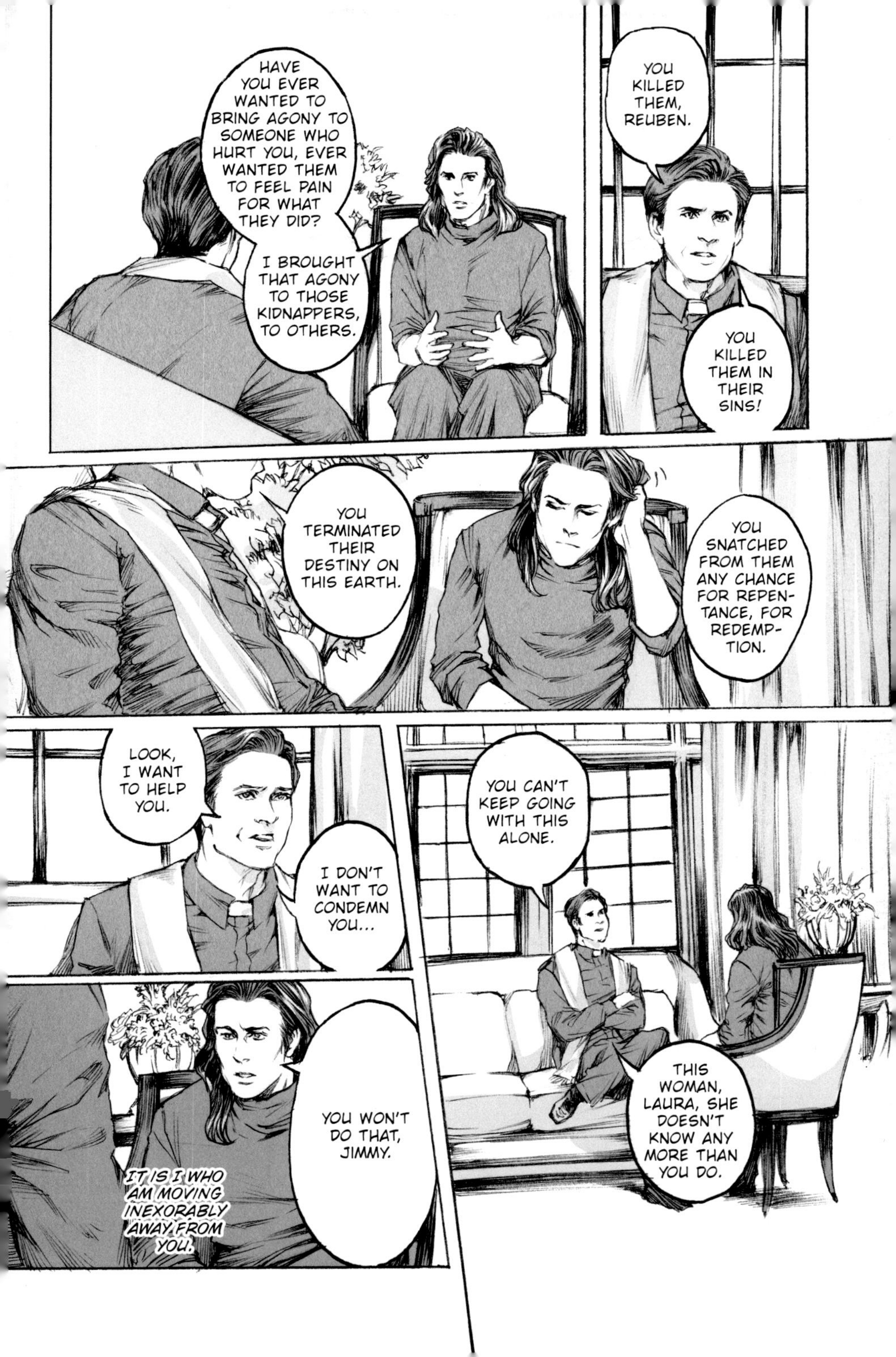
HAVE YOU EVER WANTED TO BRING AGONY TO SOMEONE WHO HURT YOU, EVER WANTED THEM TO FEEL PAIN FOR WHAT THEY DID?
I BROUGHT THAT AGONY TO THOSE KIDNAPPERS, TO OTHERS.
YOU KILLED THEM, REUBEN.
YOU KILLED THEM IN THEIR SINS!
YOU TERMINATED THEIR DESTINY ON THIS EARTH.
YOU SNATCHED FROM THEM ANY CHANCE FOR REPENTANCE, FOR REDEMPTION.
LOOK, I WANT TO HELP YOU.
I DON'T WANT TO CONDEMN YOU...
YOU CAN'T KEEP GOING WITH THIS ALONE.
THIS WOMAN, LAURA, SHE DOESN'T KNOW ANY MORE THAN YOU DO.
YOU WON'T DO THAT, JIMMY.
IT IS I WHO AM MOVING INEXORABLY AWAY FROM YOU.

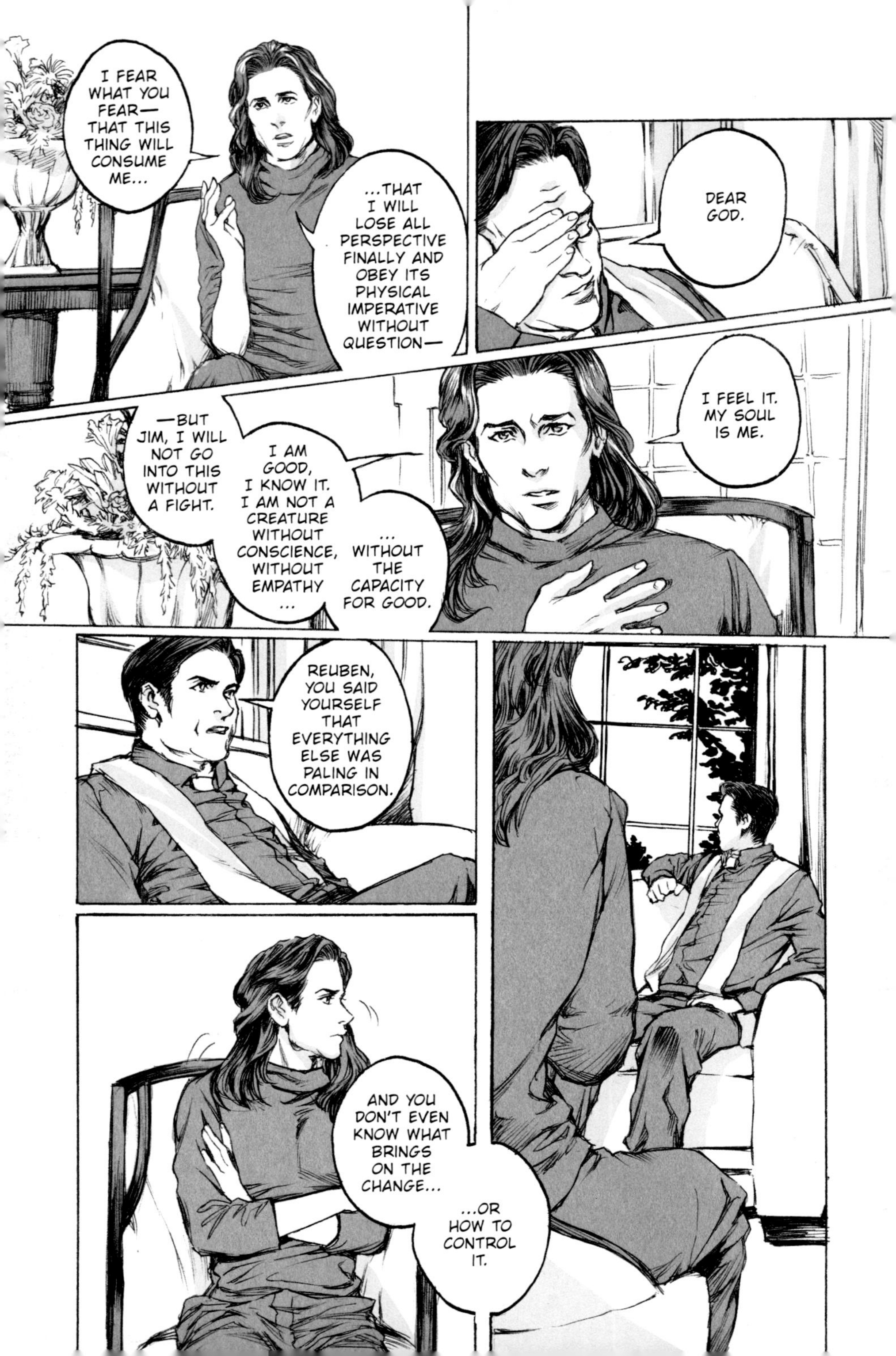
I FEAR WHAT YOU FEAR—THAT THIS THING WILL CONSUME ME...
...THAT I WILL LOSE ALL PERSPECTIVE FINALLY AND OBEY ITS PHYSICAL IMPERATIVE WITHOUT QUESTION—
DEAR GOD.
—BUT JIM, I WILL NOT GO INTO THIS WITHOUT A FIGHT.
I AM GOOD, I KNOW IT. I AM NOT A CREATURE WITHOUT CONSCIENCE, WITHOUT EMPATHY...
...WITHOUT THE CAPACITY FOR GOOD.
I FEEL IT. MY SOUL IS ME.
REUBEN, YOU SAID YOURSELF THAT EVERYTHING ELSE WAS PALING IN COMPARISON.
AND YOU DON'T EVEN KNOW WHAT BRINGS ON THE CHANGE...
...OR HOW TO CONTROL IT.

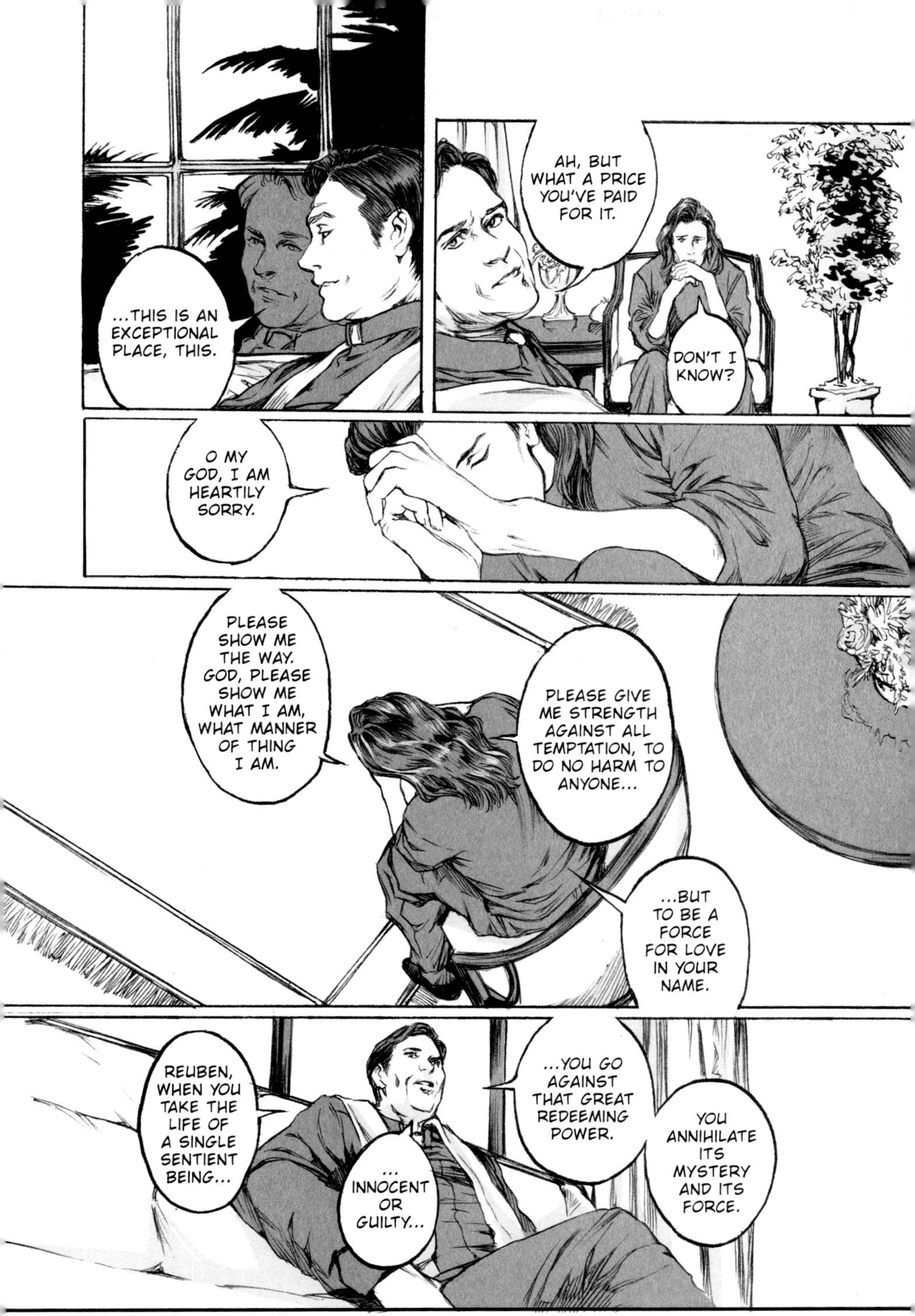
...THIS IS AN EXCEPTIONAL PLACE, THIS.
AH, BUT WHAT A PRICE YOU'VE PAID FOR IT.
DON'T I KNOW?
O MY GOD, I AM HEARTILY SORRY.
PLEASE SHOW ME THE WAY. GOD, PLEASE SHOW ME WHAT I AM, WHAT MANNER OF THING I AM.
PLEASE GIVE ME STRENGTH AGAINST ALL TEMPTATION, TO DO NO HARM TO ANYONE...
...BUT TO BE A FORCE FOR LOVE IN YOUR NAME.
REUBEN, WHEN YOU TAKE THE LIFE OF A SINGLE SENTIENT BEING...
...INNOCENT OR GUILTY...
...YOU GO AGAINST THAT GREAT REDEEMING POWER.
YOU ANNIHILATE ITS MYSTERY AND ITS FORCE.

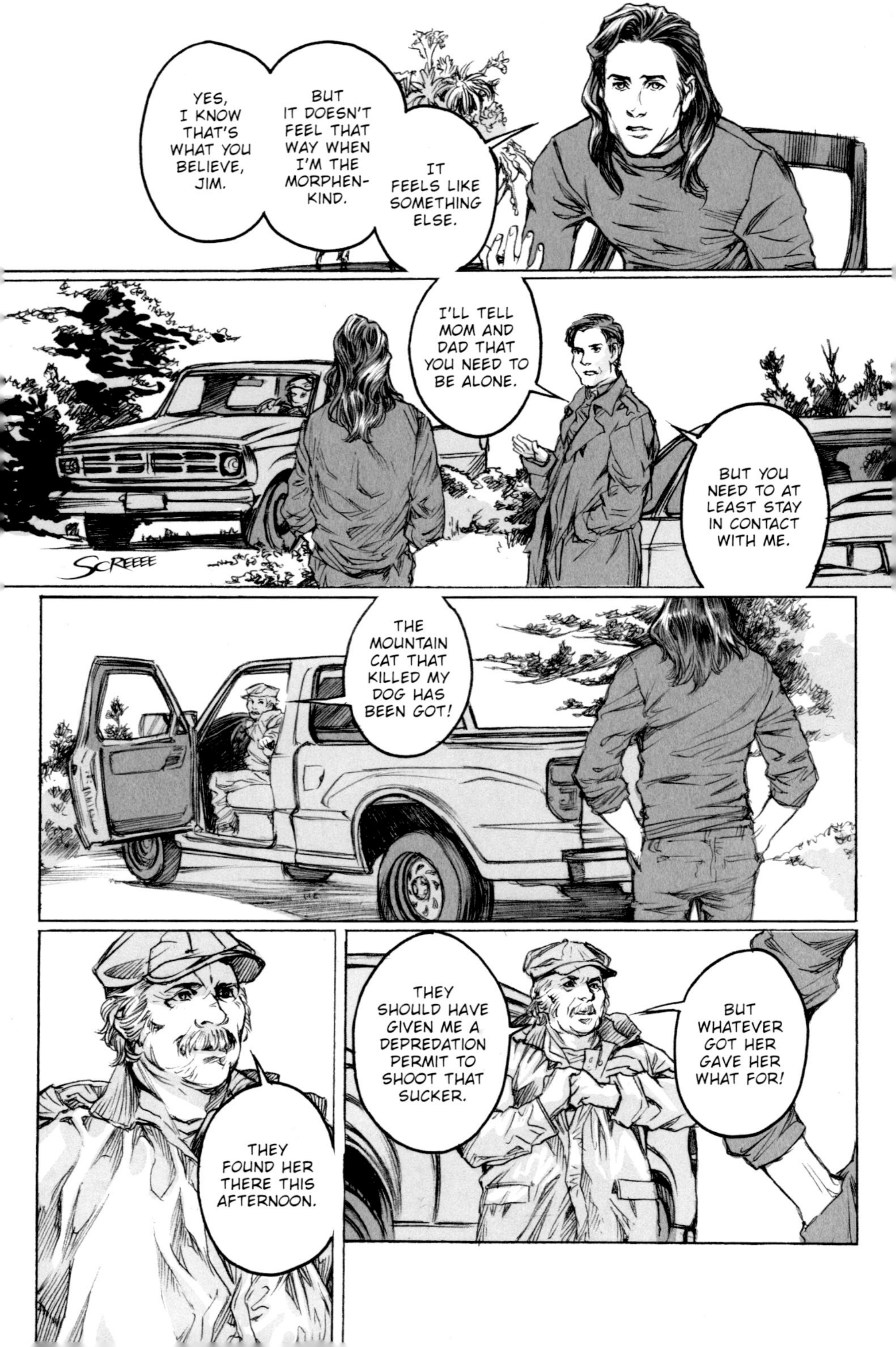
YES, I KNOW THAT'S WHAT YOU BELIEVE, JIM.
BUT IT DOESN'T FEEL THAT WAY WHEN I'M THE MORPHEN-KIND.
IT FEELS LIKE SOMETHING ELSE.
I'LL TELL MOM AND DAD THAT YOU NEED TO BE ALONE.
BUT YOU NEED TO AT LEAST STAY IN CONTACT WITH ME.
SCREEEE
THE MOUNTAIN CAT THAT KILLED MY DOG HAS BEEN GOT!
THEY FOUND HER THERE THIS AFTERNOON.
THEY SHOULD HAVE GIVEN ME A DEPREDATION PERMIT TO SHOOT THAT SUCKER.
BUT WHATEVER GOT HER GAVE HER WHAT FOR!

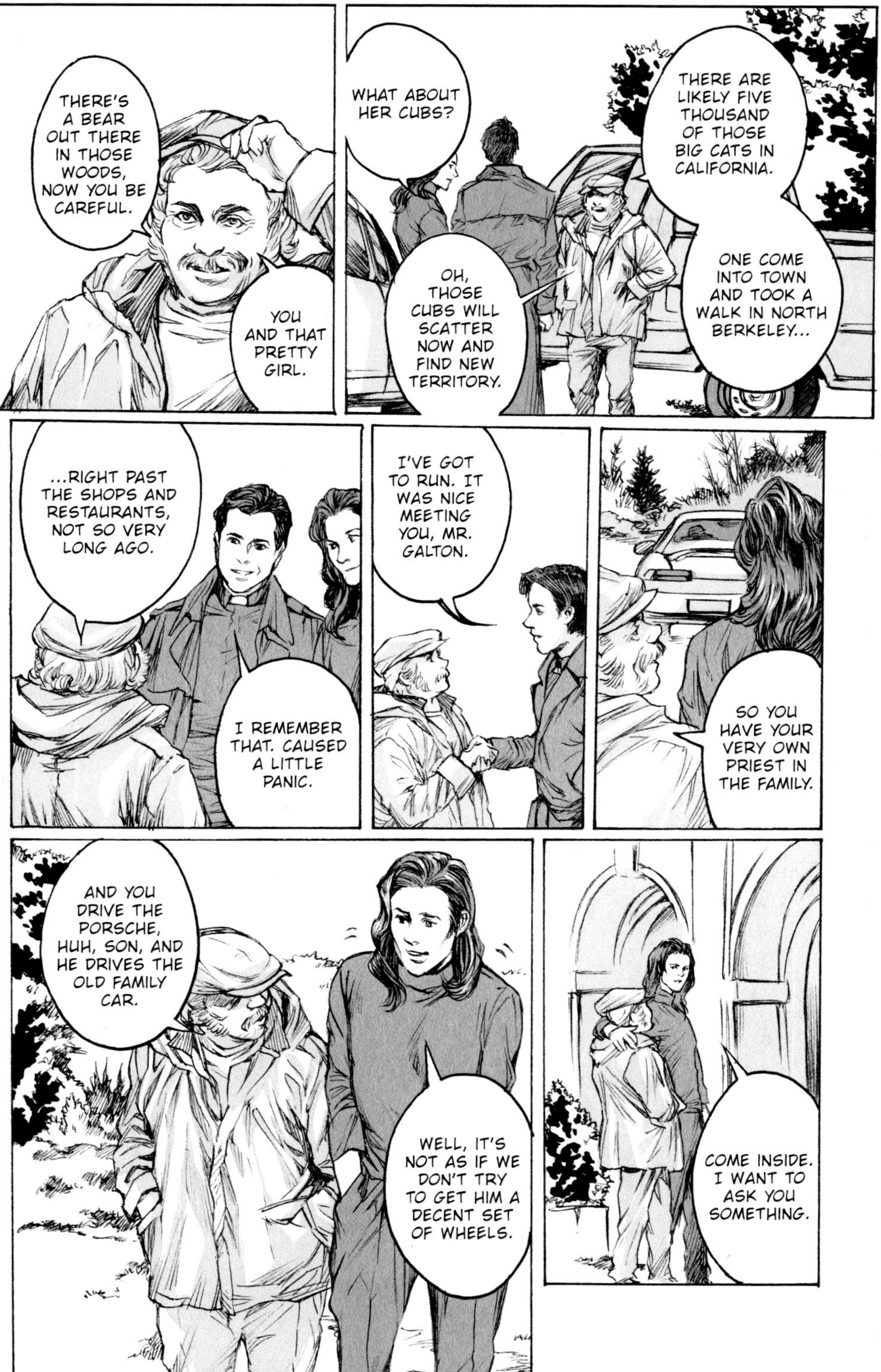
THERE'S A BEAR OUT THERE IN THOSE WOODS, NOW YOU BE CAREFUL.
YOU AND THAT PRETTY GIRL.
WHAT ABOUT HER CUBS?
OH, THOSE CUBS WILL SCATTER NOW AND FIND NEW TERRITORY.
THERE ARE LIKELY FIVE THOUSAND OF THOSE BIG CATS IN CALIFORNIA.
ONE COME INTO TOWN AND TOOK A WALK IN NORTH BERKELEY...
...RIGHT PAST THE SHOPS AND RESTAURANTS, NOT SO VERY LONG AGO.
I REMEMBER THAT. CAUSED A LITTLE PANIC.
I'VE GOT TO RUN. IT WAS NICE MEETING YOU, MR. GALTON.
SO YOU HAVE YOUR VERY OWN PRIEST IN THE FAMILY.
AND YOU DRIVE THE PORSCHE, HUH, SON, AND HE DRIVES THE OLD FAMILY CAR.
WELL, IT'S NOT AS IF WE DON'T TRY TO GET HIM A DECENT SET OF WHEELS.
COME INSIDE. I WANT TO ASK YOU SOMETHING.

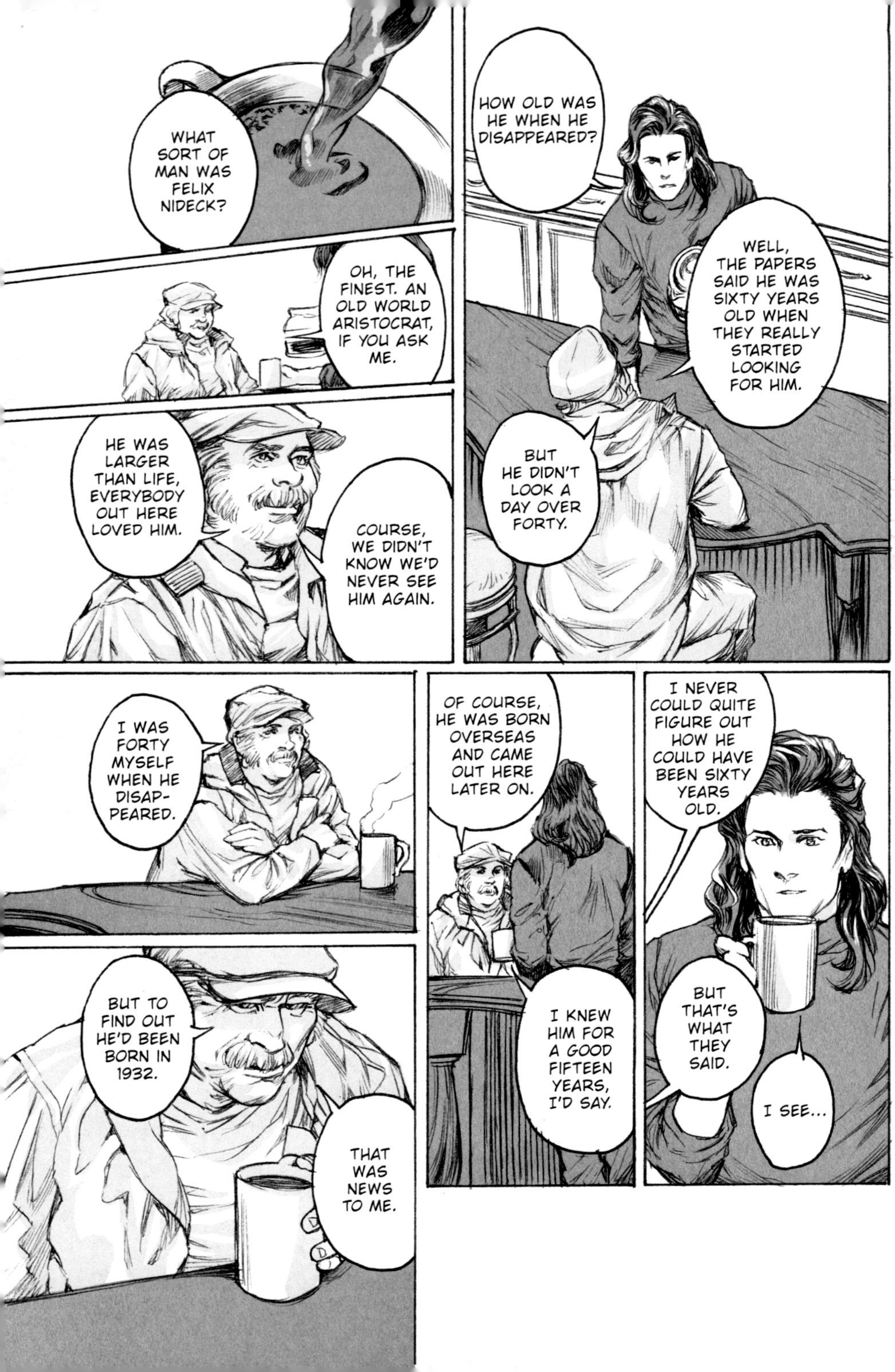
WHAT SORT OF MAN WAS FELIX NIDECK?
HOW OLD WAS HE WHEN HE DISAPPEARED?
OH, THE FINEST. AN OLD WORLD ARISTOCRAT, IF YOU ASK ME.
HE WAS LARGER THAN LIFE, EVERYBODY OUT HERE LOVED HIM.
COURSE, WE DIDN'T KNOW WE'D NEVER SEE HIM AGAIN.
WELL, THE PAPERS SAID HE WAS SIXTY YEARS OLD WHEN THEY REALLY STARTED LOOKING FOR HIM.
BUT HE DIDN'T LOOK A DAY OVER FORTY.
I WAS FORTY MYSELF WHEN HE DISAP-PEARED.
BUT TO FIND OUT HE'D BEEN BORN IN 1932.
THAT WAS NEWS TO ME.
OF COURSE, HE WAS BORN OVERSEAS AND CAME OUT HERE LATER ON.
I KNEW HIM FOR A GOOD FIFTEEN YEARS, I'D SAY.
I NEVER COULD QUITE FIGURE OUT HOW HE COULD HAVE BEEN SIXTY YEARS OLD.
BUT THAT'S WHAT THEY SAID.
I SEE...

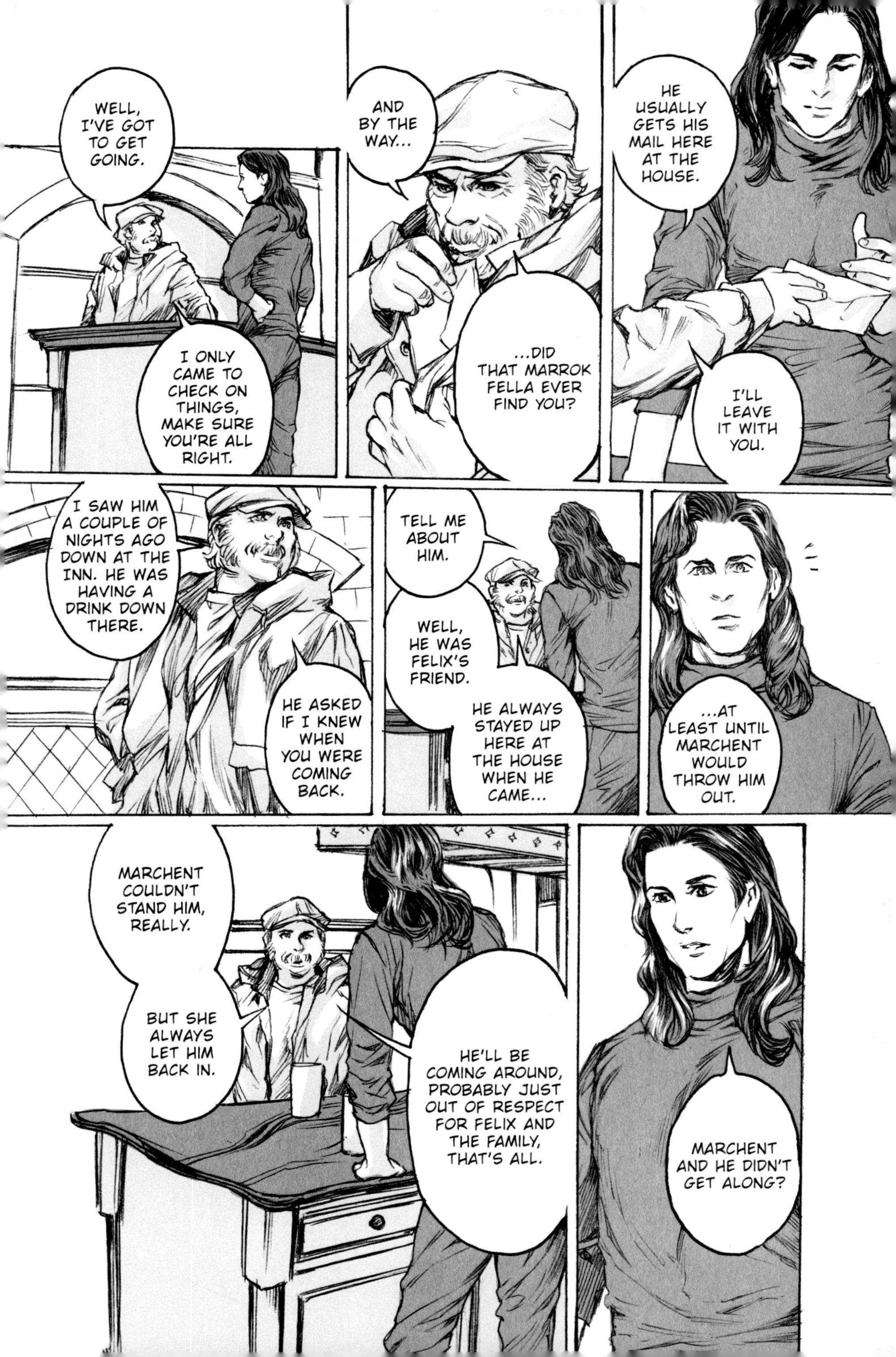

WELL, I'VE GOT TO GET GOING.
I ONLY CAME TO CHECK ON THINGS, MAKE SURE YOU'RE ALL RIGHT.
AND BY THE WAY...
...DID THAT MARROK FELLA EVER FIND YOU?
HE USUALLY GETS HIS MAIL HERE AT THE HOUSE.
I'LL LEAVE IT WITH YOU.
I SAW HIM A COUPLE OF NIGHTS AGO DOWN AT THE INN. HE WAS HAVING A DRINK DOWN THERE.
HE ASKED IF I KNEW WHEN YOU WERE COMING BACK.
TELL ME ABOUT HIM.
WELL, HE WAS FELIX'S FRIEND.
HE ALWAYS STAYED UP HERE AT THE HOUSE WHEN HE CAME...
...AT LEAST UNTIL MARCHENT WOULD THROW HIM OUT.
MARCHENT COULDN'T STAND HIM, REALLY.
BUT SHE ALWAYS LET HIM BACK IN.
HE'LL BE COMING AROUND, PROBABLY JUST OUT OF RESPECT FOR FELIX AND THE FAMILY, THAT'S ALL.
MARCHENT AND HE DIDN'T GET ALONG?

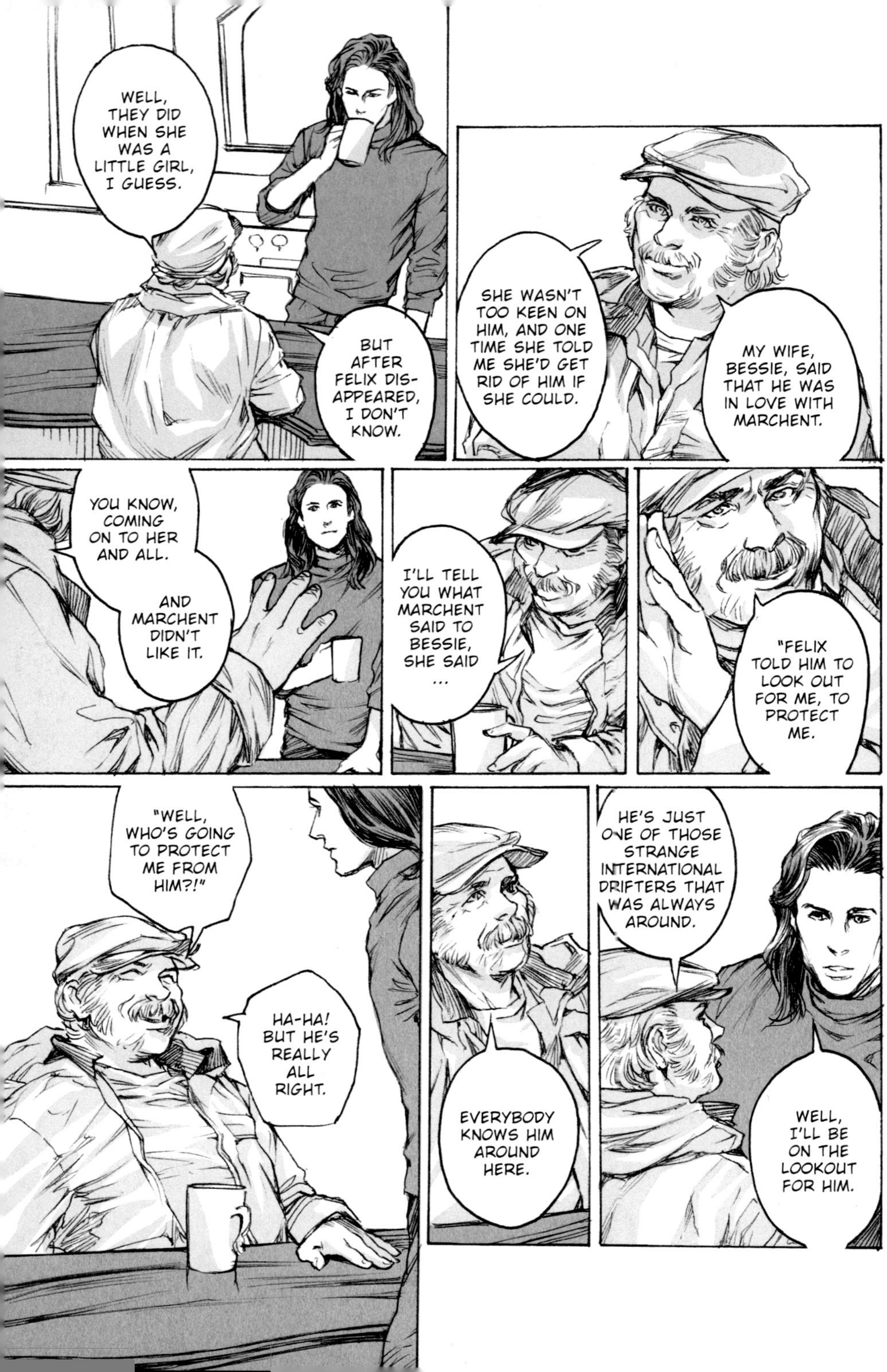
WELL, THEY DID WHEN SHE WAS A LITTLE GIRL, I GUESS.
BUT AFTER FELIX DIS-APPEARED, I DON'T KNOW.
MY WIFE, BESSIE, SAID THAT HE WAS IN LOVE WITH MARCHENT.
SHE WASN'T TOO KEEN ON HIM, AND ONE TIME SHE TOLD ME SHE'D GET RID OF HIM IF SHE COULD.
YOU KNOW, COMING ON TO HER AND ALL.
AND MARCHENT DIDN'T LIKE IT.
I'LL TELL YOU WHAT MARCHENT SAID TO BESSIE, SHE SAID ...
"FELIX TOLD HIM TO LOOK OUT FOR ME, TO PROTECT ME.
"WELL, WHO'S GOING TO PROTECT ME FROM HIM?!"
HA-HA! BUT HE'S REALLY ALL RIGHT.
EVERYBODY KNOWS HIM AROUND HERE.
HE'S JUST ONE OF THOSE STRANGE INTERNATIONAL DRIFTERS THAT WAS ALWAYS AROUND.
WELL, I'LL BE ON THE LOOKOUT FOR HIM.

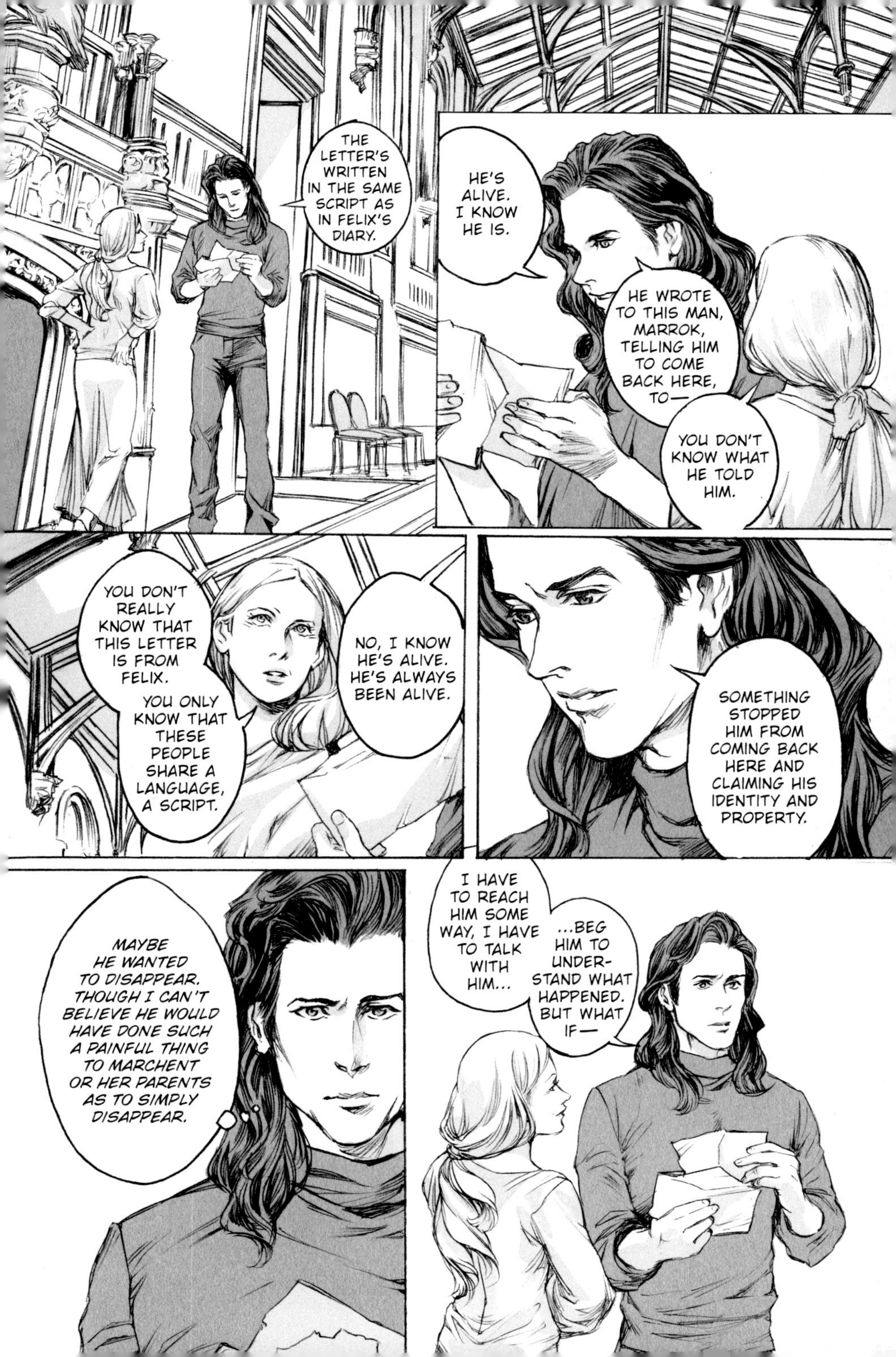

THE LETTER'S WRITTEN IN THE SAME SCRIPT AS IN FELIX'S DIARY.
HE'S ALIVE. I KNOW HE IS.
HE WROTE TO THIS MAN, MARROK, TELLING HIM TO COME BACK HERE, TO—
YOU DON'T KNOW WHAT HE TOLD HIM.
YOU DON'T REALLY KNOW THAT THIS LETTER IS FROM FELIX.
YOU ONLY KNOW THAT THESE PEOPLE SHARE A LANGUAGE, A SCRIPT.
NO, I KNOW HE'S ALIVE. HE'S ALWAYS BEEN ALIVE.
SOMETHING STOPPED HIM FROM COMING BACK HERE AND CLAIMING HIS IDENTITY AND PROPERTY.
MAYBE HE WANTED TO DISAPPEAR. THOUGH I CAN'T BELIEVE HE WOULD HAVE DONE SUCH A PAINFUL THING TO MARCHENT OR HER PARENTS AS TO SIMPLY DISAPPEAR.
I HAVE TO REACH HIM SOME WAY, I HAVE TO TALK WITH HIM...
...BEG HIM TO UNDER-STAND WHAT HAPPENED. BUT WHAT IF—

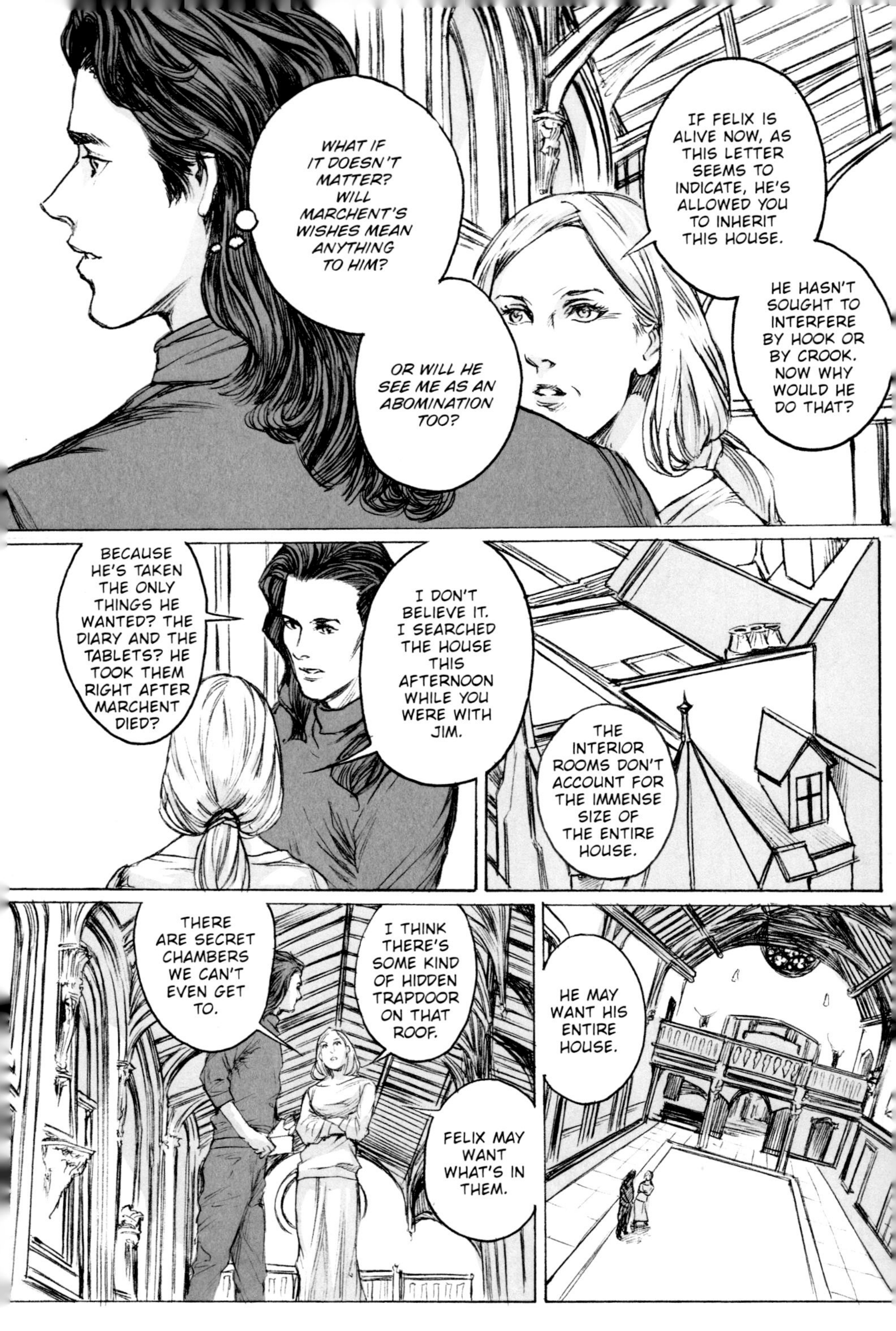
WHAT IF IT DOESN'T MATTER? WILL MARCHENT'S WISHES MEAN ANYTHING TO HIM?
OR WILL HE SEE ME AS AN ABOMINATION TOO?
IF FELIX IS ALIVE NOW, AS THIS LETTER SEEMS TO INDICATE, HE'S ALLOWED YOU TO INHERIT THIS HOUSE.
HE HASN'T SOUGHT TO INTERFERE BY HOOK OR BY CROOK. NOW WHY WOULD HE DO THAT?
BECAUSE HE'S TAKEN THE ONLY THINGS HE WANTED? THE DIARY AND THE TABLETS? HE TOOK THEM RIGHT AFTER MARCHENT DIED?
I DON'T BELIEVE IT. I SEARCHED THE HOUSE THIS AFTERNOON WHILE YOU WERE WITH JIM.
THE INTERIOR ROOMS DON'T ACCOUNT FOR THE IMMENSE SIZE OF THE ENTIRE HOUSE.
THERE ARE SECRET CHAMBERS WE CAN'T EVEN GET TO.
I THINK THERE'S SOME KIND OF HIDDEN TRAPDOOR ON THAT ROOF.
FELIX MAY WANT WHAT'S IN THEM.
HE MAY WANT HIS ENTIRE HOUSE.

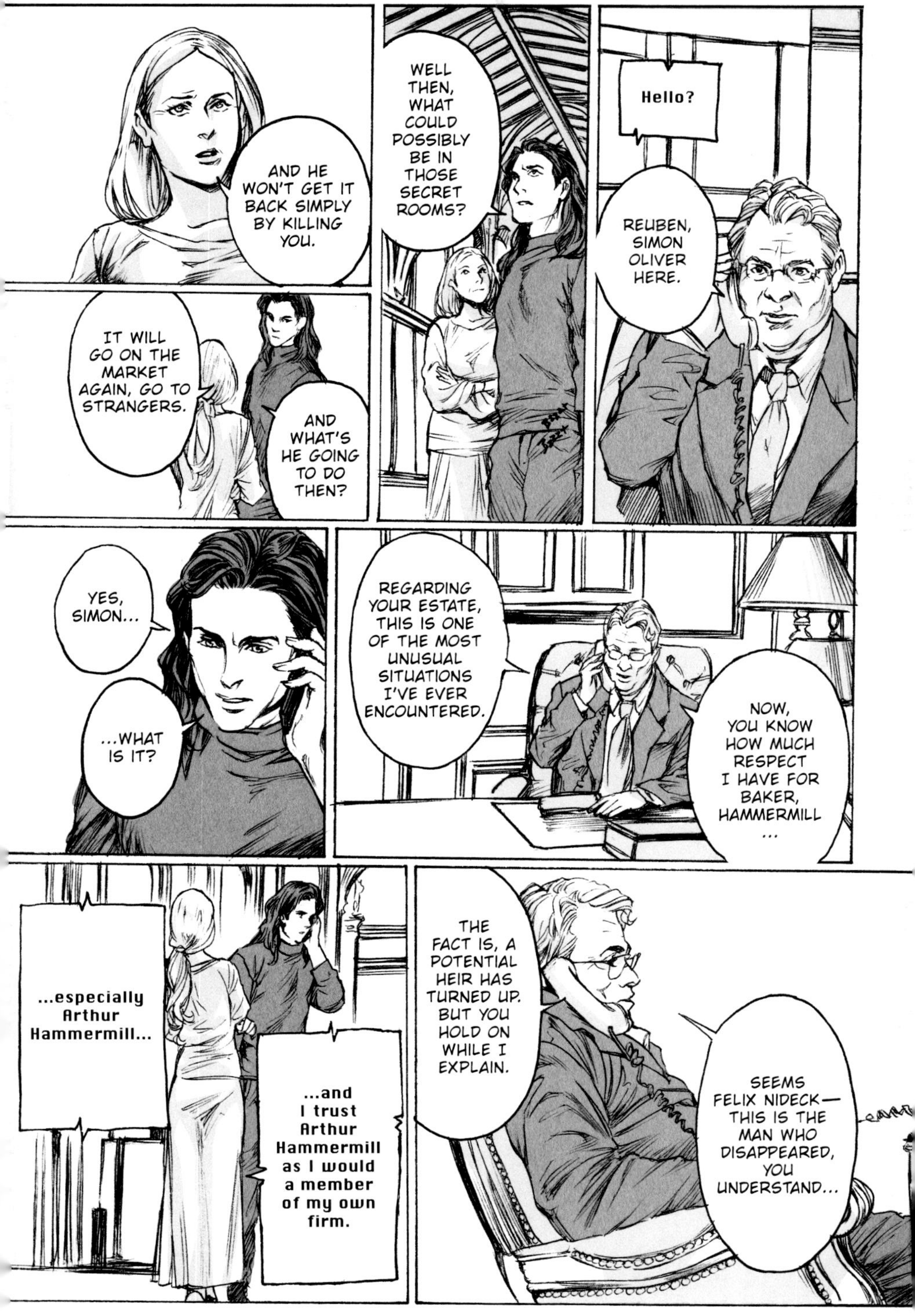
AND HE WON'T GET IT BACK SIMPLY BY KILLING YOU.
IT WILL GO ON THE MARKET AGAIN, GO TO STRANGERS.
AND WHAT'S HE GOING TO DO THEN?
WELL THEN, WHAT COULD POSSIBLY BE IN THOSE SECRET ROOMS?
Hello?
REUBEN, SIMON OLIVER HERE.
YES, SIMON...
...WHAT IS IT?
REGARDING YOUR ESTATE, THIS IS ONE OF THE MOST UNUSUAL SITUATIONS I'VE EVER ENCOUNTERED.
NOW, YOU KNOW HOW MUCH RESPECT I HAVE FOR BAKER, HAMMERMILL...
...especially Arthur Hammermill...
...and I trust Arthur Hammermill as I would a member of my own firm.
THE FACT IS, A POTENTIAL HEIR HAS TURNED UP. BUT YOU HOLD ON WHILE I EXPLAIN.
SEEMS FELIX NIDECK— THIS IS THE MAN WHO DISAPPEARED, YOU UNDERSTAND...

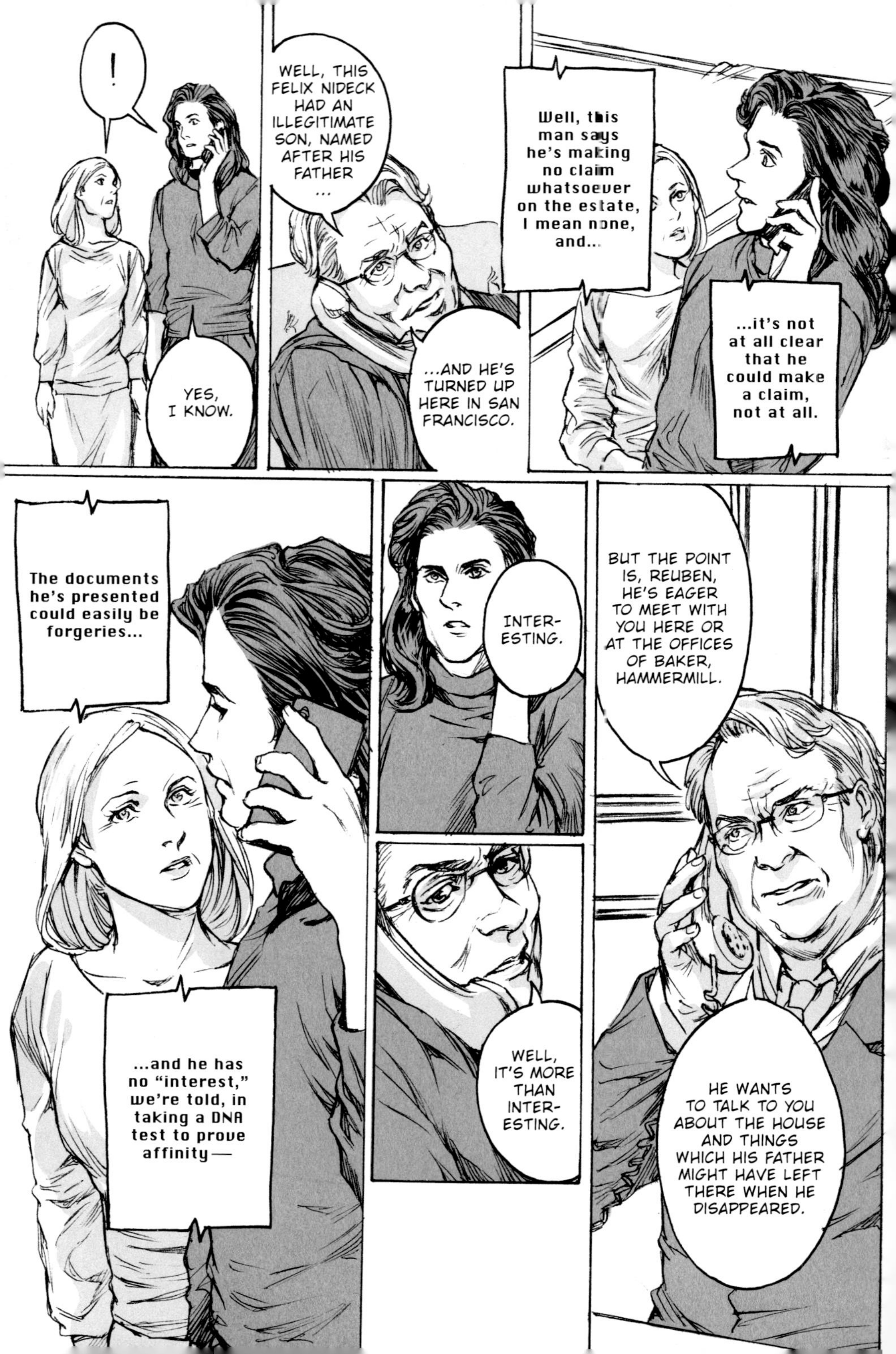
!
YES, I KNOW.
WELL, THIS FELIX NIDECK HAD AN ILLEGITIMATE SON, NAMED AFTER HIS FATHER ...
...AND HE'S TURNED UP HERE IN SAN FRANCISCO.
Well, this man says he's making no claim whatsoever on the estate, I mean none, and...
...it's not at all clear that he could make a claim, not at all.
The documents he's presented could easily be forgeries...
...and he has no "interest," we're told, in taking a DNA test to prove affinity—
INTER-ESTING.
WELL, IT'S MORE THAN INTER-ESTING.
BUT THE POINT IS, REUBEN, HE'S EAGER TO MEET WITH YOU HERE OR AT THE OFFICES OF BAKER, HAMMERMILL.
HE WANTS TO TALK TO YOU ABOUT THE HOUSE AND THINGS WHICH HIS FATHER MIGHT HAVE LEFT THERE WHEN HE DISAPPEARED.

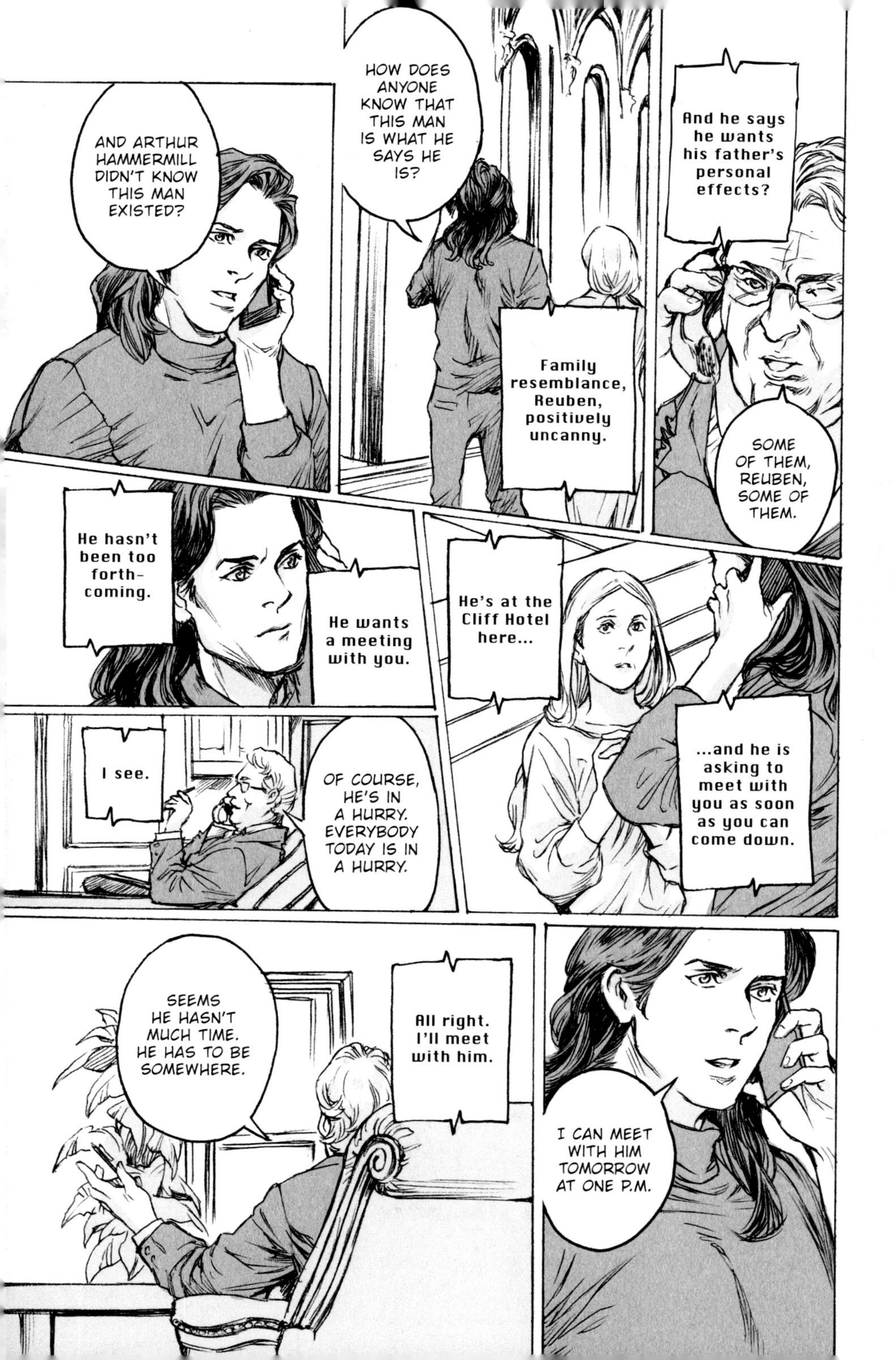
AND ARTHUR HAMMERMILL DIDN'T KNOW THIS MAN EXISTED?
HOW DOES ANYONE KNOW THAT THIS MAN IS WHAT HE SAYS HE IS?
Family resemblance, Reuben, positively uncanny.
And he says he wants his father's personal effects?
SOME OF THEM, REUBEN, SOME OF THEM.
He hasn't been too forth-coming.
He wants a meeting with you.
He's at the Cliff Hotel here...
...and he is asking to meet with you as soon as you can come down.
I see.
OF COURSE, HE'S IN A HURRY. EVERYBODY TODAY IS IN A HURRY.
SEEMS HE HASN'T MUCH TIME. HE HAS TO BE SOMEWHERE.
All right. I'll meet with him.
I CAN MEET WITH HIM TOMORROW AT ONE P.M.

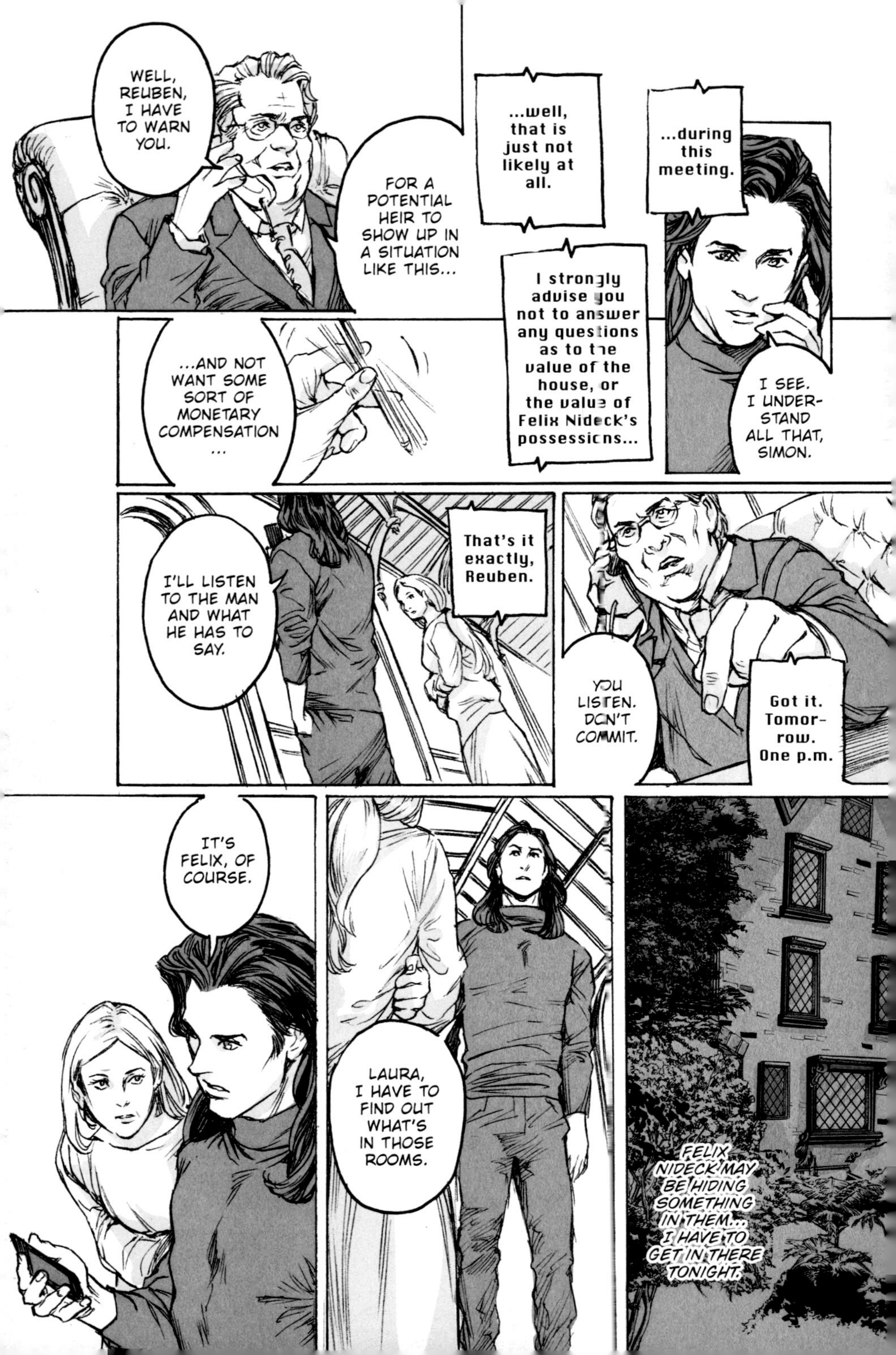
WELL, REUBEN, I HAVE TO WARN YOU.
FOR A POTENTIAL HEIR TO SHOW UP IN A SITUATION LIKE THIS...
...well, that is just not likely at all.
...during this meeting.
...AND NOT WANT SOME SORT OF MONETARY COMPENSATION ...
I strongly advise you not to answer any questions as to the value of the house, or the value of Felix Nideck's possessions...
I SEE. I UNDERSTAND ALL THAT, SIMON.
I'LL LISTEN TO THE MAN AND WHAT HE HAS TO SAY.
That's it exactly, Reuben.
YOU LISTEN. DON'T COMMIT.
Got it. Tomorrow. One p.m.
IT'S FELIX, OF COURSE.
LAURA, I HAVE TO FIND OUT WHAT'S IN THOSE ROOMS.
FELIX NIDECK MAY BE HIDING SOMETHING IN THEM... I HAVE TO GET IN THERE TONIGHT.

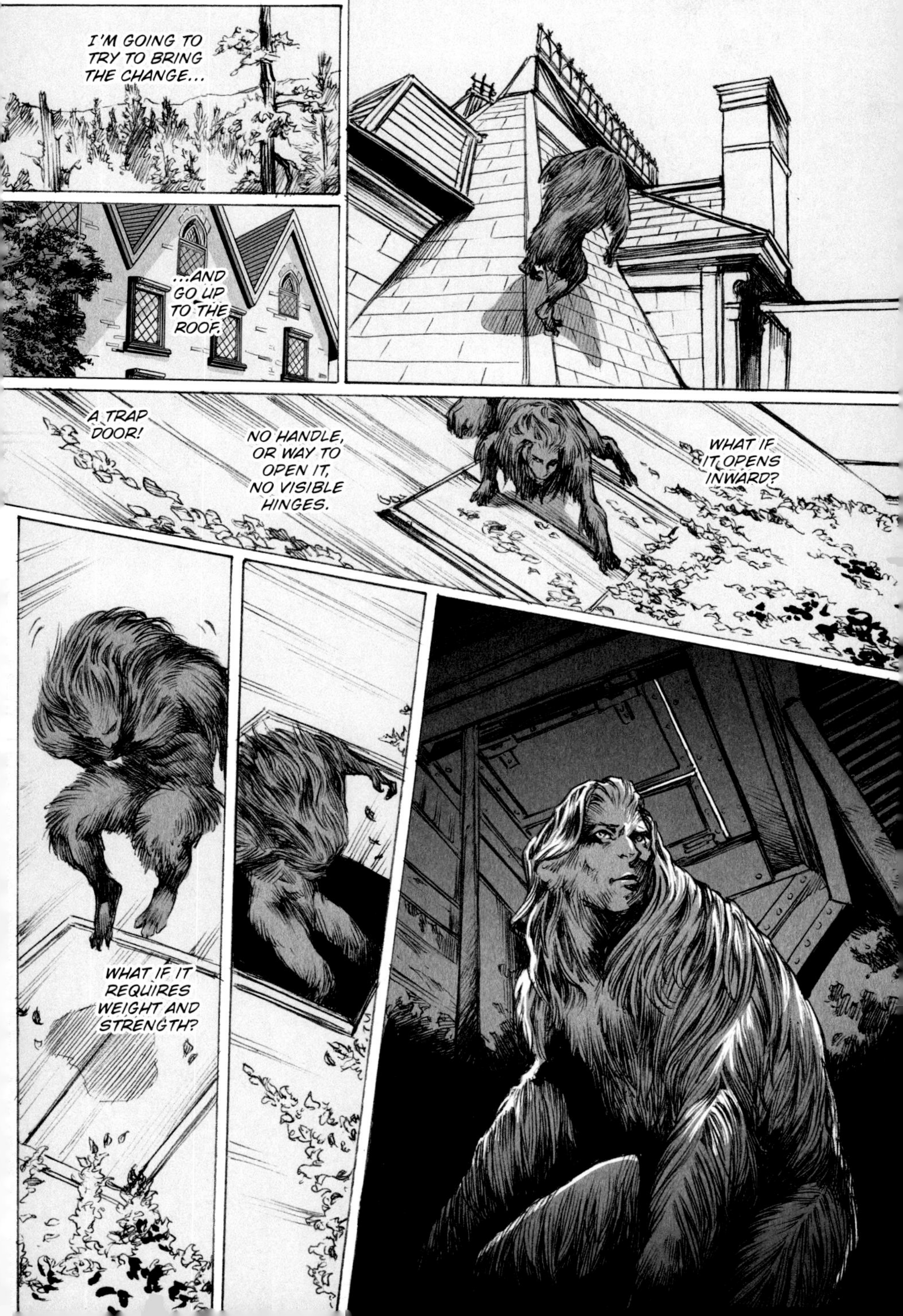
I'M GOING TO TRY TO BRING THE CHANGE...
...AND GO UP TO THE ROOF.
A TRAP DOOR!
NO HANDLE, OR WAY TO OPEN IT, NO VISIBLE HINGES.
WHAT IF IT OPENS INWARD?
WHAT IF IT REQUIRES WEIGHT AND STRENGTH?

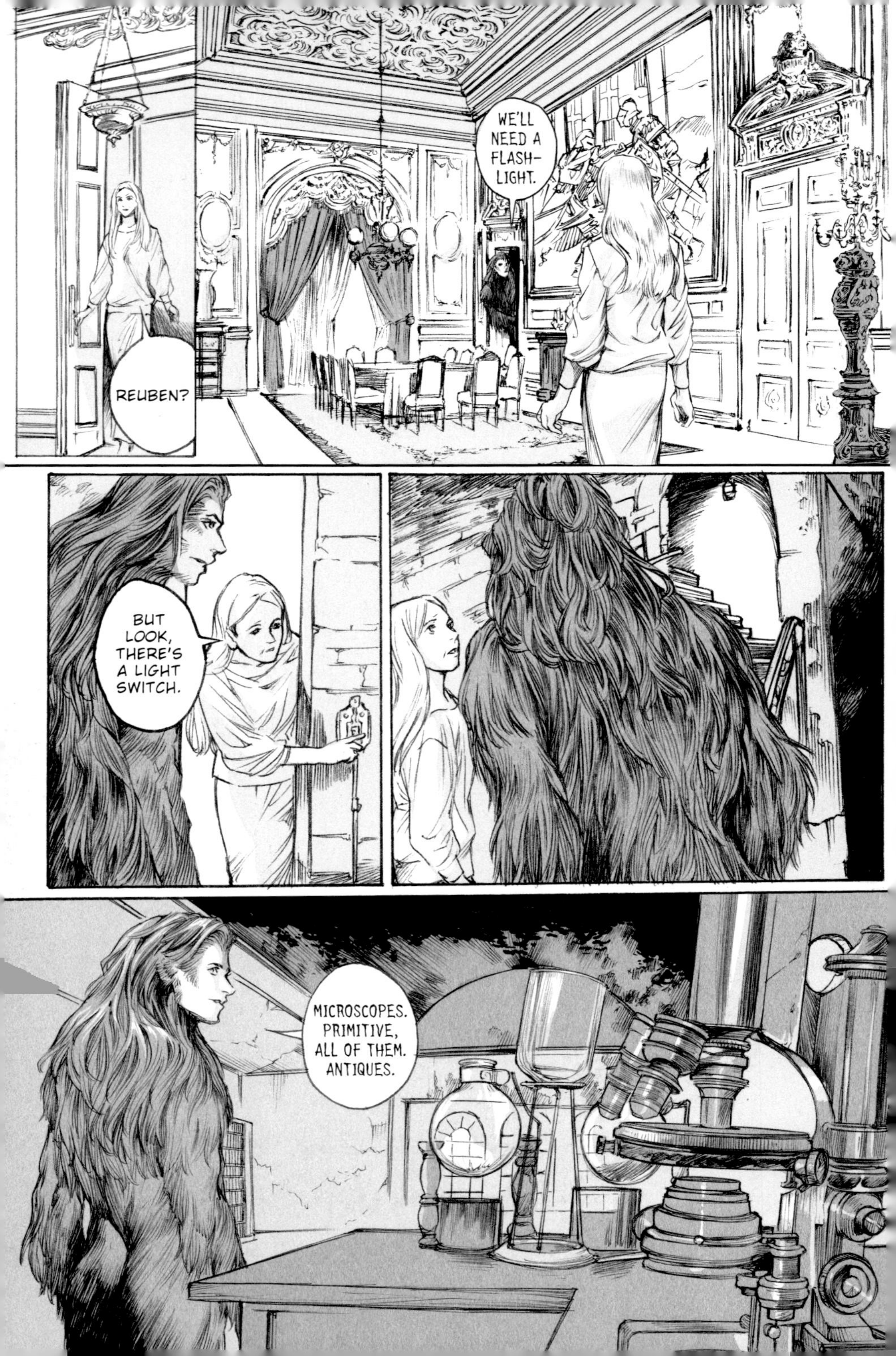
REUBEN?
WE'LL NEED A FLASH-LIGHT.
BUT LOOK, THERE'S A LIGHT SWITCH.
MICROSCOPES. PRIMITIVE, ALL OF THEM. ANTIQUES.

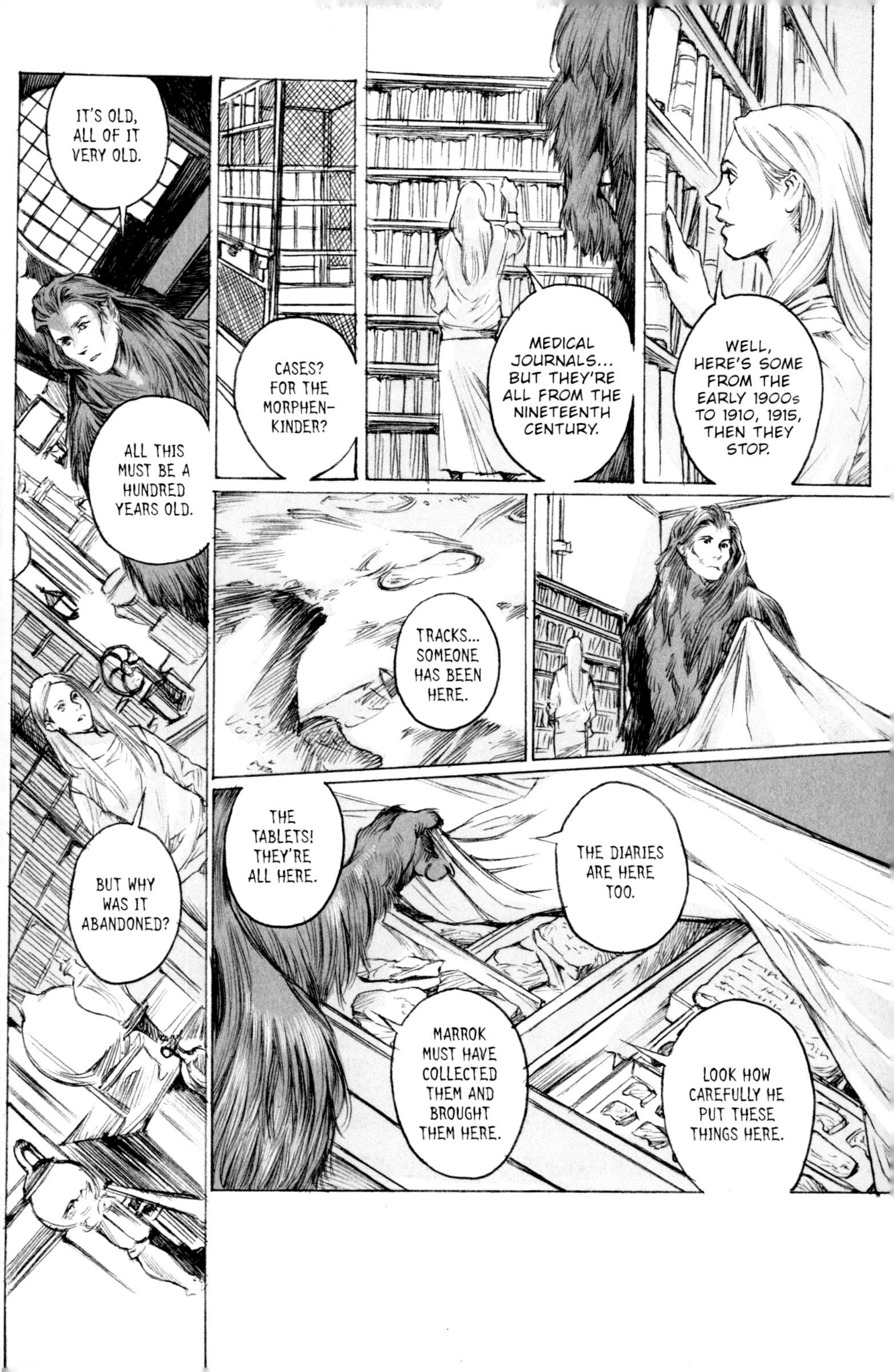
IT'S OLD, ALL OF IT VERY OLD.
ALL THIS MUST BE A HUNDRED YEARS OLD.
BUT WHY WAS IT ABANDONED?
CASES? FOR THE MORPHEN-KINDER?
MEDICAL JOURNALS... BUT THEY'RE ALL FROM THE NINETEENTH CENTURY.
WELL, HERE'S SOME FROM THE EARLY 1900s TO 1910, 1915, THEN THEY STOP.
TRACKS... SOMEONE HAS BEEN HERE.
THE TABLETS! THEY'RE ALL HERE.
THE DIARIES ARE HERE TOO.
MARROK MUST HAVE COLLECTED THEM AND BROUGHT THEM HERE.
LOOK HOW CAREFULLY HE PUT THESE THINGS HERE.

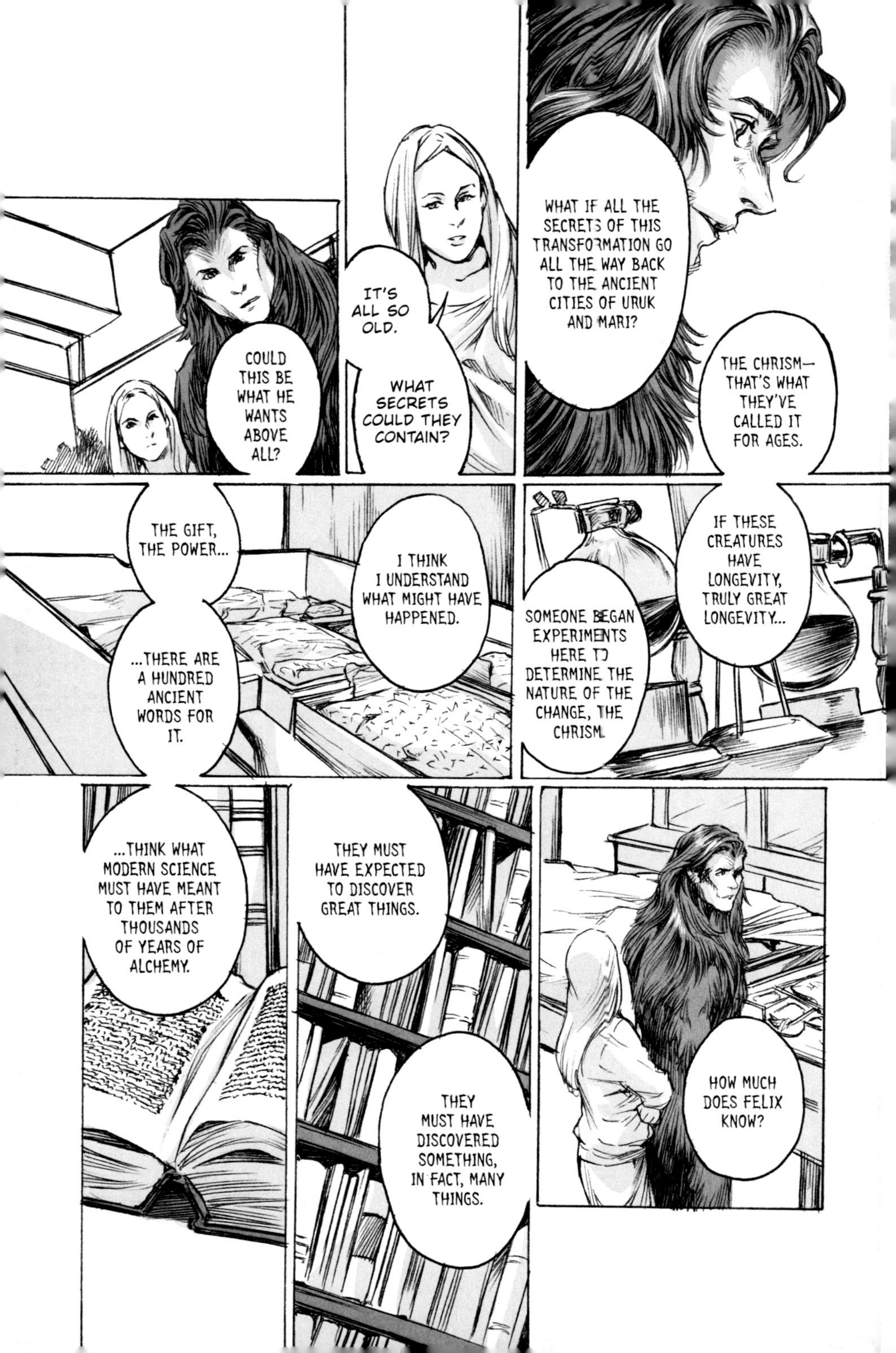
COULD THIS BE WHAT HE WANTS ABOVE ALL?
IT'S ALL SO OLD.
WHAT SECRETS COULD THEY CONTAIN?
WHAT IF ALL THE SECRETS OF THIS TRANSFORMATION GO ALL THE WAY BACK TO THE ANCIENT CITIES OF URUK AND MARI?
THE CHRISM—THAT'S WHAT THEY'VE CALLED IT FOR AGES.
THE GIFT, THE POWER...
...THERE ARE A HUNDRED ANCIENT WORDS FOR IT.
I THINK I UNDERSTAND WHAT MIGHT HAVE HAPPENED.
IF THESE CREATURES HAVE LONGEVITY, TRULY GREAT LONGEVITY...
SOMEONE BEGAN EXPERIMENTS HERE TO DETERMINE THE NATURE OF THE CHANGE, THE CHRISM.
...THINK WHAT MODERN SCIENCE MUST HAVE MEANT TO THEM AFTER THOUSANDS OF YEARS OF ALCHEMY.
THEY MUST HAVE EXPECTED TO DISCOVER GREAT THINGS.
THEY MUST HAVE DISCOVERED SOMETHING, IN FACT, MANY THINGS.
HOW MUCH DOES FELIX KNOW?

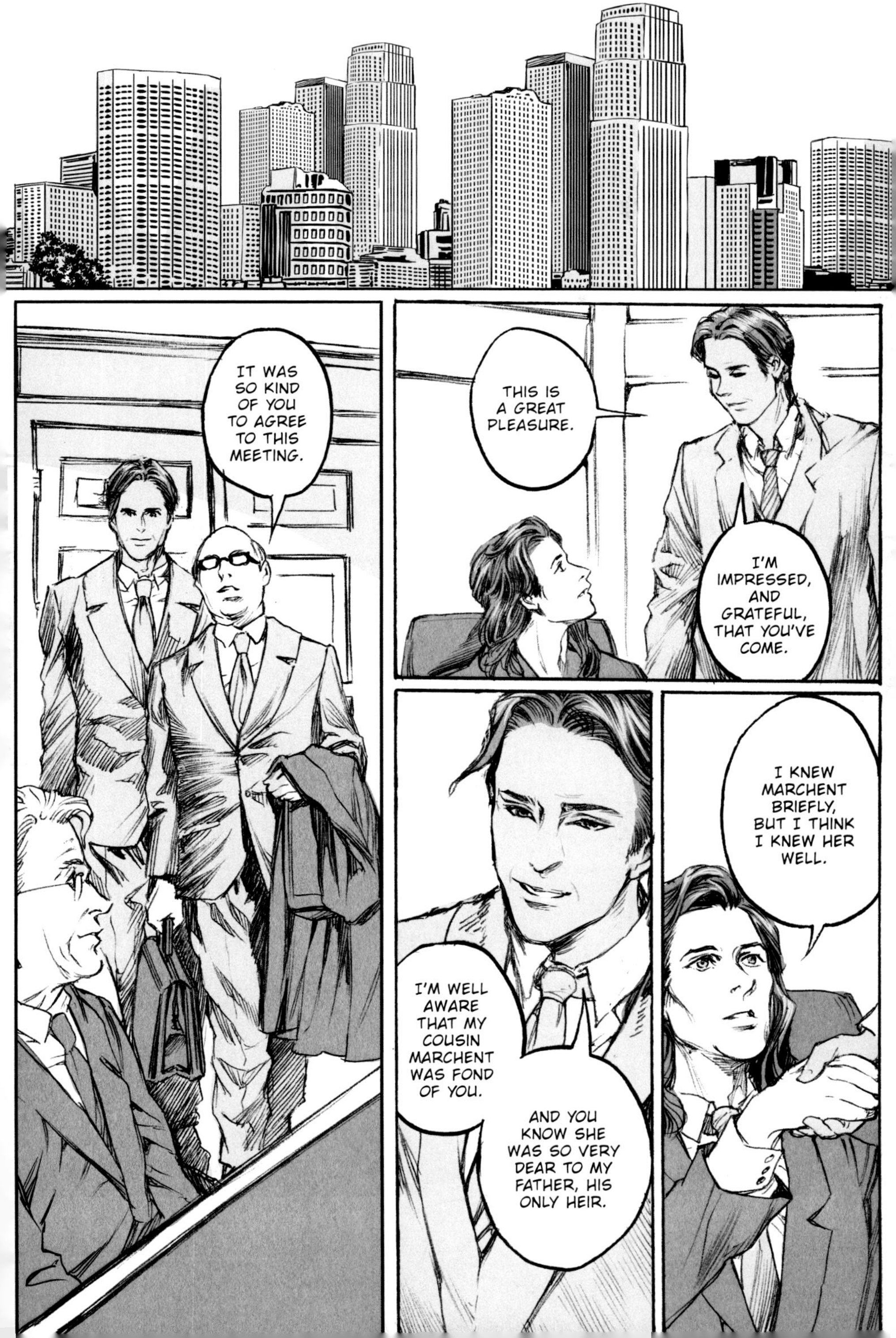

IT WAS SO KIND OF YOU TO AGREE TO THIS MEETING.
THIS IS A GREAT PLEASURE.
I'M IMPRESSED, AND GRATEFUL, THAT YOU'VE COME.
I'M WELL AWARE THAT MY COUSIN MARCHENT WAS FOND OF YOU.
AND YOU KNOW SHE WAS SO VERY DEAR TO MY FATHER, HIS ONLY HEIR.
I KNEW MARCHENT BRIEFLY, BUT I THINK I KNEW HER WELL.

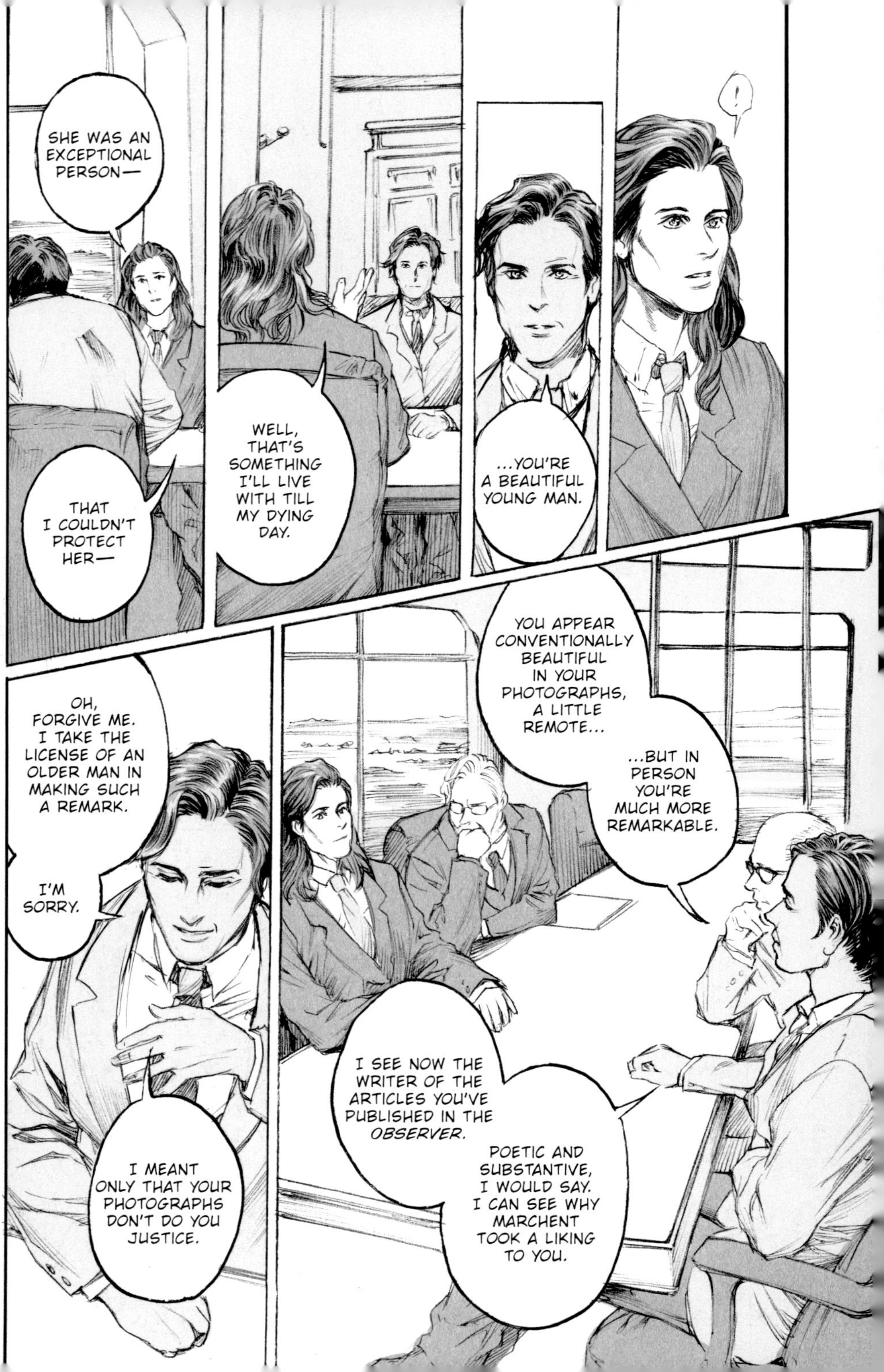
SHE WAS AN EXCEPTIONAL PERSON—
THAT I COULDN'T PROTECT HER—
WELL, THAT'S SOMETHING I'LL LIVE WITH TILL MY DYING DAY.
...YOU'RE A BEAUTIFUL YOUNG MAN.
!
YOU APPEAR CONVENTIONALLY BEAUTIFUL IN YOUR PHOTOGRAPHS, A LITTLE REMOTE...
...BUT IN PERSON YOU'RE MUCH MORE REMARKABLE.
OH, FORGIVE ME. I TAKE THE LICENSE OF AN OLDER MAN IN MAKING SUCH A REMARK.
I'M SORRY.
I MEANT ONLY THAT YOUR PHOTOGRAPHS DON'T DO YOU JUSTICE.
I SEE NOW THE WRITER OF THE ARTICLES YOU'VE PUBLISHED IN THE *OBSERVER*.
POETIC AND SUBSTANTIVE, I WOULD SAY. I CAN SEE WHY MARCHENT TOOK A LIKING TO YOU.

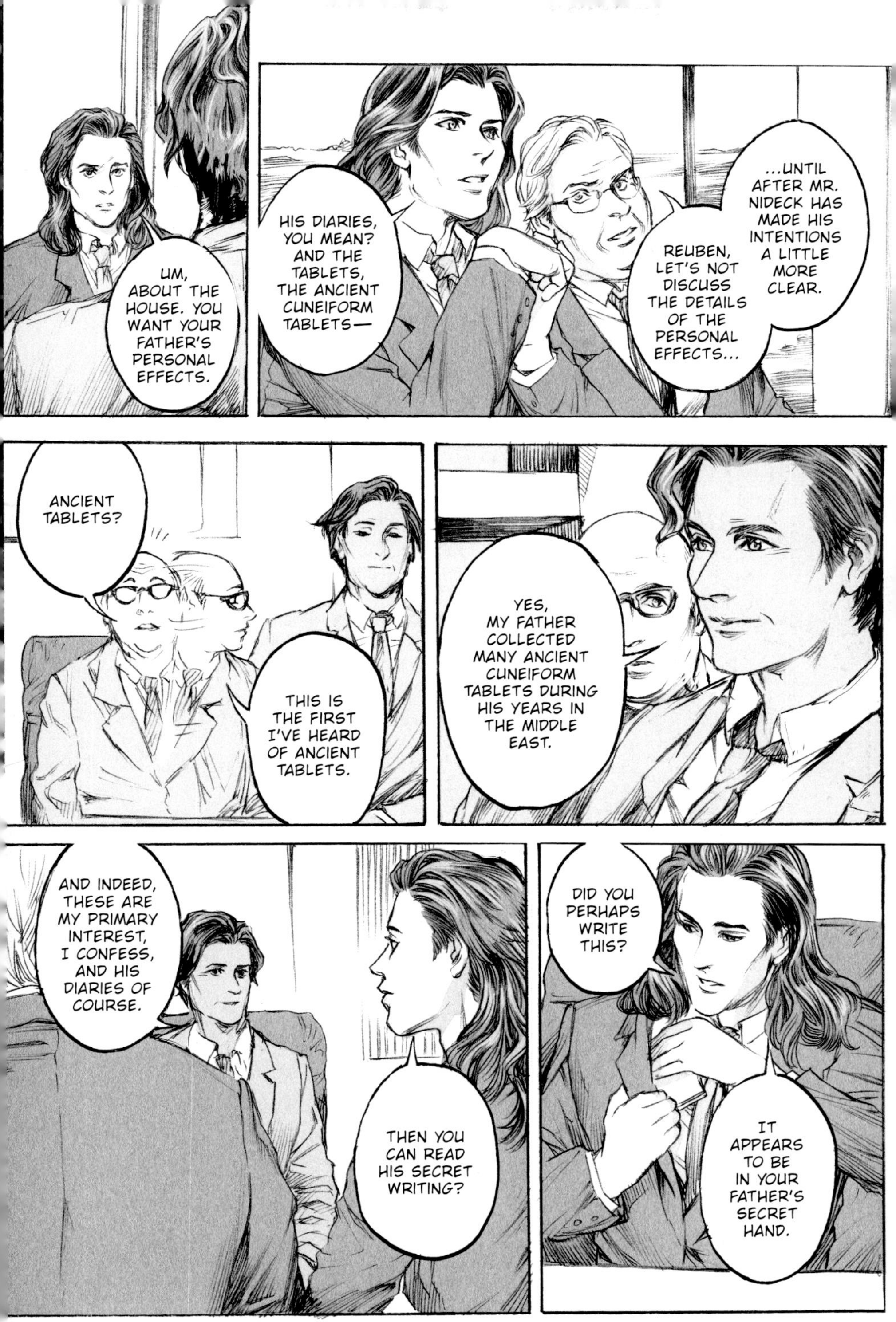
UM, ABOUT THE HOUSE. YOU WANT YOUR FATHER'S PERSONAL EFFECTS.
HIS DIARIES, YOU MEAN? AND THE TABLETS, THE ANCIENT CUNEIFORM TABLETS—
REUBEN, LET'S NOT DISCUSS THE DETAILS OF THE PERSONAL EFFECTS...
...UNTIL AFTER MR. NIDECK HAS MADE HIS INTENTIONS A LITTLE MORE CLEAR.
ANCIENT TABLETS?
THIS IS THE FIRST I'VE HEARD OF ANCIENT TABLETS.
YES, MY FATHER COLLECTED MANY ANCIENT CUNEIFORM TABLETS DURING HIS YEARS IN THE MIDDLE EAST.
AND INDEED, THESE ARE MY PRIMARY INTEREST, I CONFESS, AND HIS DIARIES OF COURSE.
THEN YOU CAN READ HIS SECRET WRITING?
DID YOU PERHAPS WRITE THIS?
IT APPEARS TO BE IN YOUR FATHER'S SECRET HAND.

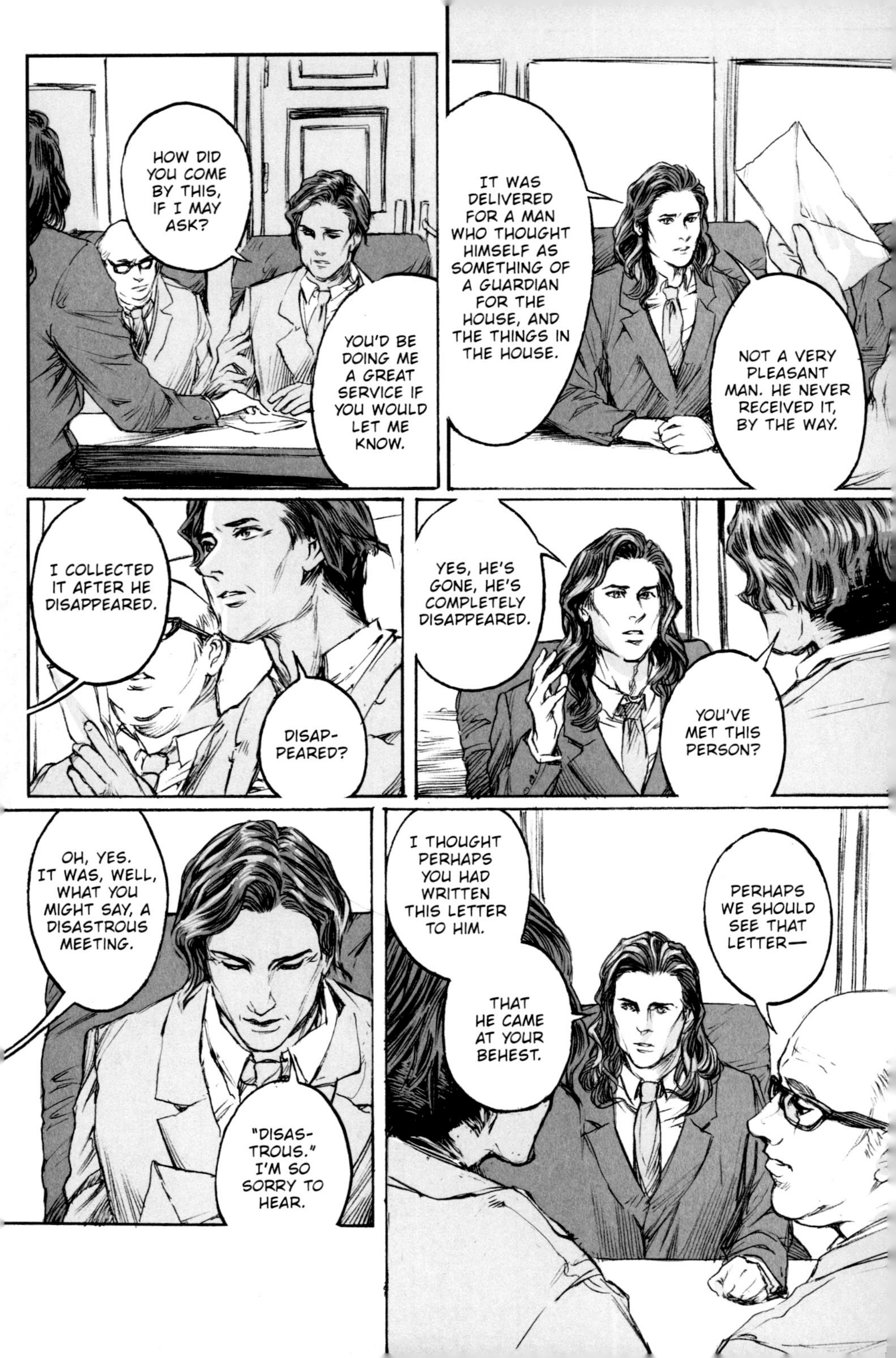
HOW DID YOU COME BY THIS, IF I MAY ASK?
YOU'D BE DOING ME A GREAT SERVICE IF YOU WOULD LET ME KNOW.
IT WAS DELIVERED FOR A MAN WHO THOUGHT HIMSELF AS SOMETHING OF A GUARDIAN FOR THE HOUSE, AND THE THINGS IN THE HOUSE.
NOT A VERY PLEASANT MAN. HE NEVER RECEIVED IT, BY THE WAY.
I COLLECTED IT AFTER HE DISAPPEARED.
DISAP-PEARED?
YES, HE'S GONE, HE'S COMPLETELY DISAPPEARED.
YOU'VE MET THIS PERSON?
OH, YES. IT WAS, WELL, WHAT YOU MIGHT SAY, A DISASTROUS MEETING.
"DISAS-TROUS." I'M SO SORRY TO HEAR.
I THOUGHT PERHAPS YOU HAD WRITTEN THIS LETTER TO HIM.
THAT HE CAME AT YOUR BEHEST.
PERHAPS WE SHOULD SEE THAT LETTER—

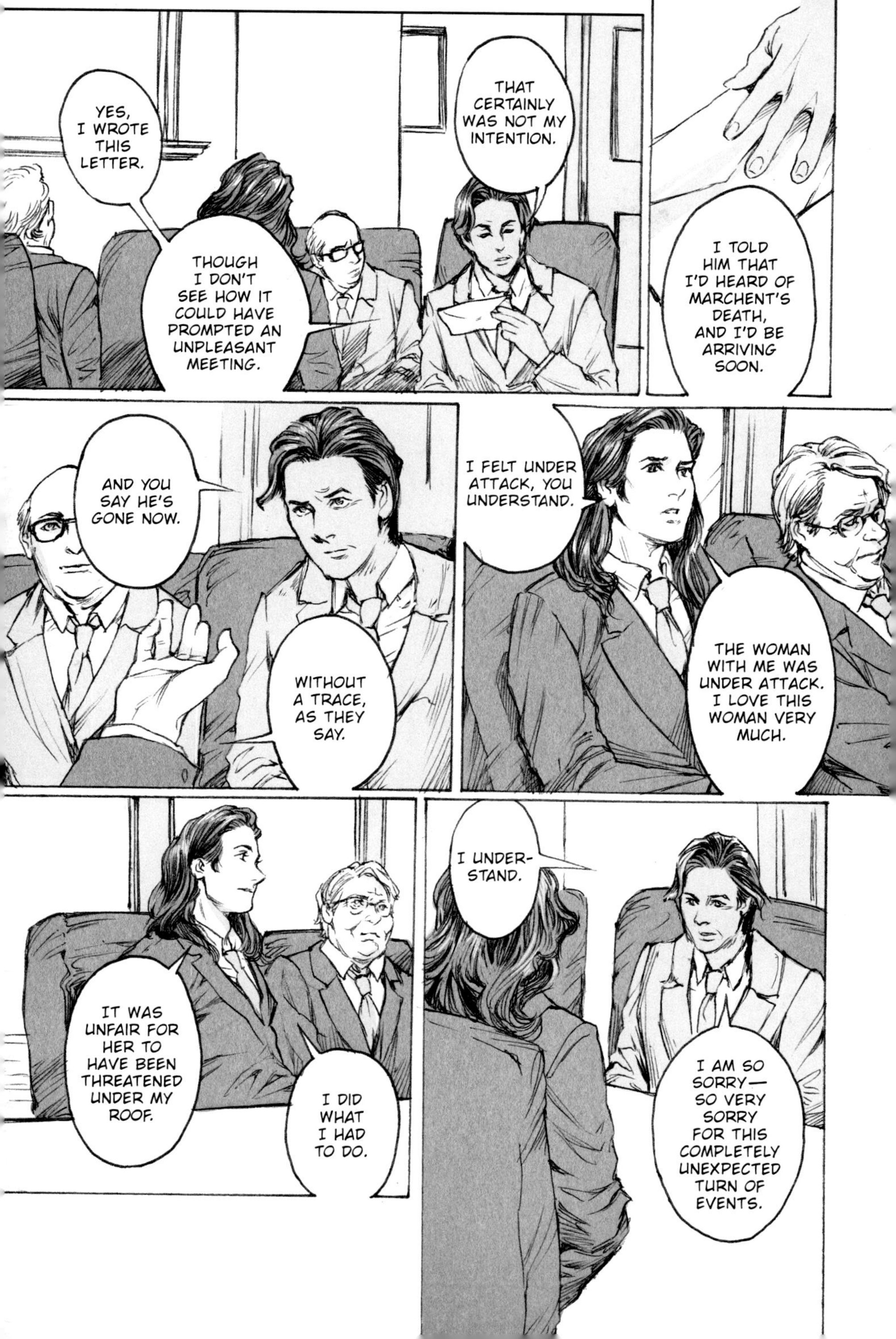
YES, I WROTE THIS LETTER.
THOUGH I DON'T SEE HOW IT COULD HAVE PROMPTED AN UNPLEASANT MEETING.
THAT CERTAINLY WAS NOT MY INTENTION.
I TOLD HIM THAT I'D HEARD OF MARCHENT'S DEATH, AND I'D BE ARRIVING SOON.
AND YOU SAY HE'S GONE NOW.
WITHOUT A TRACE, AS THEY SAY.
I FELT UNDER ATTACK, YOU UNDERSTAND.
THE WOMAN WITH ME WAS UNDER ATTACK. I LOVE THIS WOMAN VERY MUCH.
IT WAS UNFAIR FOR HER TO HAVE BEEN THREATENED UNDER MY ROOF.
I DID WHAT I HAD TO DO.
I UNDER-STAND.
I AM SO SORRY— SO VERY SORRY FOR THIS COMPLETELY UNEXPECTED TURN OF EVENTS.

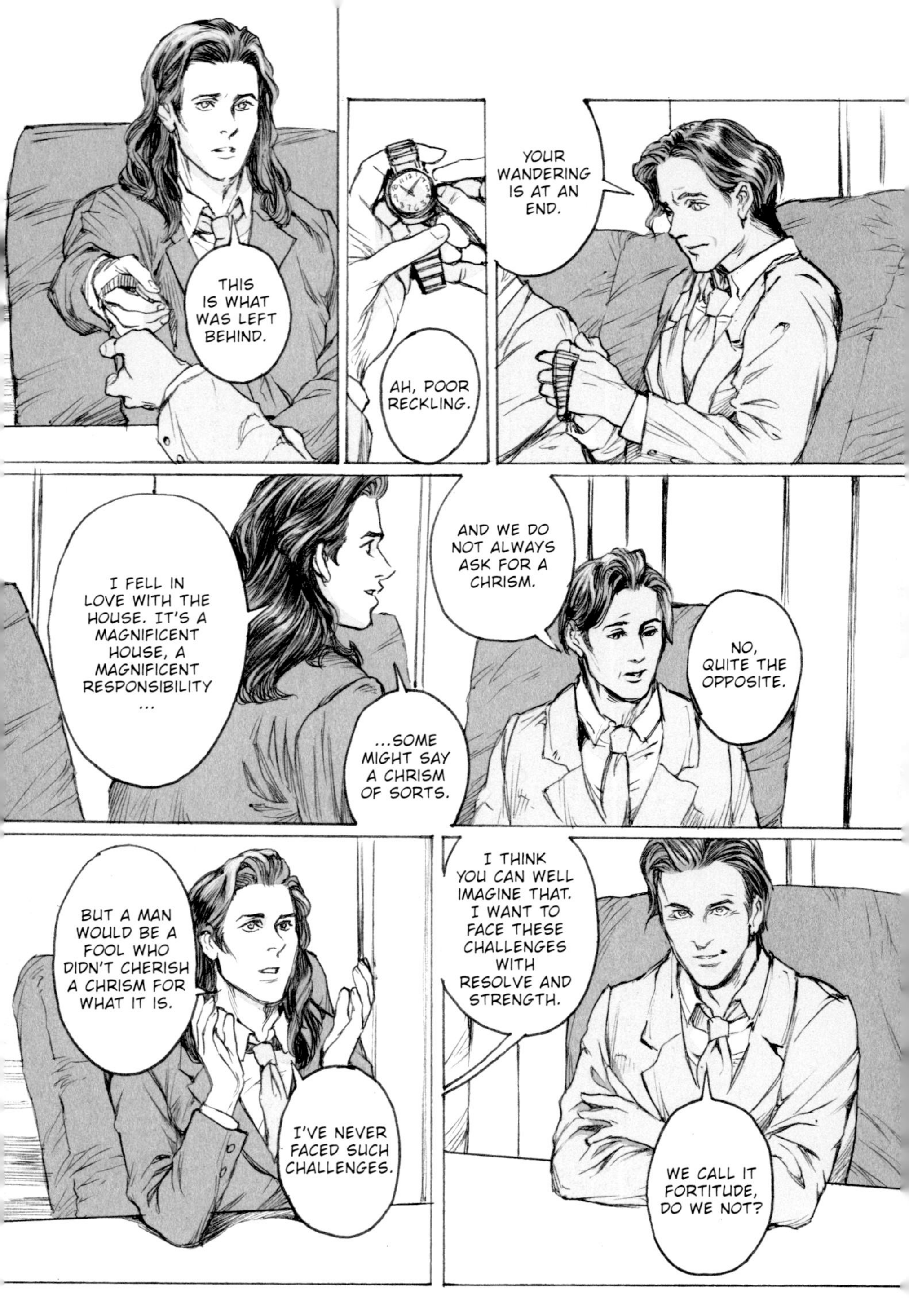
THIS IS WHAT WAS LEFT BEHIND.
AH, POOR RECKLING.
YOUR WANDERING IS AT AN END.
I FELL IN LOVE WITH THE HOUSE. IT'S A MAGNIFICENT HOUSE, A MAGNIFICENT RESPONSIBILITY ...
...SOME MIGHT SAY A CHRISM OF SORTS.
AND WE DO NOT ALWAYS ASK FOR A CHRISM.
NO, QUITE THE OPPOSITE.
BUT A MAN WOULD BE A FOOL WHO DIDN'T CHERISH A CHRISM FOR WHAT IT IS.
I'VE NEVER FACED SUCH CHALLENGES.
I THINK YOU CAN WELL IMAGINE THAT. I WANT TO FACE THESE CHALLENGES WITH RESOLVE AND STRENGTH.
WE CALL IT FORTITUDE, DO WE NOT?

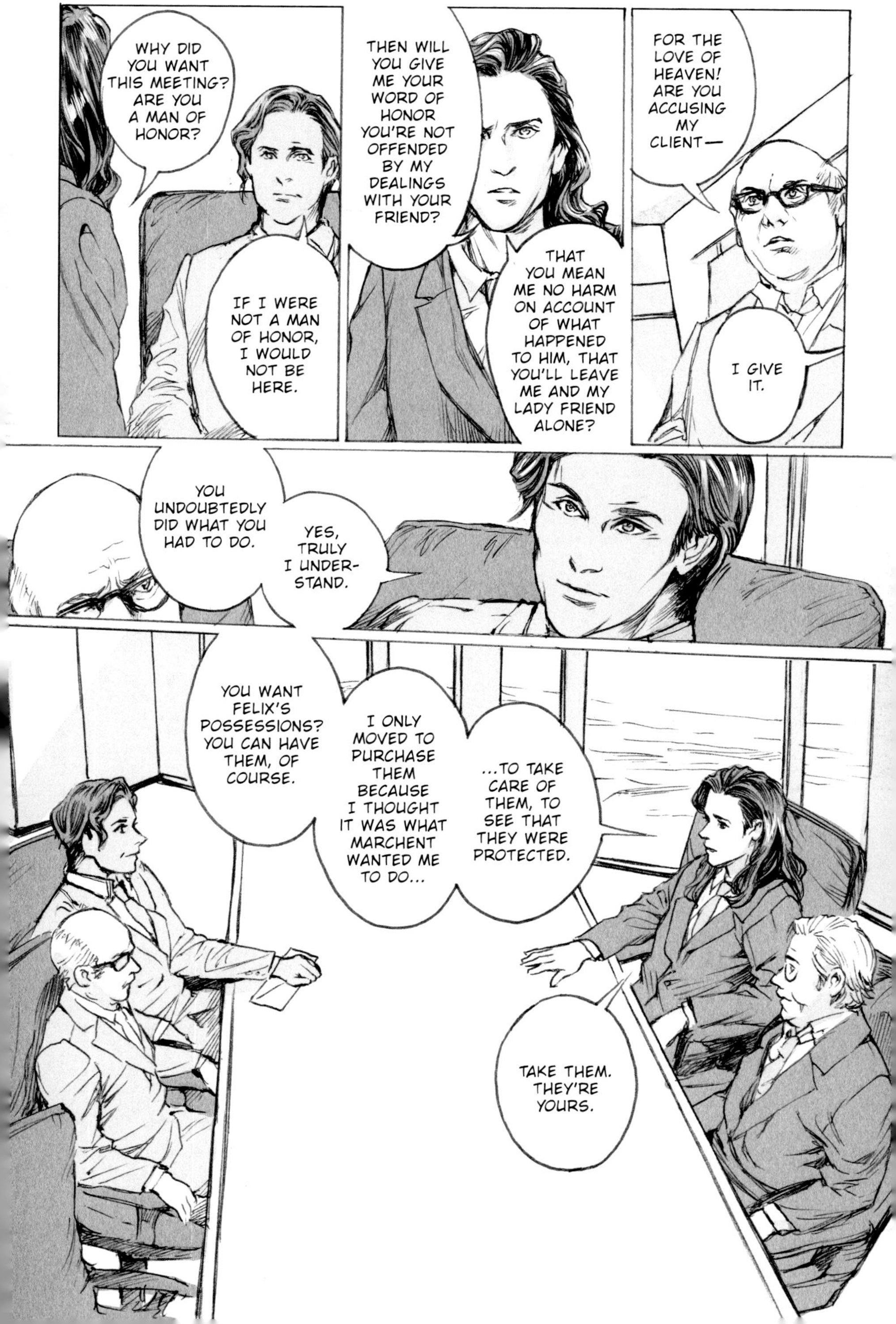
WHY DID YOU WANT THIS MEETING? ARE YOU A MAN OF HONOR?
IF I WERE NOT A MAN OF HONOR, I WOULD NOT BE HERE.
THEN WILL YOU GIVE ME YOUR WORD OF HONOR YOU'RE NOT OFFENDED BY MY DEALINGS WITH YOUR FRIEND?
THAT YOU MEAN ME NO HARM ON ACCOUNT OF WHAT HAPPENED TO HIM, THAT YOU'LL LEAVE ME AND MY LADY FRIEND ALONE?
FOR THE LOVE OF HEAVEN! ARE YOU ACCUSING MY CLIENT—
I GIVE IT.
YOU UNDOUBTEDLY DID WHAT YOU HAD TO DO.
YES, TRULY I UNDER-STAND.
YOU WANT FELIX'S POSSESSIONS? YOU CAN HAVE THEM, OF COURSE.
I ONLY MOVED TO PURCHASE THEM BECAUSE I THOUGHT IT WAS WHAT MARCHENT WANTED ME TO DO...
...TO TAKE CARE OF THEM, TO SEE THAT THEY WERE PROTECTED.
TAKE THEM. THEY'RE YOURS.

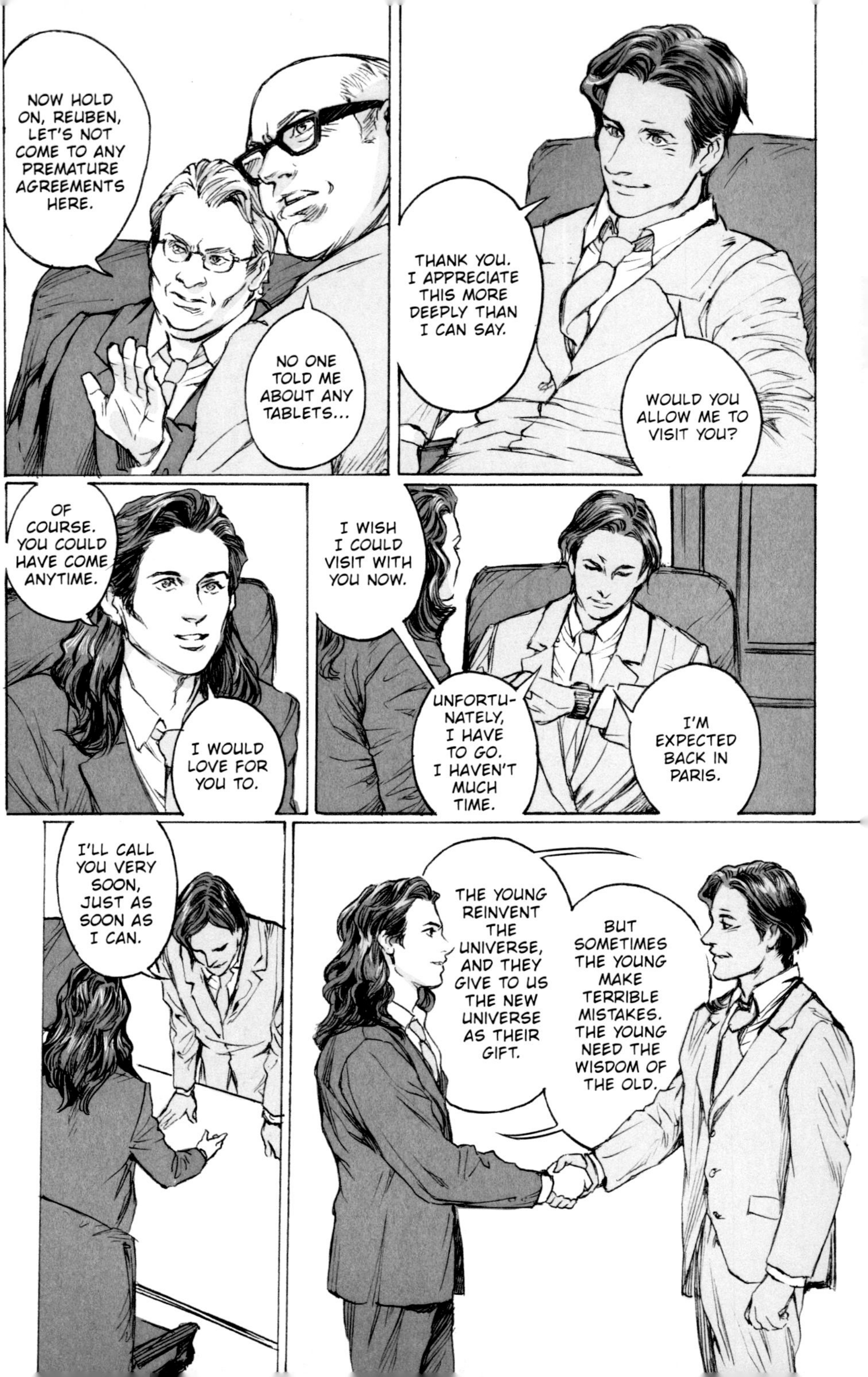
NOW HOLD ON, REUBEN, LET'S NOT COME TO ANY PREMATURE AGREEMENTS HERE.
NO ONE TOLD ME ABOUT ANY TABLETS...
THANK YOU. I APPRECIATE THIS MORE DEEPLY THAN I CAN SAY.
WOULD YOU ALLOW ME TO VISIT YOU?
OF COURSE. YOU COULD HAVE COME ANYTIME.
I WOULD LOVE FOR YOU TO.
I WISH I COULD VISIT WITH YOU NOW.
UNFORTU-NATELY, I HAVE TO GO. I HAVEN'T MUCH TIME.
I'M EXPECTED BACK IN PARIS.
I'LL CALL YOU VERY SOON, JUST AS SOON AS I CAN.
THE YOUNG REINVENT THE UNIVERSE, AND THEY GIVE TO US THE NEW UNIVERSE AS THEIR GIFT.
BUT SOMETIMES THE YOUNG MAKE TERRIBLE MISTAKES. THE YOUNG NEED THE WISDOM OF THE OLD.

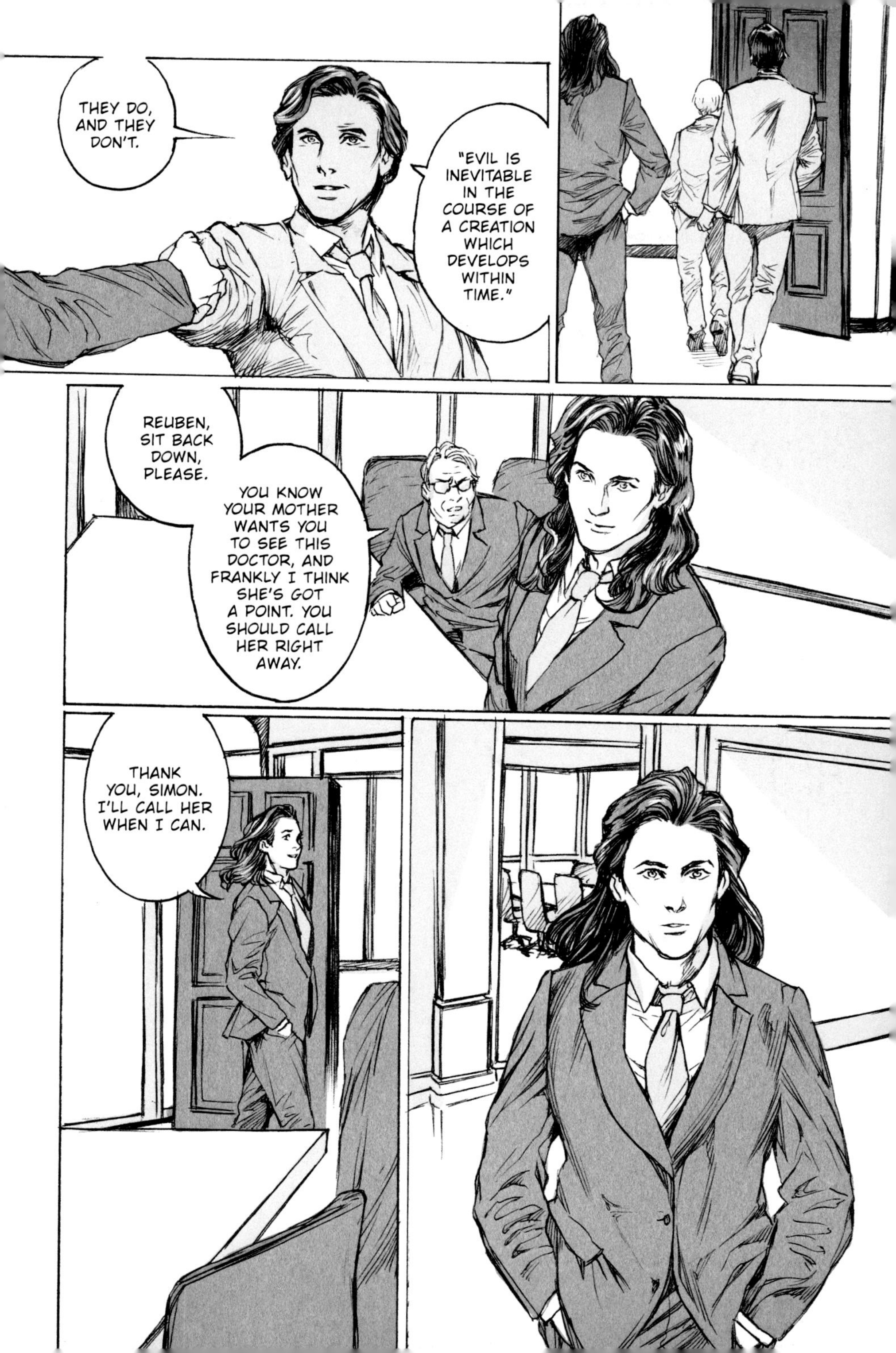
THEY DO, AND THEY DON'T.
"EVIL IS INEVITABLE IN THE COURSE OF A CREATION WHICH DEVELOPS WITHIN TIME."
REUBEN, SIT BACK DOWN, PLEASE.
YOU KNOW YOUR MOTHER WANTS YOU TO SEE THIS DOCTOR, AND FRANKLY I THINK SHE'S GOT A POINT. YOU SHOULD CALL HER RIGHT AWAY.
THANK YOU, SIMON. I'LL CALL HER WHEN I CAN.

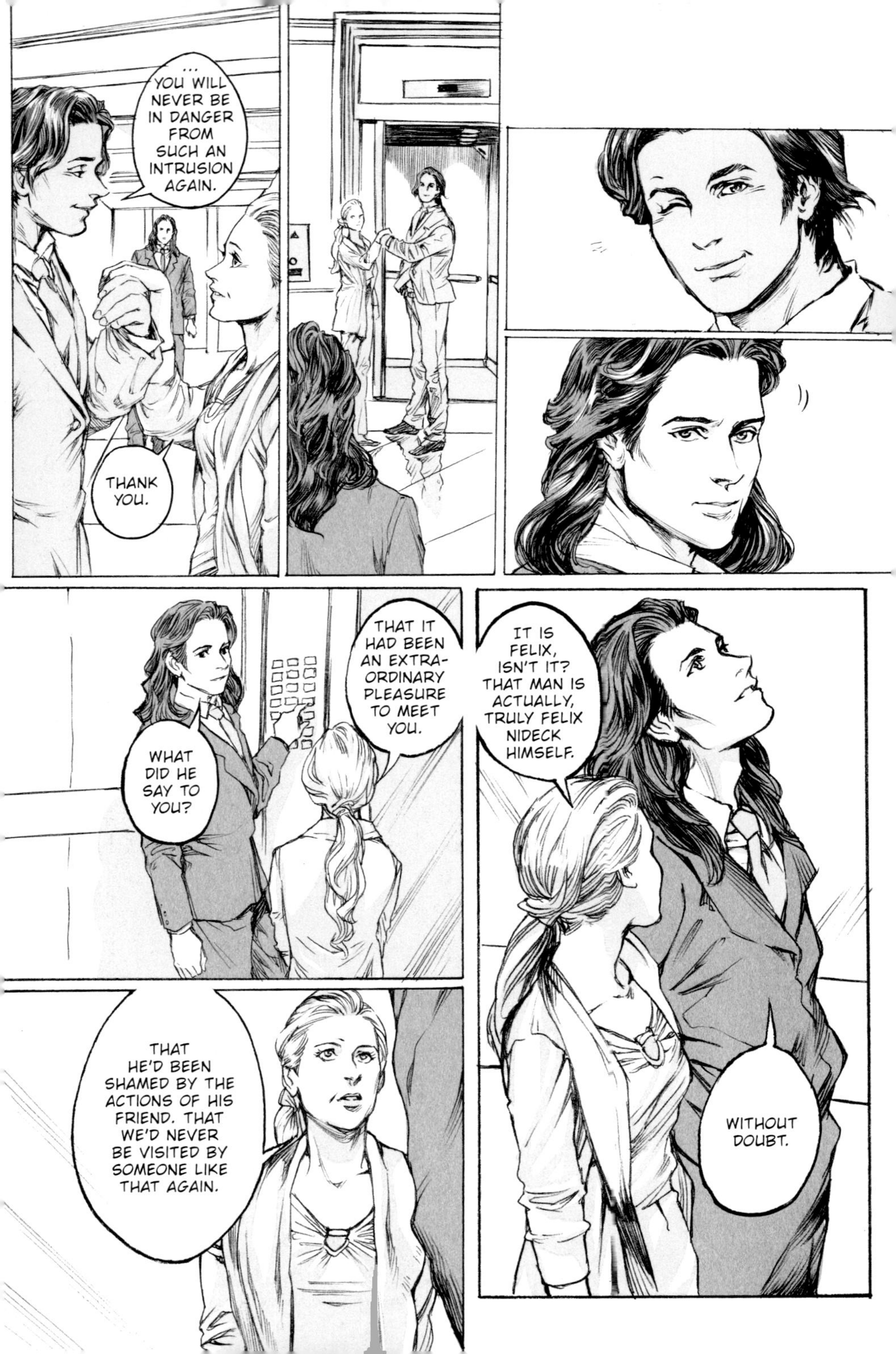
...YOU WILL NEVER BE IN DANGER FROM SUCH AN INTRUSION AGAIN.
THANK YOU.
WHAT DID HE SAY TO YOU?
THAT IT HAD BEEN AN EXTRA-ORDINARY PLEASURE TO MEET YOU.
THAT HE'D BEEN SHAMED BY THE ACTIONS OF HIS FRIEND. THAT WE'D NEVER BE VISITED BY SOMEONE LIKE THAT AGAIN.
IT IS FELIX, ISN'T IT? THAT MAN IS ACTUALLY, TRULY FELIX NIDECK HIMSELF.
WITHOUT DOUBT.

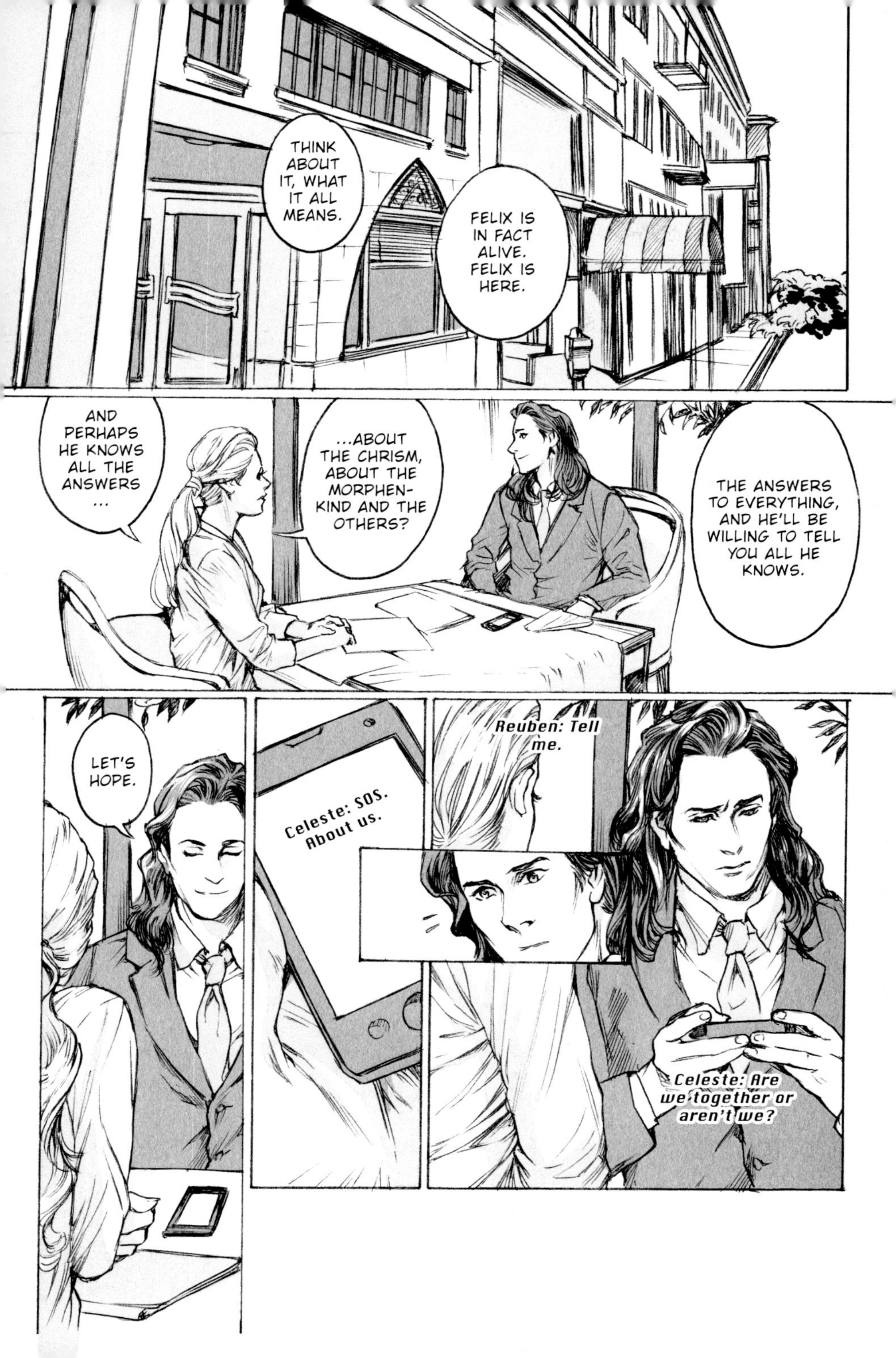
THINK ABOUT IT, WHAT IT ALL MEANS.
FELIX IS IN FACT ALIVE. FELIX IS HERE.
AND PERHAPS HE KNOWS ALL THE ANSWERS ...
...ABOUT THE CHRISM, ABOUT THE MORPHEN-KIND AND THE OTHERS?
THE ANSWERS TO EVERYTHING, AND HE'LL BE WILLING TO TELL YOU ALL HE KNOWS.
LET'S HOPE.
Celeste: SOS. About us.
Reuben: Tell me.
Celeste: Are we together or aren't we?

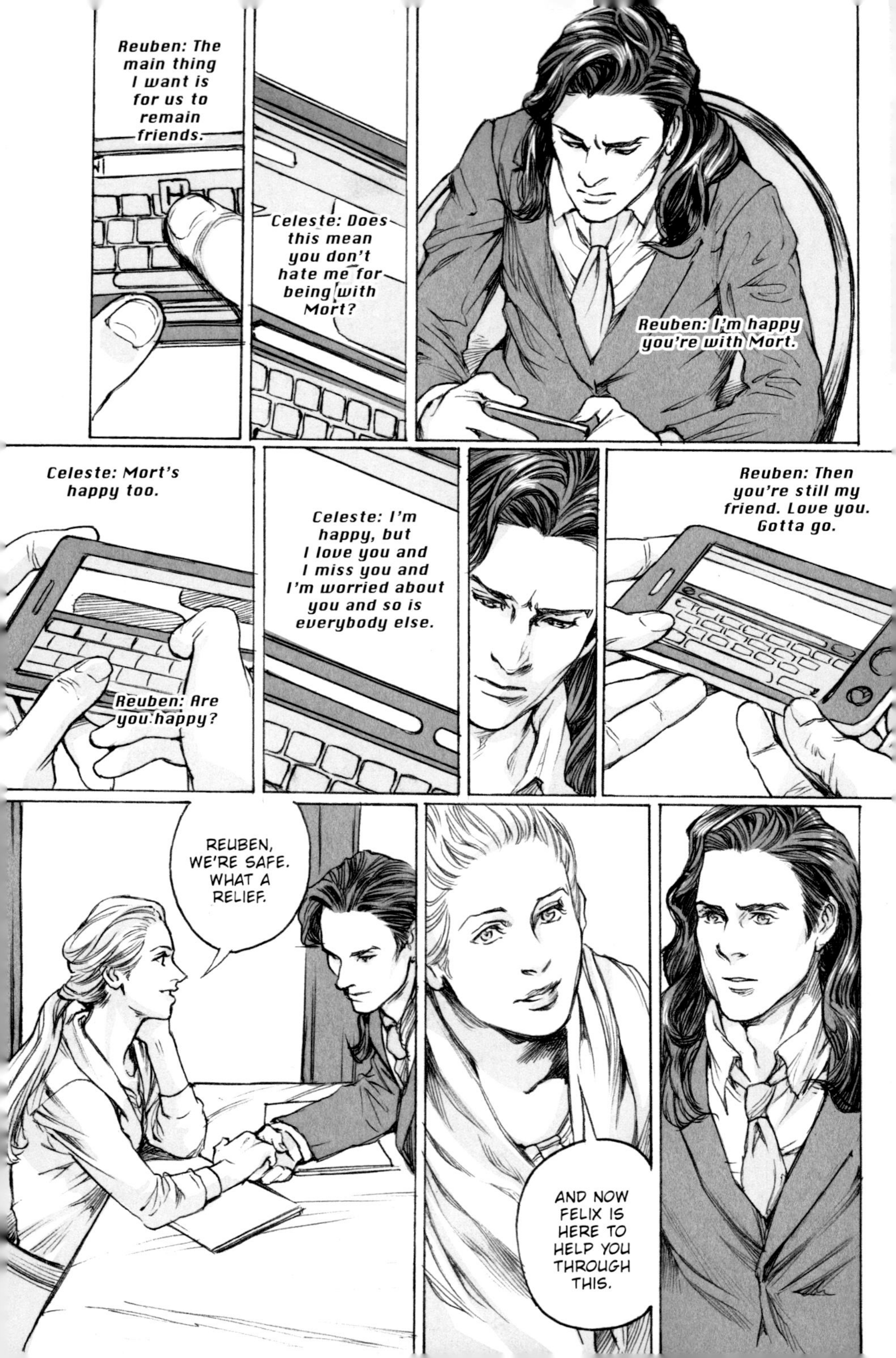
Reuben: The main thing I want is for us to remain friends.
Celeste: Does this mean you don't hate me for being with Mort?
Reuben: I'm happy you're with Mort.
Celeste: Mort's happy too.
Reuben: Are you happy?
Celeste: I'm happy, but I love you and I miss you and I'm worried about you and so is everybody else.
Reuben: Then you're still my friend. Love you. Gotta go.
REUBEN, WE'RE SAFE. WHAT A RELIEF.
AND NOW FELIX IS HERE TO HELP YOU THROUGH THIS.

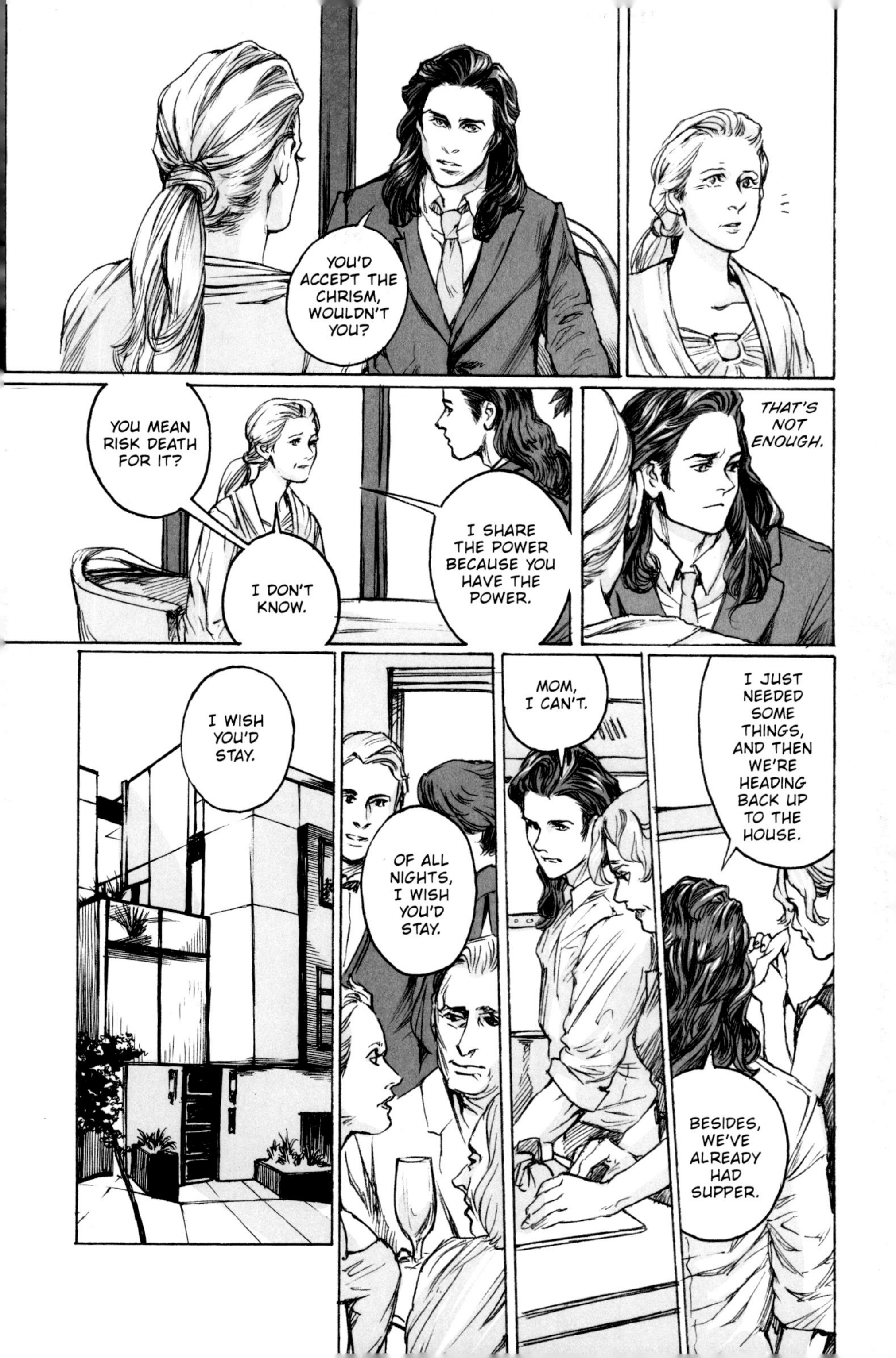
YOU'D ACCEPT THE CHRISM, WOULDN'T YOU?
YOU MEAN RISK DEATH FOR IT?
I DON'T KNOW.
I SHARE THE POWER BECAUSE YOU HAVE THE POWER.
THAT'S NOT ENOUGH.
I WISH YOU'D STAY.
OF ALL NIGHTS, I WISH YOU'D STAY.
MOM, I CAN'T.
I JUST NEEDED SOME THINGS, AND THEN WE'RE HEADING BACK UP TO THE HOUSE.
BESIDES, WE'VE ALREADY HAD SUPPER.

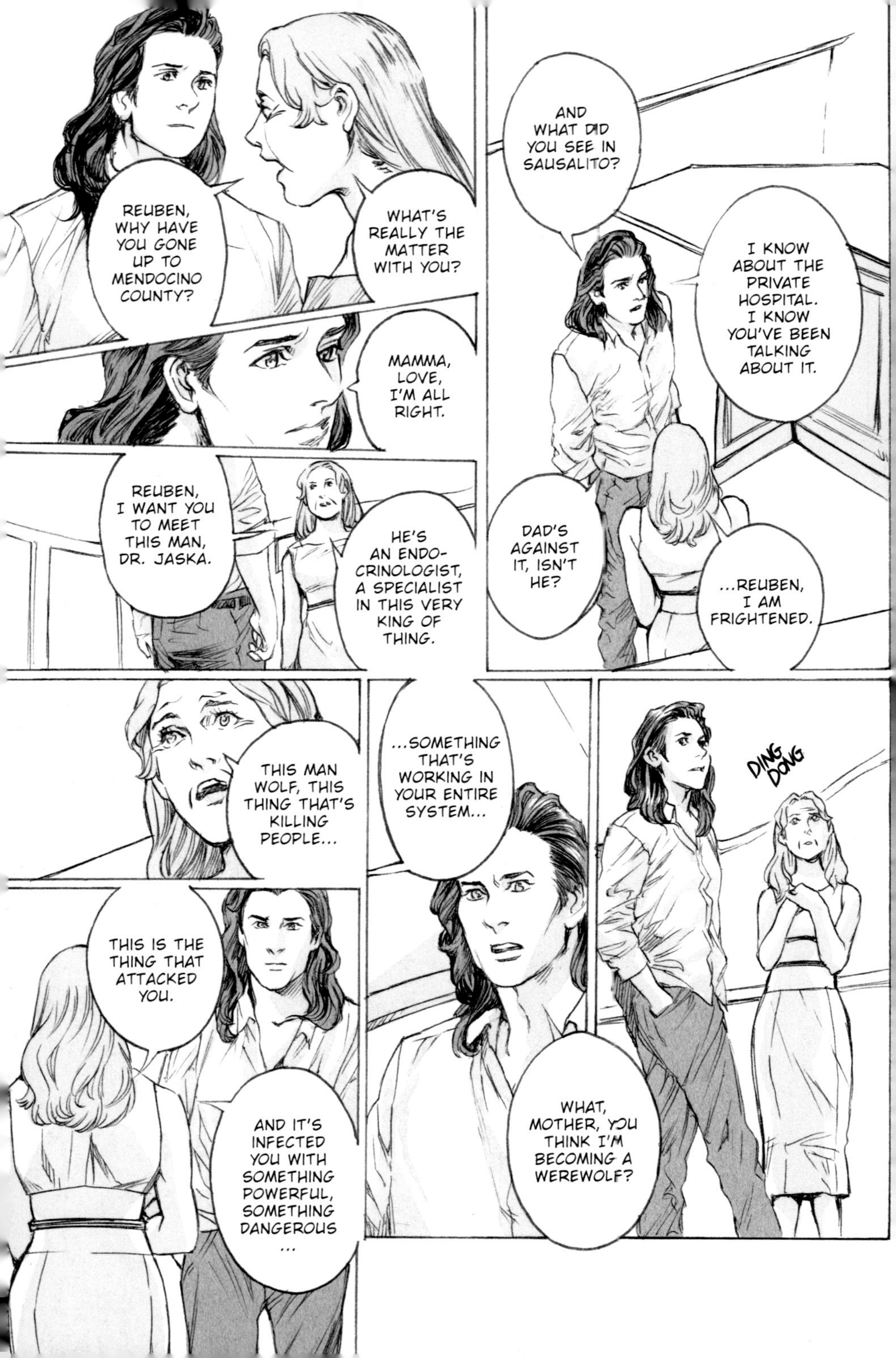

REUBEN, WHY HAVE YOU GONE UP TO MENDOCINO COUNTY?
WHAT'S REALLY THE MATTER WITH YOU?
MAMMA, LOVE, I'M ALL RIGHT.
REUBEN, I WANT YOU TO MEET THIS MAN, DR. JASKA.
HE'S AN ENDO-CRINOLOGIST, A SPECIALIST IN THIS VERY KING OF THING.
AND WHAT DID YOU SEE IN SAUSALITO?
I KNOW ABOUT THE PRIVATE HOSPITAL. I KNOW YOU'VE BEEN TALKING ABOUT IT.
DAD'S AGAINST IT, ISN'T HE?
...REUBEN, I AM FRIGHTENED.
THIS MAN WOLF, THIS THING THAT'S KILLING PEOPLE...
THIS IS THE THING THAT ATTACKED YOU.
AND IT'S INFECTED YOU WITH SOMETHING POWERFUL, SOMETHING DANGEROUS ...
...SOMETHING THAT'S WORKING IN YOUR ENTIRE SYSTEM...
WHAT, MOTHER, YOU THINK I'M BECOMING A WEREWOLF?
DING DONG

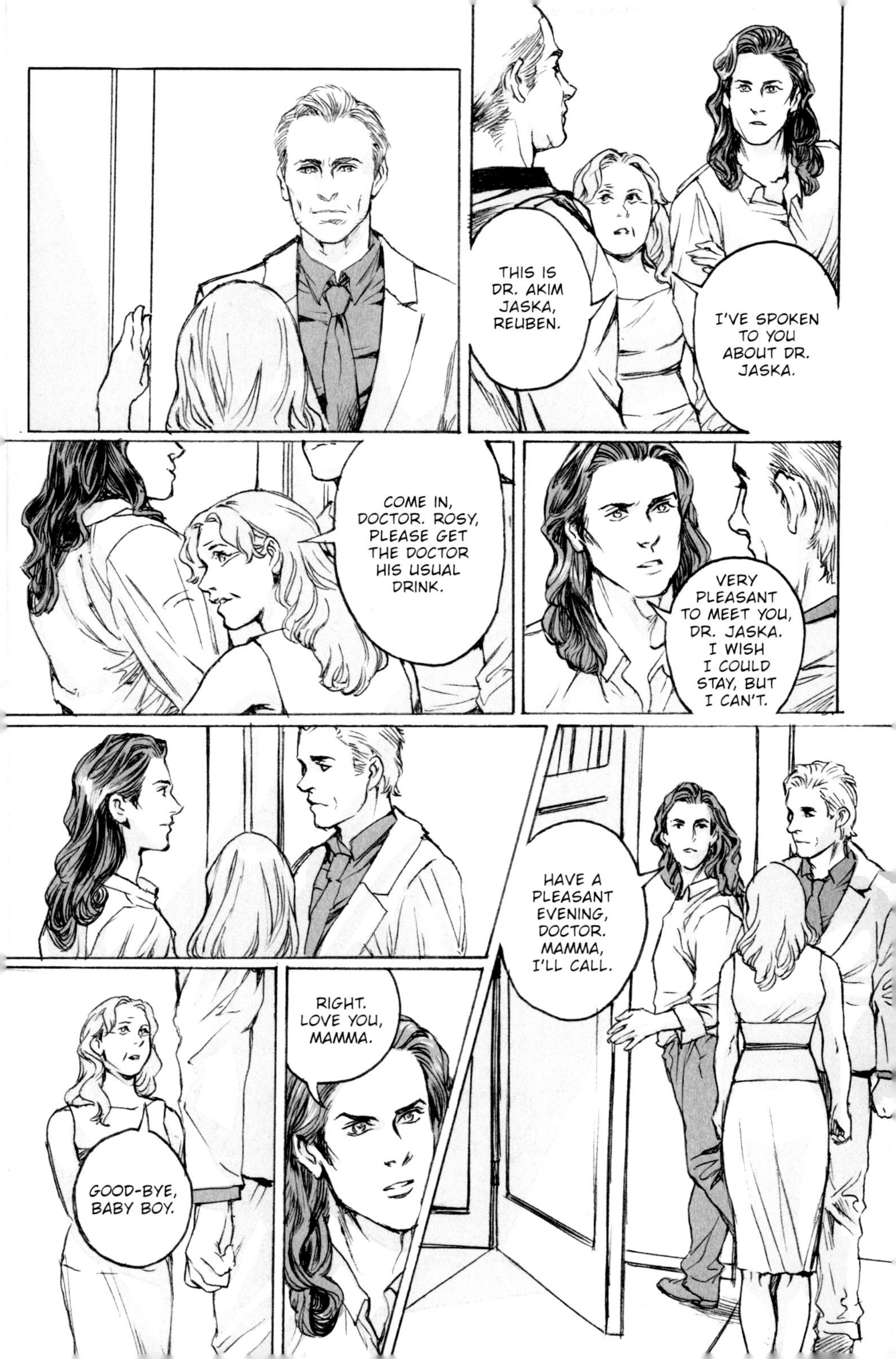
THIS IS DR. AKIM JASKA, REUBEN.
I'VE SPOKEN TO YOU ABOUT DR. JASKA.
COME IN, DOCTOR. ROSY, PLEASE GET THE DOCTOR HIS USUAL DRINK.
VERY PLEASANT TO MEET YOU, DR. JASKA. I WISH I COULD STAY, BUT I CAN'T.
HAVE A PLEASANT EVENING, DOCTOR. MAMMA, I'LL CALL.
GOOD-BYE, BABY BOY.
RIGHT. LOVE YOU, MAMMA.

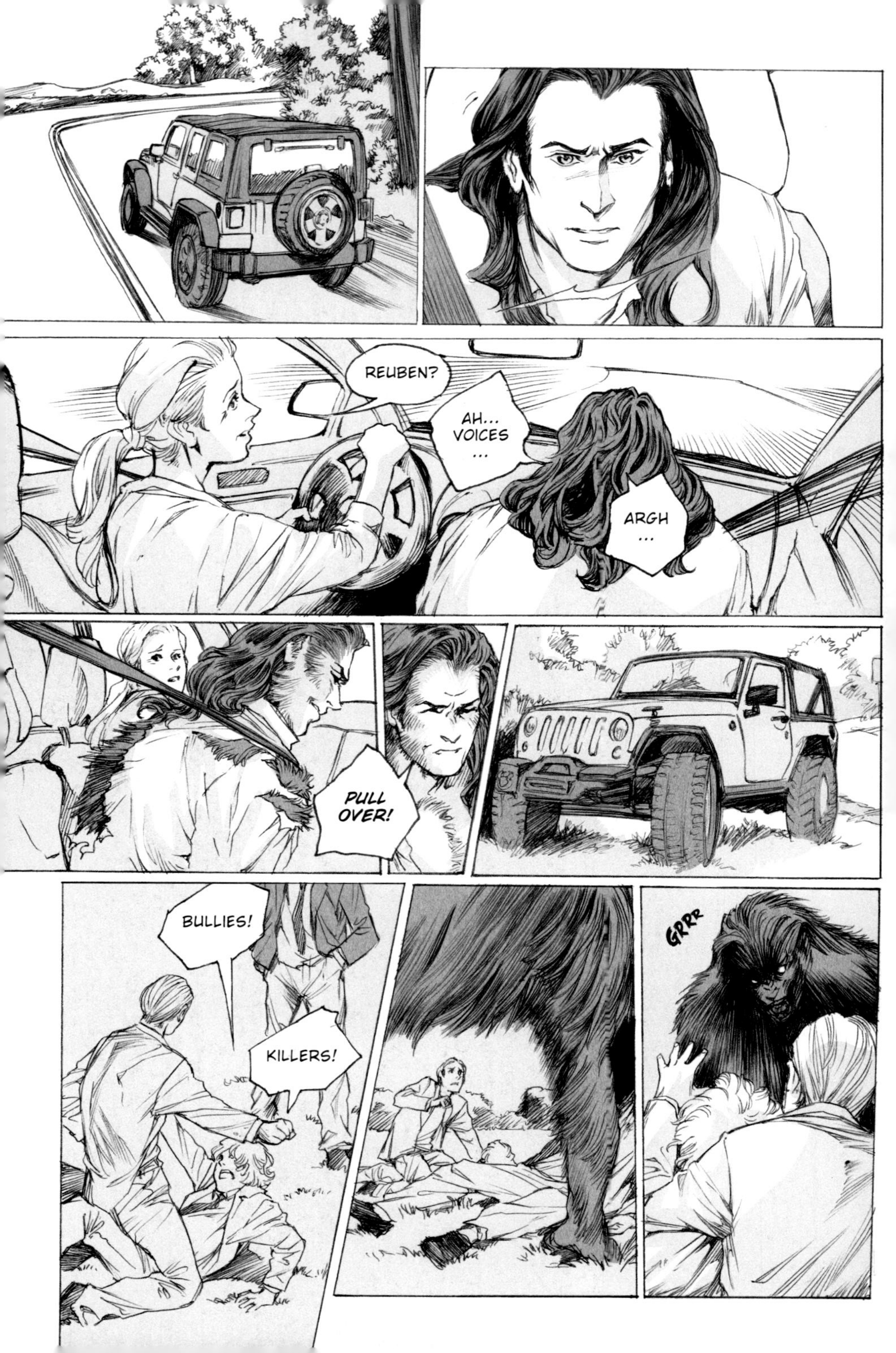
REUBEN?
AH... VOICES ...
ARGH ...
PULL OVER!
BULLIES!
KILLERS!
GRRR

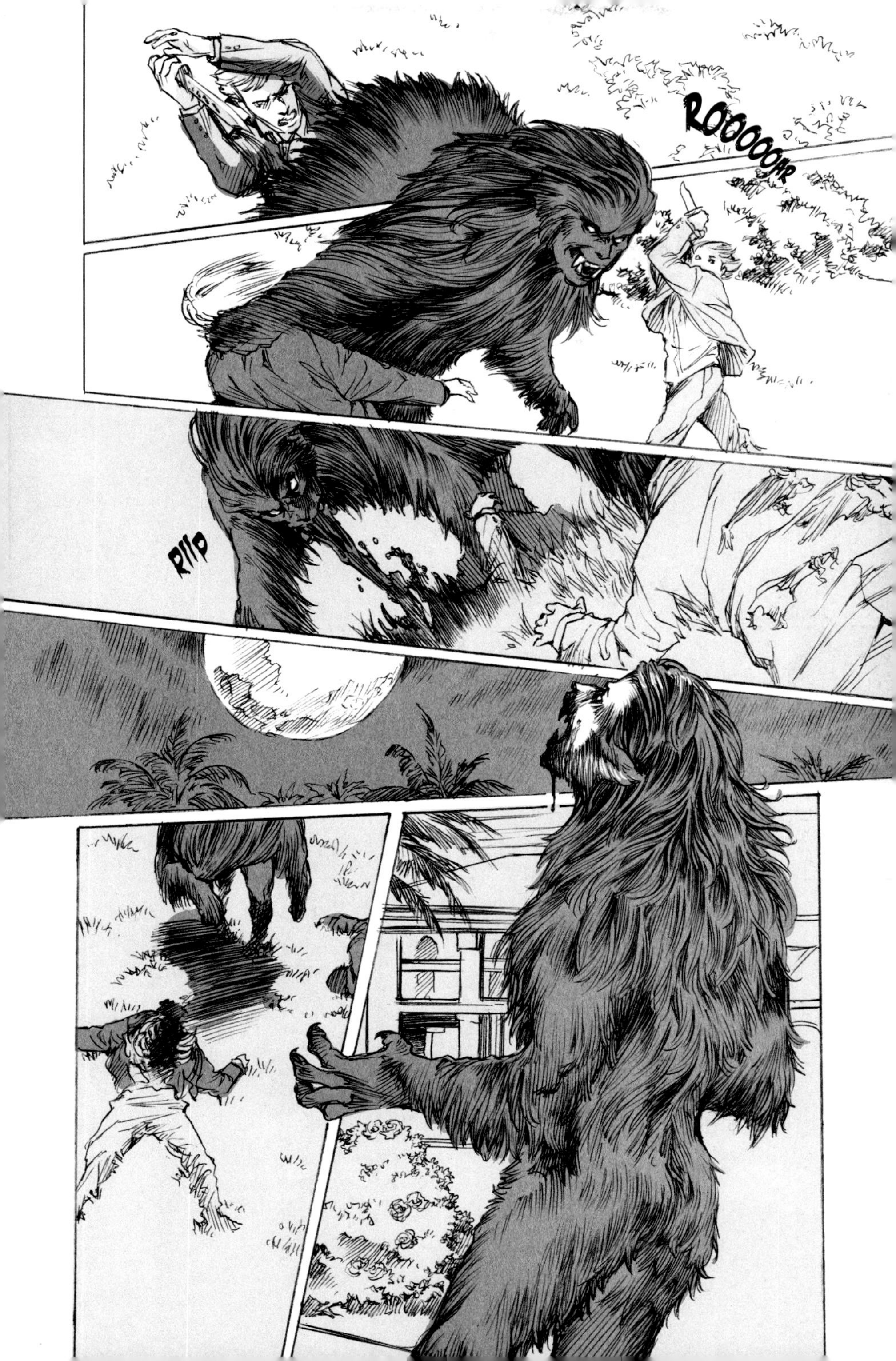
ROOOOOAR
RIIP

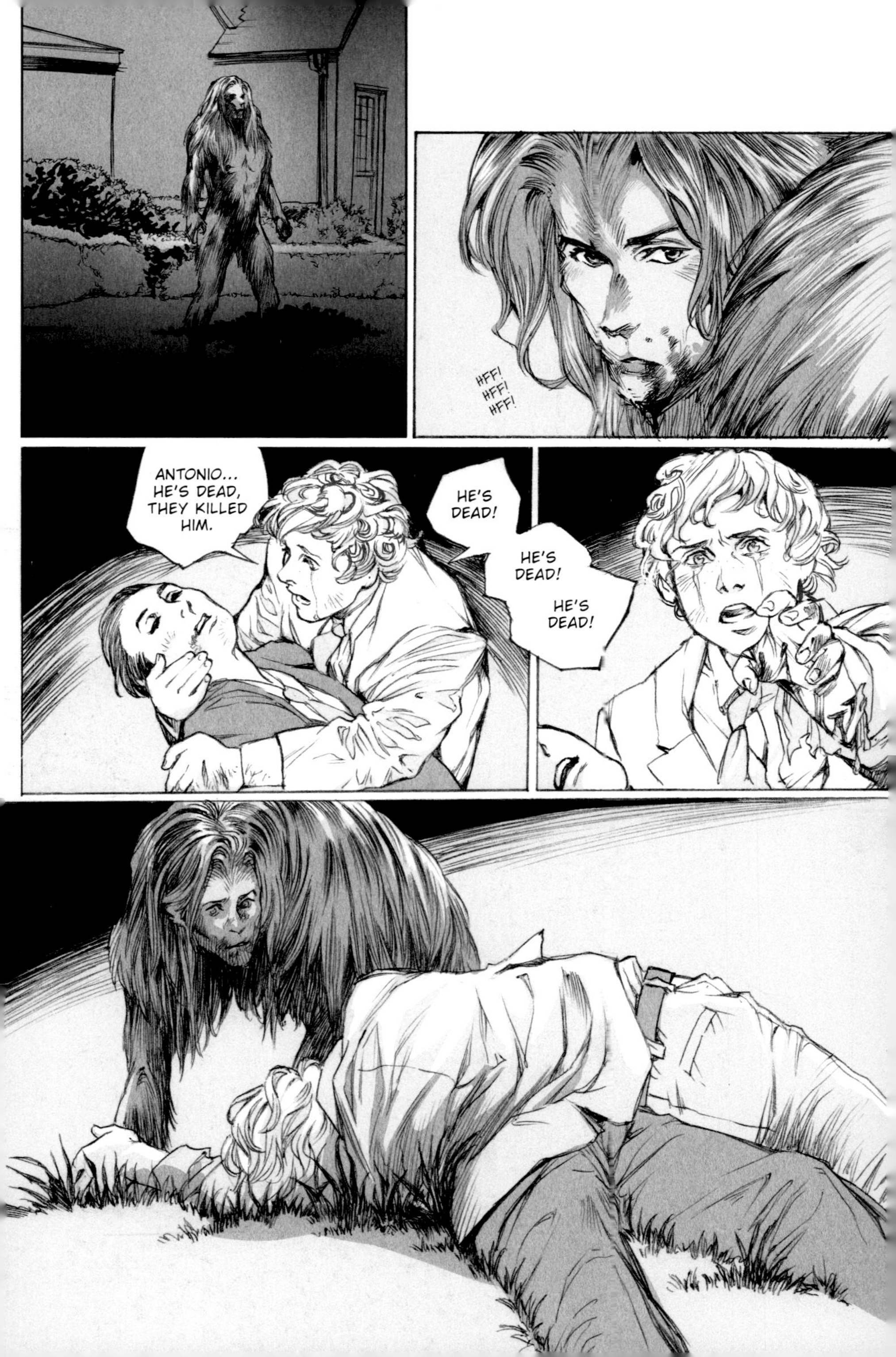
HFF!
HFF!
HFF!
ANTONIO... HE'S DEAD, THEY KILLED HIM.
HE'S DEAD!
HE'S DEAD!
HE'S DEAD!

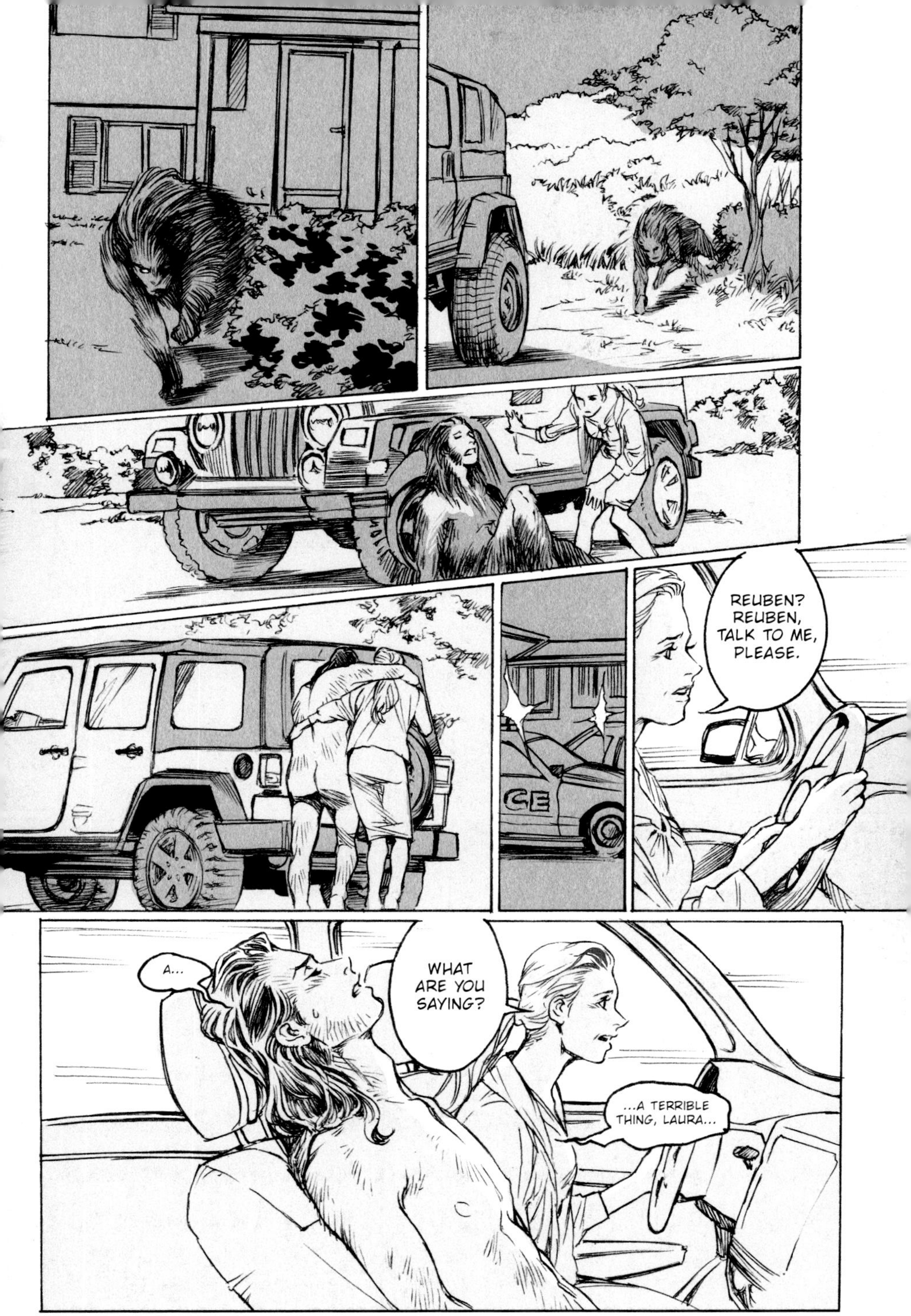
REUBEN? REUBEN, TALK TO ME, PLEASE.
A...
WHAT ARE YOU SAYING?
...A TERRIBLE THING, LAURA...

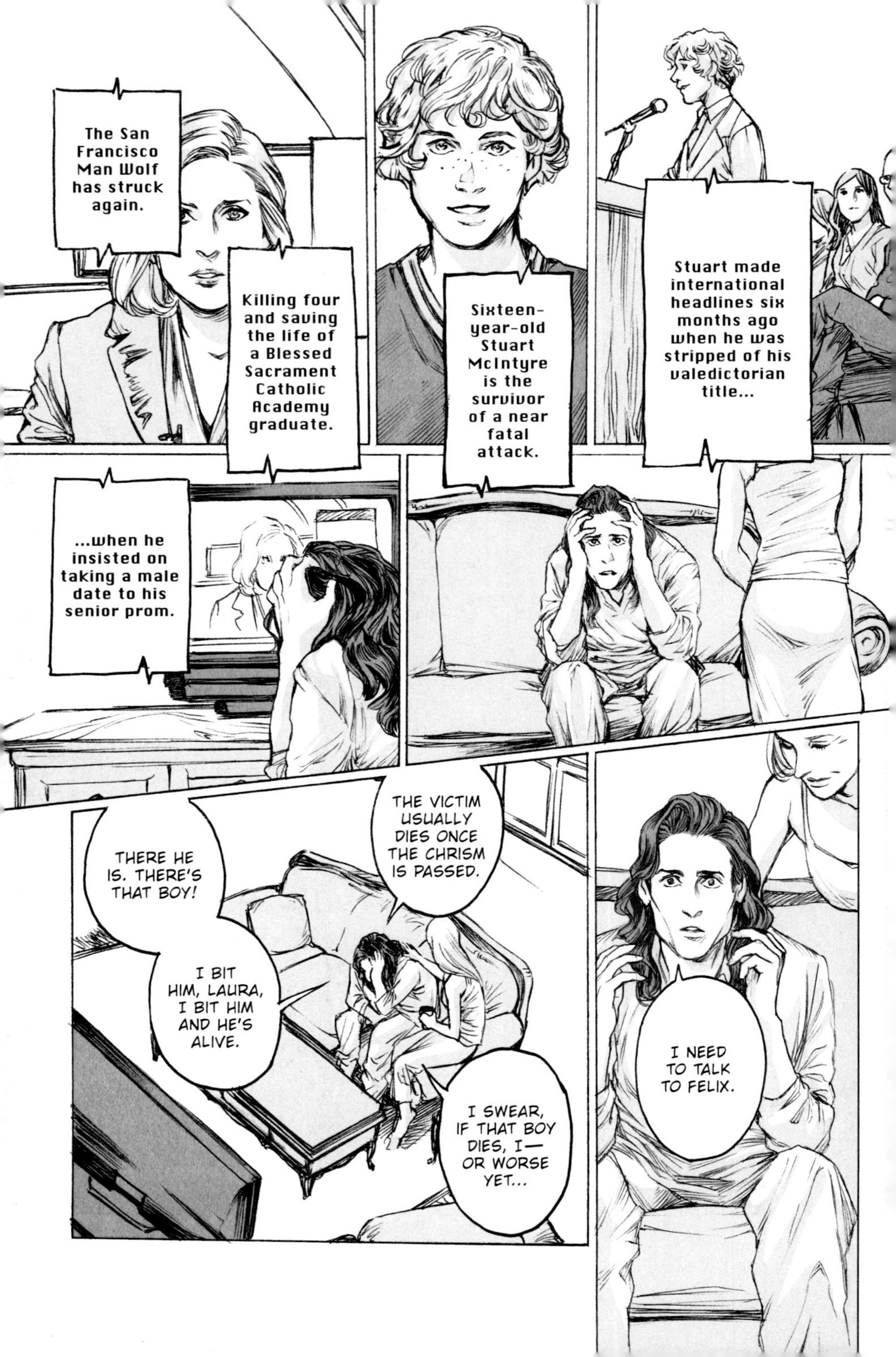
The San Francisco Man Wolf has struck again.
Killing four and saving the life of a Blessed Sacrament Catholic Academy graduate.
Sixteen-year-old Stuart McIntyre is the survivor of a near fatal attack.
Stuart made international headlines six months ago when he was stripped of his valedictorian title...
...when he insisted on taking a male date to his senior prom.
THERE HE IS. THERE'S THAT BOY!
THE VICTIM USUALLY DIES ONCE THE CHRISM IS PASSED.
I BIT HIM, LAURA, I BIT HIM AND HE'S ALIVE.
I SWEAR, IF THAT BOY DIES, I— OR WORSE YET...
I NEED TO TALK TO FELIX.

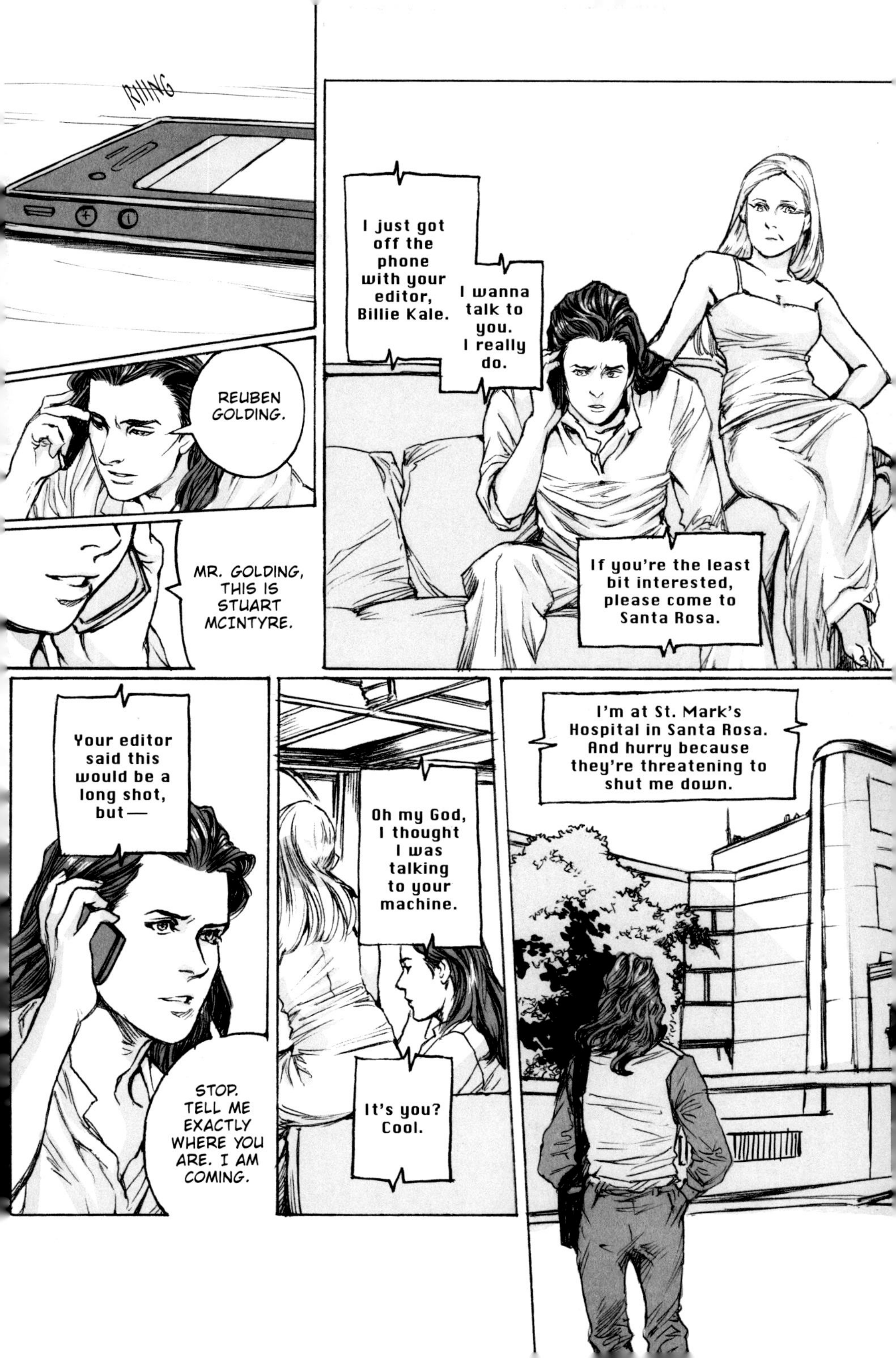
RHING
REUBEN GOLDING.
MR. GOLDING, THIS IS STUART MCINTYRE.
I just got off the phone with your editor, Billie Kale.
I wanna talk to you. I really do.
If you're the least bit interested, please come to Santa Rosa.
Your editor said this would be a long shot, but—
STOP. TELL ME EXACTLY WHERE YOU ARE. I AM COMING.
Oh my God, I thought I was talking to your machine.
It's you? Cool.
I'm at St. Mark's Hospital in Santa Rosa. And hurry because they're threatening to shut me down.

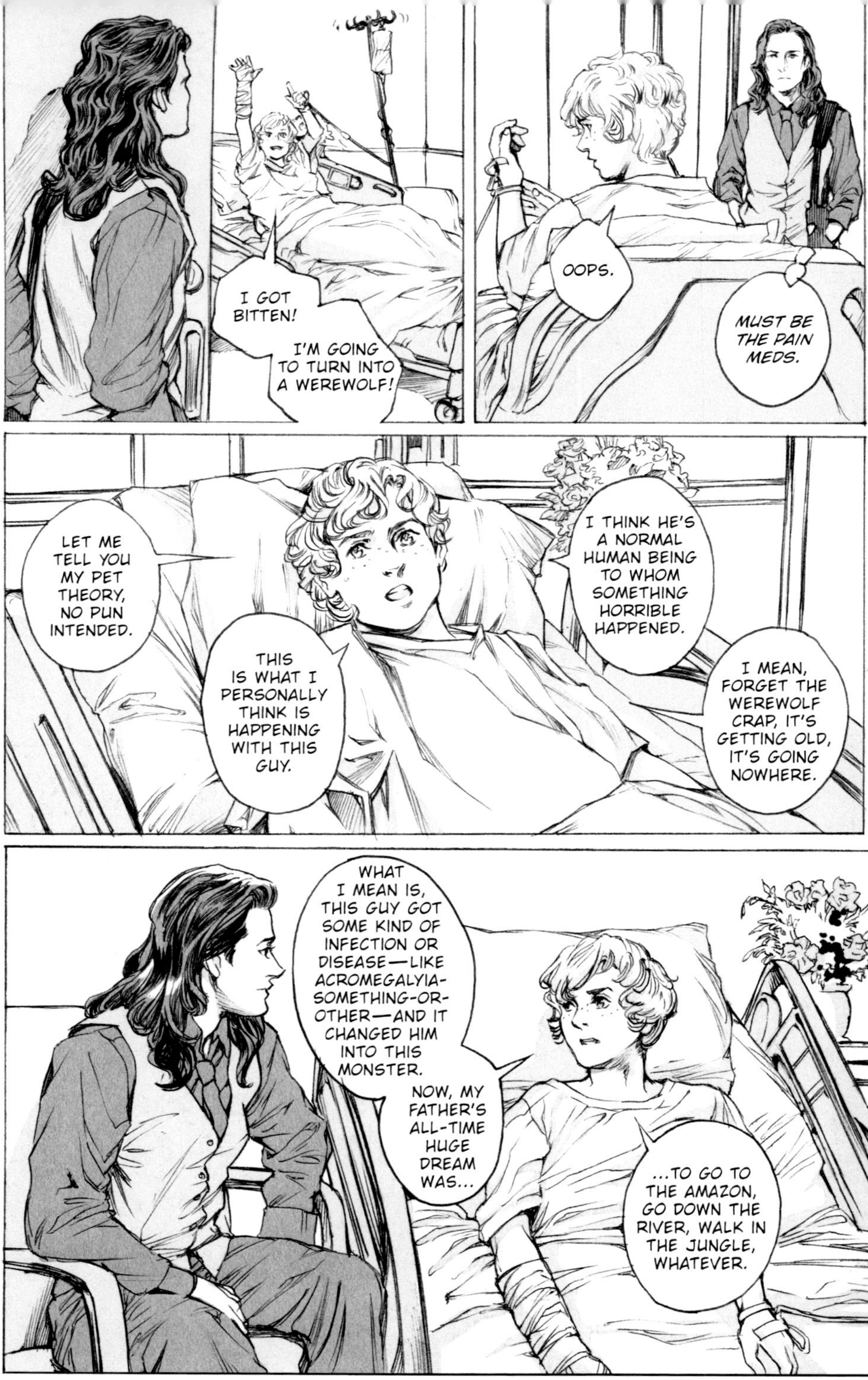
I GOT BITTEN!
I'M GOING TO TURN INTO A WEREWOLF!
OOPS.
MUST BE THE PAIN MEDS.
LET ME TELL YOU MY PET THEORY, NO PUN INTENDED.
THIS IS WHAT I PERSONALLY THINK IS HAPPENING WITH THIS GUY.
I THINK HE'S A NORMAL HUMAN BEING TO WHOM SOMETHING HORRIBLE HAPPENED.
I MEAN, FORGET THE WEREWOLF CRAP, IT'S GETTING OLD, IT'S GOING NOWHERE.
WHAT I MEAN IS, THIS GUY GOT SOME KIND OF INFECTION OR DISEASE—LIKE ACROMEGALYIA-SOMETHING-OR-OTHER—AND IT CHANGED HIM INTO THIS MONSTER.
NOW, MY FATHER'S ALL-TIME HUGE DREAM WAS...
...TO GO TO THE AMAZON, GO DOWN THE RIVER, WALK IN THE JUNGLE, WHATEVER.

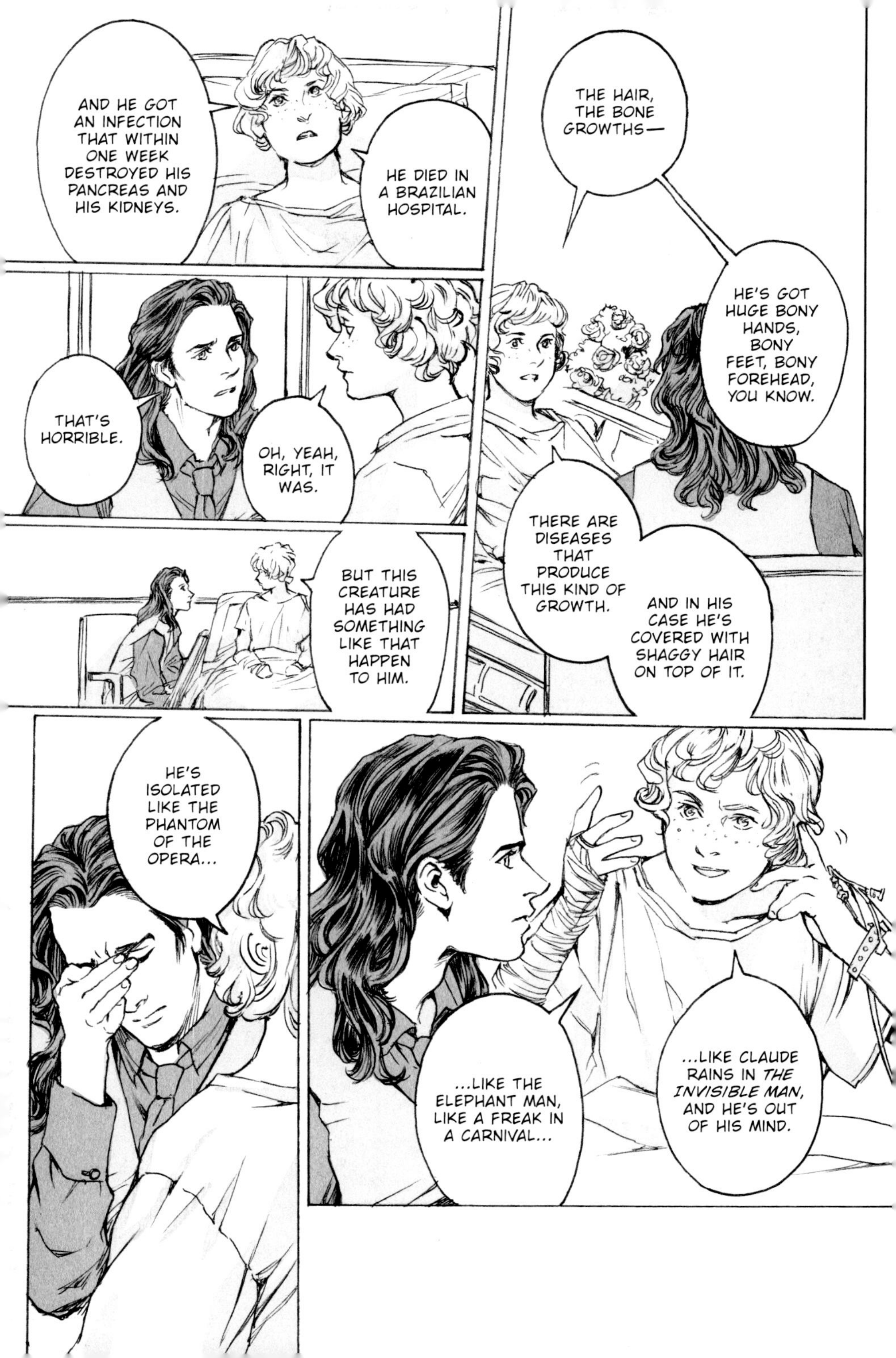
AND HE GOT AN INFECTION THAT WITHIN ONE WEEK DESTROYED HIS PANCREAS AND HIS KIDNEYS.
HE DIED IN A BRAZILIAN HOSPITAL.
THAT'S HORRIBLE.
OH, YEAH, RIGHT, IT WAS.
BUT THIS CREATURE HAS HAD SOMETHING LIKE THAT HAPPEN TO HIM.
THE HAIR, THE BONE GROWTHS—
HE'S GOT HUGE BONY HANDS, BONY FEET, BONY FOREHEAD, YOU KNOW.
THERE ARE DISEASES THAT PRODUCE THIS KIND OF GROWTH.
AND IN HIS CASE HE'S COVERED WITH SHAGGY HAIR ON TOP OF IT.
HE'S ISOLATED LIKE THE PHANTOM OF THE OPERA...
...LIKE THE ELEPHANT MAN, LIKE A FREAK IN A CARNIVAL...
...LIKE CLAUDE RAINS IN *THE INVISIBLE MAN*, AND HE'S OUT OF HIS MIND.

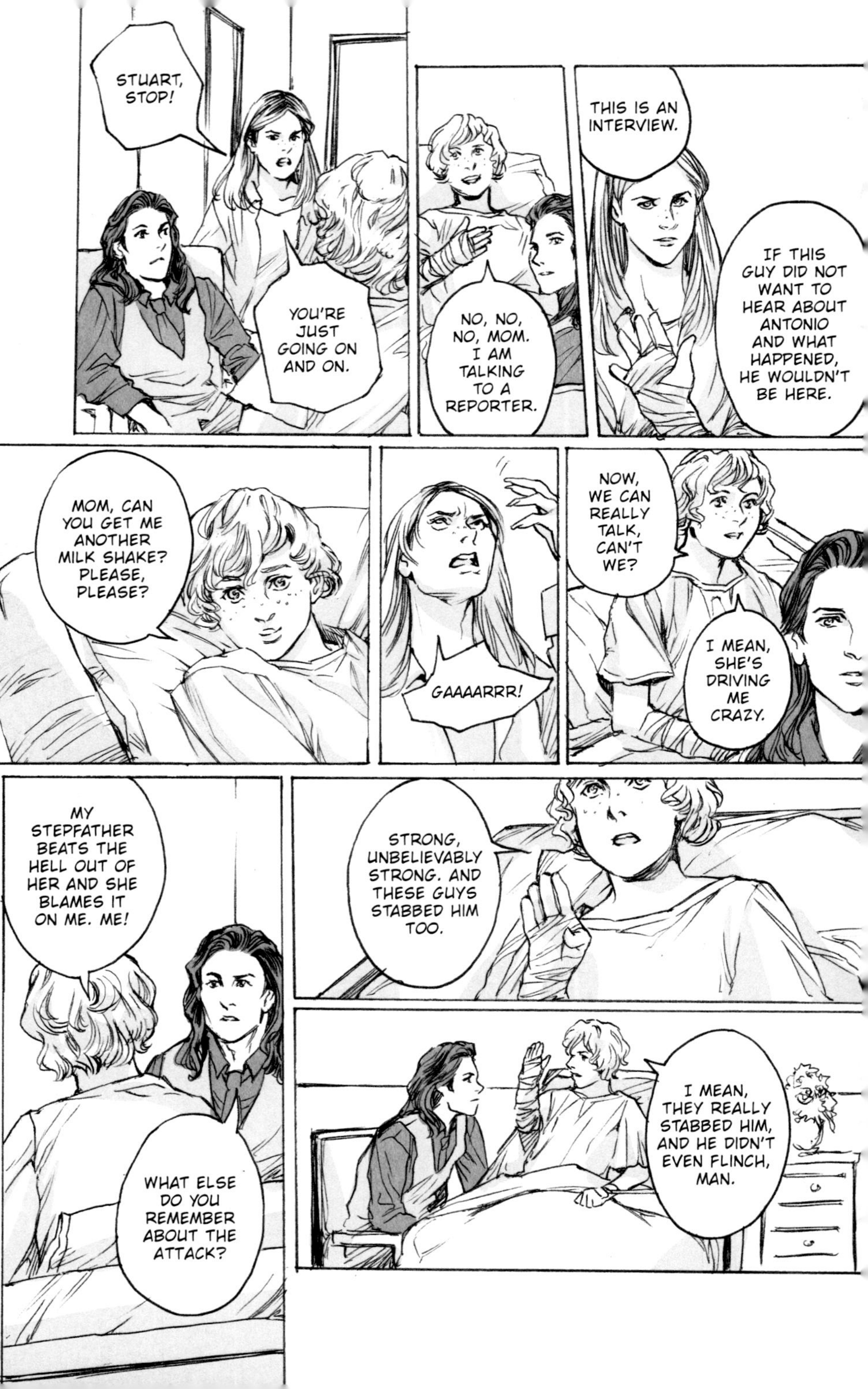
STUART, STOP!
YOU'RE JUST GOING ON AND ON.
NO, NO, NO, MOM. I AM TALKING TO A REPORTER.
THIS IS AN INTERVIEW.
IF THIS GUY DID NOT WANT TO HEAR ABOUT ANTONIO AND WHAT HAPPENED, HE WOULDN'T BE HERE.
MOM, CAN YOU GET ME ANOTHER MILK SHAKE? PLEASE, PLEASE?
GAAAARRR!
NOW, WE CAN REALLY TALK, CAN'T WE?
I MEAN, SHE'S DRIVING ME CRAZY.
MY STEPFATHER BEATS THE HELL OUT OF HER AND SHE BLAMES IT ON ME. ME!
WHAT ELSE DO YOU REMEMBER ABOUT THE ATTACK?
STRONG, UNBELIEVABLY STRONG. AND THESE GUYS STABBED HIM TOO.
I MEAN, THEY REALLY STABBED HIM, AND HE DIDN'T EVEN FLINCH, MAN.

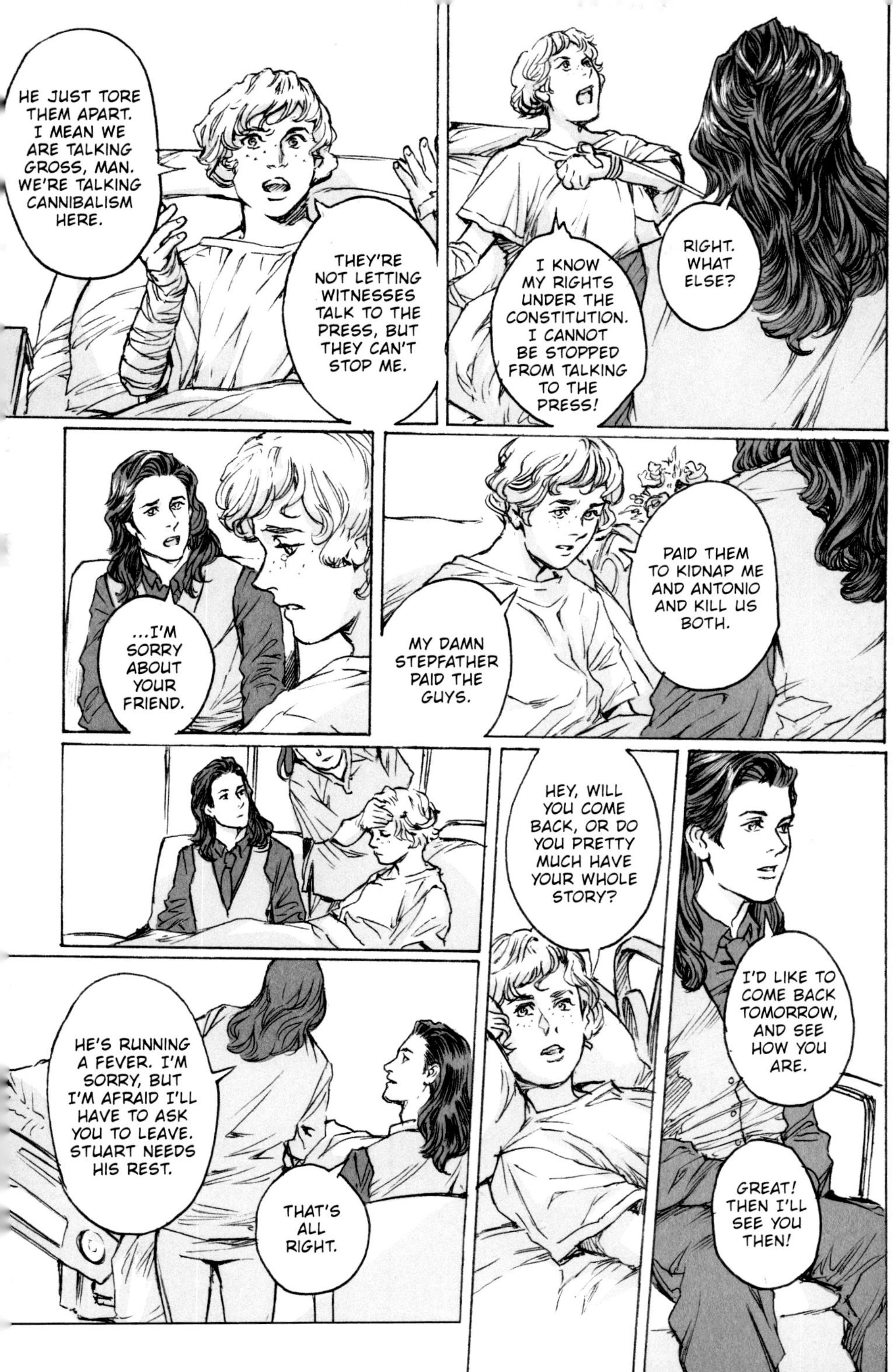
HE JUST TORE THEM APART. I MEAN WE ARE TALKING GROSS, MAN. WE'RE TALKING CANNIBALISM HERE.
THEY'RE NOT LETTING WITNESSES TALK TO THE PRESS, BUT THEY CAN'T STOP ME.
I KNOW MY RIGHTS UNDER THE CONSTITUTION. I CANNOT BE STOPPED FROM TALKING TO THE PRESS!
RIGHT. WHAT ELSE?
...I'M SORRY ABOUT YOUR FRIEND.
MY DAMN STEPFATHER PAID THE GUYS.
PAID THEM TO KIDNAP ME AND ANTONIO AND KILL US BOTH.
HEY, WILL YOU COME BACK, OR DO YOU PRETTY MUCH HAVE YOUR WHOLE STORY?
I'D LIKE TO COME BACK TOMORROW, AND SEE HOW YOU ARE.
GREAT! THEN I'LL SEE YOU THEN!
HE'S RUNNING A FEVER. I'M SORRY, BUT I'M AFRAID I'LL HAVE TO ASK YOU TO LEAVE. STUART NEEDS HIS REST.
THAT'S ALL RIGHT.

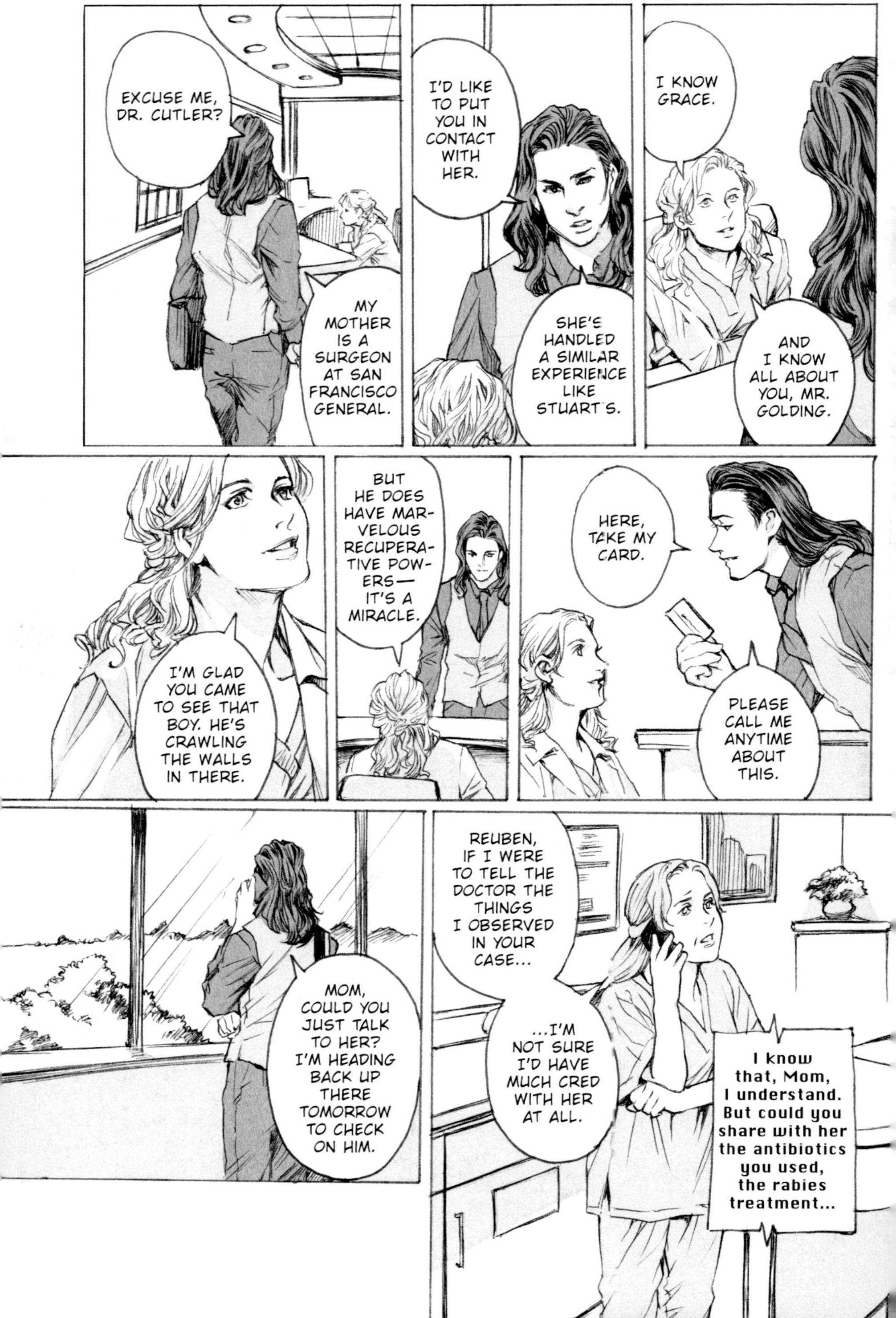
EXCUSE ME, DR. CUTLER?
MY MOTHER IS A SURGEON AT SAN FRANCISCO GENERAL.
I'D LIKE TO PUT YOU IN CONTACT WITH HER.
SHE'S HANDLED A SIMILAR EXPERIENCE LIKE STUART'S.
I KNOW GRACE.
AND I KNOW ALL ABOUT YOU, MR. GOLDING.
I'M GLAD YOU CAME TO SEE THAT BOY. HE'S CRAWLING THE WALLS IN THERE.
BUT HE DOES HAVE MARVELOUS RECUPERATIVE POWERS— IT'S A MIRACLE.
HERE, TAKE MY CARD.
PLEASE CALL ME ANYTIME ABOUT THIS.
MOM, COULD YOU JUST TALK TO HER? I'M HEADING BACK UP THERE TOMORROW TO CHECK ON HIM.
REUBEN, IF I WERE TO TELL THE DOCTOR THE THINGS I OBSERVED IN YOUR CASE...
...I'M NOT SURE I'D HAVE MUCH CRED WITH HER AT ALL.
I know that, Mom, I understand. But could you share with her the antibiotics you used, the rabies treatment...

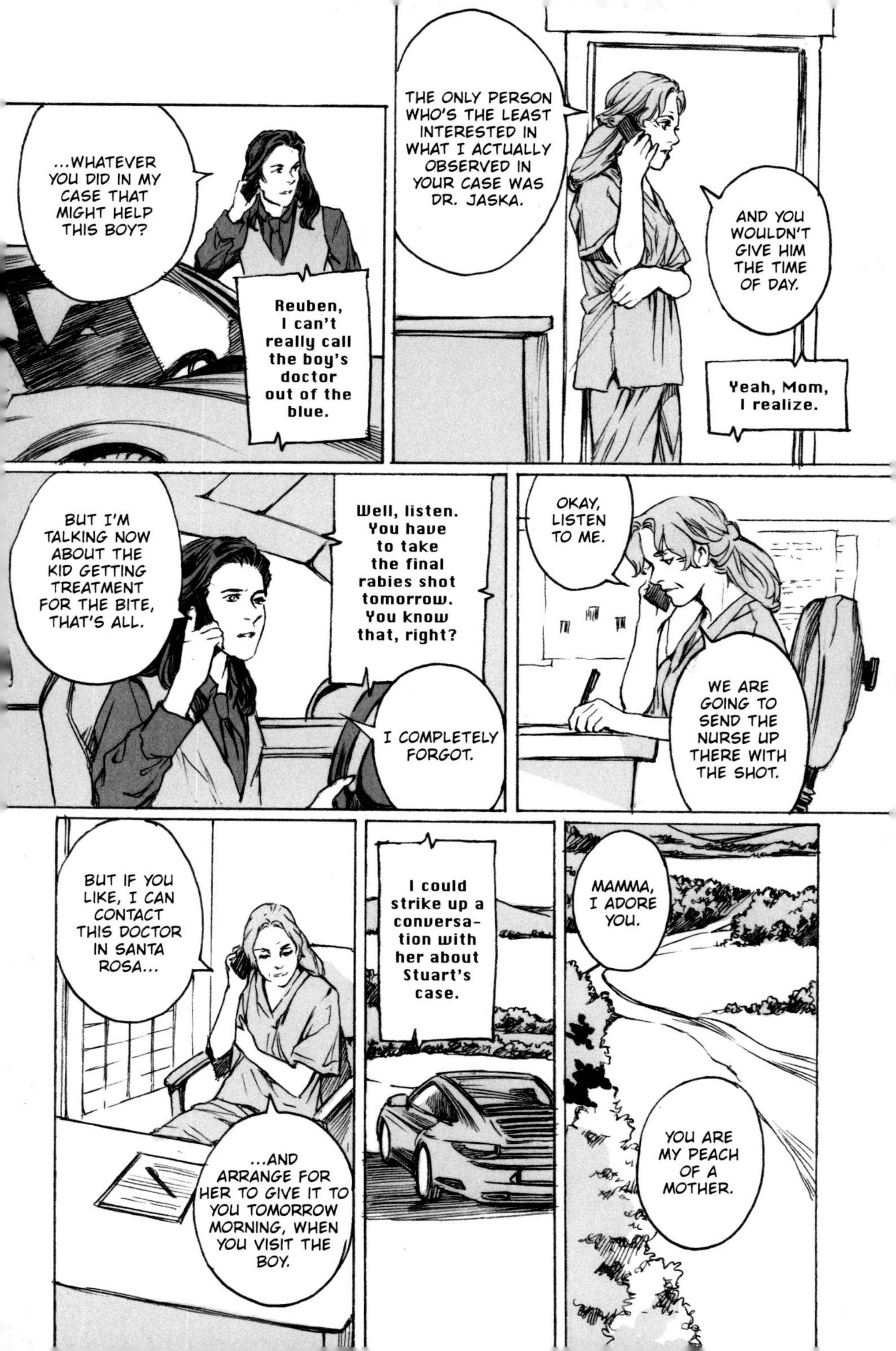
...WHATEVER YOU DID IN MY CASE THAT MIGHT HELP THIS BOY?
Reuben, I can't really call the boy's doctor out of the blue.
THE ONLY PERSON WHO'S THE LEAST INTERESTED IN WHAT I ACTUALLY OBSERVED IN YOUR CASE WAS DR. JASKA.
AND YOU WOULDN'T GIVE HIM THE TIME OF DAY.
Yeah, Mom, I realize.
BUT I'M TALKING NOW ABOUT THE KID GETTING TREATMENT FOR THE BITE, THAT'S ALL.
Well, listen. You have to take the final rabies shot tomorrow. You know that, right?
I COMPLETELY FORGOT.
OKAY, LISTEN TO ME.
WE ARE GOING TO SEND THE NURSE UP THERE WITH THE SHOT.
BUT IF YOU LIKE, I CAN CONTACT THIS DOCTOR IN SANTA ROSA...
...AND ARRANGE FOR HER TO GIVE IT TO YOU TOMORROW MORNING, WHEN YOU VISIT THE BOY.
I could strike up a conversa-tion with her about Stuart's case.
MAMMA, I ADORE YOU.
YOU ARE MY PEACH OF A MOTHER.

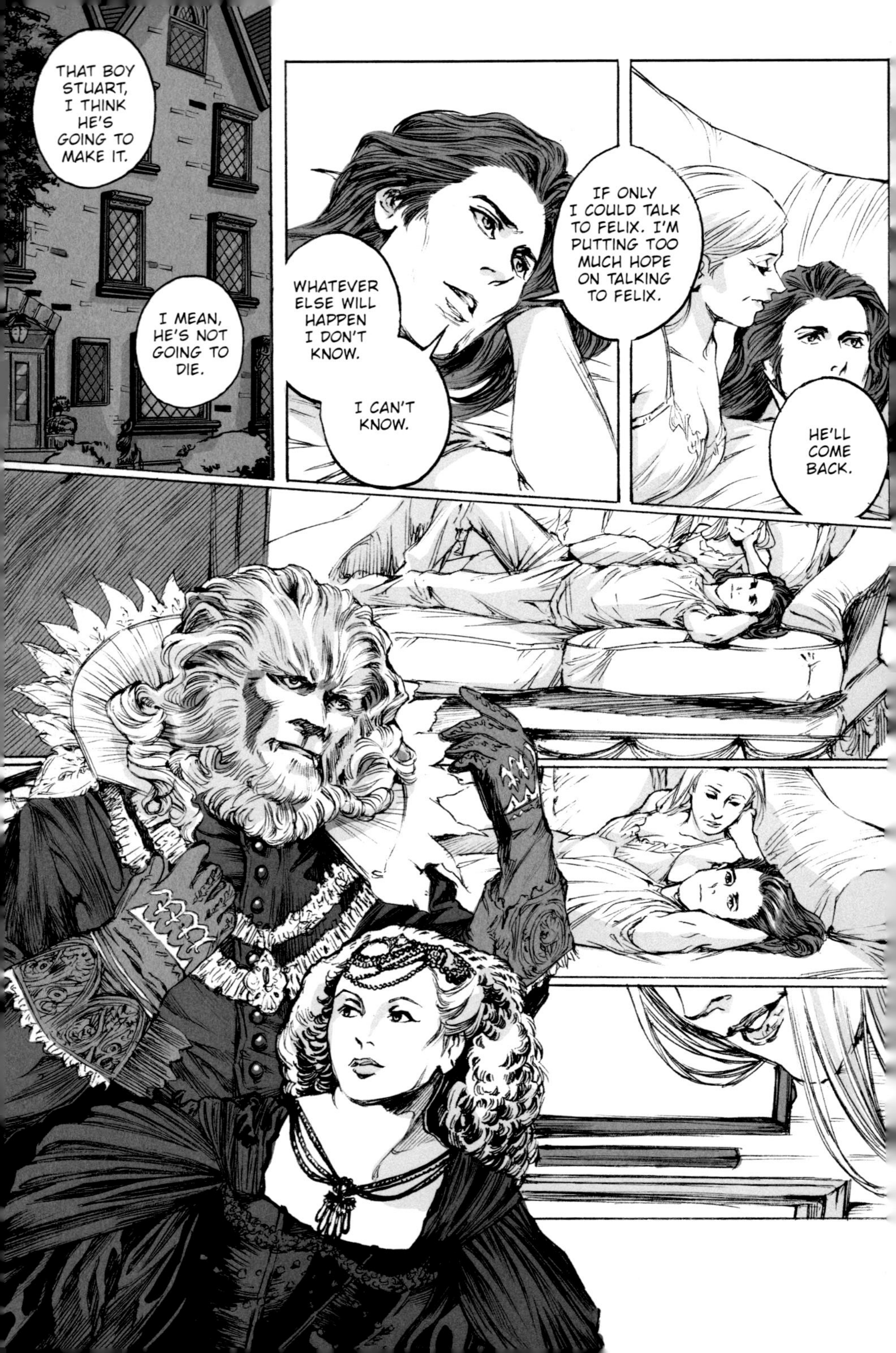

THAT BOY STUART, I THINK HE'S GOING TO MAKE IT.
I MEAN, HE'S NOT GOING TO DIE.
WHATEVER ELSE WILL HAPPEN I DON'T KNOW.
I CAN'T KNOW.
IF ONLY I COULD TALK TO FELIX. I'M PUTTING TOO MUCH HOPE ON TALKING TO FELIX.
HE'LL COME BACK.

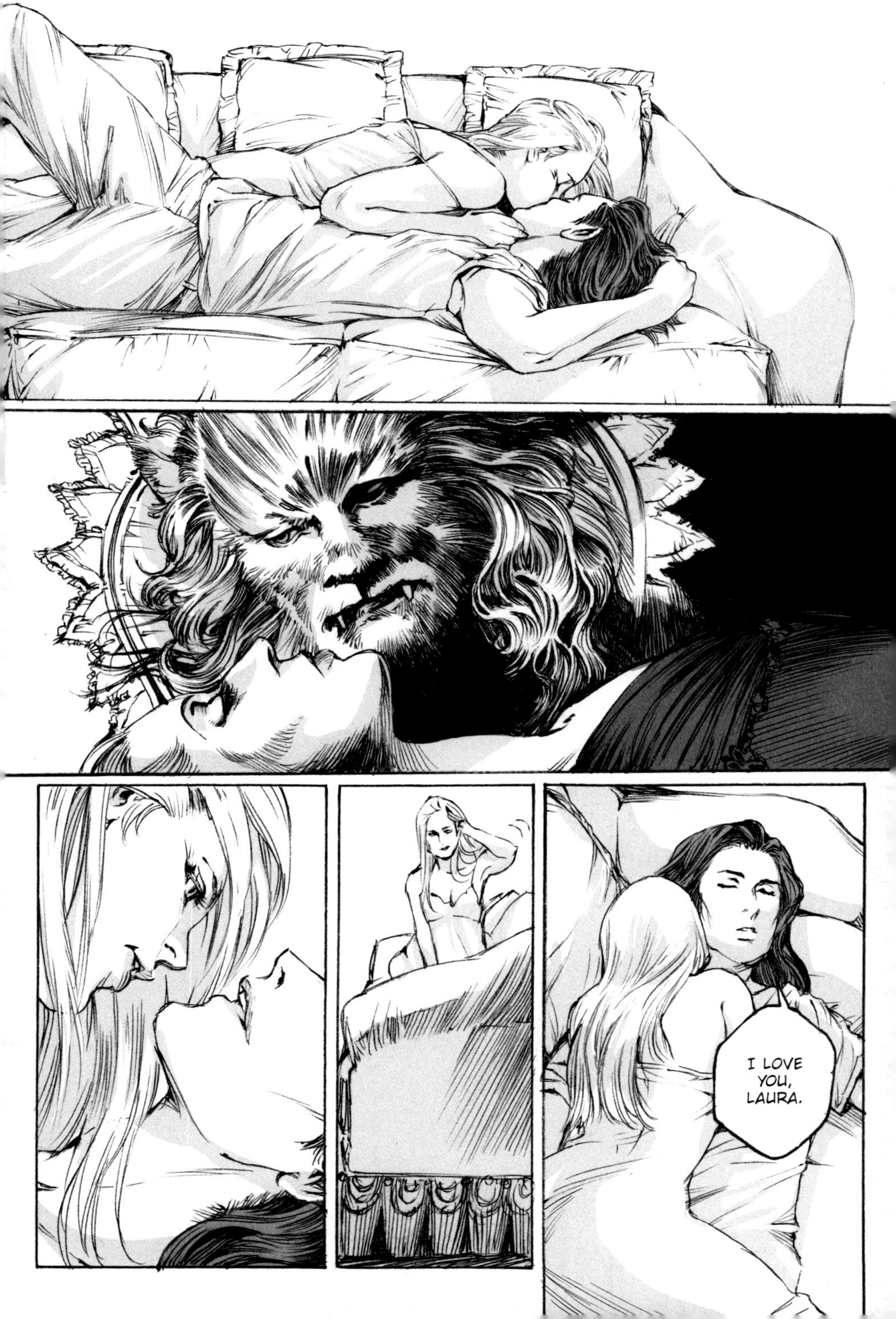
I LOVE YOU, LAURA.

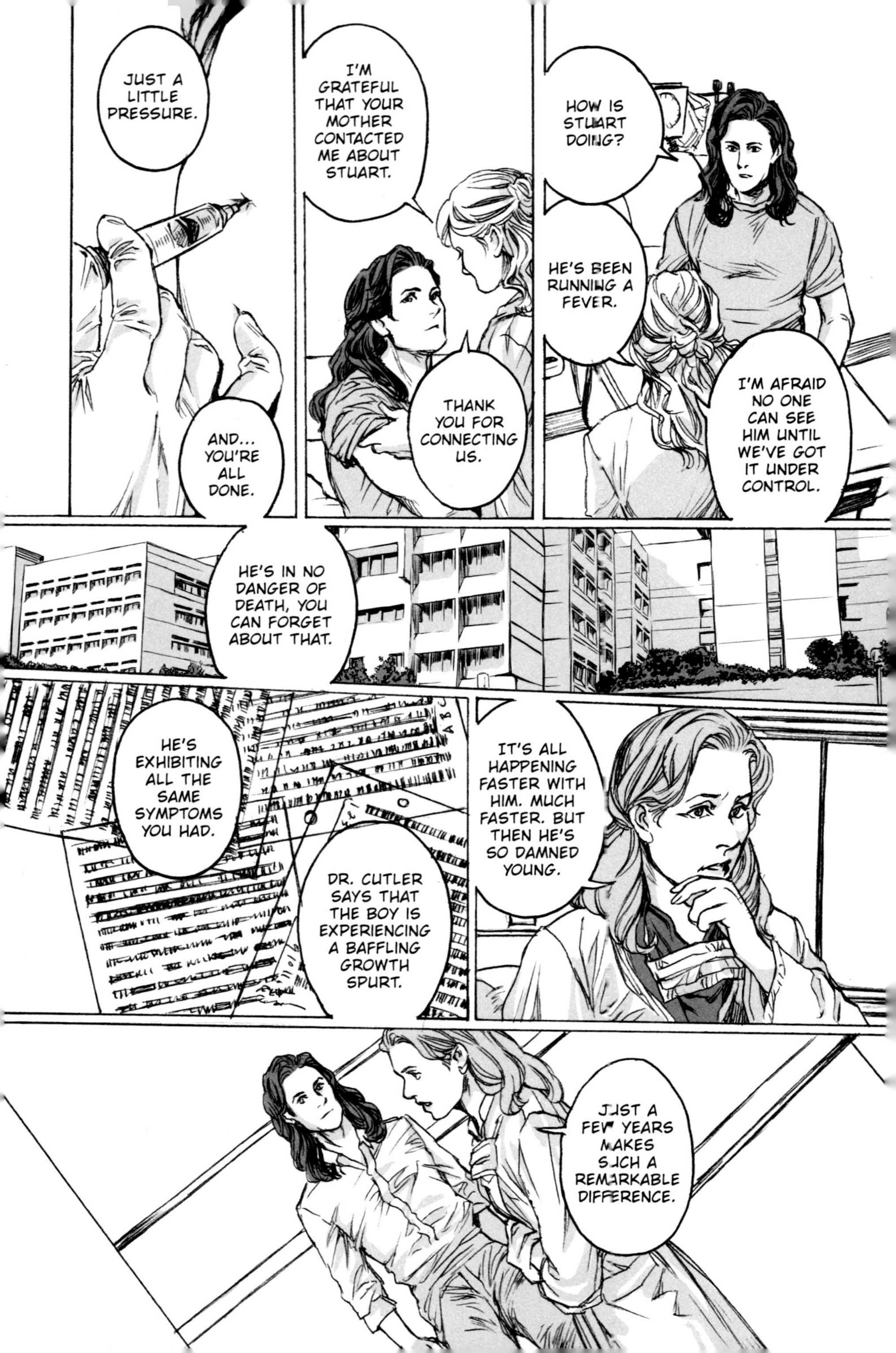
JUST A LITTLE PRESSURE.
AND... YOU'RE ALL DONE.
I'M GRATEFUL THAT YOUR MOTHER CONTACTED ME ABOUT STUART.
THANK YOU FOR CONNECTING US.
HOW IS STUART DOING?
HE'S BEEN RUNNING A FEVER.
I'M AFRAID NO ONE CAN SEE HIM UNTIL WE'VE GOT IT UNDER CONTROL.
HE'S IN NO DANGER OF DEATH, YOU CAN FORGET ABOUT THAT.
HE'S EXHIBITING ALL THE SAME SYMPTOMS YOU HAD.
DR. CUTLER SAYS THAT THE BOY IS EXPERIENCING A BAFFLING GROWTH SPURT.
IT'S ALL HAPPENING FASTER WITH HIM. MUCH FASTER. BUT THEN HE'S SO DAMNED YOUNG.
JUST A FEW YEARS MAKES SUCH A REMARKABLE DIFFERENCE.

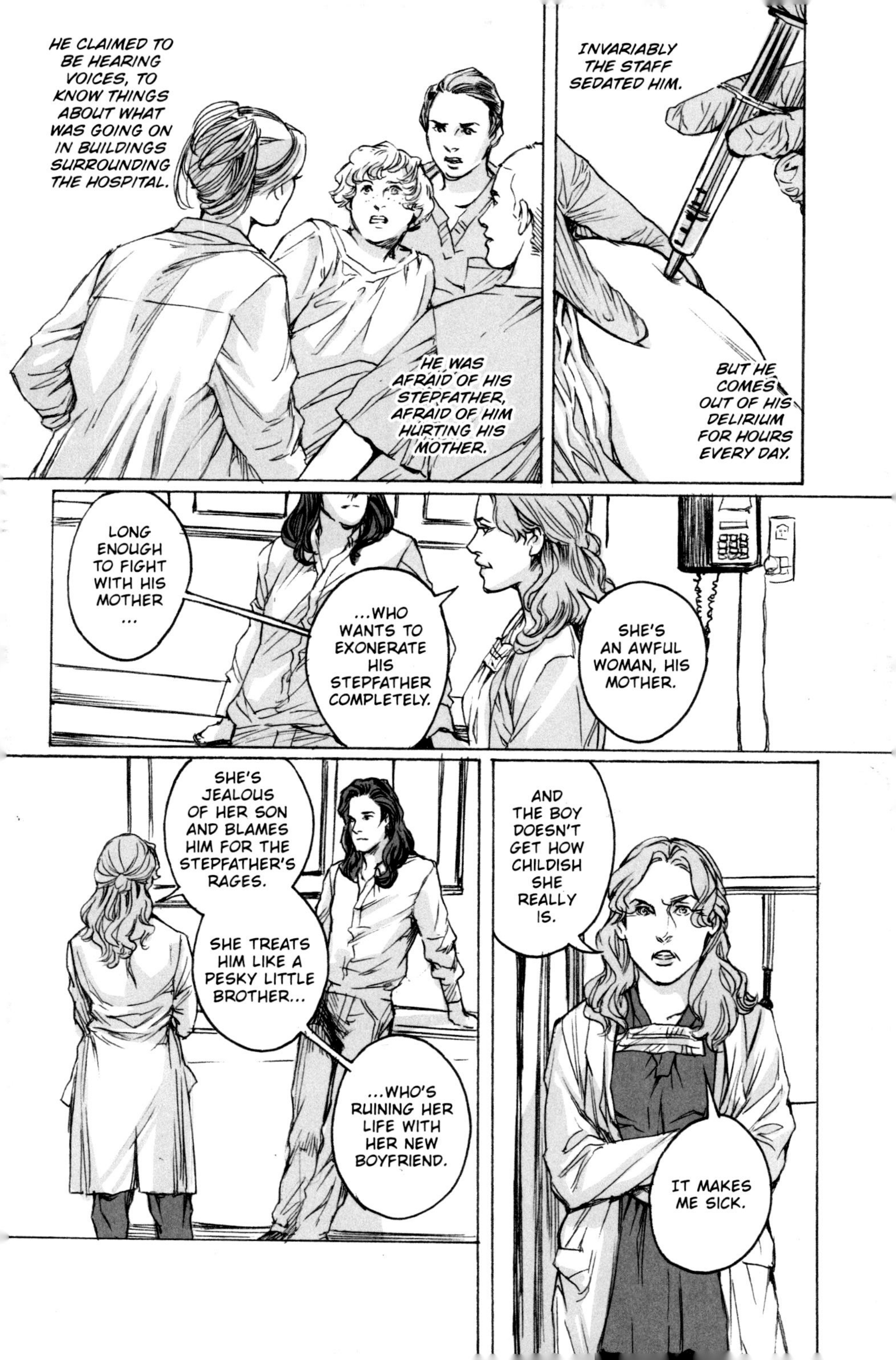
HE CLAIMED TO BE HEARING VOICES, TO KNOW THINGS ABOUT WHAT WAS GOING ON IN BUILDINGS SURROUNDING THE HOSPITAL.
HE WAS AFRAID OF HIS STEPFATHER, AFRAID OF HIM HURTING HIS MOTHER.
INVARIABLY THE STAFF SEDATED HIM.
BUT HE COMES OUT OF HIS DELIRIUM FOR HOURS EVERY DAY.
LONG ENOUGH TO FIGHT WITH HIS MOTHER ...
...WHO WANTS TO EXONERATE HIS STEPFATHER COMPLETELY.
SHE'S AN AWFUL WOMAN, HIS MOTHER.
SHE'S JEALOUS OF HER SON AND BLAMES HIM FOR THE STEPFATHER'S RAGES.
SHE TREATS HIM LIKE A PESKY LITTLE BROTHER...
...WHO'S RUINING HER LIFE WITH HER NEW BOYFRIEND.
AND THE BOY DOESN'T GET HOW CHILDISH SHE REALLY IS.
IT MAKES ME SICK.

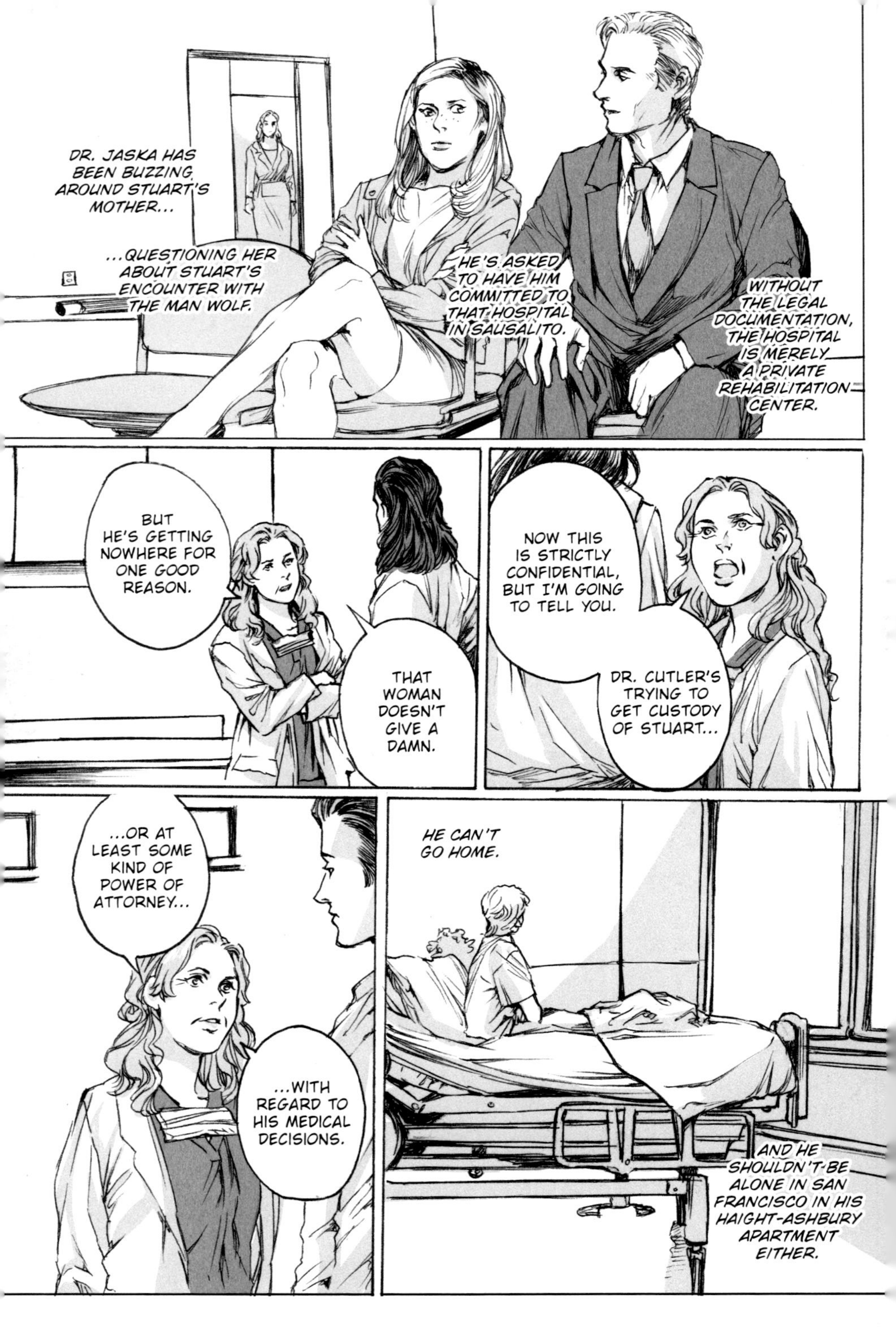
DR. JASKA HAS BEEN BUZZING AROUND STUART'S MOTHER...
...QUESTIONING HER ABOUT STUART'S ENCOUNTER WITH THE MAN WOLF.
HE'S ASKED TO HAVE HIM COMMITTED TO THAT HOSPITAL IN SAUSALITO.
WITHOUT THE LEGAL DOCUMENTATION, THE HOSPITAL IS MERELY A PRIVATE REHABILITATION CENTER.
BUT HE'S GETTING NOWHERE FOR ONE GOOD REASON.
THAT WOMAN DOESN'T GIVE A DAMN.
NOW THIS IS STRICTLY CONFIDENTIAL, BUT I'M GOING TO TELL YOU.
DR. CUTLER'S TRYING TO GET CUSTODY OF STUART...
...OR AT LEAST SOME KIND OF POWER OF ATTORNEY...
...WITH REGARD TO HIS MEDICAL DECISIONS.
HE CAN'T GO HOME.
AND HE SHOULDN'T BE ALONE IN SAN FRANCISCO IN HIS HAIGHT-ASHBURY APARTMENT EITHER.

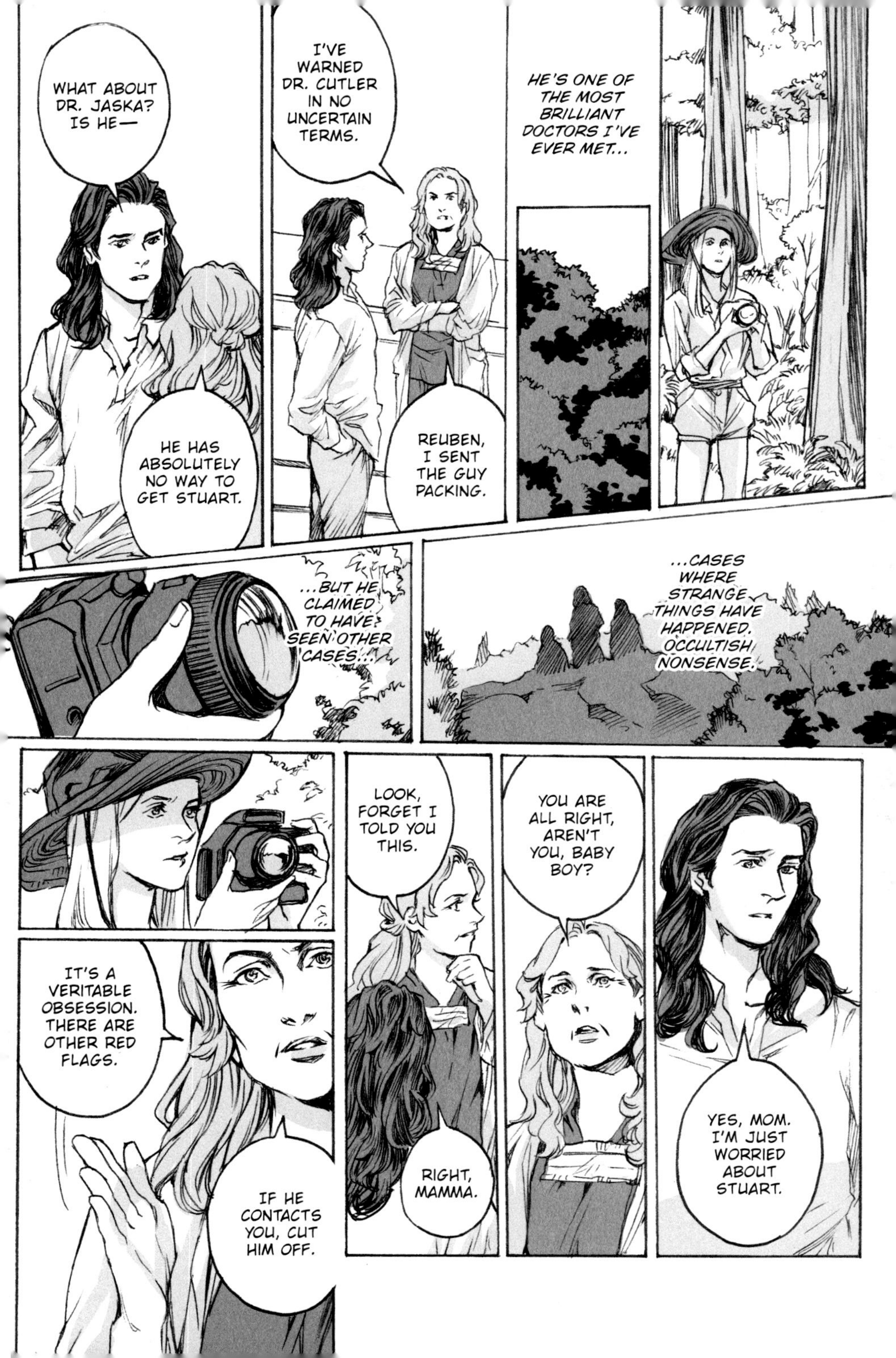
WHAT ABOUT DR. JASKA? IS HE—
HE HAS ABSOLUTELY NO WAY TO GET STUART.
I'VE WARNED DR. CUTLER IN NO UNCERTAIN TERMS.
REUBEN, I SENT THE GUY PACKING.
HE'S ONE OF THE MOST BRILLIANT DOCTORS I'VE EVER MET...
...BUT HE CLAIMED TO HAVE SEEN OTHER CASES...
...CASES WHERE STRANGE THINGS HAVE HAPPENED. OCCULTISH NONSENSE.
IT'S A VERITABLE OBSESSION. THERE ARE OTHER RED FLAGS.
IF HE CONTACTS YOU, CUT HIM OFF.
LOOK, FORGET I TOLD YOU THIS.
RIGHT, MAMMA.
YOU ARE ALL RIGHT, AREN'T YOU, BABY BOY?
YES, MOM. I'M JUST WORRIED ABOUT STUART.

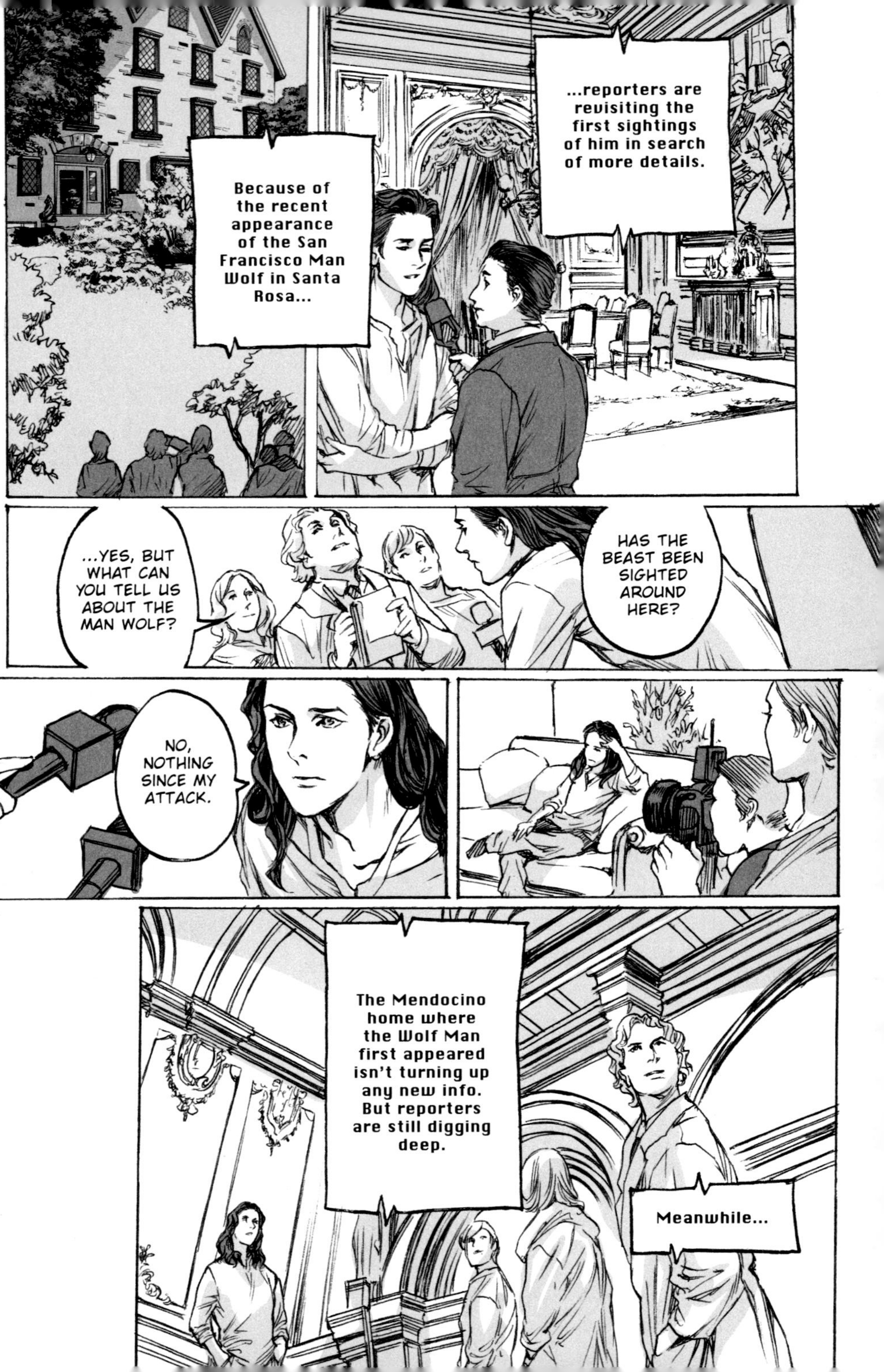
Because of the recent appearance of the San Francisco Man Wolf in Santa Rosa...
...reporters are revisiting the first sightings of him in search of more details.
...YES, BUT WHAT CAN YOU TELL US ABOUT THE MAN WOLF?
HAS THE BEAST BEEN SIGHTED AROUND HERE?
NO, NOTHING SINCE MY ATTACK.
The Mendocino home where the Wolf Man first appeared isn't turning up any new info. But reporters are still digging deep.
Meanwhile...

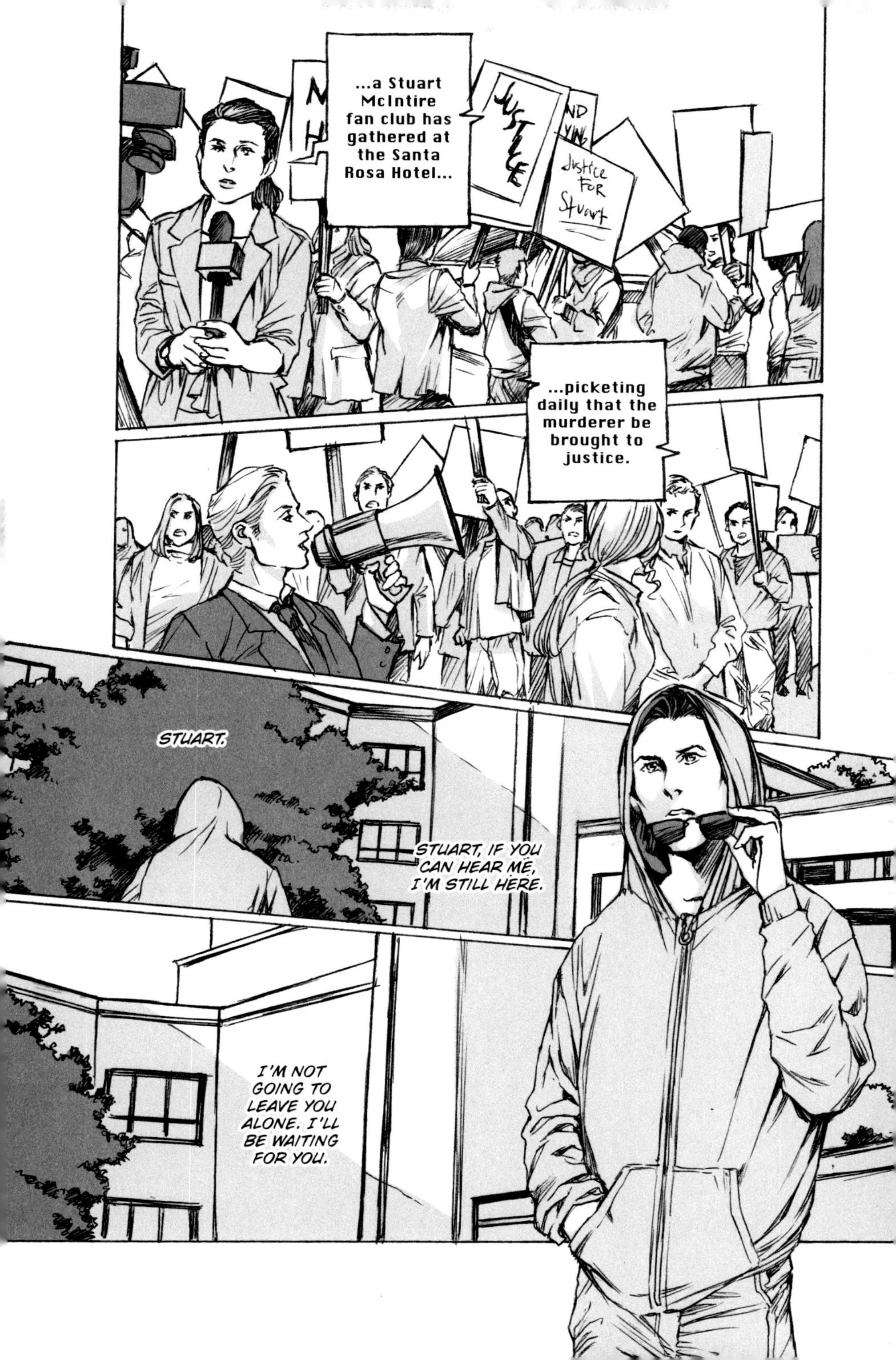
...a Stuart McIntire fan club has gathered at the Santa Rosa Hotel...
JUSTICE
Justice For Stuart
...picketing daily that the murderer be brought to justice.
STUART.
STUART, IF YOU CAN HEAR ME, I'M STILL HERE.
I'M NOT GOING TO LEAVE YOU ALONE. I'LL BE WAITING FOR YOU.

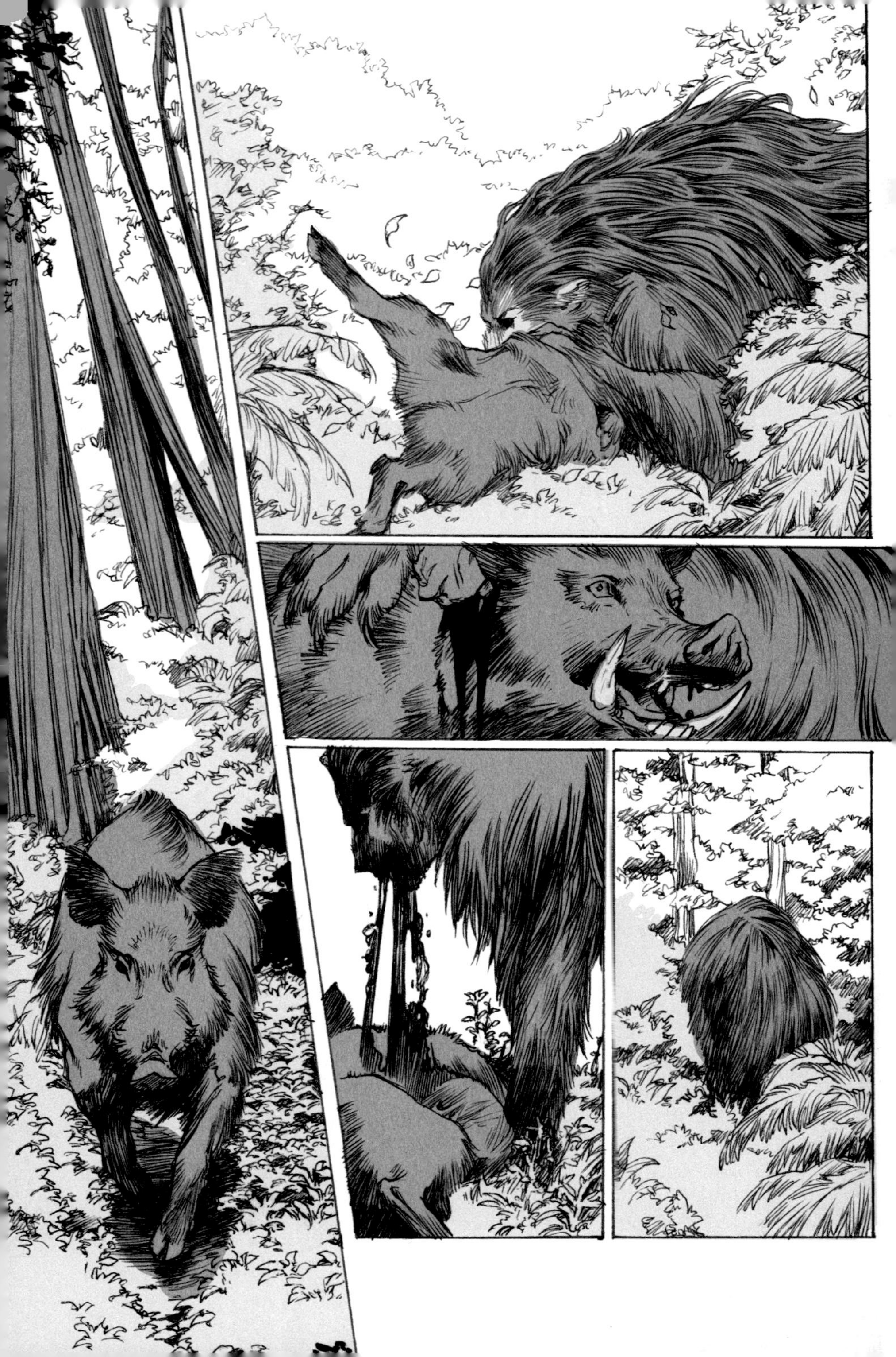

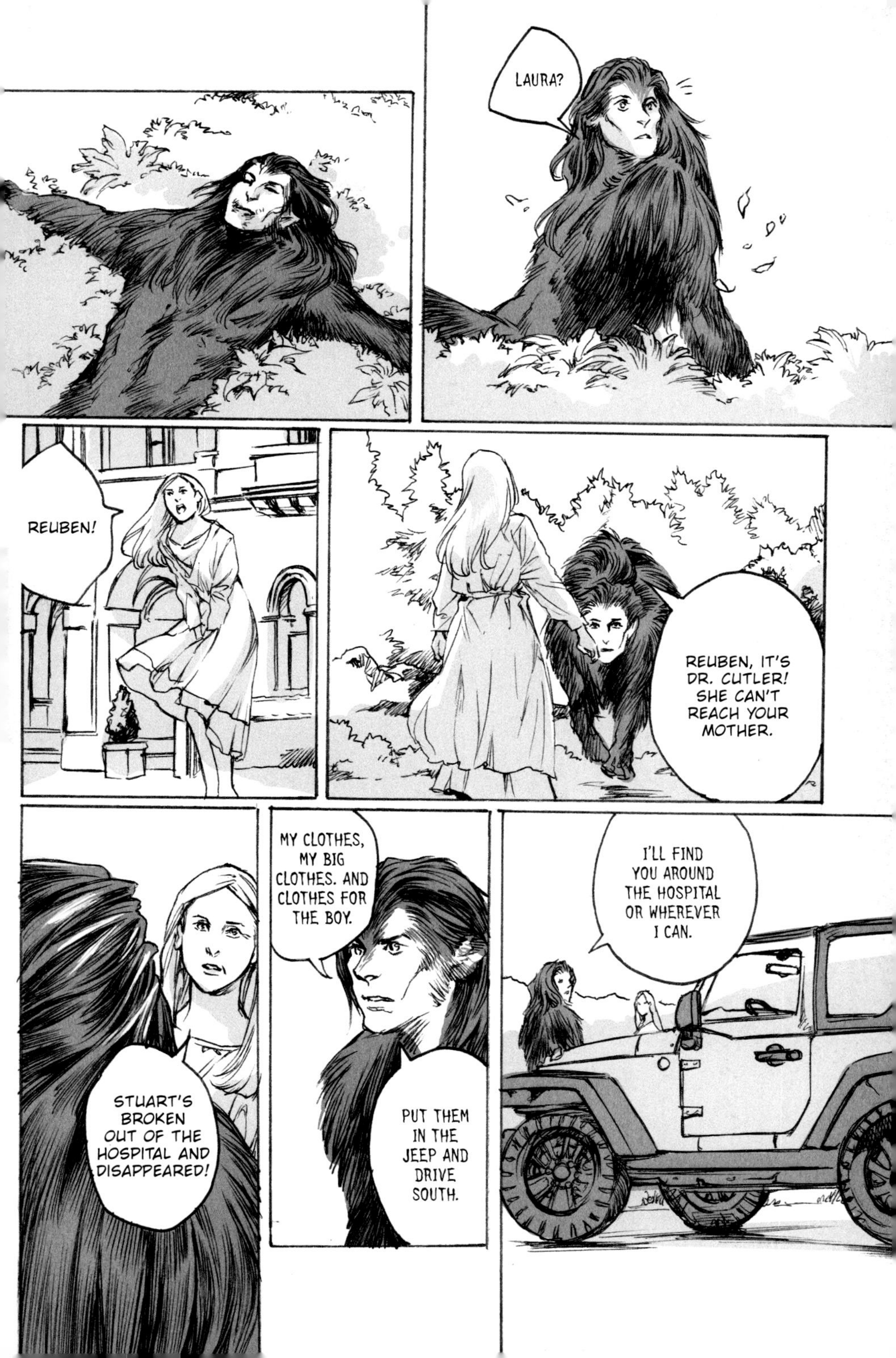
LAURA?
REUBEN!
REUBEN, IT'S DR. CUTLER! SHE CAN'T REACH YOUR MOTHER.
STUART'S BROKEN OUT OF THE HOSPITAL AND DISAPPEARED!
MY CLOTHES, MY BIG CLOTHES. AND CLOTHES FOR THE BOY.
PUT THEM IN THE JEEP AND DRIVE SOUTH.
I'LL FIND YOU AROUND THE HOSPITAL OR WHEREVER I CAN.

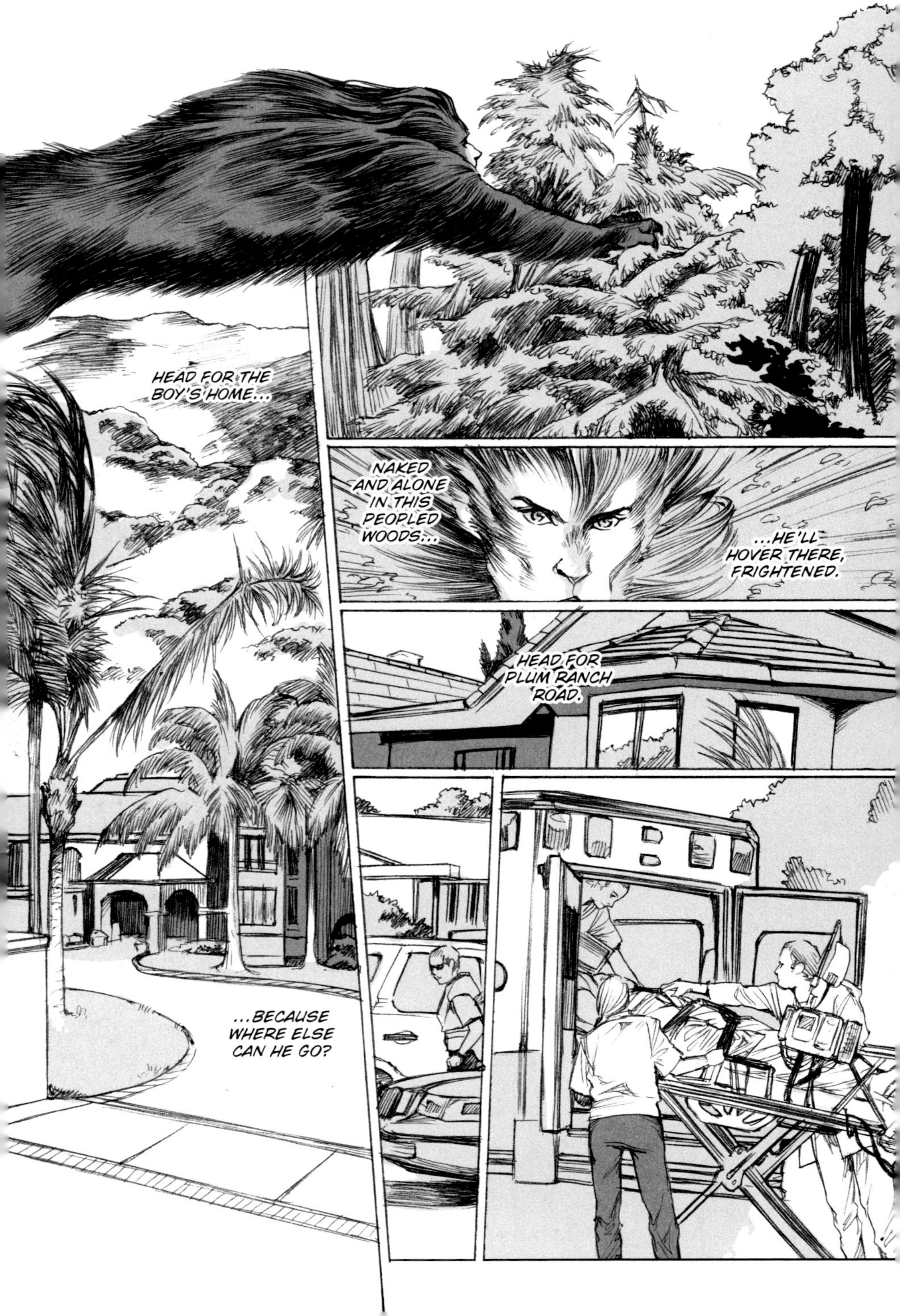
HEAD FOR THE BOY'S HOME...
NAKED AND ALONE IN THIS PEOPLED WOODS...
...HE'LL HOVER THERE, FRIGHTENED.
HEAD FOR PLUM RANCH ROAD.
...BECAUSE WHERE ELSE CAN HE GO?

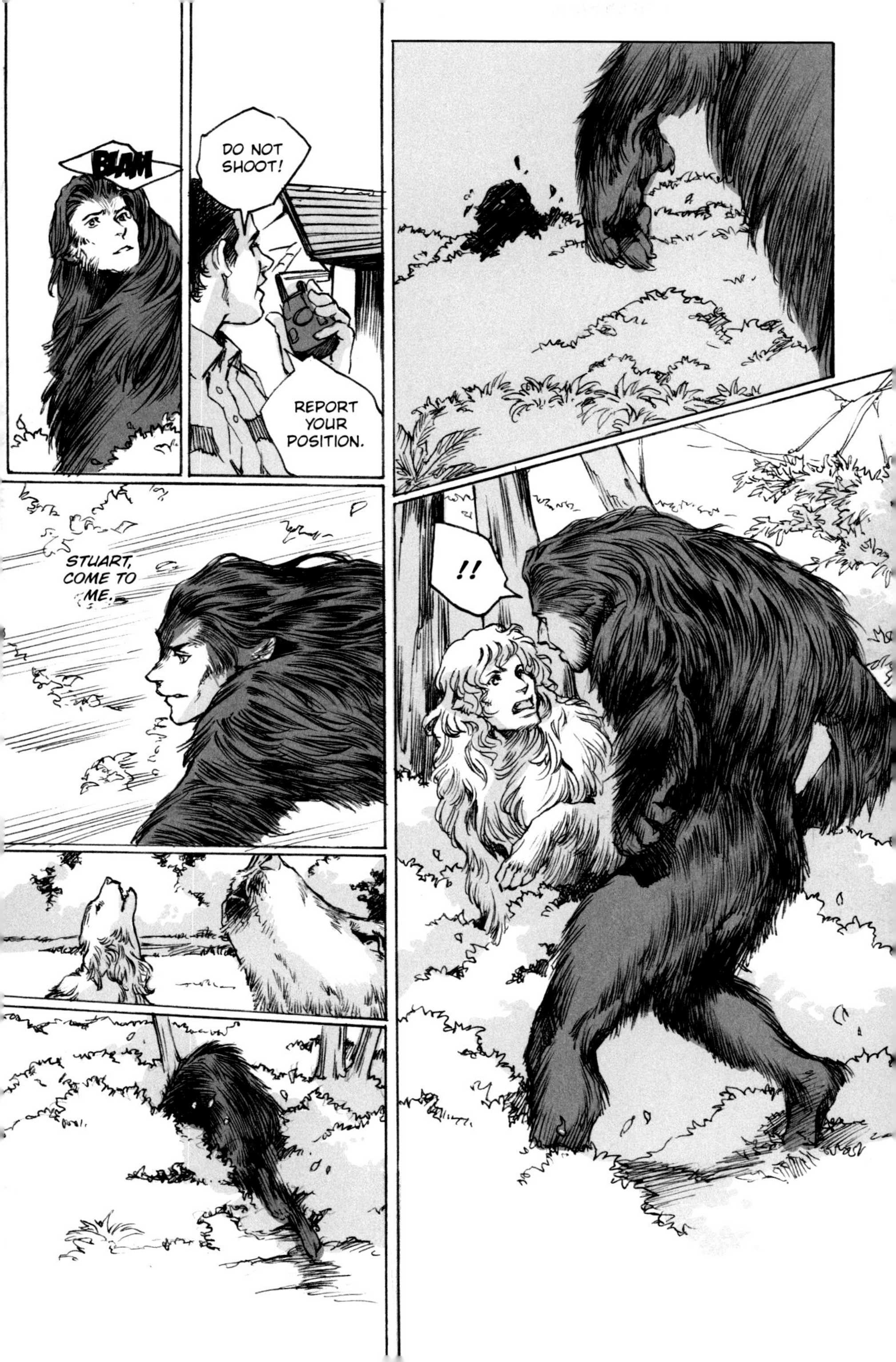
BLAM
DO NOT SHOOT!
REPORT YOUR POSITION.
STUART, COME TO ME.
!!

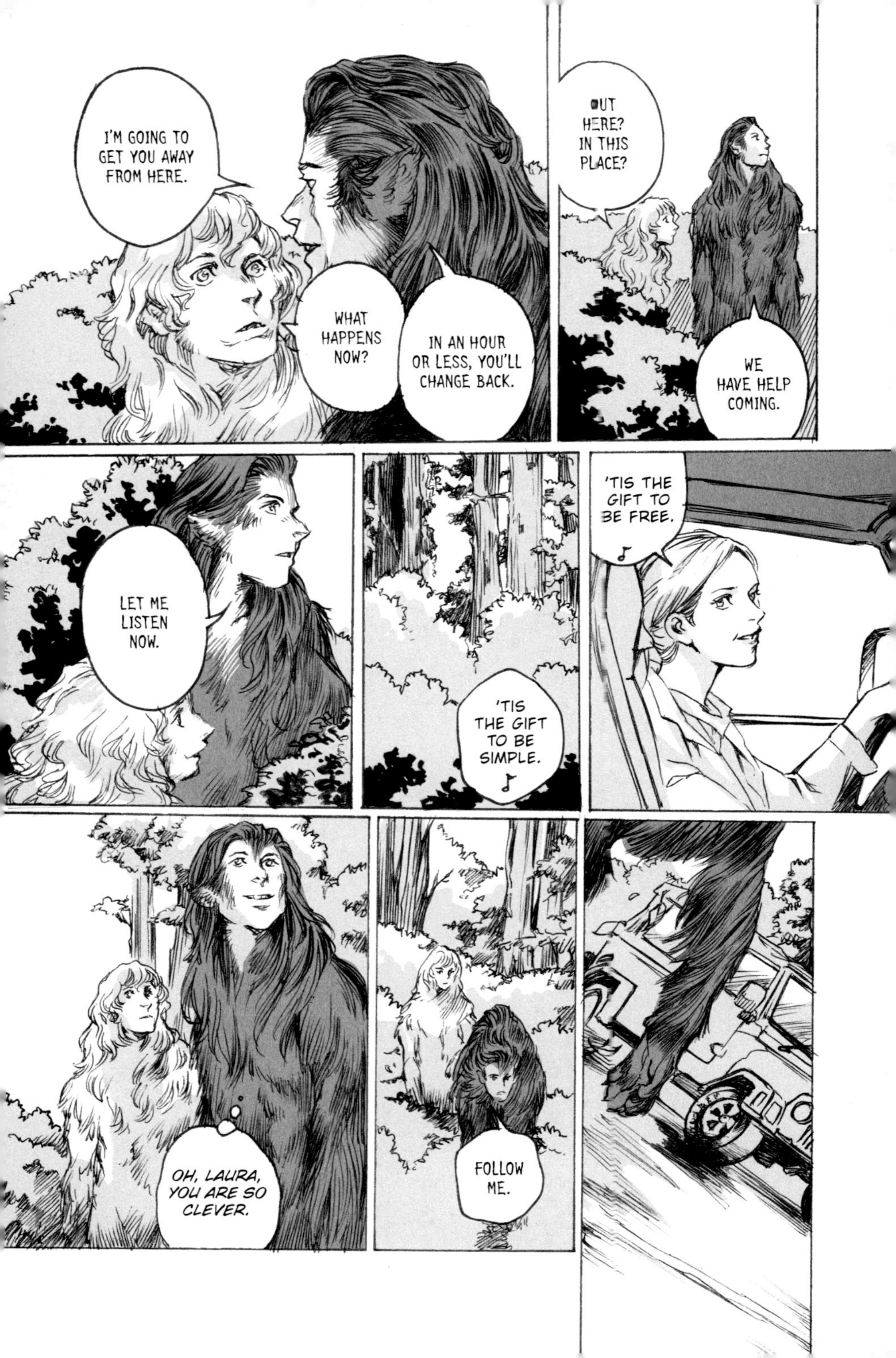
I'M GOING TO GET YOU AWAY FROM HERE.
WHAT HAPPENS NOW?
IN AN HOUR OR LESS, YOU'LL CHANGE BACK.
OUT HERE? IN THIS PLACE?
WE HAVE HELP COMING.
LET ME LISTEN NOW.
'TIS THE GIFT TO BE SIMPLE.
'TIS THE GIFT TO BE FREE.
OH, LAURA, YOU ARE SO CLEVER.
FOLLOW ME.

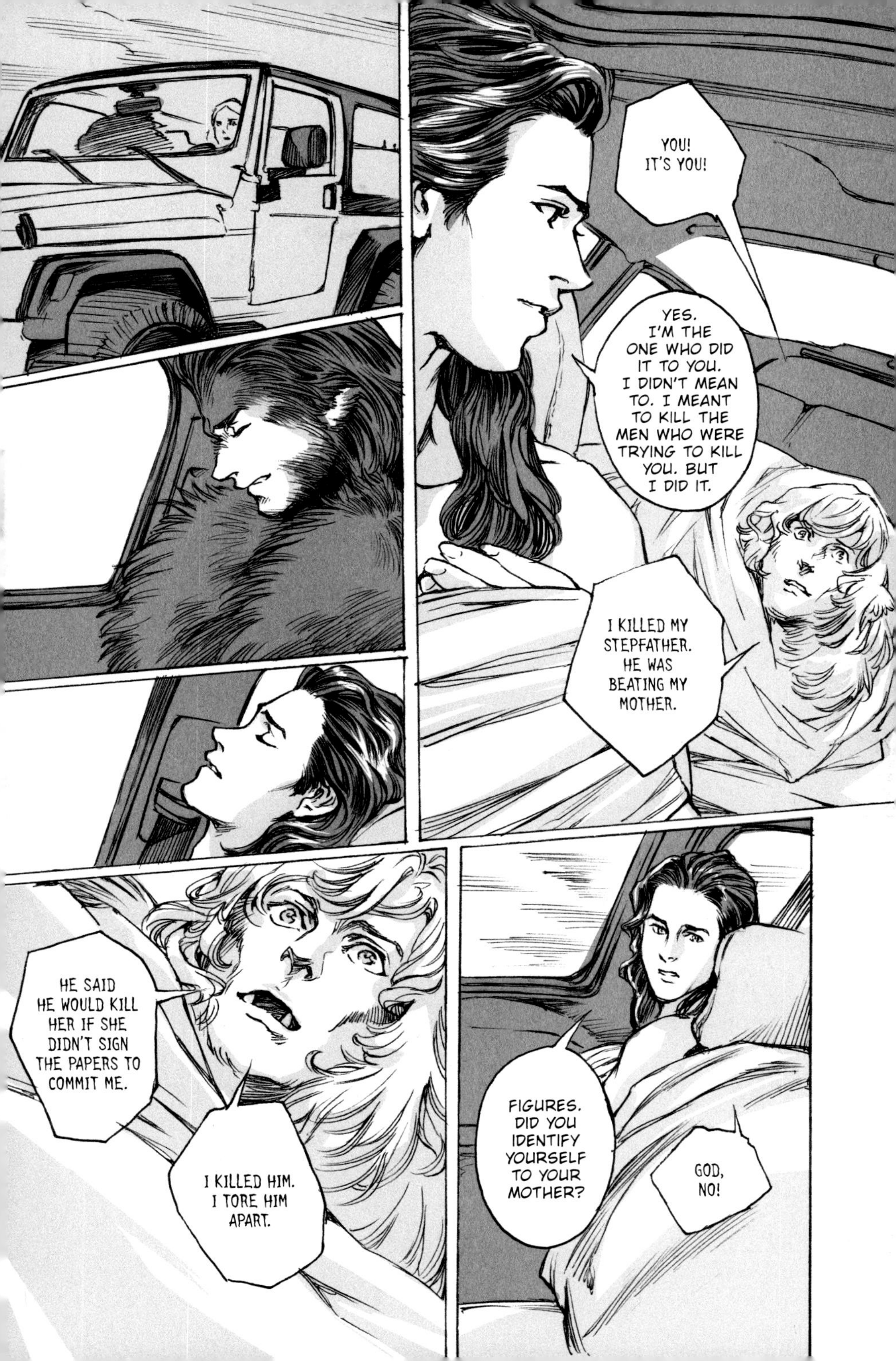
YOU! IT'S YOU!
YES. I'M THE ONE WHO DID IT TO YOU. I DIDN'T MEAN TO. I MEANT TO KILL THE MEN WHO WERE TRYING TO KILL YOU. BUT I DID IT.
I KILLED MY STEPFATHER. HE WAS BEATING MY MOTHER.
HE SAID HE WOULD KILL HER IF SHE DIDN'T SIGN THE PAPERS TO COMMIT ME.
I KILLED HIM. I TORE HIM APART.
FIGURES. DID YOU IDENTIFY YOURSELF TO YOUR MOTHER?
GOD, NO!

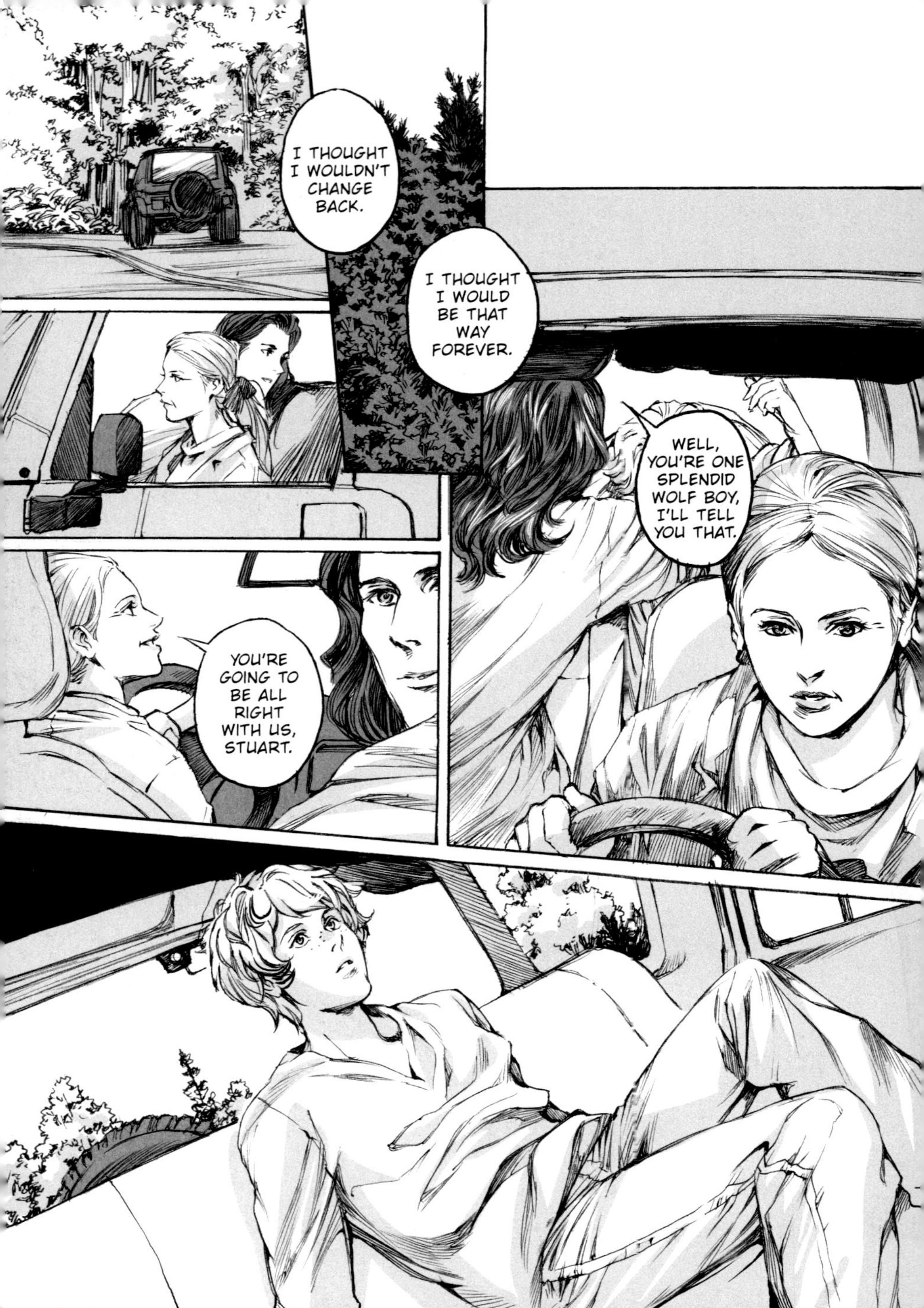
I THOUGHT I WOULDN'T CHANGE BACK.
I THOUGHT I WOULD BE THAT WAY FOREVER.
YOU'RE GOING TO BE ALL RIGHT WITH US, STUART.
WELL, YOU'RE ONE SPLENDID WOLF BOY, I'LL TELL YOU THAT.

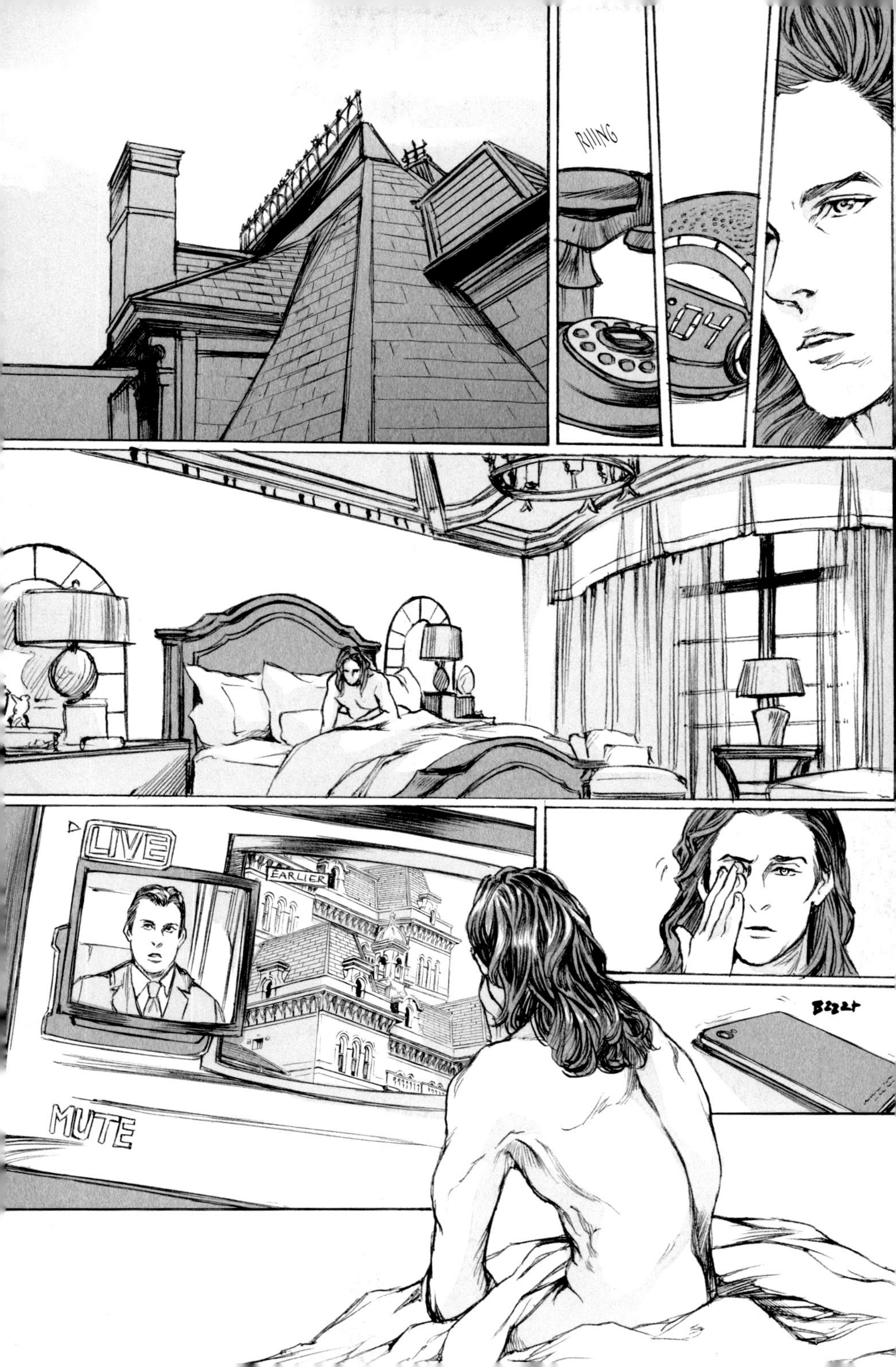
RIIING
LIVE
EARLIER
MUTE
BZZZT

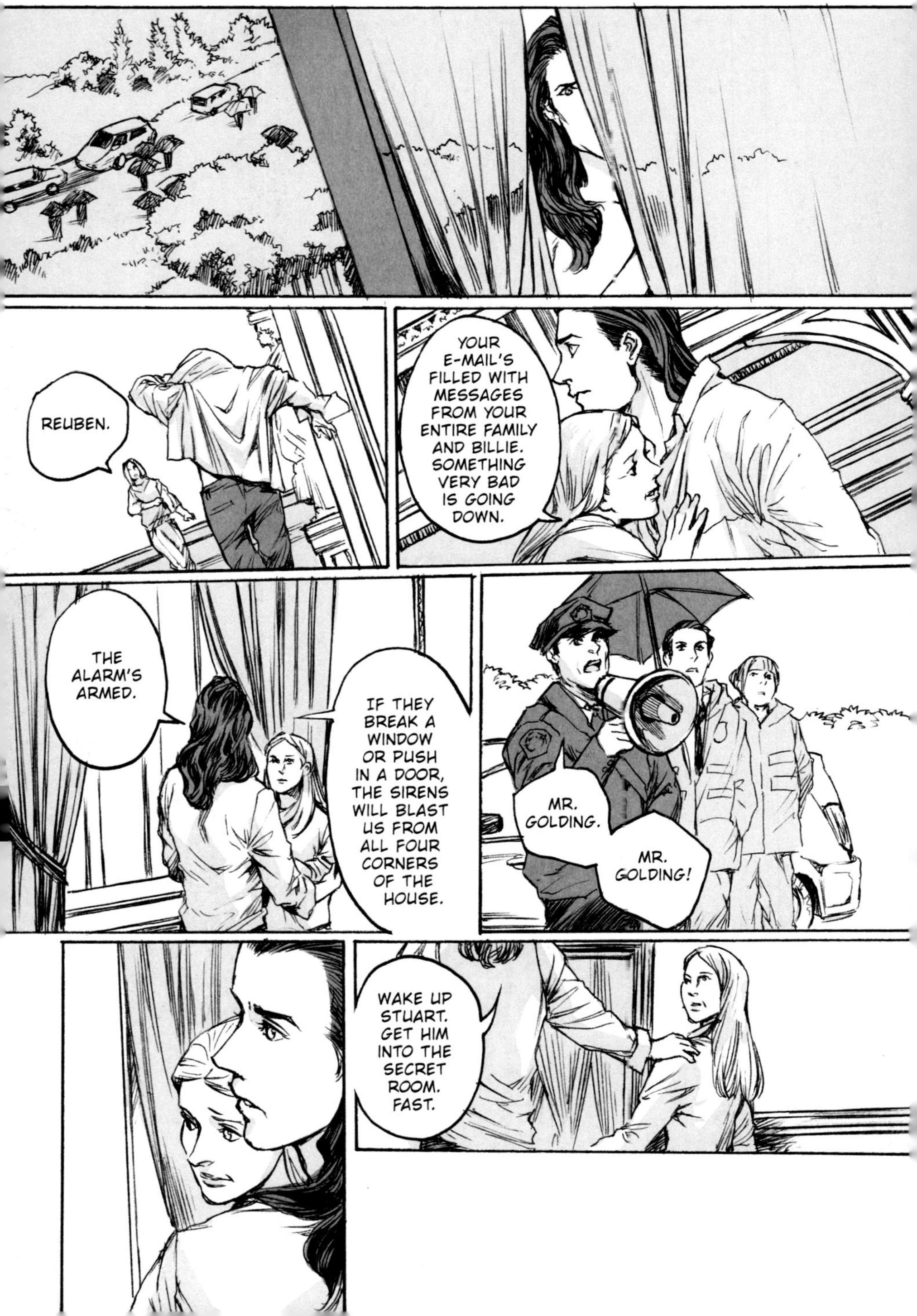
REUBEN.
YOUR E-MAIL'S FILLED WITH MESSAGES FROM YOUR ENTIRE FAMILY AND BILLIE. SOMETHING VERY BAD IS GOING DOWN.
THE ALARM'S ARMED.
IF THEY BREAK A WINDOW OR PUSH IN A DOOR, THE SIRENS WILL BLAST US FROM ALL FOUR CORNERS OF THE HOUSE.
MR. GOLDING.
MR. GOLDING!
WAKE UP STUART. GET HIM INTO THE SECRET ROOM. FAST.

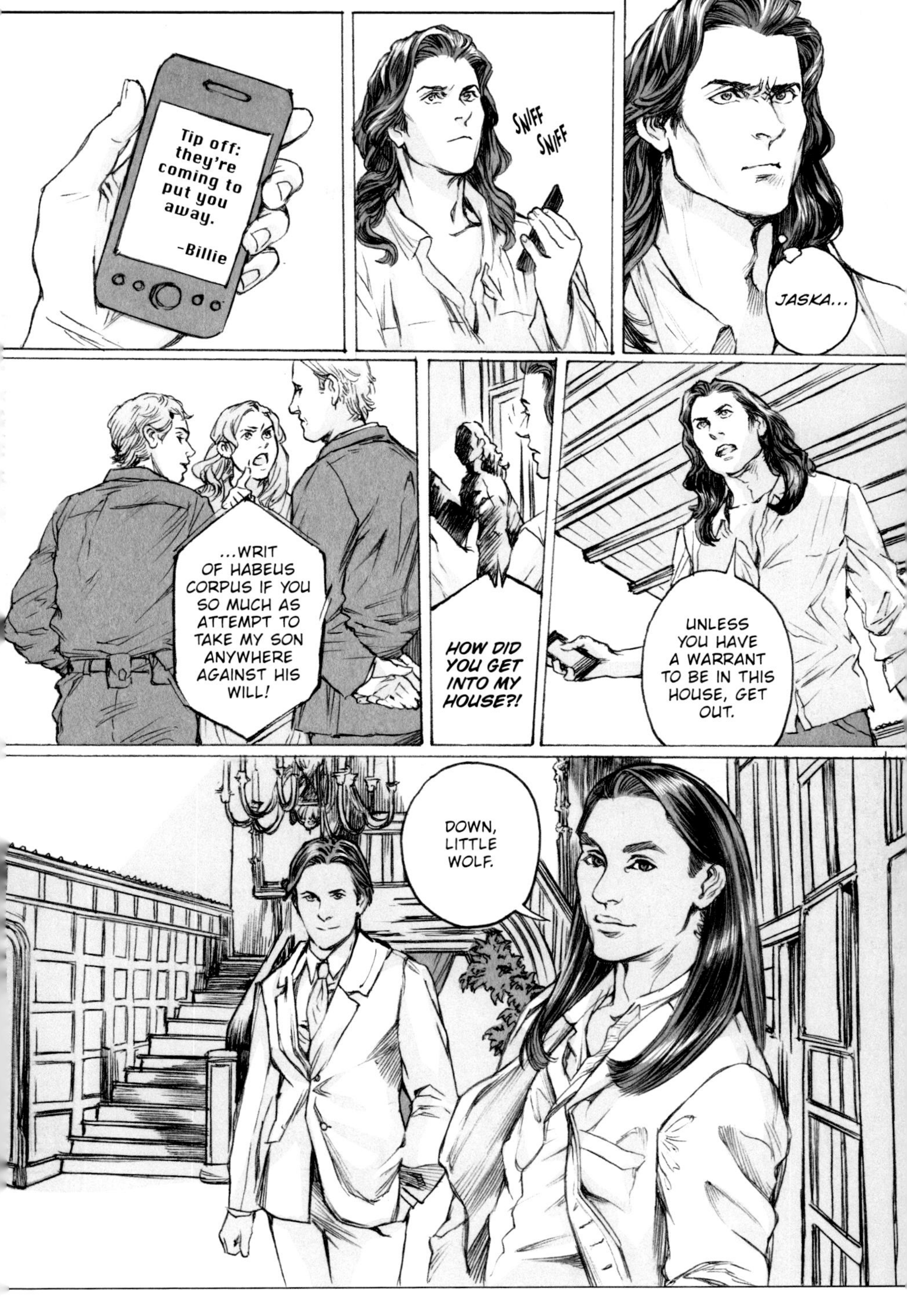
Tip off: they're coming to put you away.
-Billie
SNIFF SNIFF
JASKA...
...WRIT OF HABEUS CORPUS IF YOU SO MUCH AS ATTEMPT TO TAKE MY SON ANYWHERE AGAINST HIS WILL!
HOW DID YOU GET INTO MY HOUSE?!
UNLESS YOU HAVE A WARRANT TO BE IN THIS HOUSE, GET OUT.
DOWN, LITTLE WOLF.

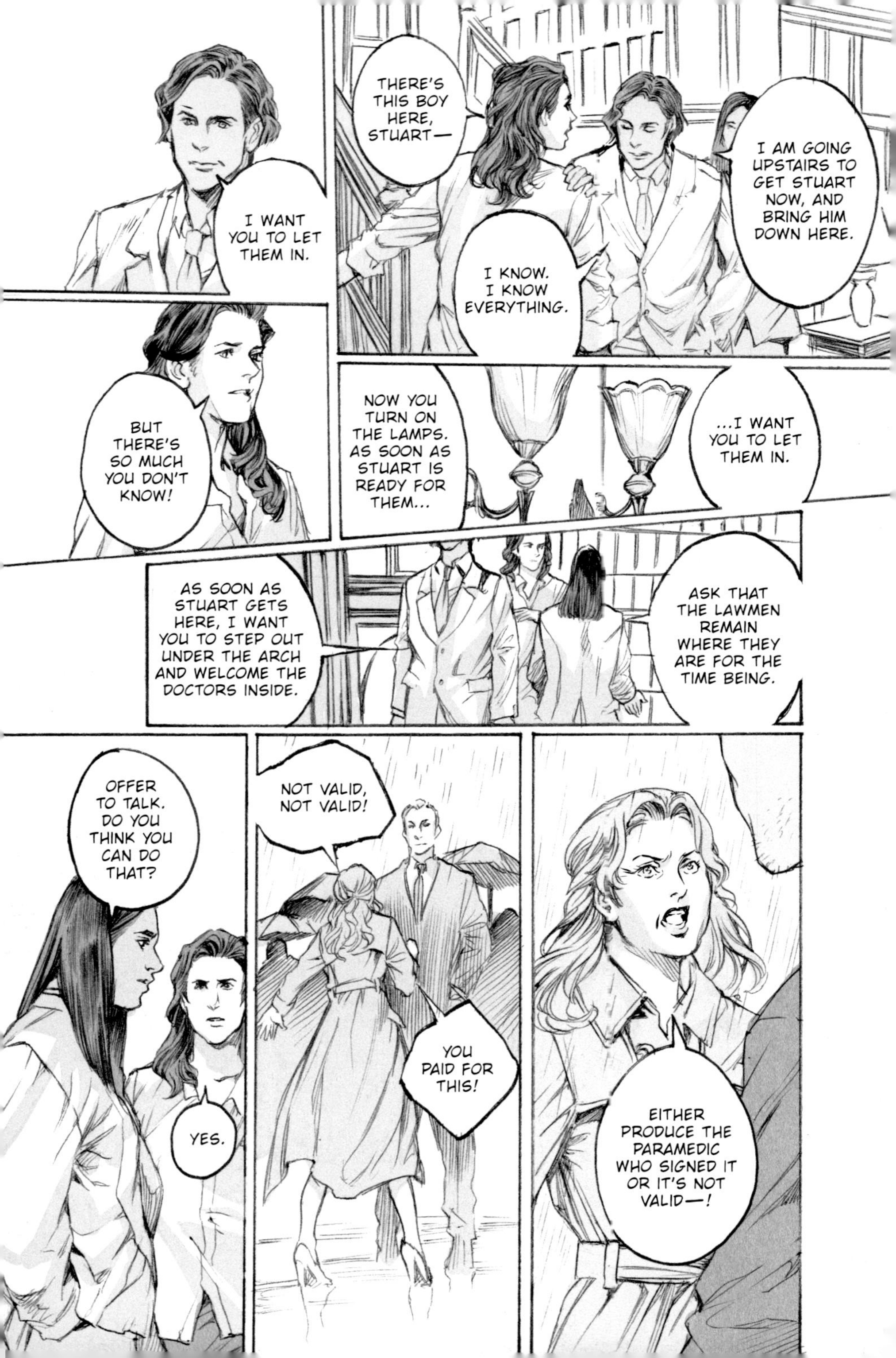
I WANT YOU TO LET THEM IN.
THERE'S THIS BOY HERE, STUART—
I KNOW. I KNOW EVERYTHING.
I AM GOING UPSTAIRS TO GET STUART NOW, AND BRING HIM DOWN HERE.
BUT THERE'S SO MUCH YOU DON'T KNOW!
NOW YOU TURN ON THE LAMPS. AS SOON AS STUART IS READY FOR THEM...
...I WANT YOU TO LET THEM IN.
AS SOON AS STUART GETS HERE, I WANT YOU TO STEP OUT UNDER THE ARCH AND WELCOME THE DOCTORS INSIDE.
ASK THAT THE LAWMEN REMAIN WHERE THEY ARE FOR THE TIME BEING.
OFFER TO TALK. DO YOU THINK YOU CAN DO THAT?
YES.
NOT VALID, NOT VALID!
YOU PAID FOR THIS!
EITHER PRODUCE THE PARAMEDIC WHO SIGNED IT OR IT'S NOT VALID—!

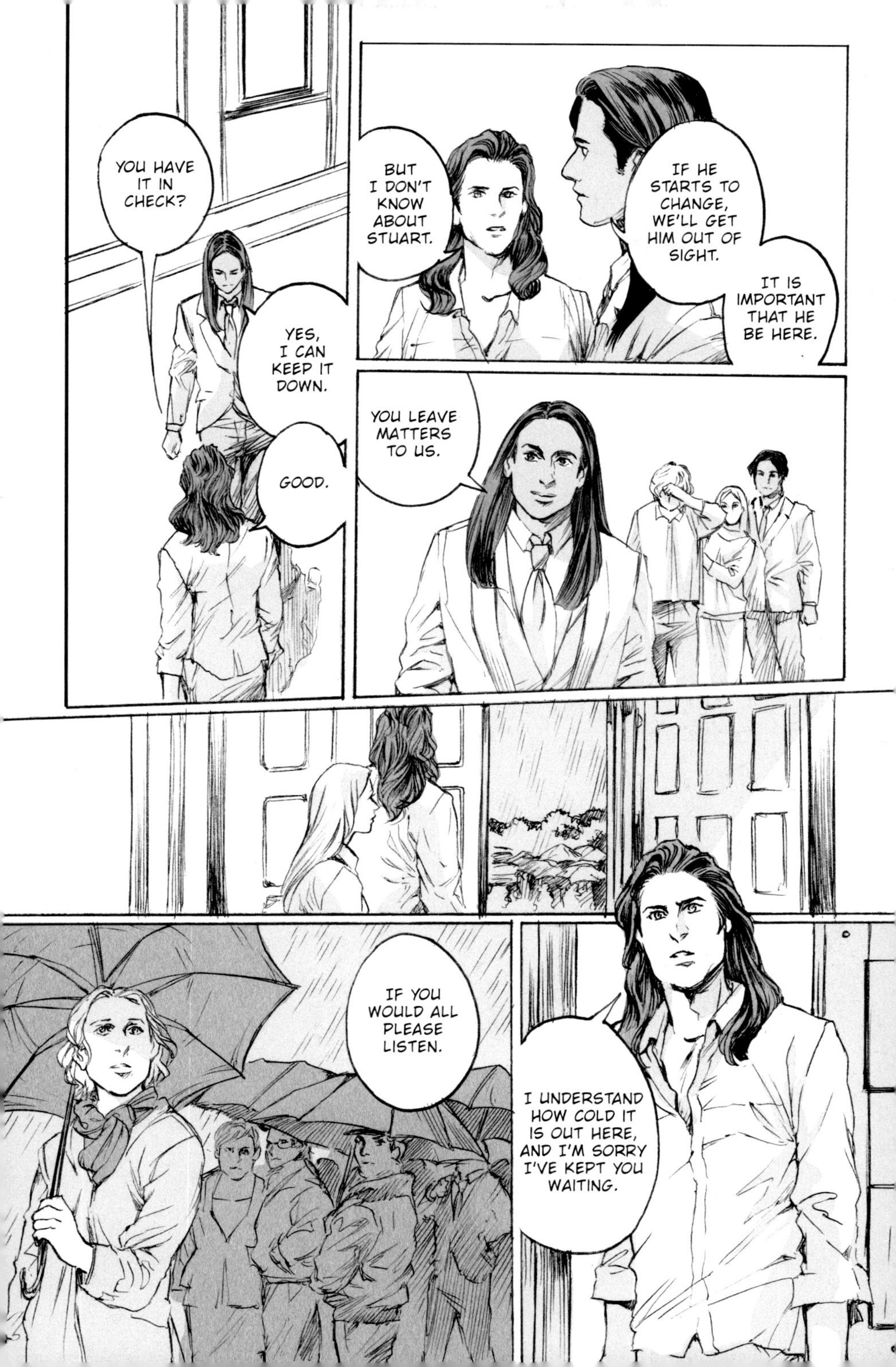
YOU HAVE IT IN CHECK?
YES, I CAN KEEP IT DOWN.
GOOD.
BUT I DON'T KNOW ABOUT STUART.
IF HE STARTS TO CHANGE, WE'LL GET HIM OUT OF SIGHT.
IT IS IMPORTANT THAT HE BE HERE.
YOU LEAVE MATTERS TO US.
IF YOU WOULD ALL PLEASE LISTEN.
I UNDERSTAND HOW COLD IT IS OUT HERE, AND I'M SORRY I'VE KEPT YOU WAITING.

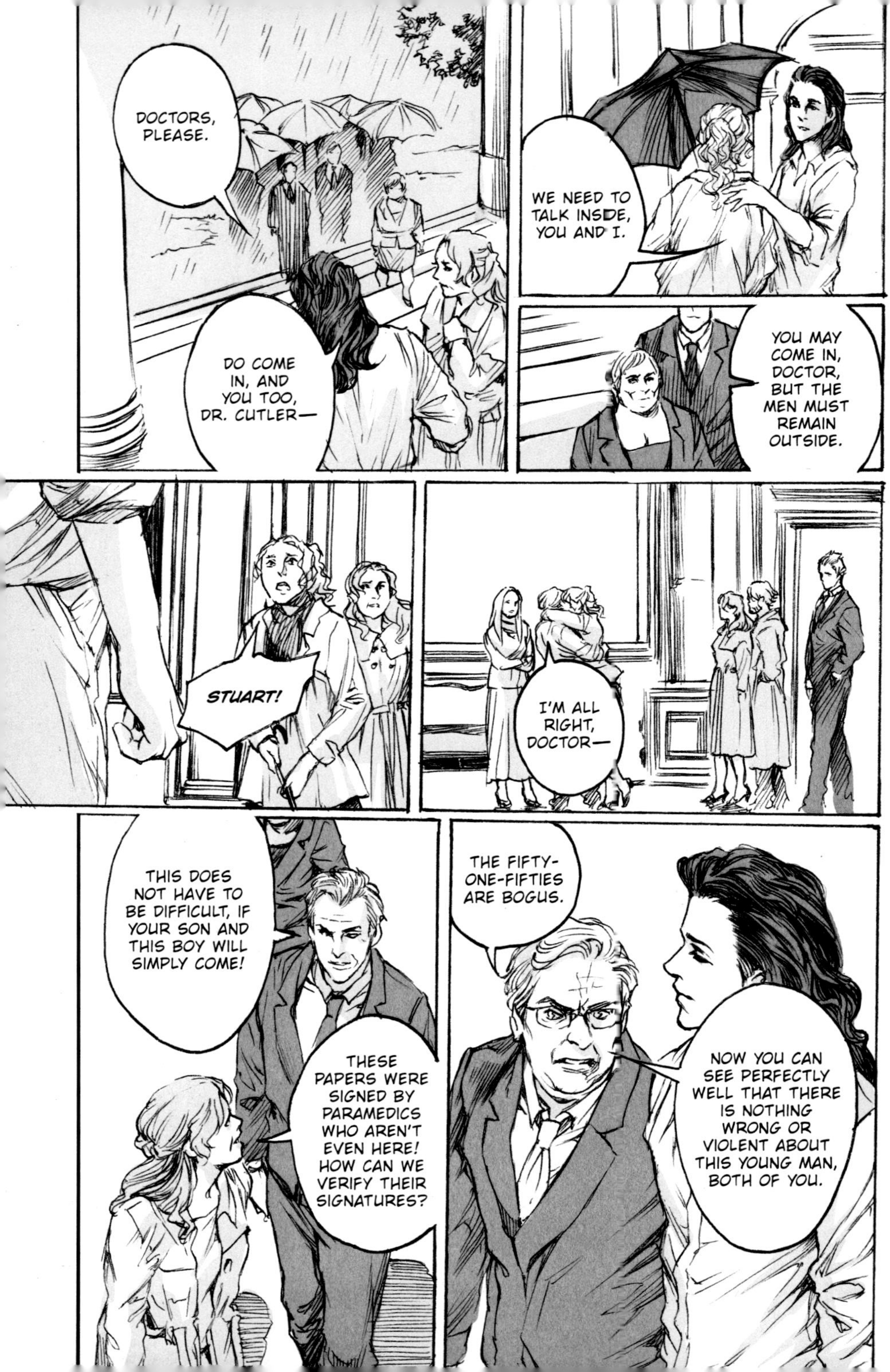
DOCTORS, PLEASE.
DO COME IN, AND YOU TOO, DR. CUTLER—
WE NEED TO TALK INSIDE, YOU AND I.
YOU MAY COME IN, DOCTOR, BUT THE MEN MUST REMAIN OUTSIDE.
STUART!
I'M ALL RIGHT, DOCTOR—
THIS DOES NOT HAVE TO BE DIFFICULT, IF YOUR SON AND THIS BOY WILL SIMPLY COME!
THESE PAPERS WERE SIGNED BY PARAMEDICS WHO AREN'T EVEN HERE! HOW CAN WE VERIFY THEIR SIGNATURES?
THE FIFTY-ONE-FIFTIES ARE BOGUS.
NOW YOU CAN SEE PERFECTLY WELL THAT THERE IS NOTHING WRONG OR VIOLENT ABOUT THIS YOUNG MAN, BOTH OF YOU.

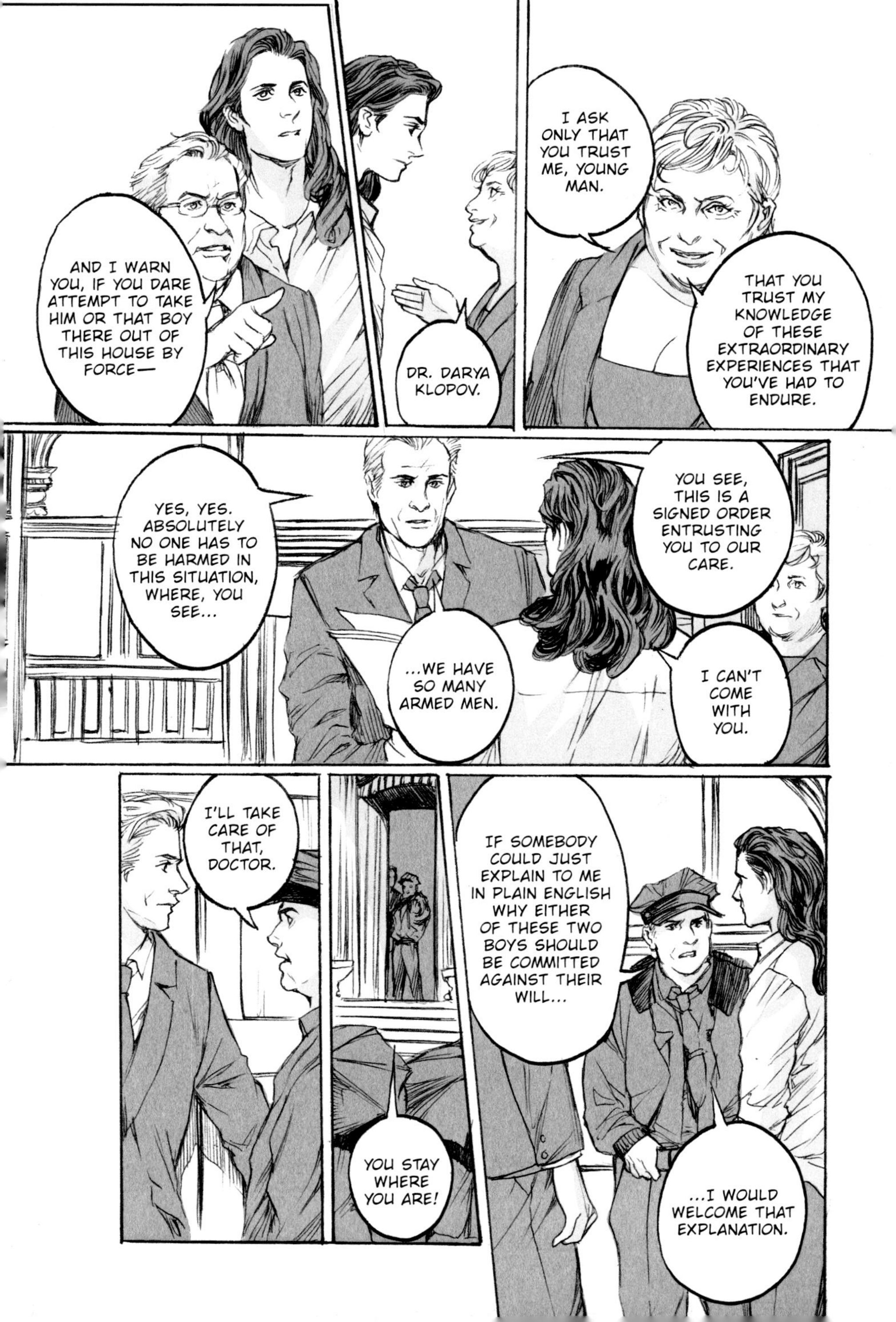
AND I WARN YOU, IF YOU DARE ATTEMPT TO TAKE HIM OR THAT BOY THERE OUT OF THIS HOUSE BY FORCE—
DR. DARYA KLOPOV.
I ASK ONLY THAT YOU TRUST ME, YOUNG MAN.
THAT YOU TRUST MY KNOWLEDGE OF THESE EXTRAORDINARY EXPERIENCES THAT YOU'VE HAD TO ENDURE.
YES, YES. ABSOLUTELY NO ONE HAS TO BE HARMED IN THIS SITUATION, WHERE, YOU SEE...
...WE HAVE SO MANY ARMED MEN.
YOU SEE, THIS IS A SIGNED ORDER ENTRUSTING YOU TO OUR CARE.
I CAN'T COME WITH YOU.
I'LL TAKE CARE OF THAT, DOCTOR.
YOU STAY WHERE YOU ARE!
IF SOMEBODY COULD JUST EXPLAIN TO ME IN PLAIN ENGLISH WHY EITHER OF THESE TWO BOYS SHOULD BE COMMITTED AGAINST THEIR WILL...
...I WOULD WELCOME THAT EXPLANATION.

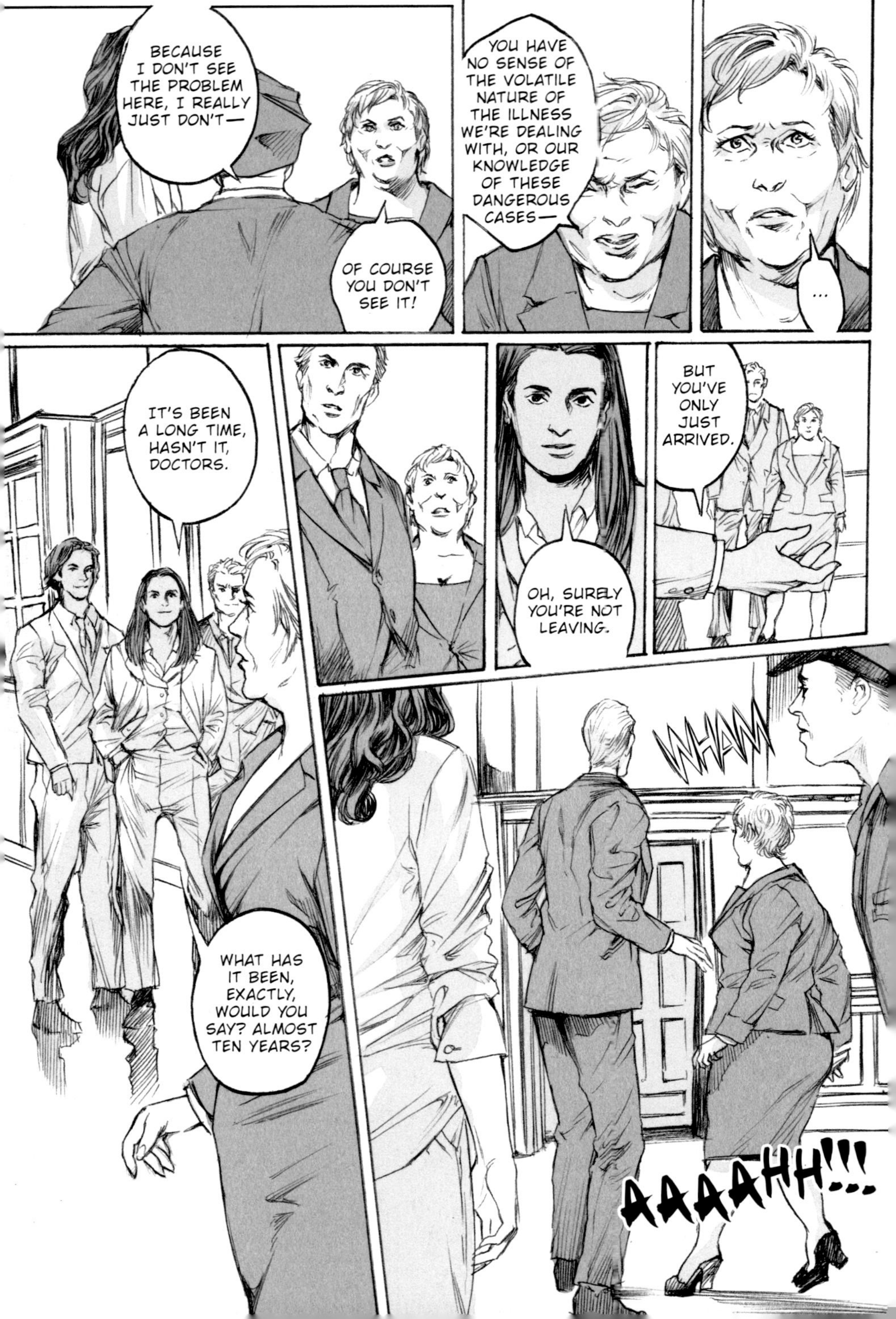
BECAUSE I DON'T SEE THE PROBLEM HERE, I REALLY JUST DON'T—
OF COURSE YOU DON'T SEE IT!
YOU HAVE NO SENSE OF THE VOLATILE NATURE OF THE ILLNESS WE'RE DEALING WITH, OR OUR KNOWLEDGE OF THESE DANGEROUS CASES—
...
IT'S BEEN A LONG TIME, HASN'T IT, DOCTORS.
OH, SURELY YOU'RE NOT LEAVING.
BUT YOU'VE ONLY JUST ARRIVED.
WHAT HAS IT BEEN, EXACTLY, WOULD YOU SAY? ALMOST TEN YEARS?
WHAM
AAAAHH!!!

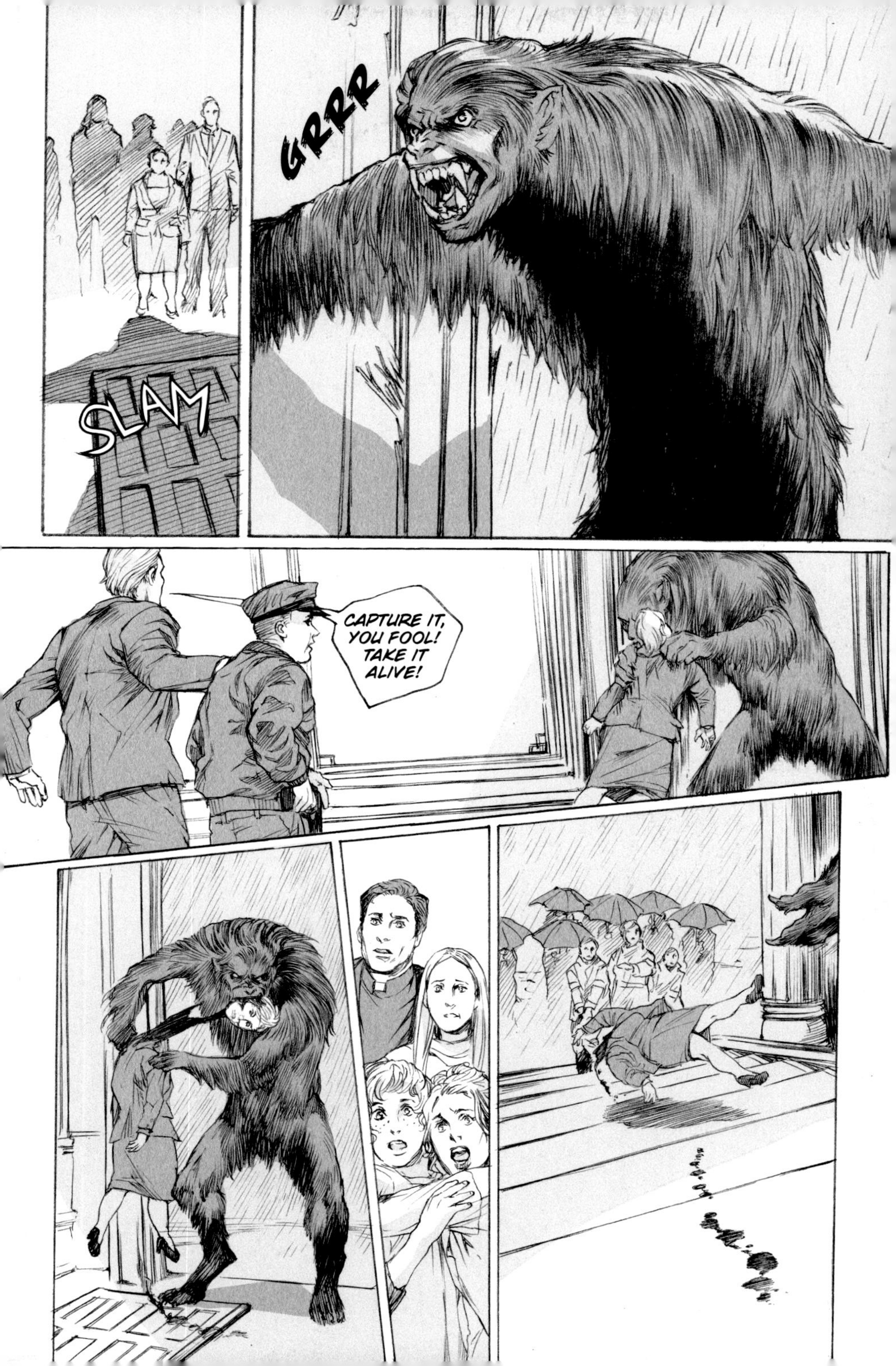
GRRR
SLAM
CAPTURE IT, YOU FOOL! TAKE IT ALIVE!

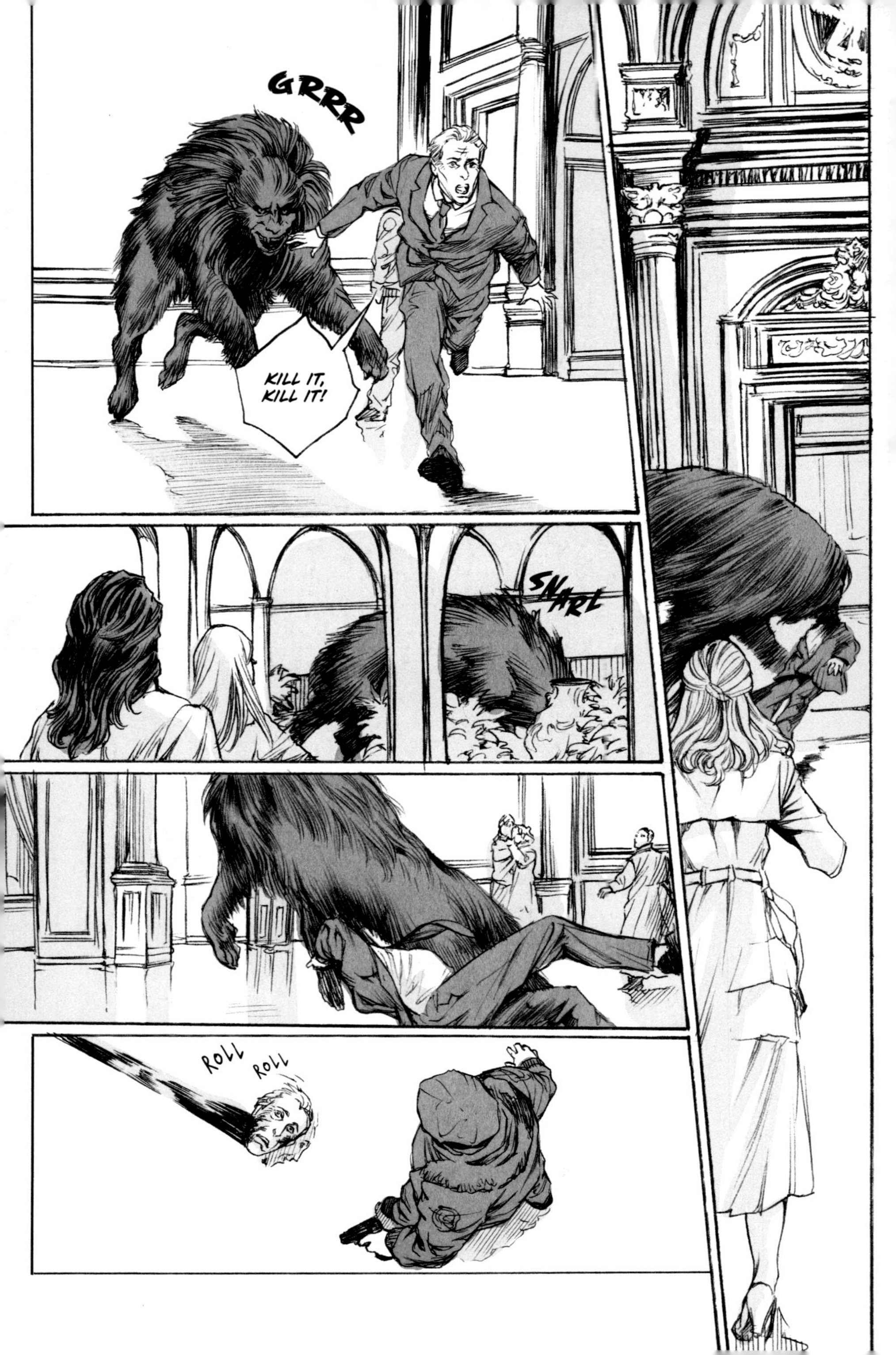
GRRR
KILL IT, KILL IT!
SNARL
ROLL
ROLL

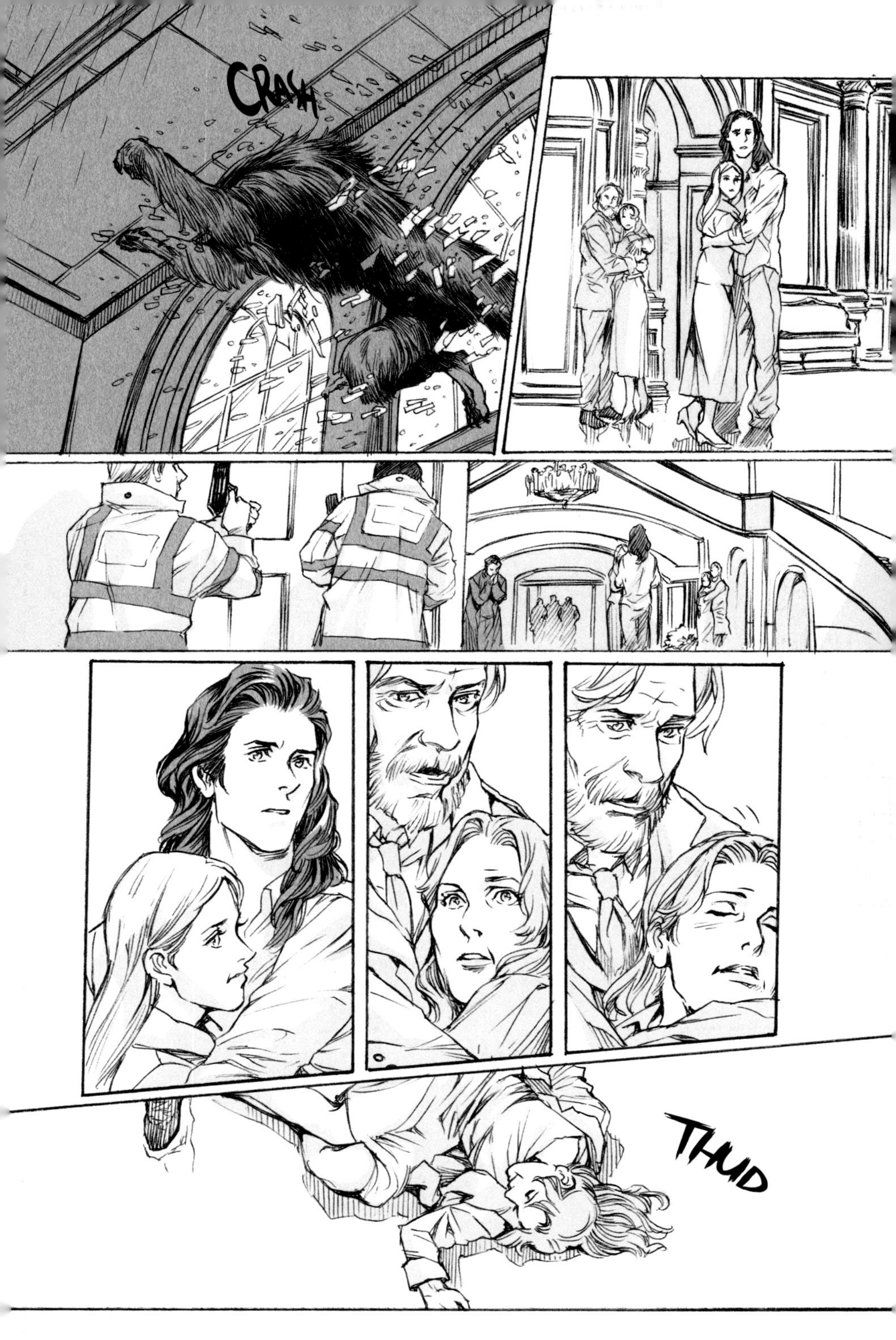
CRASH
THUD

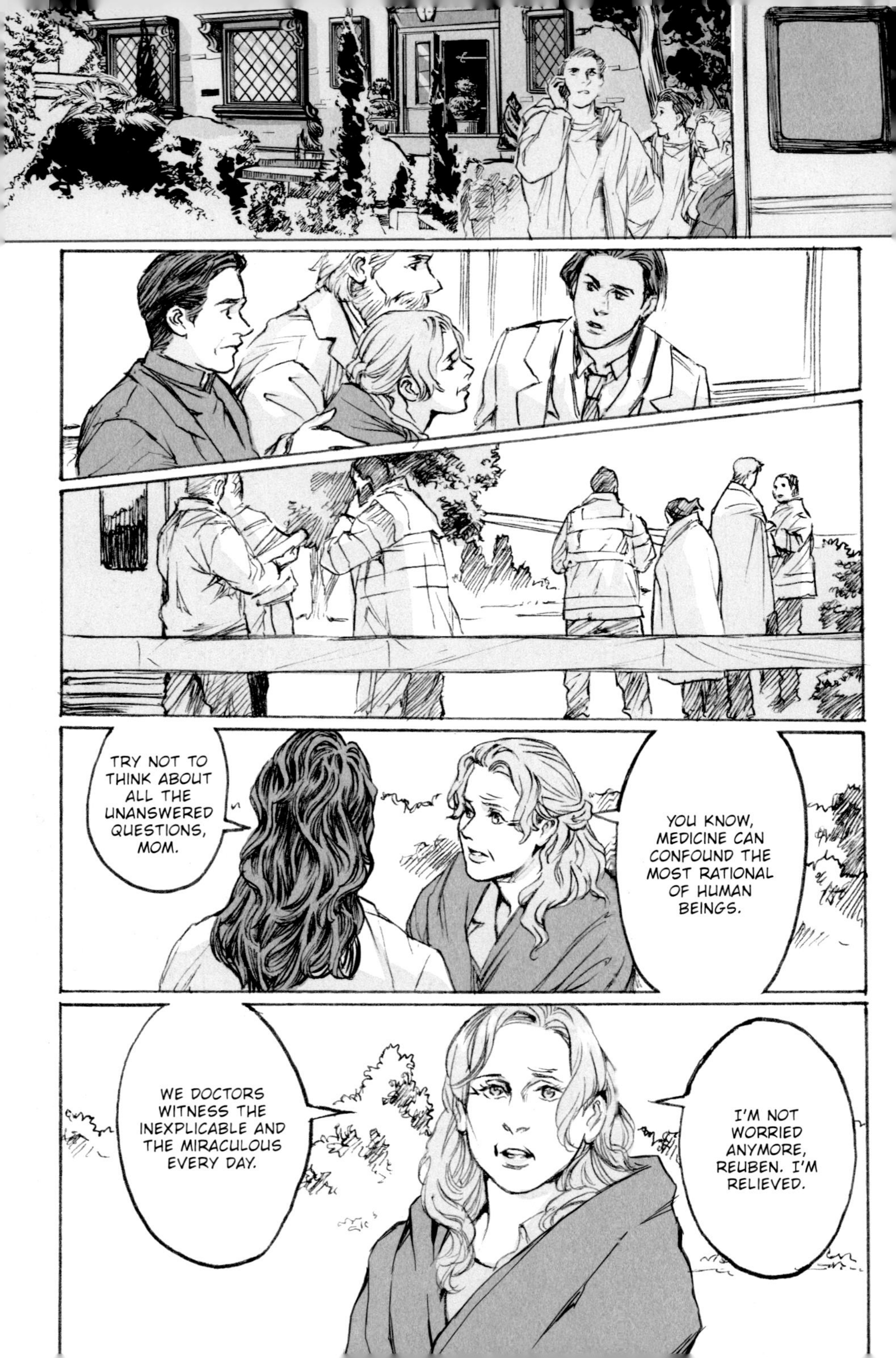
TRY NOT TO THINK ABOUT ALL THE UNANSWERED QUESTIONS, MOM.
YOU KNOW, MEDICINE CAN CONFOUND THE MOST RATIONAL OF HUMAN BEINGS.
WE DOCTORS WITNESS THE INEXPLICABLE AND THE MIRACULOUS EVERY DAY.
I'M NOT WORRIED ANYMORE, REUBEN. I'M RELIEVED.

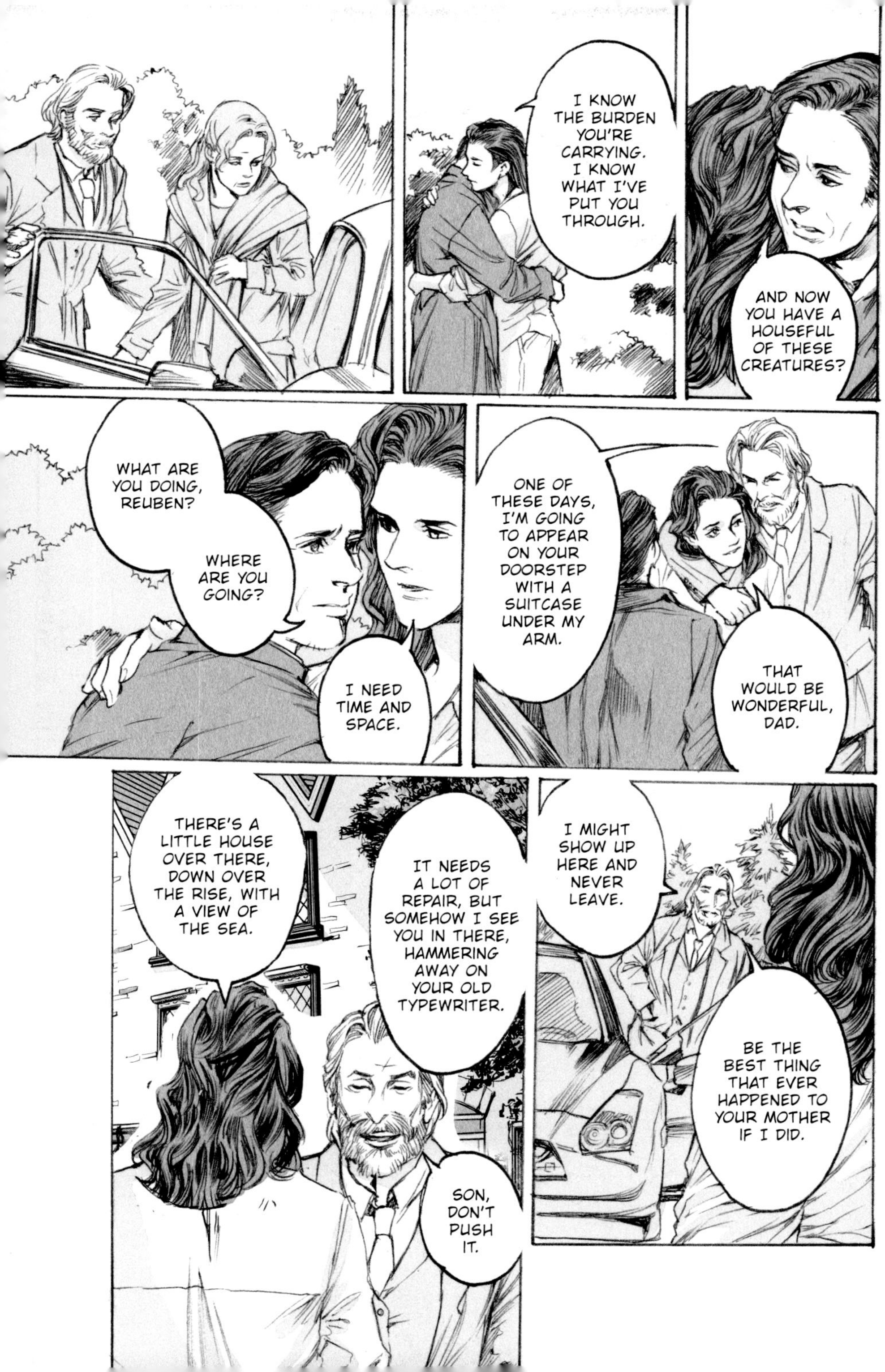
I KNOW THE BURDEN YOU'RE CARRYING. I KNOW WHAT I'VE PUT YOU THROUGH.
AND NOW YOU HAVE A HOUSEFUL OF THESE CREATURES?
WHAT ARE YOU DOING, REUBEN?
WHERE ARE YOU GOING?
I NEED TIME AND SPACE.
ONE OF THESE DAYS, I'M GOING TO APPEAR ON YOUR DOORSTEP WITH A SUITCASE UNDER MY ARM.
THAT WOULD BE WONDERFUL, DAD.
THERE'S A LITTLE HOUSE OVER THERE, DOWN OVER THE RISE, WITH A VIEW OF THE SEA.
IT NEEDS A LOT OF REPAIR, BUT SOMEHOW I SEE YOU IN THERE, HAMMERING AWAY ON YOUR OLD TYPEWRITER.
SON, DON'T PUSH IT.
I MIGHT SHOW UP HERE AND NEVER LEAVE.
BE THE BEST THING THAT EVER HAPPENED TO YOUR MOTHER IF I DID.

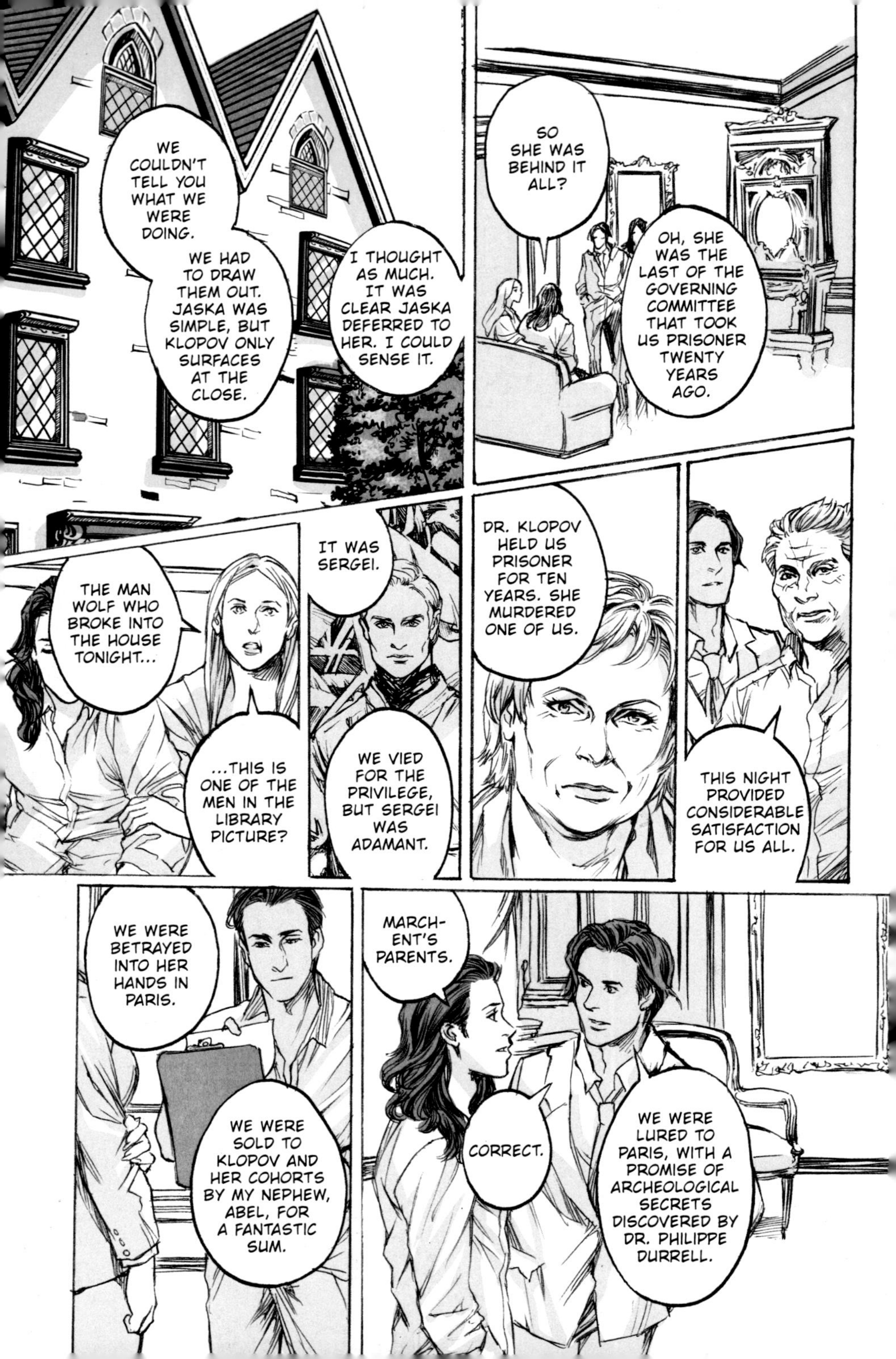
WE COULDN'T TELL YOU WHAT WE WERE DOING.
WE HAD TO DRAW THEM OUT. JASKA WAS SIMPLE, BUT KLOPOV ONLY SURFACES AT THE CLOSE.
I THOUGHT AS MUCH. IT WAS CLEAR JASKA DEFERRED TO HER. I COULD SENSE IT.
SO SHE WAS BEHIND IT ALL?
OH, SHE WAS THE LAST OF THE GOVERNING COMMITTEE THAT TOOK US PRISONER TWENTY YEARS AGO.
THE MAN WOLF WHO BROKE INTO THE HOUSE TONIGHT...
...THIS IS ONE OF THE MEN IN THE LIBRARY PICTURE?
IT WAS SERGEI.
WE VIED FOR THE PRIVILEGE, BUT SERGEI WAS ADAMANT.
DR. KLOPOV HELD US PRISONER FOR TEN YEARS. SHE MURDERED ONE OF US.
THIS NIGHT PROVIDED CONSIDERABLE SATISFACTION FOR US ALL.
WE WERE BETRAYED INTO HER HANDS IN PARIS.
WE WERE SOLD TO KLOPOV AND HER COHORTS BY MY NEPHEW, ABEL, FOR A FANTASTIC SUM.
MARCH-ENT'S PARENTS.
CORRECT.
WE WERE LURED TO PARIS, WITH A PROMISE OF ARCHEOLOGICAL SECRETS DISCOVERED BY DR. PHILIPPE DURRELL.

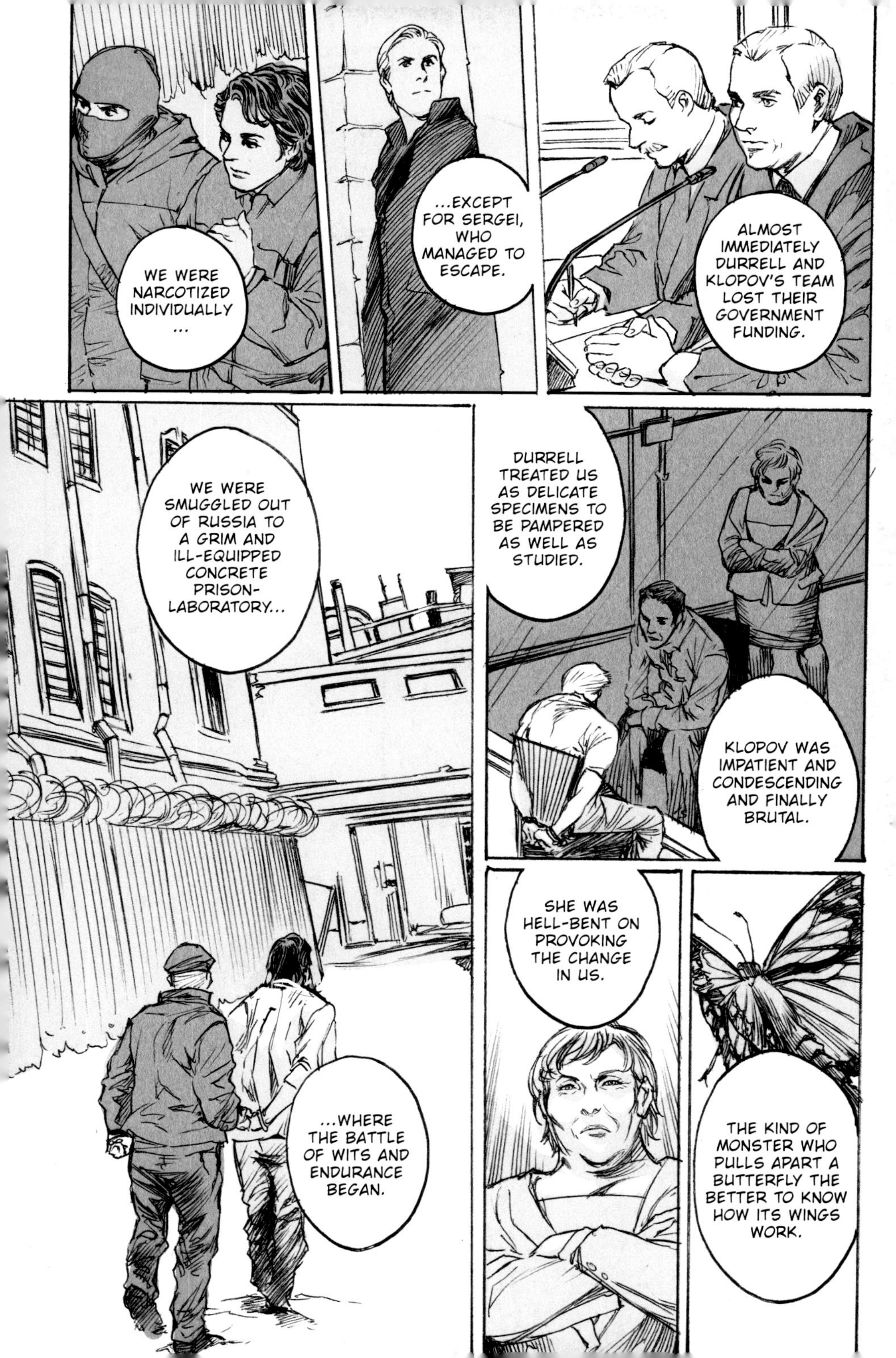
WE WERE NARCOTIZED INDIVIDUALLY ...
...EXCEPT FOR SERGEI, WHO MANAGED TO ESCAPE.
ALMOST IMMEDIATELY DURRELL AND KLOPOV'S TEAM LOST THEIR GOVERNMENT FUNDING.
WE WERE SMUGGLED OUT OF RUSSIA TO A GRIM AND ILL-EQUIPPED CONCRETE PRISON-LABORATORY...
...WHERE THE BATTLE OF WITS AND ENDURANCE BEGAN.
DURRELL TREATED US AS DELICATE SPECIMENS TO BE PAMPERED AS WELL AS STUDIED.
KLOPOV WAS IMPATIENT AND CONDESCENDING AND FINALLY BRUTAL.
SHE WAS HELL-BENT ON PROVOKING THE CHANGE IN US.
THE KIND OF MONSTER WHO PULLS APART A BUTTERFLY THE BETTER TO KNOW HOW ITS WINGS WORK.

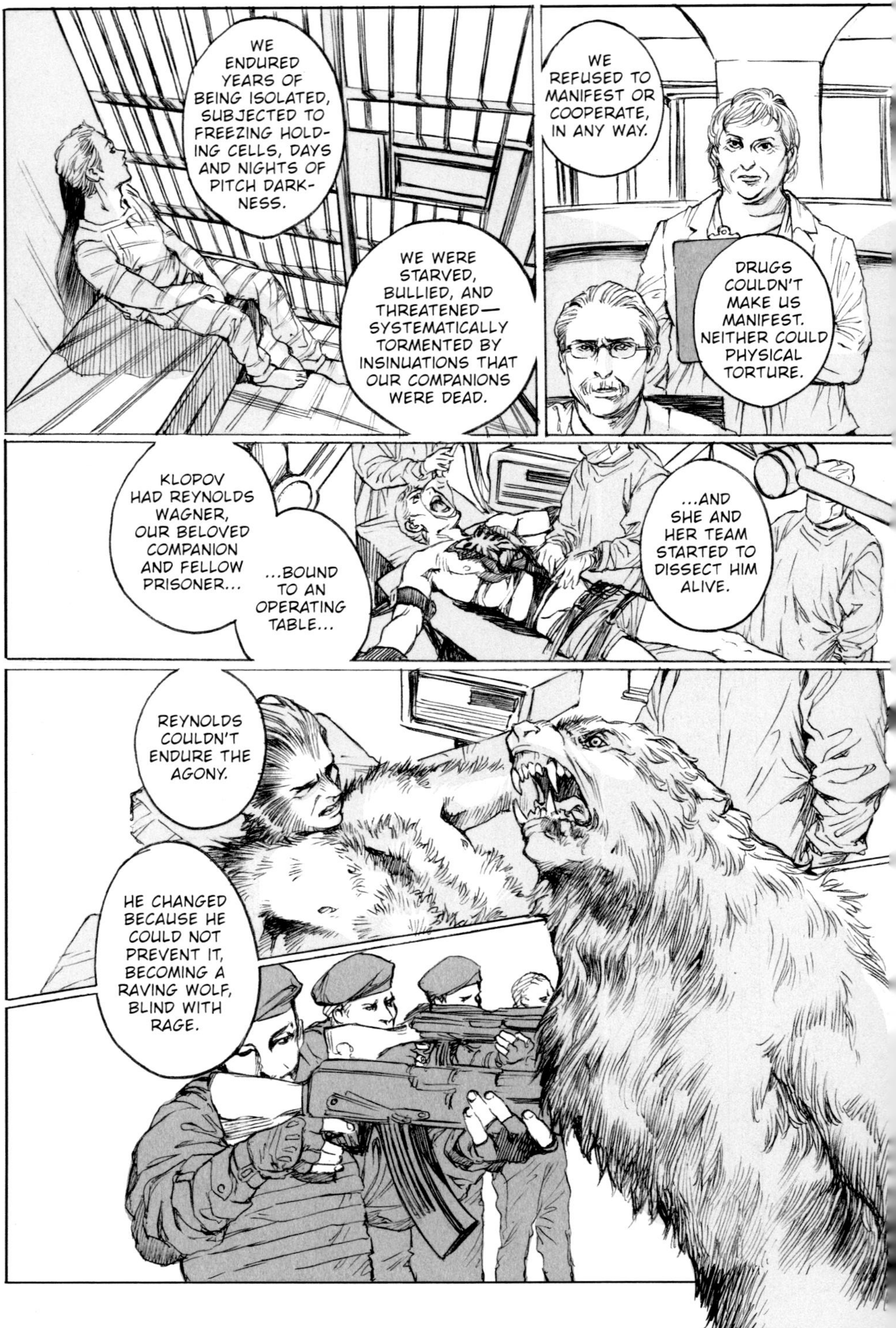
WE ENDURED YEARS OF BEING ISOLATED, SUBJECTED TO FREEZING HOLDING CELLS, DAYS AND NIGHTS OF PITCH DARKNESS.
WE WERE STARVED, BULLIED, AND THREATENED—SYSTEMATICALLY TORMENTED BY INSINUATIONS THAT OUR COMPANIONS WERE DEAD.
WE REFUSED TO MANIFEST OR COOPERATE, IN ANY WAY.
DRUGS COULDN'T MAKE US MANIFEST. NEITHER COULD PHYSICAL TORTURE.
KLOPOV HAD REYNOLDS WAGNER, OUR BELOVED COMPANION AND FELLOW PRISONER...
...BOUND TO AN OPERATING TABLE...
...AND SHE AND HER TEAM STARTED TO DISSECT HIM ALIVE.
REYNOLDS COULDN'T ENDURE THE AGONY.
HE CHANGED BECAUSE HE COULD NOT PREVENT IT, BECOMING A RAVING WOLF, BLIND WITH RAGE.

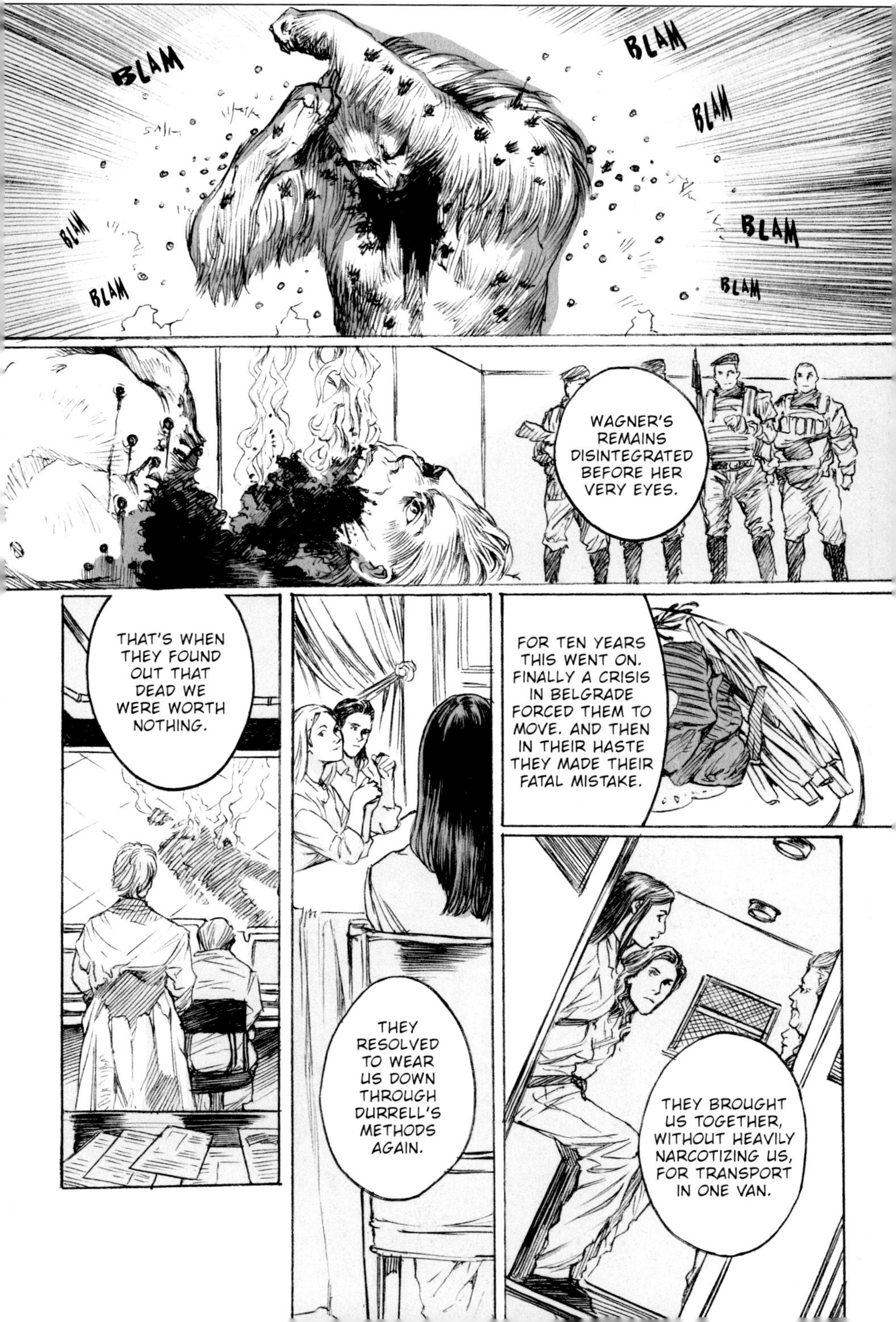
BLAM
BLAM
BLAM
BLAM
BLAM
BLAM
BLAM
WAGNER'S REMAINS DISINTEGRATED BEFORE HER VERY EYES.
THAT'S WHEN THEY FOUND OUT THAT DEAD WE WERE WORTH NOTHING.
THEY RESOLVED TO WEAR US DOWN THROUGH DURRELL'S METHODS AGAIN.
FOR TEN YEARS THIS WENT ON. FINALLY A CRISIS IN BELGRADE FORCED THEM TO MOVE. AND THEN IN THEIR HASTE THEY MADE THEIR FATAL MISTAKE.
THEY BROUGHT US TOGETHER, WITHOUT HEAVILY NARCOTIZING US, FOR TRANSPORT IN ONE VAN.

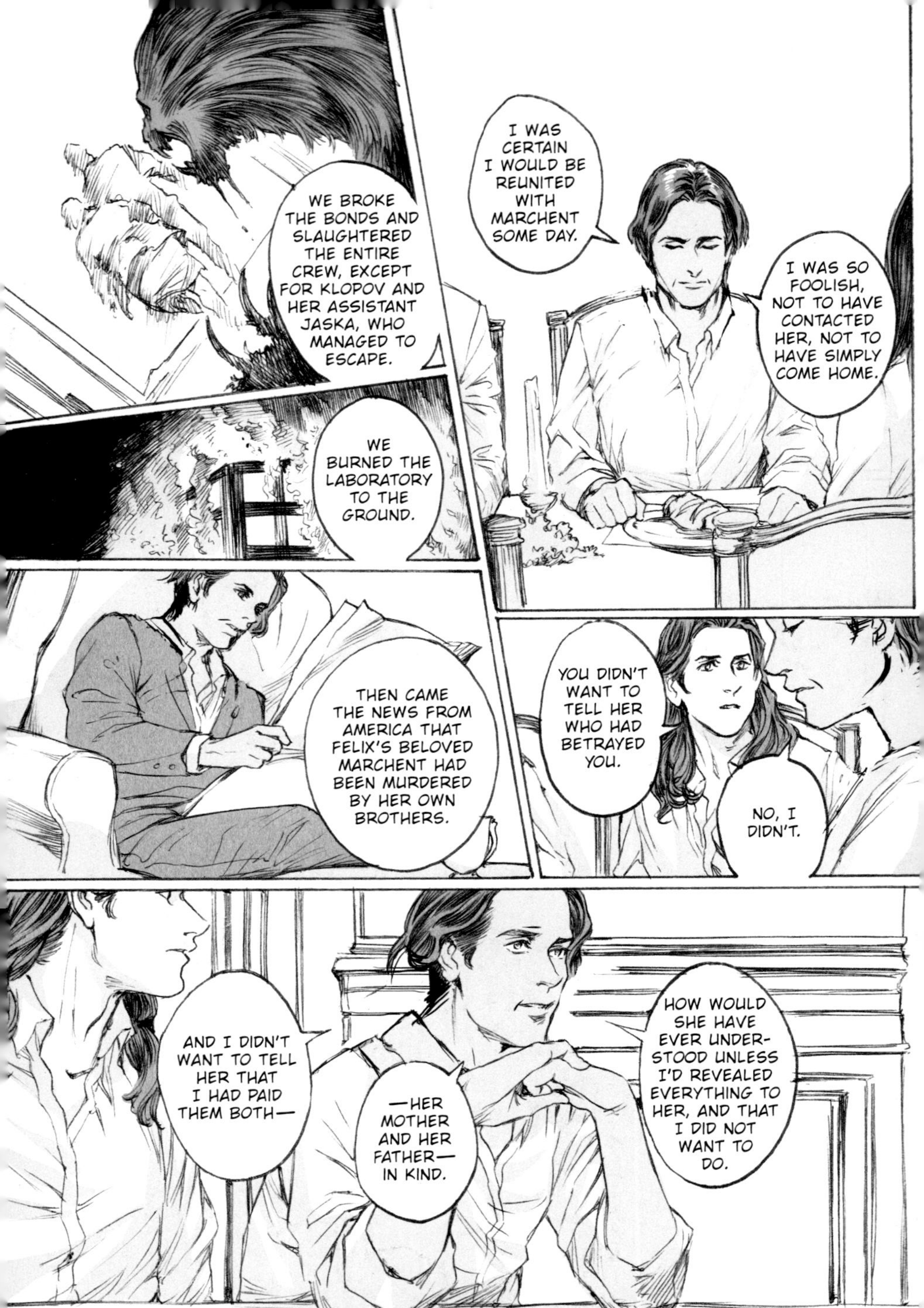
WE BROKE THE BONDS AND SLAUGHTERED THE ENTIRE CREW, EXCEPT FOR KLOPOV AND HER ASSISTANT JASKA, WHO MANAGED TO ESCAPE.
I WAS CERTAIN I WOULD BE REUNITED WITH MARCHENT SOME DAY.
I WAS SO FOOLISH, NOT TO HAVE CONTACTED HER, NOT TO HAVE SIMPLY COME HOME.
WE BURNED THE LABORATORY TO THE GROUND.
THEN CAME THE NEWS FROM AMERICA THAT FELIX'S BELOVED MARCHENT HAD BEEN MURDERED BY HER OWN BROTHERS.
YOU DIDN'T WANT TO TELL HER WHO HAD BETRAYED YOU.
NO, I DIDN'T.
AND I DIDN'T WANT TO TELL HER THAT I HAD PAID THEM BOTH—
—HER MOTHER AND HER FATHER—IN KIND.
HOW WOULD SHE HAVE EVER UNDER-STOOD UNLESS I'D REVEALED EVERYTHING TO HER, AND THAT I DID NOT WANT TO DO.

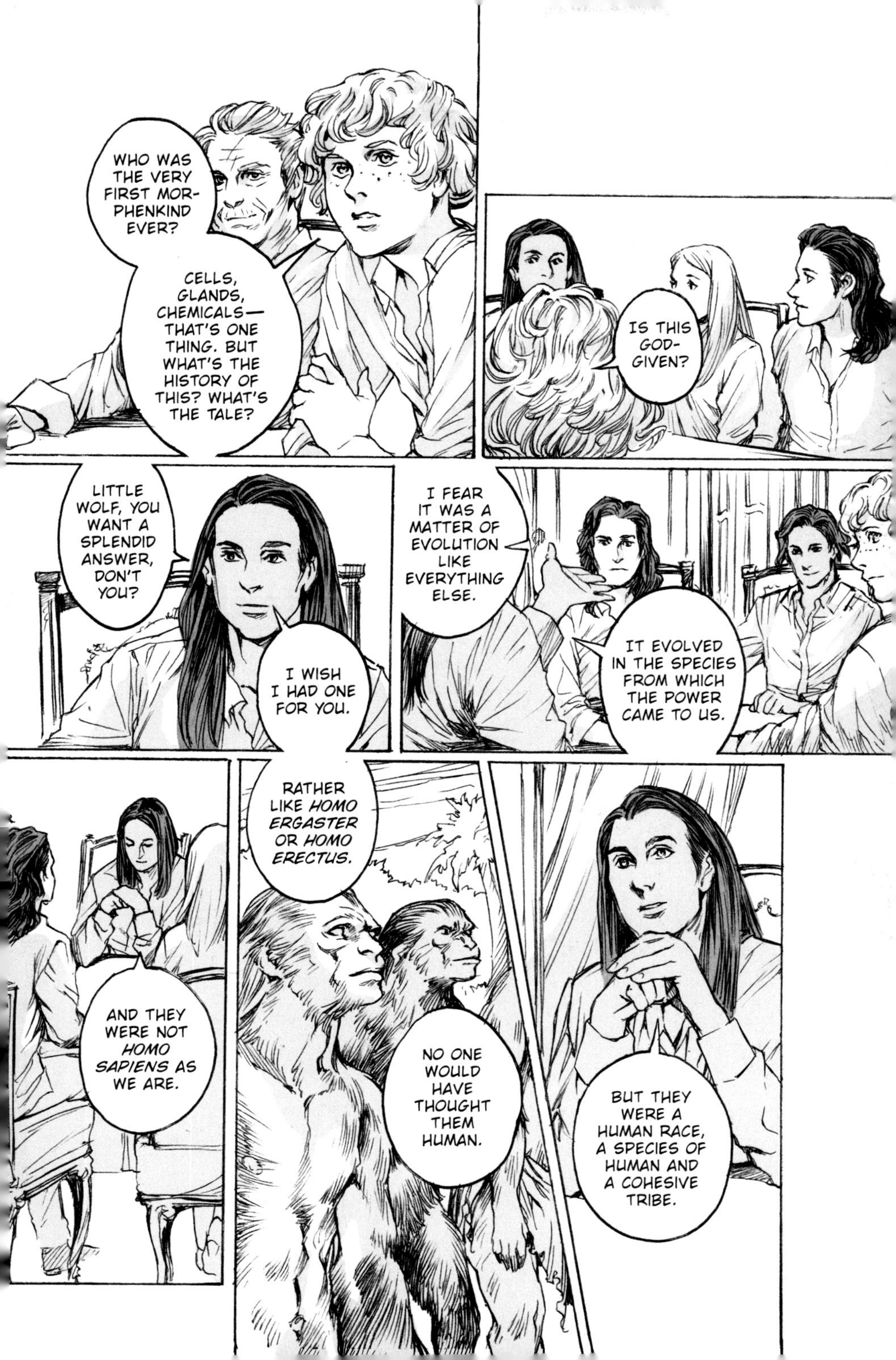
WHO WAS THE VERY FIRST MORPHENKIND EVER?
CELLS, GLANDS, CHEMICALS— THAT'S ONE THING. BUT WHAT'S THE HISTORY OF THIS? WHAT'S THE TALE?
IS THIS GOD-GIVEN?
LITTLE WOLF, YOU WANT A SPLENDID ANSWER, DON'T YOU?
I WISH I HAD ONE FOR YOU.
I FEAR IT WAS A MATTER OF EVOLUTION LIKE EVERYTHING ELSE.
IT EVOLVED IN THE SPECIES FROM WHICH THE POWER CAME TO US.
RATHER LIKE *HOMO ERGASTER* OR *HOMO ERECTUS*.
AND THEY WERE NOT *HOMO SAPIENS* AS WE ARE.
NO ONE WOULD HAVE THOUGHT THEM HUMAN.
BUT THEY WERE A HUMAN RACE, A SPECIES OF HUMAN AND A COHESIVE TRIBE.

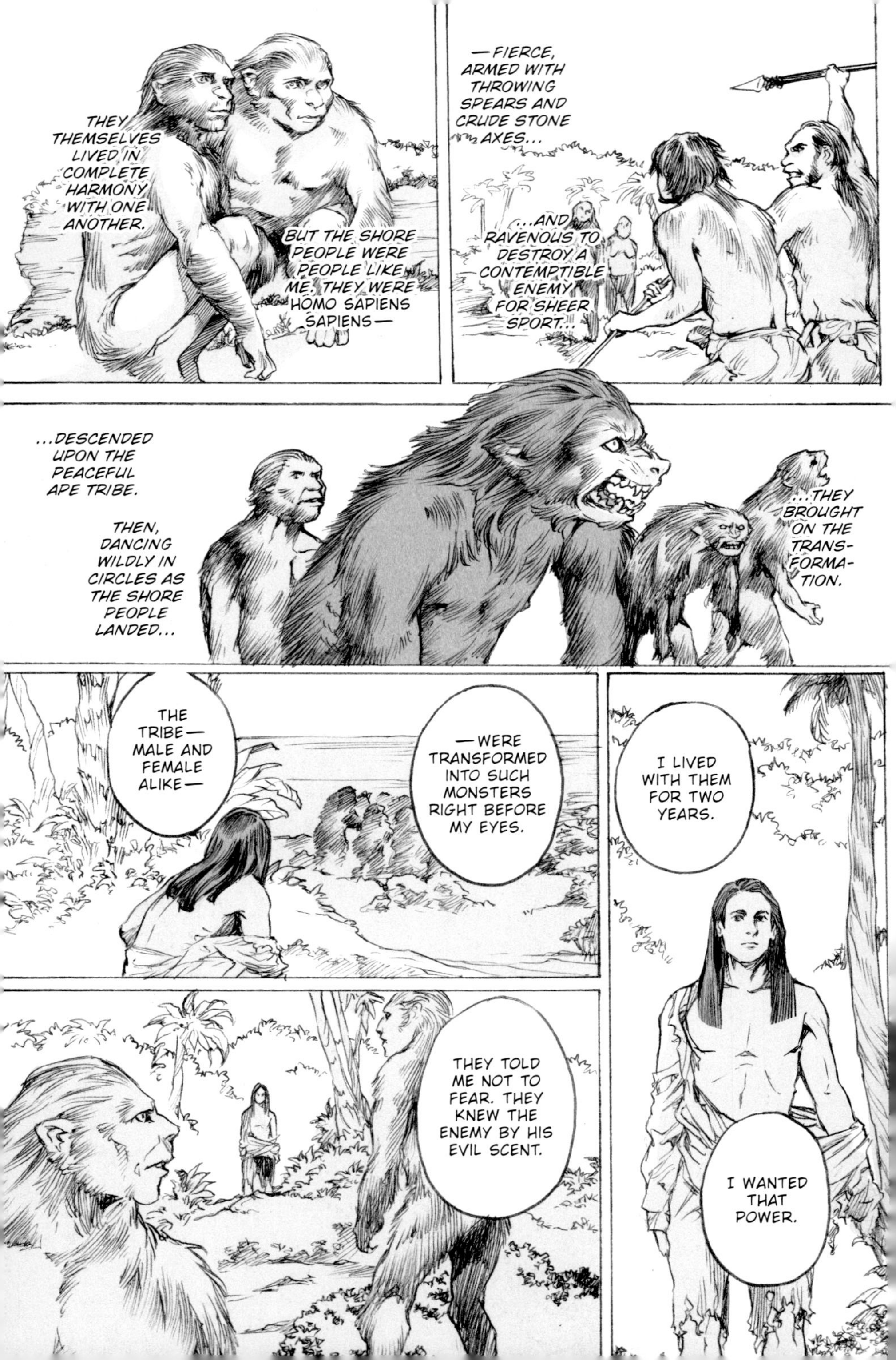
THEY THEMSELVES LIVED IN COMPLETE HARMONY WITH ONE ANOTHER.
BUT THE SHORE PEOPLE WERE PEOPLE LIKE ME. THEY WERE HOMO SAPIENS SAPIENS—
—FIERCE, ARMED WITH THROWING SPEARS AND CRUDE STONE AXES...
...AND RAVENOUS TO DESTROY A CONTEMPTIBLE ENEMY FOR SHEER SPORT...
...DESCENDED UPON THE PEACEFUL APE TRIBE.
THEN, DANCING WILDLY IN CIRCLES AS THE SHORE PEOPLE LANDED...
...THEY BROUGHT ON THE TRANS-FORMA-TION.
THE TRIBE— MALE AND FEMALE ALIKE—
—WERE TRANSFORMED INTO SUCH MONSTERS RIGHT BEFORE MY EYES.
I LIVED WITH THEM FOR TWO YEARS.
I WANTED THAT POWER.
THEY TOLD ME NOT TO FEAR. THEY KNEW THE ENEMY BY HIS EVIL SCENT.

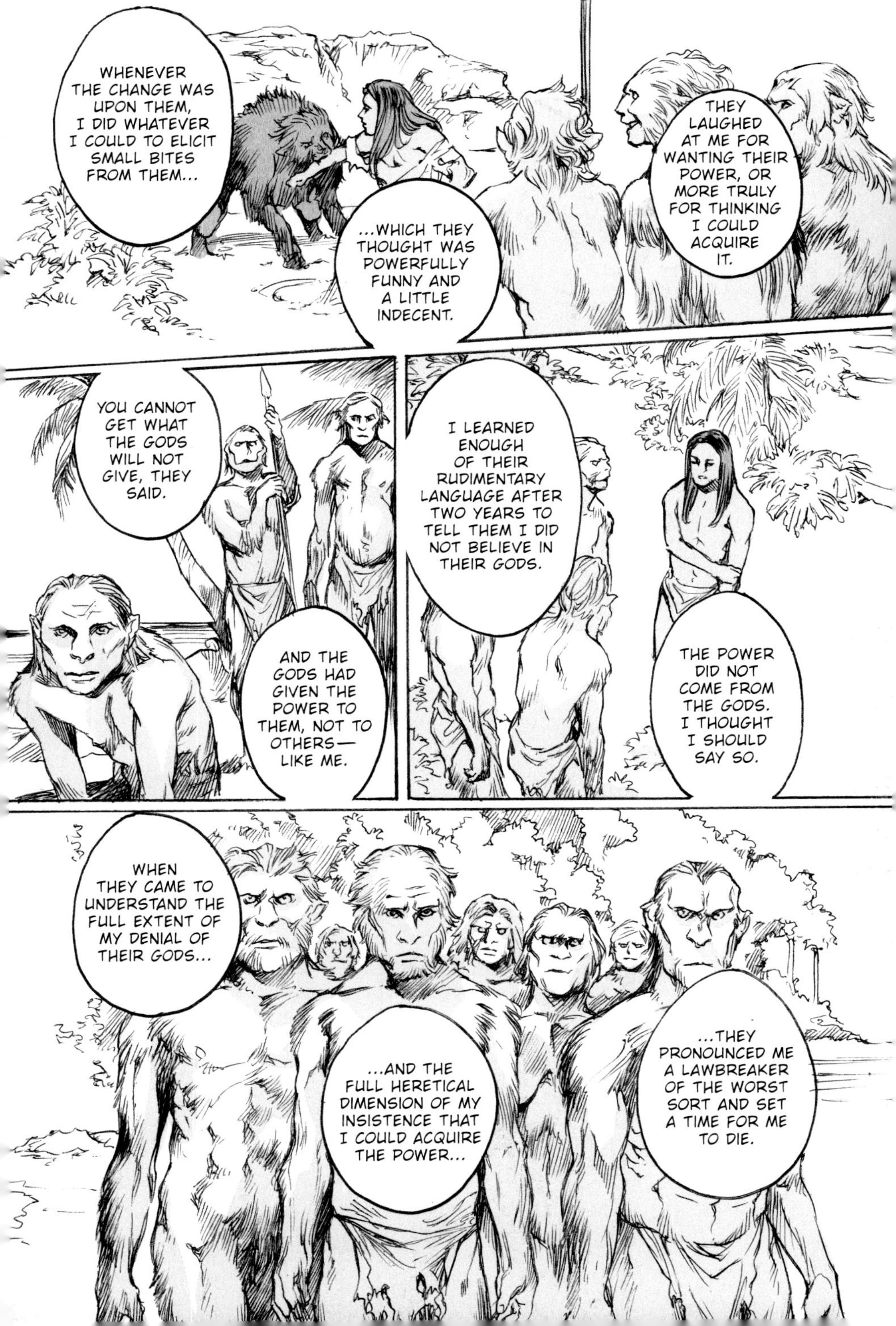
WHENEVER THE CHANGE WAS UPON THEM, I DID WHATEVER I COULD TO ELICIT SMALL BITES FROM THEM...
...WHICH THEY THOUGHT WAS POWERFULLY FUNNY AND A LITTLE INDECENT.
THEY LAUGHED AT ME FOR WANTING THEIR POWER, OR MORE TRULY FOR THINKING I COULD ACQUIRE IT.
YOU CANNOT GET WHAT THE GODS WILL NOT GIVE, THEY SAID.
AND THE GODS HAD GIVEN THE POWER TO THEM, NOT TO OTHERS—LIKE ME.
I LEARNED ENOUGH OF THEIR RUDIMENTARY LANGUAGE AFTER TWO YEARS TO TELL THEM I DID NOT BELIEVE IN THEIR GODS.
THE POWER DID NOT COME FROM THE GODS. I THOUGHT I SHOULD SAY SO.
WHEN THEY CAME TO UNDERSTAND THE FULL EXTENT OF MY DENIAL OF THEIR GODS...
...AND THE FULL HERETICAL DIMENSION OF MY INSISTENCE THAT I COULD ACQUIRE THE POWER...
...THEY PRONOUNCED ME A LAWBREAKER OF THE WORST SORT AND SET A TIME FOR ME TO DIE.

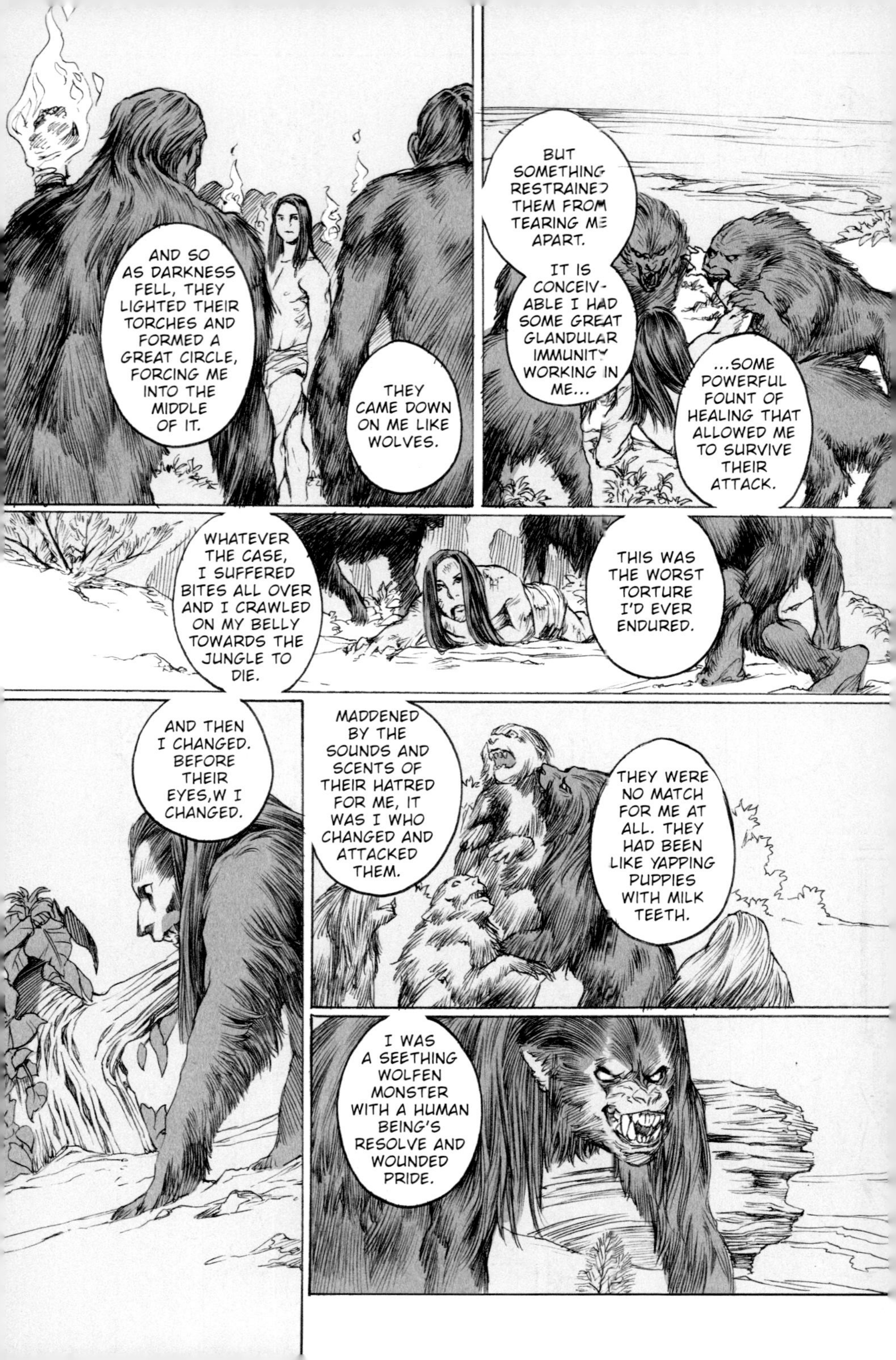
AND SO AS DARKNESS FELL, THEY LIGHTED THEIR TORCHES AND FORMED A GREAT CIRCLE, FORCING ME INTO THE MIDDLE OF IT.
THEY CAME DOWN ON ME LIKE WOLVES.
BUT SOMETHING RESTRAINED THEM FROM TEARING ME APART.
IT IS CONCEIV-ABLE I HAD SOME GREAT GLANDULAR IMMUNITY WORKING IN ME...
...SOME POWERFUL FOUNT OF HEALING THAT ALLOWED ME TO SURVIVE THEIR ATTACK.
WHATEVER THE CASE, I SUFFERED BITES ALL OVER AND I CRAWLED ON MY BELLY TOWARDS THE JUNGLE TO DIE.
THIS WAS THE WORST TORTURE I'D EVER ENDURED.
AND THEN I CHANGED. BEFORE THEIR EYES,W I CHANGED.
MADDENED BY THE SOUNDS AND SCENTS OF THEIR HATRED FOR ME, IT WAS I WHO CHANGED AND ATTACKED THEM.
THEY WERE NO MATCH FOR ME AT ALL. THEY HAD BEEN LIKE YAPPING PUPPIES WITH MILK TEETH.
I WAS A SEETHING WOLFEN MONSTER WITH A HUMAN BEING'S RESOLVE AND WOUNDED PRIDE.

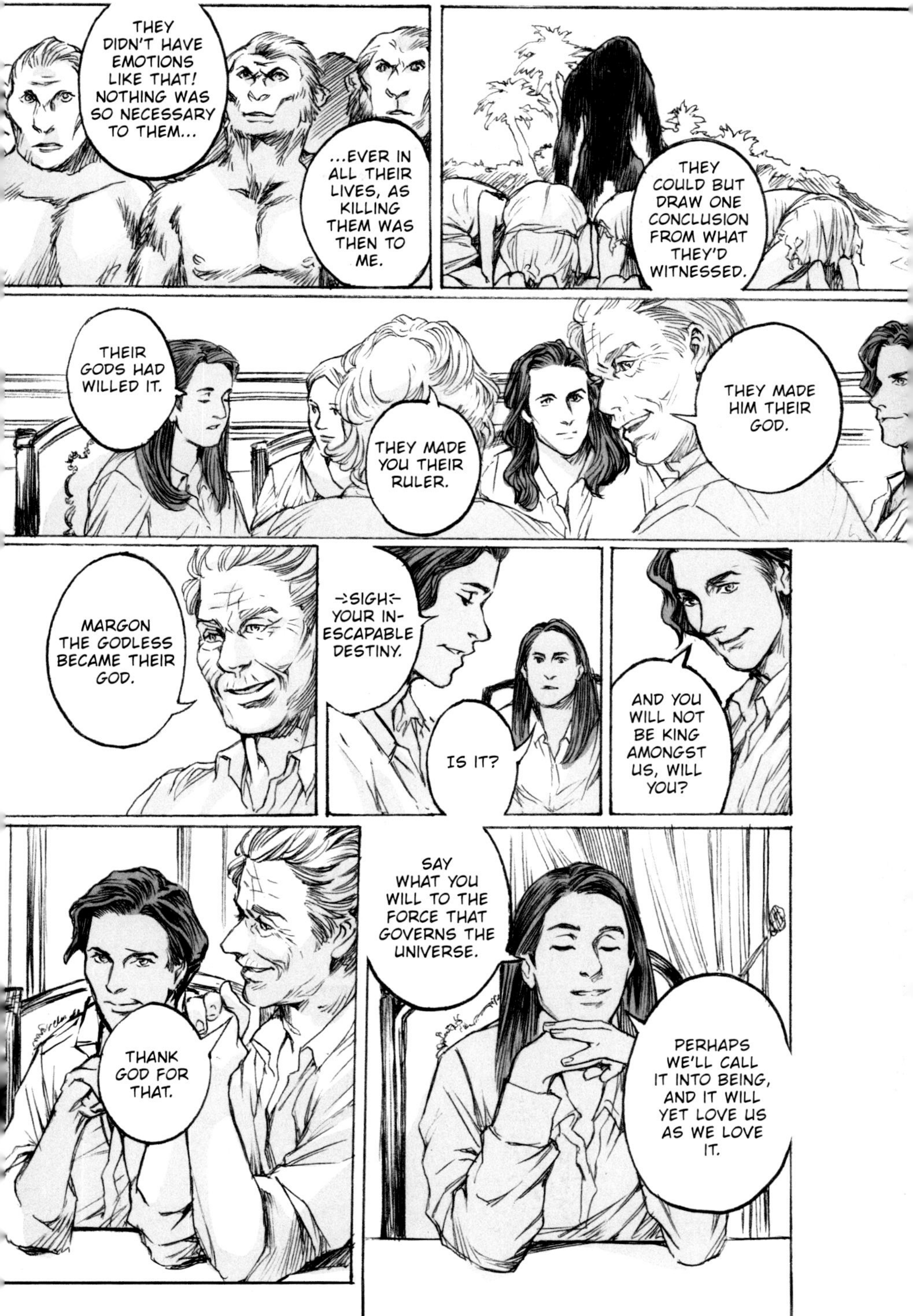
THEY DIDN'T HAVE EMOTIONS LIKE THAT! NOTHING WAS SO NECESSARY TO THEM...
...EVER IN ALL THEIR LIVES, AS KILLING THEM WAS THEN TO ME.
THEY COULD BUT DRAW ONE CONCLUSION FROM WHAT THEY'D WITNESSED.
THEIR GODS HAD WILLED IT.
THEY MADE YOU THEIR RULER.
THEY MADE HIM THEIR GOD.
MARGON THE GODLESS BECAME THEIR GOD.
-:-SIGH-:- YOUR IN-ESCAPABLE DESTINY.
IS IT?
AND YOU WILL NOT BE KING AMONGST US, WILL YOU?
THANK GOD FOR THAT.
SAY WHAT YOU WILL TO THE FORCE THAT GOVERNS THE UNIVERSE.
PERHAPS WE'LL CALL IT INTO BEING, AND IT WILL YET LOVE US AS WE LOVE IT.

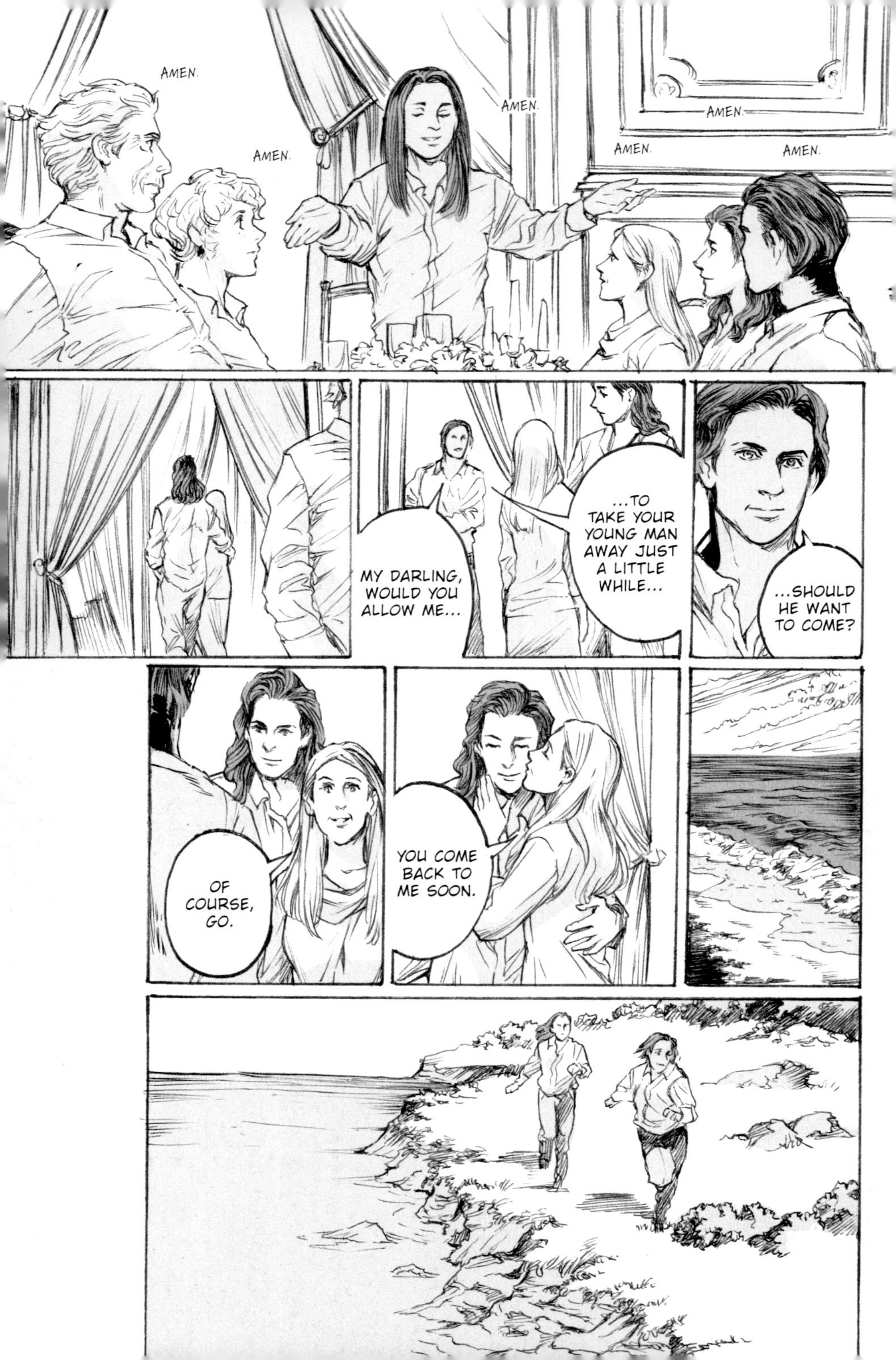
AMEN.
AMEN.
AMEN.
AMEN.
AMEN.
AMEN.
MY DARLING, WOULD YOU ALLOW ME...
...TO TAKE YOUR YOUNG MAN AWAY JUST A LITTLE WHILE...
...SHOULD HE WANT TO COME?
OF COURSE, GO.
YOU COME BACK TO ME SOON.

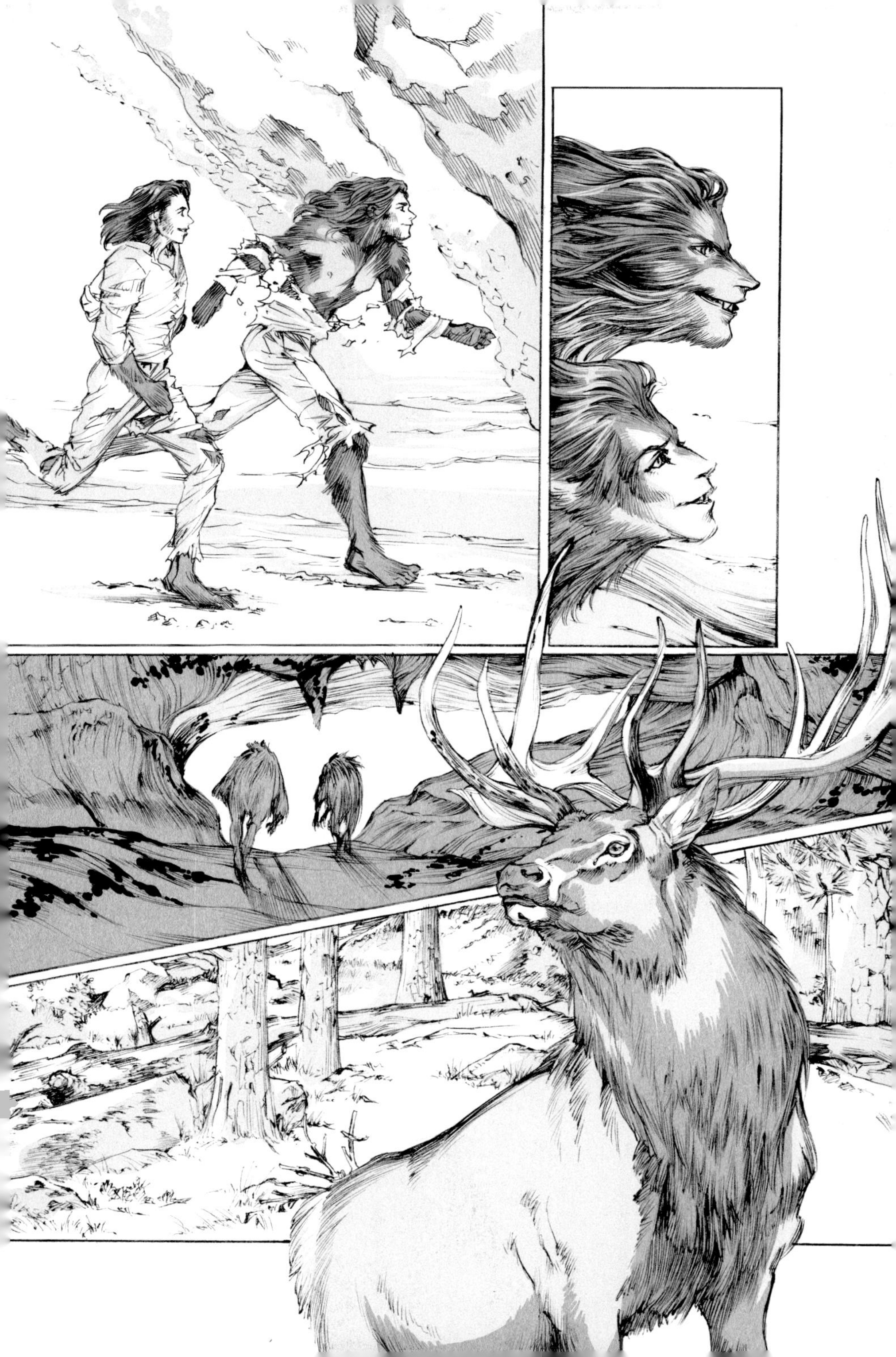

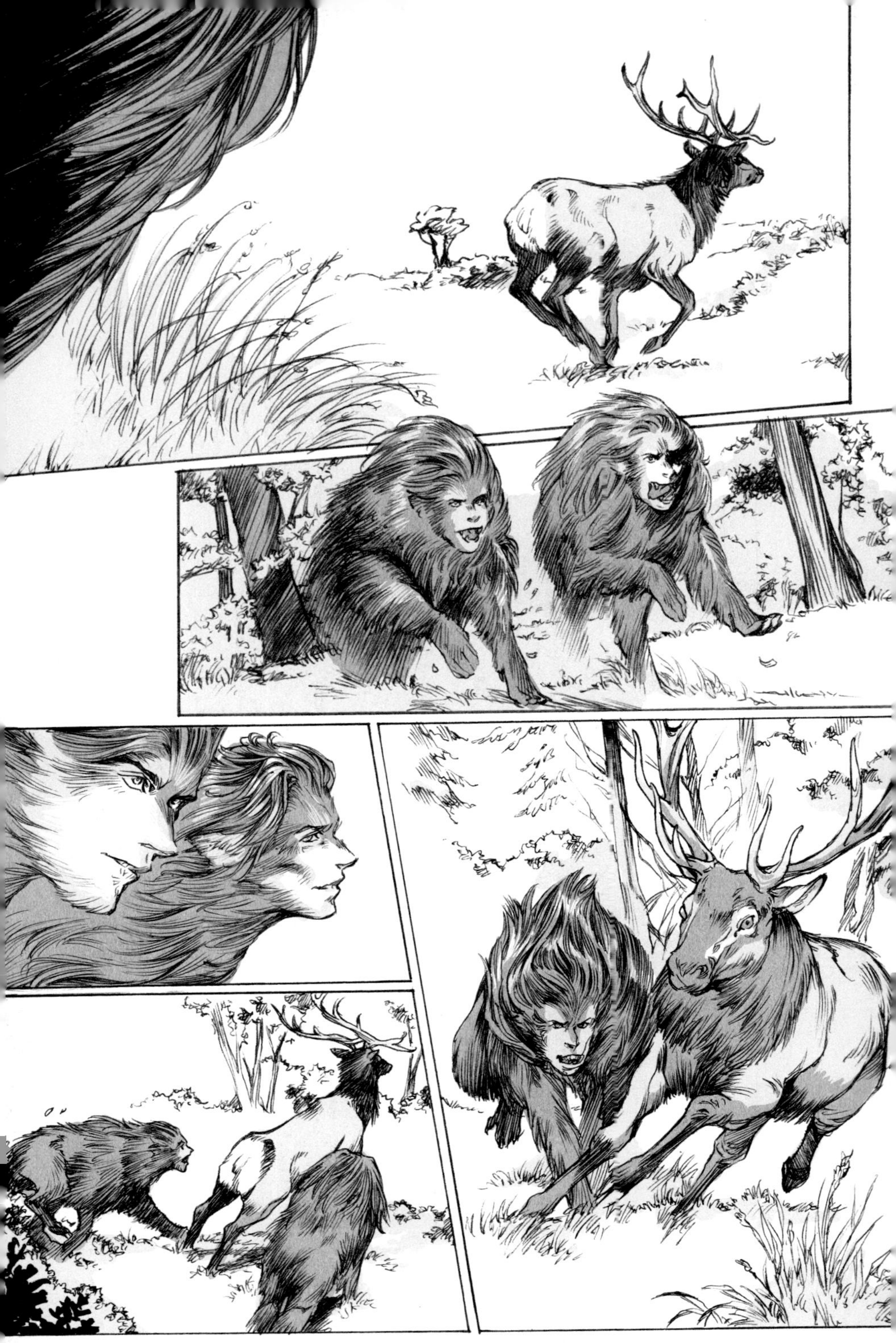

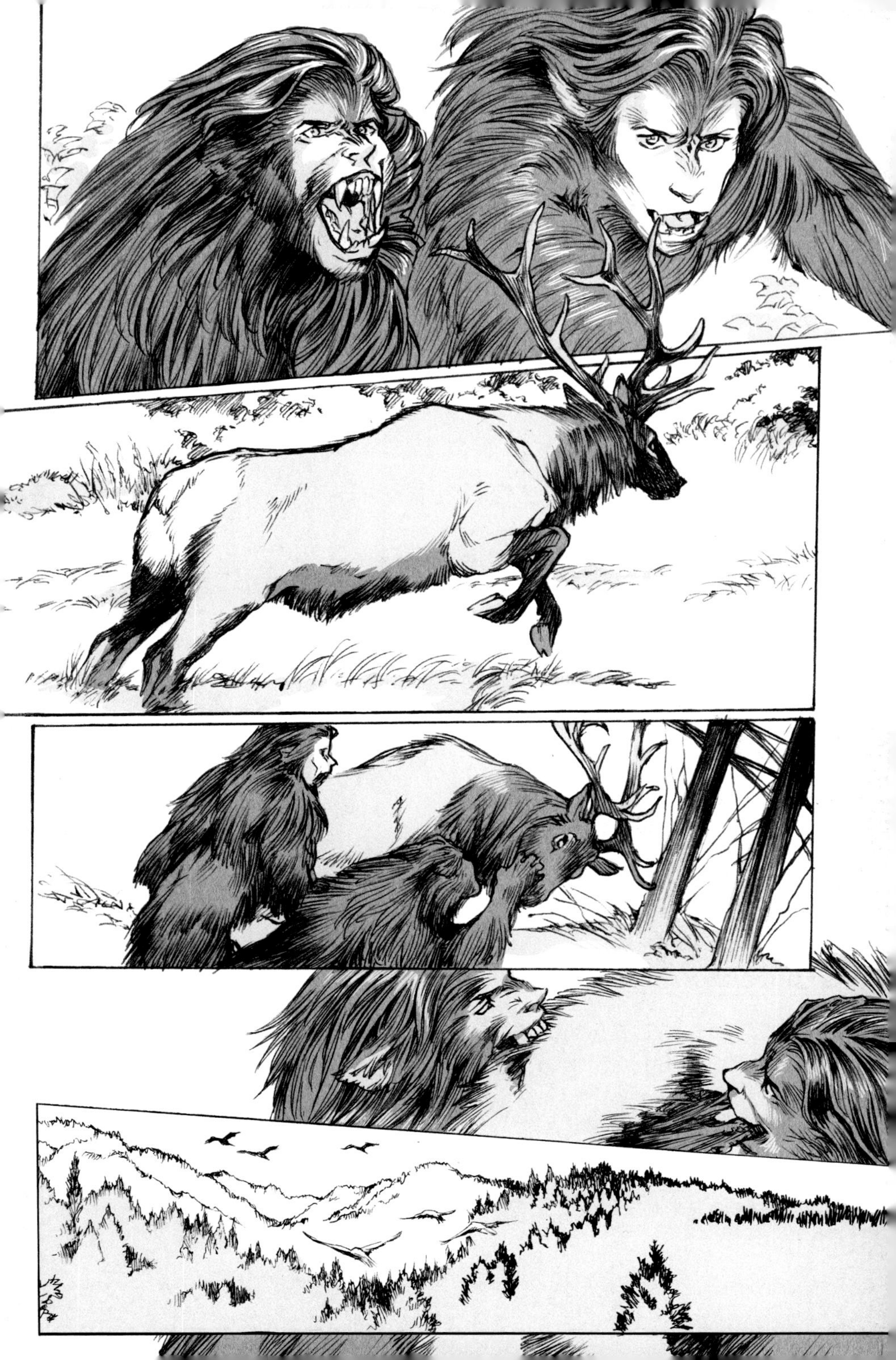

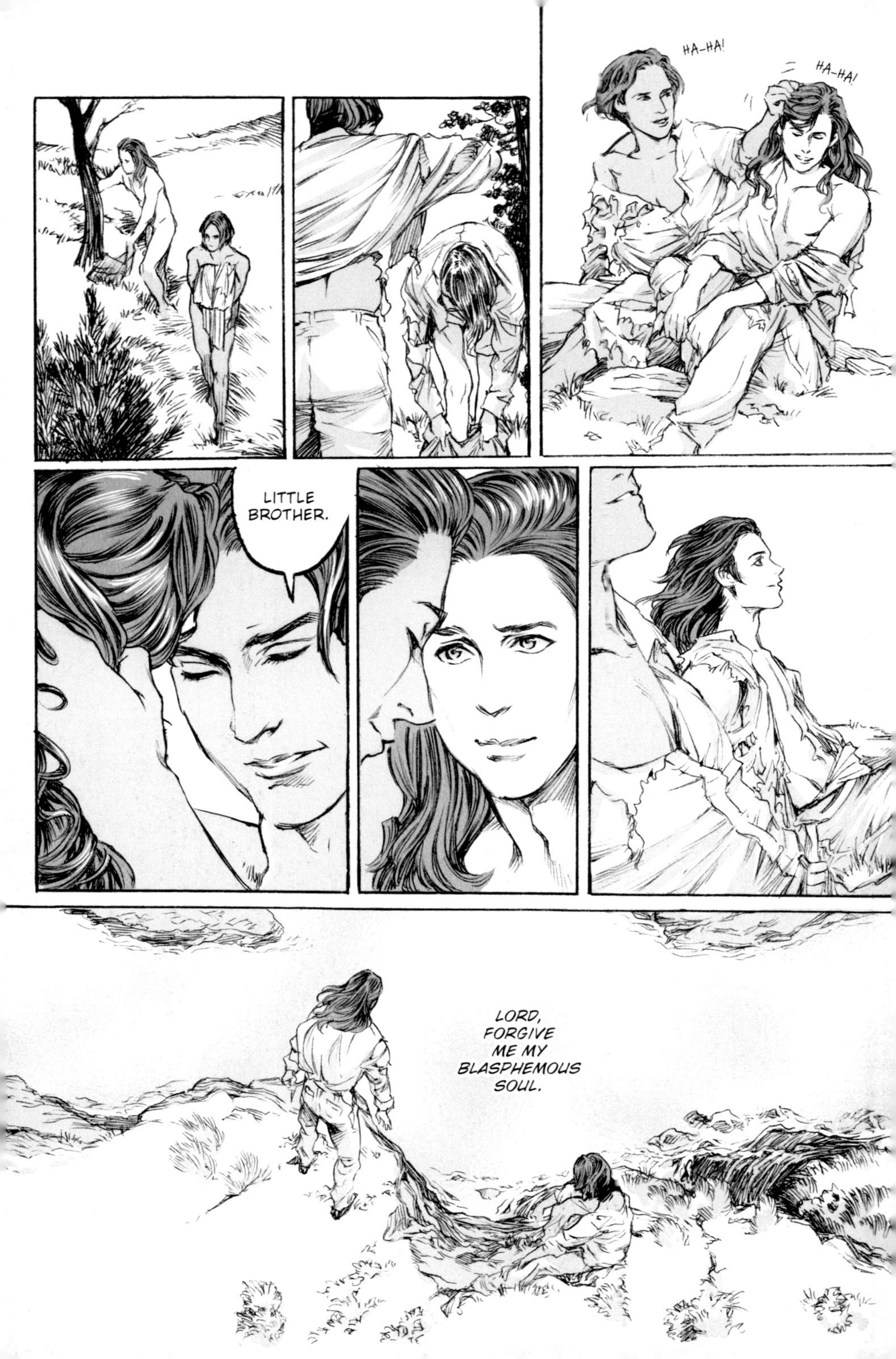
HA-HA!
HA-HA!
LITTLE BROTHER.
LORD, FORGIVE ME MY BLASPHEMOUS SOUL.

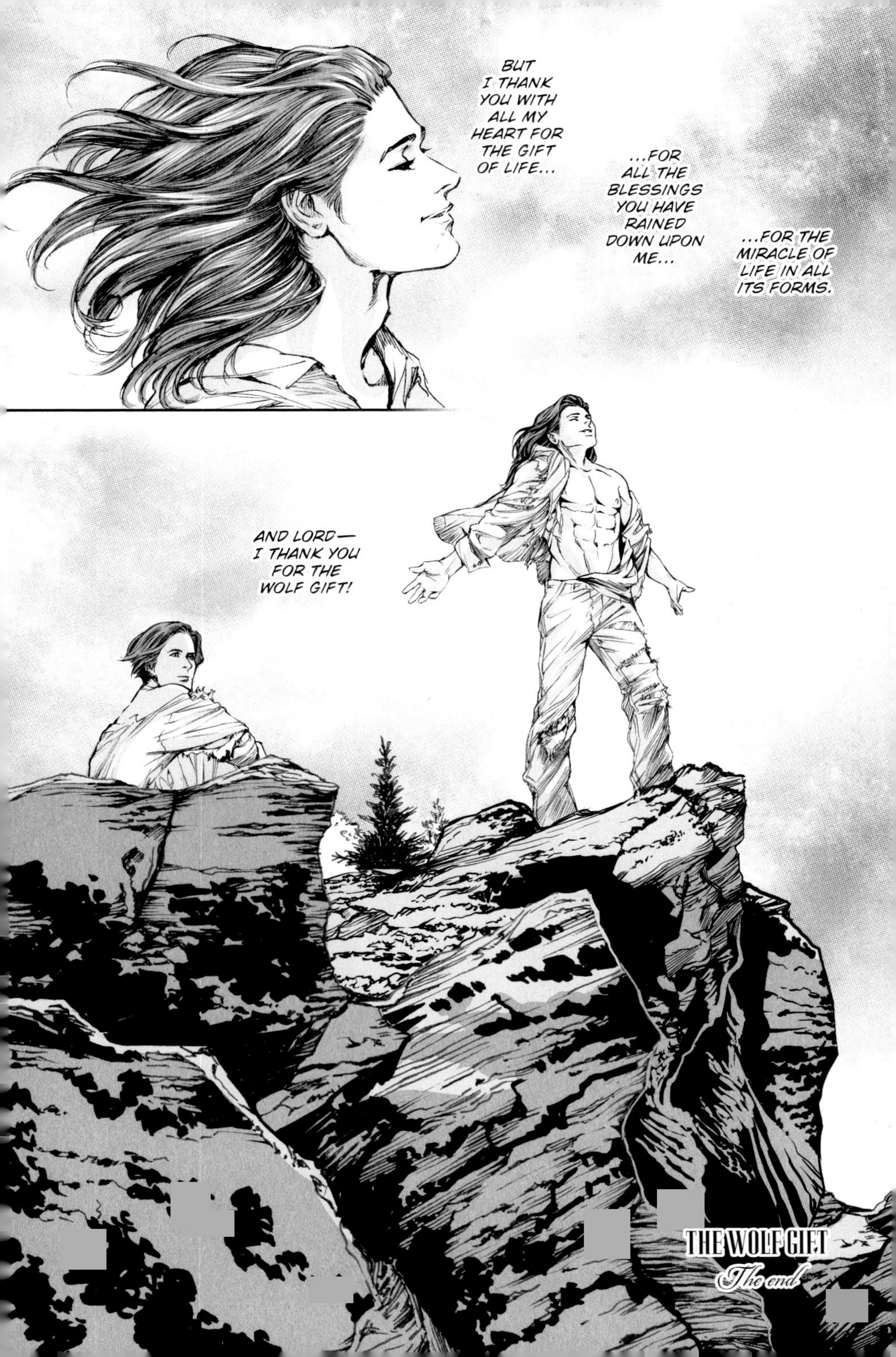
BUT I THANK YOU WITH ALL MY HEART FOR THE GIFT OF LIFE...
...FOR ALL THE BLESSINGS YOU HAVE RAINED DOWN UPON ME...
...FOR THE MIRACLE OF LIFE IN ALL ITS FORMS.
AND LORD— I THANK YOU FOR THE WOLF GIFT!
THE WOLF GIFT
The end